Books by Richard Gordon

JACK
THE
RIPPER

JACK
THE
RIPPER

Richard Gordon, pseud. of
Gordon Stanley Ostlere

ATHENEUM

New York

1980

Open your eyes and look round you on the strange
melodrama of life.

J. Leckie, *Life and Religion*

Copyright © 1980 by Richard Gordon Ltd.
All rights reserved
Manufactured by Fairfield Graphics, Fairfield, Pennsylvania
ISBN 0-689-11101-0
Library of Congress catalog card number 80-66000
First Printing July 1980
Second Printing November 1980

JACK
THE
RIPPER

SHORTLY BEFORE NOON on Friday, February 10, 1888 –
the year everyone called 'the three eights' – two doctors
shared a hansom from the foot of Harley Street to India
Road. It was a bitter morning of sparse flying snow, the
smoke which streamed from London chimney-pots bending
in the wind like corn.

They had been operating in a Cavendish Square nursing
home, where frenzied preparations had begun with the thin
dawn. The ceilings thumped with shifted furniture, the stairs
clanged with metal basins and brass cans of boiling water.
The bustling nurses neglected inmates unsentenced to the
knife, the surgeon was presaged by heavy black leather bags
of instruments in a separate cab.

The patient was a woman, who walked downstairs in her
nightdress, dropped her slippers, climbed on the operating
table in a room with lace curtains on the tall windows, and
submitted herself to chloroform. The relatives had bid their
last farewells and saved their sobs for the street, where an
Italian was playing a barrel-organ all morning. An operation
was a drama so infrequent, so seemingly callous, so chillingly
risky, it lay in the public mind little short of an execution.

The woman had a tumour of the breast, and was likely to
live. But the case the two doctors discussed was another.

'So Crown Prince Frederick of Prussia had his throat cut,'
said Bertram Randolph flippantly. He was still in his
twenties, ruddy faced and thick lipped, with large hazel eyes
and dark curly hair. 'As I saw from my *Times*, at three
o'clock yesterday afternoon in the Villa Zirio at San Remo.
But why the devil didn't Sir Morell Mackenzie perform the
operation on his own patient?'

'Come, Bertie! Be a realist,' said Oliver Wilberforce. 'Mackenzie's only at San Remo because he was sent there by the Queen. He's attending her "dear Fritz", as she calls the Crown Prince, only because the Crown Princess is her even dearer daughter Vicky. Which doesn't exactly commend Mackenzie to either the German medical profession or the German press.'

'I suppose the knighthood, which he collected at Balmoral like his railway tickets, failed to silence or even impress them?'

Oliver nodded agreement. He was five years older than Bertie Randolph, tall, lean, handsome, pale, fair-haired, his mouth as straight and thin as an incision. A fellow of the Royal College of Surgeons of England, Master of Surgery at the University of Oxford, he was newly-elected honorary surgeon to the Whitechapel Hospital. He wore a black cape with a high collar held by a chain, Bertie a brown-and-yellow check ulster. Both wore top hats, wing collars and knee-length frock coats – though fashionable grocers were adopting wing collars, no fashionable doctor dared sport a cutaway.

'So they settled for a mere nick in the neck,' observed Bertie. 'Slitting the windpipe to let dear Fritz breathe, just as you'd sweep a smoking chimney. If the Prince has got cancer of the larynx, it beats me how they funked plucking out his entire voice-box.'

'Sir Morell Mackenzie does *not* consider that Crown Prince Frederick has cancer.'

'Well, *you* know Mackenzie, I don't. It's almost a year now since he ruled out cancer, before the Prince came over for the Jubilee. He's sticking to his diagnosis with admirable tenacity – or Scots pigheadedness.'

The case was followed daily by every newspaper in Europe. Crown Prince Frederick of Prussia – liberal, temperate, compassionate, peaceable, earnest, Anglophile by marriage and admiration – was likely any day to succeed his father Emperor William I, turned ninety. The Crown Prince had caught cold in Italy at the start of the previous year, which everyone ascribed to his being lost by his coach-man without a greatcoat one chilly evening in the country. The hoarseness persisted. The fragrant inhalations, the vivid gargles were useless. In March 1887, the Crown Prince's physician-in-ordinary, the deputy medical director of the German army, the professor of clinical medicine at the University of Berlin, were all three called for consultation.

In May, the meteoric Morell Mackenzie, to older colleagues an upstart, founder of the Golden Square Throat Hospital in Soho, appeared in the Neue Palais at Potsdam. He sprayed the Prince's throat with strong cocaine, swooped with his narrow, curved, sharp steel forceps, and snapped up a morsel of vocal cord like a heron a fish. The fragment was bottled in formalin and hurried to Professor Virchow, most revered pathologist in Europe, member of the Reichstag, enemy of Bismarck, reorganizer of the Berlin drains.

Professor Virchow looked down his microscope and pronounced it not cancerous. Mackenzie readily agreed. Radical removal of the Prince's voice-box was less likely to be an operation than an assassination.

'Who did the minor operation in the end?' asked Bertie.

'According to my cypher telegram from San Remo, Dr Bramann. Who's had great experience performing tracheotomy. Though of course mostly on children suffocating from diphtheria. Anyway, Mackenzie had no choice. Bramann was sent to San Remo for that specific purpose by the old Emperor William himself.'

'There must be a dozen *Herren Professoren* from Berlin and Vienna at the Villa Zirio with their fingers down the throat of *unser Fritz*,' said Bertie lightly. 'It's a multiple misfortune to be royal and ill. One doctor's amply sufficient to kill anyone. And what a suspicious nest of reptiles those Prussians are! We all know what happened when Prince William of the upturned moustaches, *the patient's own son,* sent his pet throat specialist to sneak a report behind the backs of the medical mandarins. Didn't it misfire gloriously? Naturally, the Paris press gobbled the doctor-spy's indiscretion that the trouble really was syphilis – '

3

'Which Mackenzie instantly denied.' Oliver's voice, always severe, was impatient with Bertie's moods of breezy derision.

'Which everyone instantly disbelieved. Mankind always thinks the worst. It judges others by itself.'

'Bertie, you're outrageous! A man needs an opportunity to get syphilis, as he does to get married.'

'Don't you know the story?' asked Bertie with the cheerful malevolence of the hardened scandalmonger. 'He picked up a dose in the winter of '69, at the opening of the Suez Canal.'

'Who from?' asked Oliver sarcastically. 'The Empress Eugénie? She was there.'

'Oriental hospitality is generous and thoughtful. It was a señorita Dolores Cada, as luscious as an Andalucian pomegranate. When Mackenzie told Crown Princess Vicky his diagnosis, she slapped his face.'

'Nonsense!' Oliver's smile reminded Bertie of a crack in the ice. 'I prefer to believe that the only lasting result of those celebrations was Signor Verdi's *Aïda*.'

Lemon-yellow gloves resting on silver-capped ebony cane, Oliver stared straight ahead past the dancing hindquarters of the horse and the reins which disappeared into the hands of the top-hatted driver over their heads. He preferred to drop the conversation. The most voracious medical gossip in London was squeezed beside him on the green velvet upholstery, and a surgeon who is building a career cannot afford to drop bricks.

They had crawled through the cabs, horse-buses, carts and drays blocking Cheapside, rattled past the Bank of England along the cobbles of Threadneedle Street and reached the India Road, a mile-long, straight brick furrow across Whitechapel.

The crammed houses, blackened with fog and seacoal, each sheltered several families scraping pennies from making slippers, clocks, matchboxes, picture-frames, chopping firewood from disused planks, 'translating' old clothes. The larger buildings were once owned by weavers, now evicted by steam, the rooms wide enough for looms partitioned into

4

many. Some were sweat-shops, though the much vilified sweater was little better off than the sweated, who made gowns, shoes, hats, jewellery for the ladies of the West End, to whom they were themselves as remote and incomprehensible as the savages of the Niger.

The shops had the desperate look of selling to the poor. The steamy window of the mutton-pie man flared with yellow gas-jets, the oil shop glowed with coloured jars, the hammering cobbler made a show for ragged children. All supplemented their merchandise with sweets, cakes, small round tarts, onions and sausages, bread and dripping, temperance beverages and threepenny hats. Many traded in the secondhand furniture, clothes and bedding, pots and pans, bought cheap from the bailiffs, or from the pawnbrokers whose brass balls supplied regular punctuation to the sad story of poverty.

A tough regiment from London's army of street traders lived off the India Road. Chair-caners, tinkers, knife-grinders, glaziers. Vendors with barrows or trays of fruit, spices, ribbons, sheet-music, magazines and toffees. The baked-potato van, the muffin man with his teatime bell, the man with the fresh sixpenny rabbits dangling on the stick across his shoulder, blood dripping from their muzzles. A barrel-organ played, street acrobats tumbled, passers-by tossed halfpennies into entreating caps. There were no sand-wichmen. The inhabitants of India Road were not worth advertising to.

Oliver seeming disinclined to talk, Bertie observed the crowded pavements through the square side window of the cab. They passed one of the biggest brick buildings in Whitechapel, a toy and doll factory just closed under the pressure of cheap German imports. The dwellings were interrupted by public houses far more frequently than by schools and missions. Everyone knew that the hand of God, which created men unequal, poured upon some his gifts and left others unable to feed themselves with their sweat. Though the world's welfare rested on its perpetuating these divine distances, horror and disgust at human misery moved philanthropists to provide refreshment somewhere in between. Bertie noticed outside a sagging weatherboard house with gaping windows a knot of women in their working aprons, without bonnet or shawl in the freezing wind, all clutching jugs and some their babies, waiting for the daily missionary soup.

'The children of Israel get everywhere, don't they?' he remarked.

'Does the whole world dine with Montefioris and Rothschilds?'

'The nobs don't signify. Society would eat off gold plate with Hottentots. The tide from Russia and Poland has flooded Whitechapel. What's to stop it swamping the country?'

'Immigrant labour is cheap.'

'Oh, it's good biz, I admit, but work for Englishmen is scarce. Mind, you should see the people here, on their sabbaths and holidays. The men may be sallow, pinched, quick and furtive, gleaming with hair-oil – but the women! Eastern goddesses,' he said enthusiastically. 'Shapely figures, soft skins, in bright reds and greens and sparkling like houris with gimcrack jewellery, waving with feathers like pink ostriches, It's how my father used to describe the streets of Jodhpur or Bombay.'

'You favour starving immigrants with an attitude of amused contempt?'

'I favour everyone with it. Life in my lowly station would otherwise be unbearable.'

They jerked against the padded-leather lining of the knee-doors. The fragile-looking, black lacquered, brass-trimmed hansom, lamps above its pair of rubber-rimmed wheels like eyes, stopped abruptly for a country wain with six steaming horses, lumbering into London with felled timber from the forests of Essex. The frozen dirt in the gutters of India Road was regularly augmented with dead dogs and cats flattened by massive, iron-rimmed cartwheels. Bertie noticed how the wain crushed straw laid thick across the cobbles over mud and squashed horse-dung. Someone lay ill behind a nearby

6

upstairs window. Spreading straw across the street, muffling the knocker, were old devices to deaden the busy world in a sick man's ears – or to chide it with his presence.

'How's Mrs Wilberforce?' asked Bertie slyly. The cabhorse clipped briskly between twin brick pillars breaking the stout railings which pallisaded the Whitechapel hospital forecourt.

Hands still clasped on stick, Oliver turned his head slowly. The contradictions and complexities of his character never broke the surface of his expression, nor interrupted the civilized language of his eye. He lived under a frost of shyness, melted only by the impatient ambition which thrust him into the company of valuable men.

'How should I know?'

'You live in the same house.'

'I walk the same street as a thousand women. I cannot tell how they are, if they pass me as strangers.'

Bertie thought for a moment. 'It must be deuced uncomfortable at home. When affection walks out, there's never a vacant place at the family table. Hatred walks in and takes the seat.'

Bertie's conversation had a deadly way of unknotting the bonds of caution. 'You're right,' Oliver confided. 'I honestly shouldn't care a jot if I arrived at the hospital to hear the news that my wife had fallen downstairs and broken her neck.'

'What an uncharitable thought,' Bertie muttered. 'Luckily, I've a cure for such notions.'

'What?'

'You should permit my introducing you to a lady friend or two of mine.'

'I should not submit so estimable a colleague as yourself to so onerous an imposition.'

'You're a bally idiot. It would be a pleasurable duty. I suppose you're frightened I'd tell tales?'

'Well, you amuse me heartily by telling plenty of tales about others. Anyway, your concern is unnecessary. I'm not made like you.'

'You are. All men are. What's the difference between a

monk and a rake on the dissecting table? Not a slip of a ligament, not a thread of a nerve. A man needs the regular glow of a woman, as a flower needs the sunshine.'

They had reached the porticoed main entrance, carved with standing gods and reclining goddesses of healing. A shiny two-horse Victoria was waiting, leather hood up against the weather, a smart coachman with cockaded top-hat on the box, whip in hand, wrapped in black oilcloth from the waist down.

'Ambrose Porter-Hartley is here early,' said Oliver in surprise.

Bertie drew from his frock-coat pocket a thin gold watch, the touch of a hidden spring chiming the last hour and quarters. All Whitechapel Hospital knew his watch, of which he was boyishly proud. His mother gave it him for his twenty-first birthday, though from the engraved initials he concluded it had been resourcefully extracted from her aristocratic lover in Paris.

'Perhaps he dropped a sovereign last week, and is making time to look for it?' he suggested.

Their driver released the lever throwing open the pair of low doors. Bertie climbed down the iron steps in front of the wheels, carrying a Gladstone containing lint, a wire-framed mask and a brown vial of chloroform – the 'rag and bottle' by which surgical oblivion was dispensed. Bertie's qualification, Licentiate of the Society of Apothecaries, compared with Oliver's as the ordination of a priest to the consecration of a bishop. He was anaesthetist to the Whitechapel Hospital, a job unsought, unsung and unexacting. Bertie found it a useful stepping-stone among a busy traffic of important doctors, while building a profitable general practice in the West End. Oliver's hunger was for professional prestige. Bertie's taste was for amusement, fashion, luxury and idleness.

Oliver paid the three shillings fare. The driver unhooked a nosebag from under his perch, preferring a wait for another fare to the hope of one in the poor streets leading back to the City. The two doctors hastened up six granite steps. The portico was chiselled inside with aphorisms of Hippocrates, which had met their awed ill-comprehension when first arriving at the Whitechapel Hospital Medical School, and which now they were too busy to quote.

The hospital entrance hall was shaped like a drum. Stone-floored, its curving walls lined by vast, gleaming, jet-black boards picked in gold with the names of benefactors. Miss Ann Baker's £200 Indian Peninsular Railway Stock, Stephen Coombs Esq's £100 4½% Preference Stock of the London, Chatham and Dover Railway Co, the Whitechapel Association of Fruiterers' £32. 4s. 2d. bought immortality. A glass cupola lit the quick changing parade of doctors, nurses and patients, eyed by a porter with a face like beef and a moustache like a scrubbing-brush, in bright blue, brass-buttoned, long-skirted uniform.

The Whitechapel Hospital admitted cases from 9 to 10, accidents at all times. Operations were at 1.30 p.m. daily, visiting was allowed on Sundays from 2 p.m. to 3 p.m. and Wednesdays from 3 p.m. to 4 p.m. It had 29 sisters, 179 nurses, 678 beds, and every year treated 7,000 inpatients and 150,000 out-patients. The Whitechapel people were terrified of it. It was the place you went to die. An operation was an atrocity, to be escaped by the sharpest Cockney subterfuge. The disciplined beds were feared worse than prison cells, where the authorities kept their obligation to release you at the stated time in one piece.

As Bertie and Oliver came through the glass-panelled doors, a fat man in moleskin trousers and greasy waistcoat, snatching breath with the wheeze of old bellows, supported by a fair pale girl of about ten, his possessions bundled in a red cloth, was waiting admittance to a ward from which he struck Bertie as unlikely to return. A woman with a black shawl, sobbing as she left with an armful of male clothes, was a familiar indication of a husband who never would. A broad flagstoned corridor led to the rear of the hospital, where it split right to the medical wards, left to the surgical. A small brass-studded padded leather door, leading into the out-patients' surgery, was a short cut to the operating theatre.

9

The long surgery was chilly, illuminated by a glass roof filmed with soot, lined by brown-painted doors emblazoned in gold with the names of physicians and surgeons, leading to their white-tiled consulting-rooms. The floor was filled with black-painted benches, on which patients who had resignedly waited four hours were resigning themselves to wait four or five more. They had anyway nothing else to occupy their day. It smelt of sweat, chlorine and Eau de Cologne. The notion of germs was new, suspect and too disturbing to be seriously entertained in the older medical heads at the Whitechapel. Typhus was known to arise from ochlesis – which was Greek for overcrowding – scarlet fever and typhoid from miasmas. Chlorine was spread to destroy any mysterious contagium, and deodorants as liberally because all humanity stank, luckily not dangerously.

As Bertie hurried through the unsavoury mass of his fellow humans he saw the girl.

He grabbed Oliver's cloak. 'The fair-haired one,' he whispered excitedly. 'A Botticelli Venus, arising from the scum.'

2

JUBILEE SUMMER the year before grew warm with the strenuous celebrations. At the end of August 1887 the weather broke. A savage storm split the skies of Kent, on the night farmer Farnaby went mad, slit his wife's throat with a carver and stabbed himself through the heart.

The flashing, crashing majesty of tempest was overawed by mortal screams, catapulting their eighteen-year-old daughter Candace from her attic in the ragstone farmhouse. A vivid streak through the skylight illuminated the rickety stairs like photographer's magnesium. Her brother Jethro in his nightcap, quivering like a drumskin, was shielding his bride of the spring, pregnant as a poppy-head, her face like suet pudding.

Thundercrack faded into thudding rain, the room below menaced with silence. Candace dared open the door, fumble for the candlestick on the commode, with trembling fingers strike a vesta. Her mother was a crucifix on the bed, blood overpainting the patchwork quilt. Her father was doubled in the empty grate, dead among the fire-irons. It was Candace's first caress with the hand of murder, who was to pay her his shadowy court over the next fifteen months.

And it had been such a lovely evening.

Though likely to turn the milk, thought Candace – who everybody called Candy. As the muffled footsteps of the coming thunder frightened the birds to silence, she was in the dairy-house pouring a threepenny quart for a pair of young sisters among the hop-pickers. The hoppers appeared every August, all Cockneys, raucous, rowdy, sly, thieving, quarrelsome, clownish and drunk, hated in the village like a plague of rabbits.

As the twist of a lane wins enchantment from the English countryside like an unexpected smile from a pretty girl in the street, Blessington was discovered in a grassy dell among the hop-poles and orchards, within a web of tiny roads and the unsteady meanderings of infant rivers, amid the fat fields of the Vale of Kent which helped feed the four and a half million Londoners. Its thatched cottages of Kentish white weatherboard mingled with oast houses like russet pepper-pots, all clustering round the Goat and Bees, the smithy ringing with iron and reeking of singed hoofs, and a pair of shops selling goods in vast variety but apparently the same in both. The church was Norman, ruthlessly restored by City men planted by the railways, their roots as shallow as the forget-me-nots.

'You should come back with us to London town, dearie.' The elder sister Lizzie giggled, swinging their can of milk. 'A right good time you'd get. My word! A 'undred gentlemen would do their balls for a proper bit of frock like you.' It was a Cockney compliment – men would go mad over such a lovely girl.

'And real nice spoken too,' agreed Sal, smiling with head cocked, as though valuing a pile of ripe Kentish plums on a coster's barrow.

Candy blushed, glancing nervously across the dairy-house at her father. He sat on his three-legged stool, hat brim turned down, right cheek hard against the cow's flank, white milking-pinner over cord breeches and leather gaiters, boots thick with mulch, pulling the heavy blue-veined udders while muttering morosely to himself or the animal.

The country was not one of great dairies like the dank, mooing dales of Somerset. The milking-parlour was a thatched dry-stone shed abuzz with bluebottles, its floor thick with cow-dung. The farmyard outside encompassed scratching chickens, a sleeping lurcher, a chained billy-goat. The hop-vines beyond were alive with chattering families, smocked men in caps and curly-brimmed bowlers, broad-aproned women in black straw hats with luridly-dyed flowers, all sweaty in the heavy air, busily filling with sticky, yellow-green cones the canvas panniers slung between pairs of poles like commodious stretchers. The hoppers picked at four bushels a shilling. They lived in low, dark sheds, the walls stained with grease and smoke, full of vermin and stinks. The London Church Society sent them a missionary to preach on Sunday, and a fish dinner from the van cost threepence, which represented a lot of picking.

'But how should I get a living in London?' Candy's cornflower-blue eyes widened as she drew the sisters from her father's earshot. She had coiled straw-coloured hair as long as a mare's tail, milky forearms lamenting beetroot-red hands, the breasts beneath her plain brown dress suggesting the darling buds of May. Her shoulders as graceful as drooping fritillaries were bedecked with a bright green cotton scarf, from a waist as neat as a thistle's her apron fell to cracked and dusty boots.

'Why, you could sell the 'erbses or the vilets,' Sal told her helpfully. 'Lots of gals in Whitechapel goes down to Kent for the day, to pick the arsunts and the ment. Wiv a basket on a good pitch in the West End, she can make herself a madza caroon.'

Only Candy in the village could translate that she spoke of selling herbs and violets, hyacinths and mint for half-a-crown. The hoppers were not London vermin to her, but the colourful racy-tongued missionaries of a tantalizing civilization.

'If she's pretty,' Lizzie qualified. 'The gentlemen ain't much bothered with the flahze.' Candy nodded. Why should a West End 'swell' buy flowers in the street?

'Mind, it's 'ard. You're out past midnight to catch the trade, and don't get 'ome afore folk is going to work. I'd stop where you was, duckie,' Sal advised prudently. ' 'Opping's an 'oliday for the likes of us, wiv two or three bright pounds to show at the end of it.' Victoria's pounds shone of pure gold. 'But you 'as an 'oliday all year round, you're the one wot's touched lucky.'

'You've got to look sharp in London, no mistake,' Lizzie boasted. 'There's a gal I know of, came up from the country after a fortune, went to a women's lodging where you pays tuppence for yer doss, and two more steevers for yer scrag, or goes 'ungry – '

'Mrs Collins of Parker Street.' Sal nodded. There a bed cost twopence, and two more pennies for your food. 'Always dressed like the Christmas beef, loaded with rings and bangles, all thirty stone of 'er. Died and left a Queen's ransom.'

'This poor gal was robbed, barely left a stitch, that and the drink ... mind, I likes a drop of satin – wot you'd call gin – myself. I'll say nothing against it. She ended thrown out of an upstairs winder.'

'Was she killed?' asked Candy eagerly, finding the story no more discouragement than old soldiers' tales to a recruit hungry for glory.

'Stone dead,' Lizzie assured her.

'There's been grown men thrown out of them winders, the woman are diabolical at that kip.' Sal plucked at her sister's sleeve as farmer Farnaby came glowering from the dairy-house, pail in each hand. 'Look at 'im,' she whispered. 'You'd think 'e'd been pissing on a nettle.'

That summer had drawn a black veil of melancholy between farmer Farnaby and his kin. Scowling, surly, suspicious, calling gloomy curses on his cronies, mouthing vengeful accusations at himself, he took no delight in his bread and cheese, his bacon and beer, but sat dark hours in the ingle-nook muttering at ghosts. Blessington folk tapped their foreheads as he passed, sighing or grinning according to kindliness, or whether they had any mad relatives themselves. That midnight, his deranged mind impelled him to his deed as surely as a man falling off a cliff hits the shingle.

The blood of Farnaby's Farm soaked the *Maidstone Telegraph* and splashed the *Ashford Examiner*. It choked the lanes with the gigs and wagonettes of horrified gogglers. There was a crowner's quest, sitting in the bar-parlour of the Goat and Bees, a pair of policemen at the inn door blazoning the British constitution like the lions in Trafalgar Square. A verdict of murder and *felo de se* was pronounced like a double sentence of death.

Candy telegraphed Peter Robinson's Mourning Warehouse at Regent Street in London, who despatched ready-made outfits with fitting dressmaker, at no extra charge. The village took the day off for the funeral. With no entertainment save the sparse festivals of husbandry or church, no music but the parlour piano, few books and few able to read them, death provided the Victorians' emotional waterfall.

The family name, so appallingly besmirched by its own blood, required as many relatives as the railways might reach to follow the hearse. Gruesomeness not grief gathered a gratifying crowd in the farmhouse parlour with fly-speckled sepia-papered walls, a gilt-framed mirror over a mantel with its gaudy miscellany of chipped china, a photograph of the Queen and her dead Prince, a grey engraving of the fleet steaming in storm, a fly-paper curling stickily from the hanging brass oil-lamp, and two samplers by Candy, of the Lord's Prayer and a recipe for ginger pudding.

On the sideboard were piled plates for the funeral breakfast afterwards, bottles of spirits and a firkin of ale to steel the mourners before. Mother's body lay on trestles in the back kitchen, tactfully shrouded to the chin, in a handsome coffin to match the splendour of its passing. Everyone politely went to view, agreeing she made a lovely corpse under trying circumstances.

The hearse drove up at noon. Undertakers with a fine black-and-gold shopfront in Tunbridge Wells provided black plumes on the horses' heads, and a panoply of jet ostrich feathers carried ahead by a mute in top hat with flowing crêpe band, at a guinea extra. A crowd several times the local population enjoyed the satisfaction of watching the coffin appear, followed by the mourners masked in black-bordered handkerchiefs, the front door left wide open by custom or superstition for their return. In stiff shiny bombasine, veiled like a bee-keeper, Candy went in the churchyard to the toll of muffled bells, leather bags half-covering their clappers, so they rang loud then soft, as though echoing in Heaven.

Her father necessitated earlier disposal less formally, in

unconsecrated ground at the fixed fee of six-and-eightpence.

Candy's comfort came from the Cockneys. They were so cheerfully unimpressed with the crime. Murder in their culture was a diverting stroke of drama, as drunkenness was laughable buffoonery, a woman beaten half to death the loser of a domestic argument, rape the penalty of procrastination.

'Back 'ome in Cockneyland,' Sal told her, savouring the splendours of the funeral afterwards in the dairy-house, 'even the poorest will find ten sovs for a burial, if they 'as to starve the next week. A bloke can kick 'is old woman to the grave, but everyone forgives 'im if 'e gives her a decent funeral.'

'There was a lovely one this summer, after a big fire in our street,' Lizzie recalled sentimentally. 'Mother and eight children burnt to death. They 'ad three omnibuses taking the mourners to the cemetery, shilling there and back.'

'A band playing the Death March, and twenty policemen for the crowds,' Sal said. 'Everyone in their Sunday clothes, washed and on their best behaviour. I reckon there was some what wished they'd been burnt too, just to 'ave such a turn out.'

'Remember that little gal in Flower and Dean Street?' Lizzie said fondly. 'Dying, poor thing, ever so pretty, the neighbours clubbed to buy a wreath for her coffin. As she was still alive when it was ready, they took it to 'er bedroom so's she could enjoy it.'

'Wasn't she frightened?' asked Candy breathlessly.

'Frightened? Naw! She was very taken with the kind thought. We've all got to be put to bed one day with a Lord Lovell, ain't we?'

Candy agreed. We shall all be laid to rest with a shovel. In the year of Queen Victoria's Golden Jubilee flourished Cockney rhyming slang, which made stairs 'the apples and pears', and your wife 'the trouble and strife'.

A week later Candy told her brother she was going to London.

'And who's going to help with the farm?'

'Get a slavey from the village. My hands can find better things to do.'

Jethro sat at the parlour table with a tumbler of brandy and hot water. All Blessington noticed how the double tragedy had overstrained him. After the funeral, he had shouted at the relatives and broken the furniture. 'You'll come to a bad end.'

'What of it?' she asked pertly. 'It's so dreary and dull living here, I might as well be dead already.'

He scowled like his father. 'How can you say that? With the earth on our dear parents still fresh.'

But Candy knew that she herself did not live to be buried in Kentish clay.

In the middle of September the hoppers left. Candy packed her bundle and sewed three sovereigns into her stays. Jethro refused her money. He complained that the funeral had ruined him. The poorer Cockneys always walked, but Lizzie and Sal perched with Candy on a hay-wain as high as a house. She knew little of her companions, and discovered they were equally vague of their parents' whereabouts, or how their father was earning a living.

' 'E's as lazy as a tinker what put down 'is budget to fart,' Lizzie disclosed, indicating extreme laziness. 'P'raps they've put 'im where the omnibuses can't run over 'im.'

'In 'Olloway Gaol,' Sal explained.

They promised Candy to share their lodging-house, which was licensed and run by a 'deputy', eightpence a night, its women's dormitory with truckle-beds, a big basement kitchen where there was always a fire, the kettle singing, and somebody toasting a bloater at the grate.

'Me and me skin and blister will look after you,' Lizzie pledged herself and her sister. 'Mind, you've got to watch every bloke, no matter 'ow old or even if 'e's got a wooden leg.'

'You guard your crown and feathers, dearie, if you've still got it,' Sal counselled Candy gravely about her maidenhead. 'Why let a butcher's boy take your maid's ring? My arse! A cherry-pie like you could go up West and get twenty-five Jimmy O' Goblins for it.'

'I'm a good girl,' protested Candy, scarlet at the notion of selling her virginity for 25 sovereigns.

Sal pulled down a lower eyelid. 'My name's Walker,' she scoffed in the fashionable phrase.

The wain creaked up the Old Kent Road and across London Bridge, leaving them at Whitechapel Hay Market. They were east of the Aldgate pump, a part of the globe less familiar to many Londoners than east of Suez. The journey had taken since dawn and it was growing dusk. The cobbles were filled with waggons and carts, amid sheep and bullocks driven to London that morning, still waiting their turn for the slaughter-houses.

For fifty years, English and Irish rustics had arrived at the Hay Market in the hope of better selling their skills or muscles. Now they were overwhelmed by 60,000 'greeners' a year from Poland, Germany and Russia, who soon felt the crook of a tout round their ankles before ending in squalid lodgings among alleys and courts thick with rotting food and human excrement, where life was as hard as death easy. The Hay Market stood where Whitechapel's short High Street became the India Road, which joined the City of London to the docks and the riches of the world.

3

CANDY STARED DOWN at the white card handed her by the surgery porter. It was printed in bold capitals, and needed only a black border to pass as an undertaker's advertisement.

PATIENT OF
DR AMBROSE PORTER–HARTLEY
MA MD (CANTAB) FRCP.

In front of her was a brassbound collecting-box labelled DEPENDENT ENTIRELY ON VOLUNTARY CONTRIBUTIONS, and a white board with black lettering –

SPITTING STRICTLY PROHIBITED
EXCEPT IN SPITTOONS.

She wondered where to go.

Almost half a year had passed. Candy was first excited and scared to find people in Whitechapel as thick as the September starlings, which would rocket down to roost through every branch of an elm tree. Blessington could go a month without seeing a stranger. Here unknown faces were never out of eyesight. Men in waistcoats and caps, women in shawls and aprons, with children often ragged and generally barefoot, and their babies dotingly swaddled and bonneted, loafed in taciturn groups outside their front doors, shouted from windows, laughed and squabbled in the alleys, rubbed elbows in a pavement promenade, and passed continually packaged in cabs, carriages, horse-drawn trams and omnibuses. Poverty cannot afford privacy. The poor acted their lives as publicly as a play, which sharpened feelings, roughened tongues and deadened tenderness in the already limpingly articulate.

The misshapen among them now seemed gathered round her. Men and women hobbled on crutches, sticks and wooden legs, with bent arms, flailing limbs and crooked backs. The children were bowed with rickets and twisted from falls. Everyone was coughing and wiping noses on sleeves. Some sat moaning with their eyes shut, one man was having a fit. A woman was being led out screaming. The baby she had brought in a shawl was already dead.

Candy waited beside a fat man sprawled on one of the benches, who was snorting out gusts of beer like the doorway of a busy pub. A middle-aged woman with a man's face, in a blue dress with a bibbed apron, her collar and cuffs stifly glittering, came unexpectedly from a warm, gas-lit room lined with brass-handled drawers, in the middle a table covered with bandages and rolls of lint.

'What do you want?' she asked Candy curtly.

'If you please, Miss – '

'Not "Miss". The correct form of address is "Sister".' A silver buckle shone like an extra scolding eye from her blue belt, her dangling bunch of keys appeared daily burnished with metal-polish. A flat muslin cap was tied under her chin, the fanned-out bow deserving of a leg of mutton. 'I am Sister Surgery.' She pulled the card from Candy's entwined fingers. 'Are you clean?'

'Pretty well, I think, Sister,' she replied humbly.

'You've nits, I suppose? Everyone has nits and fleas. I'm used to those, but I don't like lice. Have you got crabs? That's the same thing, you know. Yes, you look well scrubbed,' Sister Surgery conceded. 'If you're lousy, the rule is to go home and cover yourself with mercury ointment and bake your clothes in the oven before the doctor sees you.' She handed the card back. 'Sit there and listen attentively until the nurse calls your name.' Sister shook the snoring man heartily. 'Wake up, Daddy,' she said, seemingly not finding his condition unusual.

Candy perched on the edge of the bench. A man's voice said kindly. 'Whose shop are you waiting for?'

She rose, trembling. He was the most magnificent person

ever to address her. Young, handsome, hair and cheeks gleaming, in a silk hat, smelling of violets.

'May I?' Bertie took the card. His principle for being swiftly on intimate terms with any woman was to treat char-women like countesses and vice versa. 'What's your name? How old are you?'

Candy stumbled out the information. 'Were do you live?'

'No. 4 Star Place, sir,' she said in a crushed voice. 'That's in Star Street, off the Commercial Road. I lodge with Mrs Martha Turner.'

His smile was as comforting as salve to a scald. 'What's the trouble?'

'I spat up blood, sir. I was frightened I'd got phossy jaw. I work making the lucifers.'

'How distressing. Fortunately, Dr Porter-Hartley is excellent for such conditions. Quite renowned for it, throughout Europe,' Bertie suggested encouragingly. 'Now, I've a jolly idea. Would you care to visit my consulting rooms in the West End?' Candy's eyes widened. He might have invited her to Buckingham Palace. 'I am making a special study of your sort of case, my dear. It makes no difference if the patients are poor or rich, in society or in jail. Here's my card. Any day from ten to eleven and four till six. You needn't mention it to anyone here. I'll see if I can oil the machinery.'

Bertie spoke to someone beyond a brown-painted door and hurried away without a glance. A young nurse appeared, in grey dress and apron with broad strings across her shoulders, hair lost under a triangular cap. Candy was beckoned into a small room with tiles glistening in the steady white light of the new Wellsbach mantle under a green-topped white-enamelled shade, instead of the usual batswing gas jet. A table held half a dozen tall stoppered jars of coloured fluid, a pitcher and washbasin of plain white china, and a dish with a slice of bright yellow soap. Against a desk like a schoolboy's stood a narrow, flat leather couch. The nurse drew a green baize curtain on a brass rail, dividing it from the door, indicating to Candy a wooden chair. Round the curtain hastened a young man, sallow, thickly moustached, black-haired, in a dark suit with a heavy watch-chain, a wing collar and bow tie.

He stopped short. 'By jove!' He stood rubbing his hands briskly. 'By jove!' he repeated.

He sat at the schoolroom desk, producing paper from the folder under his arm, plucking pen from inkwell.

'And why has the Whitechapel Hospital the honour of your custom?'

'The woman what I lives with once came here. When she pissed pins and needles,' Candy said expressively.

'Ah, the gonorrhoea, the clap,' he reflected. 'No more than a cold in the nose, if you watch out for the pox in the same dose. It even has its uses. Clap stops you having children, you know. Otherwise, the Whitechapel warrens would be breeding to bursting.'

She told him about the blood. She knew nothing of her body deeper than its skin. It frightened her to remember young people in Blessington who coughed a mouthful of blood, sweated, wasted, languished, died within a year – the village said it was caused by miasmas rising from damp soil. She had already visited a chemist's shop in India Road, where a doctor came once a week and left a supply of signed blank death certificates for the man to fill in as needed. The chemist told her she looked strong enough to shift 'fourteen of coals' – a stone – and sold her a bottle of red medicine.

A month later, she spat blood again into the grate. Sal and Lizzie had then disappeared. Perhaps the police were after them, perhaps they moved with the fecklessness of the root-less. She lived now in a two-roomed house, 'one up and one down', back-to-back on an unpaved court with a midden privy. The other room was shared by a carman with a broken leg which never healed after a street accident, who lived by patching old shoes with paper and paste, polishing them up, selling them 'warranted' at a shilling a pair, and hoping the buyer would be some distance away by the next rainstorm. His companion was a nimble-witted rat-catcher, as surly as his chained dogs and boxes of snapping ferrets, the couple often augmented by two noisy Italians from the colony who worked on Gatti's ice wharf.

The room Candy shared was full of scraps which Martha Turner gathered in the street with the notion they might one day prove useful – rags, string, paper, picked-clean bones, stone ginger-beer bottles, coverless books, the spoked skeletons of umbrellas. Candy and Martha made alternative use of the bed. Martha was a prostitute, never in at night. She performed her work in Nature's bedroom. She knew every nook in the walls, every archway in Whitechapel.

Martha had heard of 'medical aid' a person might apply for, and of the sick asylum in the workhouse of Bromley-atte-Bow in Poplar. She recommended the hospital as giving more medicine and less preaching. 'And the doctors there is very now-and-never,' she added, admiring that they were very clever.

'Some of my colleagues would be very interested in your case,' said the young man, eyes sparkling.

He left Candy with the grey-uniformed nurse, who commanded, 'Take your clothes off and lie down.'

'What? All of them?'

'You can keep your drawers.'

She lay on the cold couch. The door burst open, round the curtain appeared the young man with a dozen others. 'We must inspect the abdomen,' he said cheerfully, pulling down Candy's drawers below her pubic hair. 'By jove!' he said again.

The young men felt her chest, tapped it, listened with their stethoscopes. To lie naked with one man touching her was an experience unknown to Candy. A dozen was unimagined. She supposed it was doing her good.

'I say, chaps – !' One in a crimson velvet waistcoat with bright buttons held up his silver pocket-watch. 'It's on one-thirty. We'll get the thundering blazes from old Porters-Harters.'

They vanished. 'May I go, Miss?' Candy asked the nurse timidly.

'Go? Of course not. You've to see the doctor.' As Candy

glanced confusedly towards the door, she added, 'Those were the medical students.'

The nurse handed her a worn dressing-gown of grey flannel and disappeared. Candy lay on the couch, quiet as a corpse. An hour passed. Whatever might be in store was beyond fantasy.

She had often contemplated returning to Kent, but was tainted with the indecisiveness of everyone who slopped in the currents of Whitechapel life. That things must get better kept everyone going, until it became plain that things would not, when there was left only gin and the Thames. Candy took comfort – as any who still breathe – that many were worse off than herself. And Blessington would seem as dull as Lent from one Christmas to the next. Whitechapel was a beggarman's Eldorado, a starvling's Rialto. It bubbled with buying and selling. Petticoat Lane on Sunday was a bazaar, stalls improvised on cart-tilts and shutters across orange boxes. The top of Brick Lane, by the Great Eastern railway station, was a market for racing pigeons, canaries, pet rabbits, guinea-pigs. Commercial Street was jammed by night with noisy, rollicking, cursing, ogling saunterers, costers shouting fiercely under flaring naptha the worth of shoddy clothes, catsmeat, patent braces, chipped china, flashy jewellery, miraculous cure-alls and false teeth. Brass wedding-rings sold a dozen a day, hoodwinking husbands with the real one pawned for drink.

Candy had watched open-mouthed the greasy-aproned salesman reducing his price by a penny a shout, until a bystander's proffered coppers had the fillet of fish slapped into newspaper and wrapped like a conjuring trick. Edging the crowd were small tents with fairground games, oyster sellers with barrels. Serpenting through it went racing tipsters and pickpockets, inseparable from any assembly in London, but harvesting sparsely where the poor were living off the poor.

The Jews sold, the Gentiles bought, and the illusion of snatching a bargain was irresistible. Londoners thought Whitechapel the frontier post between Western civilization and Eastern barbarism. Though it was an insignificant area

24

of the capital, under a mile across, pressed by teeming Shore-ditch, Bethnal Green and Poplar against the cleanly thoroughfares of the City, where men thought of money only in the abstract.

Next door to her first lodging was a brothel, a tumble-down house of three or four rooms indicated by Sal and Lizzie as offhandedly as a post office. A dozen women lived there, supporting their bullies, seldom sober or long out of jail. One November night came screams, one harlot reeled into their kitchen bleeding. A man of too good appearance and too little sense had been lured next door, robbed of money and watch, killed the bully and near killed the girl. The police never found him nor bothered much looking.

Candy made twelve shillings a week at the match factory, working from nine in the morning to eight at night. Lizzie and Sal did sweatshop tailoring, trouser-finishing at three-pence a pair, varying with glueing up dolls at tuppence ha'penny a gross. All were glad of any work, when a job at fifteen shillings a week had five hundred men after it.

She existed on bread-and-jam, condensed milk, stewed eels, everlasting tea at three-farthings a pinch, and treacle – a favourite of the poor, flavoursome and cheap. Every one had so little money, they went to the shops often, for minute quantities. Candy sometimes treated herself to 'the ordinary' – fixed price meat and vegetables, a shilling at the eating house in Houndsditch – or to a savoury pink saveloy for a penny at the stall. When she was down to ha'pence, a cook-shop on the corner of Fashion Street sold hefty ha'penny dough-puddings, warmed by steam rising through holes like the roof of a busy railway station. Or pease pudding at the pork butcher's, who pinched her behind and poured into her basin a spoonful of gravy from the joint roasting for rich customers.

Candy had met Martha Turner with Sal and Lizzie at a pub in Artillery Street. Like many in Whitechapel, it was seemly and hushed, couples chatting or courting in nooks on the sawdust-covered floor, the fat sateened landlady ex-uding respectability. Slips of children came with jugs for their parents' supper beer, at three-ha'pence a pint – more palatable, less poisonous than the water. Publicans attracted their custom with sweets, bribery condemned every Sunday when the Salvation Army marched outside, blowing the Devil back to Hell with trombones.

'Martha's a gay girl,' Lizzie explained. 'She's on the game.'

Martha was thirty-five, gaunt, raw handed, dirty. She took her tuppenny dram of gin, stroking and gently pinching Candy as though a prize leg of mutton awaiting a customer. 'You're a real game-cock, ain't yer, lovey? Why work for a sweater? A gal like you could 'ave a fortune, from men giving you hard for soft.'

Candy smiled. She thought it a pretty way of saying what men did to a girl.

'P'raps she don't want to open Eve's custom house,' suggested Sal, grinning broadly.

'What's the point, keeping up the shutters when you can be as gay as a goose in the gutter?' asked Martha glumly.

Martha called in the lodging-house kitchen every evening for a mug of tea. Candy moved to her hovel in the New Year, because she knew she was disliked among the rough women as finicky and lardy-dardy, and life without her two protectors Sal and Lizzie might turn perilous.

The nurse reappeared in the tiled room from another door. 'Farnaby.'

Candy followed into a long yellow-walled room with rows of benches, filled by a hundred dark-suited young men. A pair of six-spoked gas-jets hung from the ceiling like huge brass spiders. There was another leather couch, and a blackboard on an easel with a meaningless drawing in chalk. Beside stood a short fat man about forty, with sleek black hair, side-whiskers thick as doorknockers, skin as pale as lard and cheeks which wobbled as he talked. He wore a fine frock coat, a high collar and a black satin stock. The nurse silently pressed Candy on an isolated hard chair. Every eye on the benches was upon her. She remembered a dream, on the music-hall stage with every word of her lines forgotten.

'Whose is she?' The gentleman in the frock coat gazed

into the hall. The first young man was bustling forward, papers in hand. He read aloud for several minutes, to Candy as incomprehensibly as the Polish, German and other tongues echoing round her ears in Whitechapel.

'Haemoptysis,' declared the frock-coated man solemnly to the benches. 'The poet John Keats, a qualified doctor, gentlemen ...' He shook a fat finger. 'Though disadvantaged by education not at the Whitechapel Hospital, but at Guy's Hospital – '

There was a burst of loud laughter.

'Keats exclaimed when he expectorated similarly, "That drop of blood is my death warrant. I must die." ' Ambrose Porter-Hartley let it be known that he was a man of culture and of current affairs, as of science. 'We immediately think of – ?'

'Phthisis,' thundered the eager response.

He nodded, stroking his smooth chin. 'Yet we have heard from Mr Grimes, the clerk, that the blood in this woman's case was not frothy. No. Nor did it continue in ever-darkening pellets for hours, or even days. Not at all. So she may not be condemned to expectorating unto the grave, buoyed by *spes phthisica*, the strange hope of such patients when there is nothing to hope for.' His tones were melancholy. 'Expound to us, Mr Grimes, the causes of phthisis.'

'Heredity, sir.'

'Indeed. The offspring of the phthisical suffer a grave tendency to the disease, doubtless from some delicacy of the tissues. The tubercular diathesis is revealed by certain characteristics.' He had not yet looked at Candy, but bestowed a glance in her direction. 'There is the dark, often beautiful, tubercular type. There is the fair, coarse-skinned scrofulous type, to which this woman belongs. More causes?'

'Deficiency of food and fresh air, sir,' the student continued.

'Exactly. Overcrowding. Exhausting toil. Frequent childbearing, the debilitating drain of lactation. Exposure to wet and damp, excessive indulgence in alcoholic drink, syphilitic cachexia ... in short, the earmarks of the labouring classes,

27

among which the disease is rife, compared to those of gentle birth.'

'What about germs, sir?' exclaimed the student in the crimson velvet waistcoat, from the front row.

Dr Ambrose Porter-Hartley gave a loud sigh. 'Germs!' He might have been referring to contemptible foreigners. 'Germs,' he repeated, as though contemplating the nebulous mysteries of the universe. 'Germs,' he muttered, as though savouring a good joke.

'That phthisis was contagious has been suggested since the days of the great Arabian physician Avicenna, in the first century after the birth of Our Lord,' he expounded. 'From the Black Forest now comes a voice somewhat lesser. Phthisis is a destructive disease of the lung, gentlemen, occasioned by the formation of tubercules. Dr Koch speculates that these tubercules are incited by some "bacillus",' he said sneeringly, 'entering the mucus passages. It apparently resembles a rod, with bright spots at each end. Dr Koch has seen it. I have not. Spores of various sorts frequently contaminate microscopical preparations. And Germans have as unfortunate a capacity to create a science from the haphazard, as a philosophy from the obvious.'

To Candy's alarm, he abruptly grabbed her hand. 'This woman is a matchmaker – not of the drawing-room sort – '

There was another clap of laughter.

'We might expect her to have phosphorous burns on her fingers.' He turned the hand as though it were disembodied. 'Were she a seamstress, the left index finger would reveal roughening from constant pricking with the needle. Copyists have a corn on the middle finger, made by the pen. Photographers' fingers are blackened with nitrate of silver, coachmen have a roughened thumb and index finger from pressure of reins and whip, violinists suffer corns on the fingertips of the left hand.'

Ambrose dropped Candy's, as of no interest. 'Shoemakers have a pit in the lower breastbone, from the pressure of the last, gentlemen. Tailors work with their legs crossed and body bent, thus the thorax projects over the abdomen and they develop soft tumours on the ankles. Bricklayers, turners and coppersmiths develop flattened finger-tips. Such stigmata are useful in determining occupation, particularly of a dead body.'

The nurse stepped from behind and slipped down Candy's dressing-gown. A loud gasp came from the onlookers. She shifted nervously on the chair. Was something terrible wrong with her, instantly visible to these learned gentlemen?

The man in the frock coat placed a strip of ivory in various parts of her chest, striking it with a small ivory hammer. Then he listened through a polished wooden tube which reminded Candy of a hunting horn.

'No dull note by the plexor and pleximeter. No râles. no cogwheel respiration, no *bruit de pot fêlé*, no cavitation. Well? How do we proceed?'

'Wait and see if there's another haemoptysis, sir,' said Mr Grimes.

'That is the *experimentum crucis*,' agreed Ambrose, having the fondness for a Latin expression as Bertie had for a schoolboy one. 'Treatment?' he enquired, as the nurse covered her up.

'Change of climate, sir,' said the student in the bright waistcoat.

'South Africa or Egypt?' Ambrose demanded sarcastically. 'Only in my Harley Street rooms may I prescribe ladies and gentlemen of tubercular tendency a six months' voyage. In a sailing vessel,' he emphasized. 'In steam vessels, the conditions may be the reverse of satisfactory. This woman must be contented with a tonic.' He took a pen from a pewter inkpot on a high desk like a book-keeper's. 'I shall exhibit quinine, with iron the *ajuvans*, rhubarb the *corrigens* and *infusium quassiae* as the *constituens*.'

He handed a slip of blue paper to the nurse, who conducted Candy into the small tiled room. No one during the consultation had addressed her a word.

Bertie had not stopped thinking of her.

The operating theatre at the Whitechapel Hospital was the size of a Mayfair drawing-room, green-painted, with a pair of kitchen sinks served by robust pipes and brass taps. A marble-topped table was piled with neatly folded towels, a shelf had bottles varying in size and colour, a slate in a wooden frame held the operating-list, the frosted-glass windows with decorative cartwheel fanlights were open all summer to the busy traffic of Ropewalk Lane. A small coke stove burnt perpetually, like a sacred flame. The older surgeons preferred red-hot irons to stop the bleeding, as their predecessors under Queen Elizabeth.

In one corner stood a tall, polished deal cupboard, containing hooks with the painted names of the hospital's surgeons. Five years before, frock coats hung there, too worn for society and saved for operating, stiff with blood and pus, and the stiffer they were the better the operator's practice. At the bottom was a pail of sand and a coal-shovel. When the surgeon found the floor sticky with blood, he had a nurse scatter a few shovelfuls across the boards.

It was always crowded. Theatre sister, staff nurse and young probationer wore their distinguishing uniforms. The students wore street clothes. Oliver and Tomkins the house-surgeon wore white aprons, tied round the neck like carpenters', and linen sleeve-covers. They worked with bare hands and forearms, rinsing off the blood in china basins at their elbows. Bertie was in his shirt sleeves, dropping chloroform from a small, brown-tinted bottle on lint over the patient's face. The man was covered by a sheet stained with blood, on which lay instruments and a pair of small enamel bowls containing hot water and bloody sponges. They were amputating his right arm for gangrene, following a compound fracture after a fall at work in the nearby docks. Most operations were on the body's exterior or extremities. The abdomen had not yet opened up its riches to the surgeon.

A student was pumping the plunger of a small domed brass canister like a blowlamp. This was Professor Lister's spray, which doused the surgical wound, instruments and operators' fingers in carbolic. Only Oliver at the White-chapel Hospital used it, to be thought either eccentric or youthfully impressionable. Some surgeons were ready to admit that bacteria existed. None, that they caused disease. Cleanliness in the operating theatre was derided as affectedly ladylike. Did the butcher scrub his chopping-block, or a headsman first clean his nails?

Oliver tied the arteries with silk, sawed through the bones of the humerus above the elbow and joined the flapping skin over the end with hempen thread, as a cook sewed a stuffed goose. The stump was dressed with charpie – narrow, fringed strips of torn linen, soaked in oil. The patient was dispatched unconscious to the ward, on a brown-painted stretcher with high sides on a pair of wheels like a handcart, which looked strong enough to stall an ox. Bertie hurried back to the out-patients' surgery, calculating his chance of catching Candy. She was queuing with a dozen others at the dispensary hatch.

'Nurse told me to come back here if I spat more blood, sir,' she told him respectfully. 'Otherwise, I was to take the physic.'

Bertie glanced at the blue paper, grinning.

'Oh, the red medicine. It'll do you no end of good, I'm sure. It's a treat to swallow compared to the green, and doesn't begin to match the nastiness of the brown. You've still got my card?'

'Yes, sir.'

'You're coming?'

'I'll try, sir.'

'Try hard. You may hear something to your advantage – as solicitors say when one of their clients has carved up uncommonly well.'

Glancing hastily to assure himself unseen, he patted her behind and hurried away.

4

Dr Thomas Dalhouse opened the letter bearing the German stamp with a thumbnail stained green and violet by dye. It was the following Tuesday morning, shortly after nine o'clock. The second post had arrived. Her Majesty's postmen, in brass-buttoned blue serge and shiny-peaked shakos, scurried around London with canvas mailbags sewn by Her Majesty's prisoners, making eleven deliveries a day, snatching sleep in hourly naps on post office floors.

Dr Dalhouse was the same age as Bertie Randolph. He was short and pasty-faced, with a long smooth chin, a sharp nose, and pale hair which he could never decide to plaster back with pomade and look dignified, or retain in its natural quiff and look a little sporty. His serge suit was thick, worn and well-pressed, his linen clean but frayed, his watch-chain heavy gold, betokening a legacy. He wore substantial boots, one with a small patch, he hoped unnoticeable. He had the look of a grocer's assistant dressed for church.

Tom Dalhouse stood before a newly lit fire in a small triangular room among the complicated architecture at the back of Whitechapel Hospital. Under the window ran a laboratory bench with a small square sink and a Bunsen burner, with flasks and racks of test-tubes stoppered by tow. A brass microscope with a double eye-piece stood amid small china dishes and some glass jars – like those used for potted meat – containing human organs in white spirit. The Whitechapel Hospital conscientiously cut up its dead. Doctors have never won sufficient credit from their patients for willingness to learn from their mistakes.

The hospital paid poorly for this service. Unlike surgery and medicine, where a patient would gladly give guineas for the loss of a lump or an ague, pathology had no commercial value. Tom was demonstrator in morbid anatomy. He could never afford to marry for years. He could barely afford to live as it was. This dispiriting thought returned to him as he heard the door open and deliberately kept his eyes hard on the letter.

He had still che expense of ploddingly learning German from an emigré Jewish schoolmaster in India Road. Any scientist needed a grasp of that language to flourish. After some minutes mental translation, he gave a businesslike nod, folded the paper, slipped it in his pocket, and bestowed his attention on the newcomer.

'It's from Professor Koch. From Berlin. The leading bacteriologist in the world. In his own hand,' he announced impressively. 'He was pleased to express interest in my paper on erysipelas in the *British Medical Journal*, the reprint of which I ventured to send him.'

'Well, now, isn't that nice?' Dr Janet Veale was in her mid-twenties. Her bright red hair was coiled in a chignon, she had straight brows over hazel eyes, a kindly face and freckles on her milky complexion like nutmeg on wholesome junket. She wore a dress of grey-and-silver striped cotton with a lace collar. She displayed no jewellery, not even a ring. She smelt early in the day of household soap, which inflamed Tom like all the perfumes of Arabia.

Janet Veale was his newly-appointed assistant in forensic medicine. In London, the law and medicine were as disinclined to mix as the oily and acid components of a prescription. The Inns of Court and the Royal Colleges of Surgeons and Physicians, with their robes and their maces and their banquets, were too jealous of their own privileges and too distrustful of each others'. The science of forensic pathology originated in the dry minds of Scots attorneys and doctors, who practised with as little pomp as they worshipped, and would dine happily on a herring in oatmeal. The first professor in medical jurisprudence was created in Edinburgh in 1806, the world's first book on it published there thirty years later. When the Whitechapel

33

Hospital decided to cultivate this ripening speciality, it looked to Edinburgh for its practitioner.

Tom was first shocked, then panicky, that his new assistant should be a lady. He had never thought about female doctors, only about the problem of medical education for women. He believed it one to be faced with extreme caution. How could a gentleman of his refined feelings, he wondered agitatedly, discuss across the sexes what must be uttered with freedom between two doctors? The practice of medicine demanded woman's acquaintance with so many matters she were better left in total ignorance for life.

He considered the excess of female population would better seek its outlet in nursing. The ministry of women was of help, of sympathy. She was a natural nurse, because of the natural surrender of her judgement to the male, and her natural inplicit obedience to him. Then Tom had grown dreadfully muddled, and fallen in love with her, and not slept or eaten properly for weeks.

'Bacteriology! There lies the future of medical science.' Tom was some inches shorter than Janet. He looked up with quiff erect. 'Think of the thundering great discoveries which are being made almost daily, Dr Veale. The bacteria of leprosy discovered by Hansen, the Norwegian. The cause of gonorrhoea by Albert Neiser. Of pneumonia by the great Pasteur. Of glanders by Löffler. Of diptheria by Klebs. Of tetanus by Nicolaier. Of Malta fever by Sir David Bruce. Of cerebrospinal meningitis by Anton Weichselbaum of Vienna. *This* is the bacillus of typhoid fever – ' He flourished from the table a test-tube of pink liquid. 'Discovered by Carl Eberth of Halle. The very tubercule bacillus itself has been unmasked by my correspondent of this morning, Robert Koch.'

Tom replaced the test-tube in the rack. He wanted to excite and impress her with his overwhelming knowledge, as a prizefighter his muscles to a barmaid.

'There certainly seems a disease for every germ, as there's a punishment for every sin,' Janet said comfortably. She stood with hands clasped, wearing the soft smile which materialized so often between Tom and his test-tubes or his solitary supper.

'I suppose that's one way of looking at it. Nobody can believe any longer that microbes arise by spontaneous generation from dead organic matter. It was shown by Fransesco Redi as long ago as 1668 that maggots don't appear on putrefying flesh if the flies were kept off. Though there's plenty of otherwise learned physicians in this hospital, and every other in London, who don't seem to have grasped the idea yet.'

'If you ask me, Dr Dalhouse,' she said with her usual frankness, suggestive of an intimacy which made the nape of his neck tingle,' the doctors don't *want* to believe in microbes. They're only bothersome nuisances to their set ideas, like mice to an old cook in a kitchen.'

'I could not have put it better,' he conceded. 'Professor Koch, who wrote to me today,' he repeated, tapping his jacket pocket, 'discovered five years ago that cholera was caused by a germ. He was head of the German Cholera Comimssion to Egypt, and got a hundred thousand marks for his pains from the old Emperor. But what a dusty answer I should get, if I suggested to the distinguished doctors walking our corridors that the cause of cholera was something microscopic, shaped like a comma.'

He glared, wishing to appear the outraged man of science, but resembled a grocer's assistant accused of giving short weight.

'Ah, me, Dr Dalhouse,' she sympathized. 'Scientific discovery progresses with the ponderousness of a hay-wain, when it should flash like the electric telegraph.'

'Precisely, Dr Veale. Meanwhile, my obdurate colleagues go on believing that cholera is caused by the miasma from bad drains, and that the epidemic abates when the body is exhausted of some mysterious food on which some equally unknown contagium must feed to live. Dr Veale,' he commanded, 'repeat to me Koch's postulates.'

Gazing at his boots, she said as a catechism, 'One, the microbe must be found in all cases of the disease. Two, it

35

must be grown outside the body. Three, these microbes must in turn produce the disease in susceptible animals. Only if these principles are fulfilled, may any particular microbe be accepted as the cause of any particular disease.'

'Excellent, Dr Veale!'

'Thank you, Dr Dalhouse.'

'I'm sure the day will not be too far distant,' he condescended, 'when women practitioners will be permitted to appear in the same medical *Register* as us males, rather than being included among foreigners and colonials. Today, I should like you for the first time in this hospital to perform the post-mortems,' he continued impressively. He found post-mortems a bore. The study of germs, forever splitting in two until they could cover the earth with an invisible deadly film, better fitted a man of his professional and social nonentity.

She gazed at him excitedly. 'I shall assist with the first, a murder,' he announced, 'which is as common in Whitechapel as a wedding. The cry "Murder!" is heard in these parts as regularly as the shout of the rag-and-bone man, though it's usually only a woman being knocked about by her chap. This case is a female, of the unfortunate class.' They had started walking along the stone-flagged corridor outside. 'Aged forty-five or so. Name, Emma Smith. Lived in George Street, across at Spitalfields Market. A widow, or so she gave out. Most Whitechapel widows have absconded husbands.'

Tom opened a door to a small cobbled, irregularly shaped yard at the rear of the hospital. A line of flagstones, pierced by an iron-covered manhole, crossed to a green-painted double door leading into Ropewalk Lane, which ran parallel to the north bank of the Thames. This was the 'fever gate', through which infected cases were brought to the isolation ward, with its incinerator sporting a thick black stove-pipe.

'You've made a good breakfast?' Tom asked. She nodded. 'No post-mortem should ever be conducted on an empty stomach,' he counselled. 'For an exhumation, which is often a disgusting proceeding, it is well to take a little spirits.'

Opposite the isolation ward was the mortuary, an octagonal brick building with a slate roof, the size of a farm-labourer's cottage. Lancet windows pierced the sides, the roof was capped by a yellow-painted lantern to admit daylight, a stove-pipe jutted from one corner. A uniformed policeman was waiting outside, with a stolid, red-faced man in gingery overcoat and a brown bowler hat. 'Detective Inspector Frederick Abberline?' Tom greeted him. 'From Scotland Yard? Haven't we met here before?'

'That's right, sir. I was inspector of the Whitechapel division of police, before I was promoted.'

'So you know the ground?'

'Every inch, sir.'

'Any arrest?'

'A matter of time, sir. This is the coroner's officer.' Inspector Abberline nodded towards the policeman. 'Inquest fixed for Saturday morning, Coroner Macdonald, sitting at the Working Lads' Institute.'

'We don't have inquests in Scotland,' Janet told him, on being introduced. 'The Procurator-Fiscal sits in private.'

'We had five hundred inquests in Whitechapel alone last year,' Tom recalled as all four entered, sounding proud of it.

The mortuary was divided by a pitch-pine wall into two parts. The front was larger, three empty coffins stacked on end in one corner, another two on the stone floor containing bodies, lids not screwed down. A trestle table covered with American cloth held the shrouded corpses of three adults and four children.

Tom Dalhouse led through an inner door to the post-mortem room. One wall was covered with shelves of large bottles, some containing coloured liquid, some human organs. The corner had a chopping-block, worn and blood-tinged like a butcher's. The room was cold, the stove being newly lit. Gas flared from the roof. On a trestle table were arranged an ebony-handled knife as long as a bayonet, scissors, cutting-forceps, a foot-rule, a conical glass graduated in drachams, a stone jar stoppered with tow, some square green pickle jars, pen and ink and scarlet sealing-wax. In the centre was a zinc-topped table with an arrow-pattern of rivulets, sloped so that they drained through a hole into a pail on the floor.

'Good day to you, Hans,' said Tom, busily removing his jacket.

A powerfully built young man with cropped fair hair, in a long leather apron like the blacksmith's, held a bucket in one hand and soapy sponge in the other. On the table lay the naked corpse of a dark-haired woman, her flesh in flabby folds, her breasts like half-empty tobacco pouches.

'I have finished washing the body,' he said, in a German accent. He nodded towards a pile of dirty rags in the corner. 'There's the clothes. Her shawl was soaked with blood.'

Hans gave a final wipe to the pale, cold skin as tenderly as a caress, a delicacy unexpected of his burly shoulders. He gently smoothed the hair away from her unseeing eyes. Tom had noticed how the mortuary attendant afforded his subjects the sensibility of a lover. Tom was glad for him to enjoy his work. The hospital paid him only twelve shillings a week.

Tom rolled up his sleeves, donning a leather apron stained with blood, handing another to Janet as she slipped the sleeves of her grey dress above the elbows. The two police officers stood by the door, notebooks drawn.

'First, the external aspect of the body,' Tom reminded her. 'We must never be too impatient to open the parcel when the wrappings may give us valuable information. What do you see, Dr Veale?'

'A black eye, Dr Dalhouse.'

'A not uncommon condition. There is quite an epidemic among the ladies of Whitechapel,' Tom told her waggishly. 'Any incised wounds?'

'Her ear.'

'Any more?' Janet shook her head. 'Look.' He tugged open the woman's legs, which was difficult through rigor mortis. 'See?'

'Her vagina's been cut into. Well, fancy that.'

'Exactly.' Displaying the corpse's private parts to Janet gave Tom such insuppressible excitement he feared he might shudder. 'From the house-surgeon's notes, the weapon was inserted through the pudenum muliebre, to incise the membrana perinalis, opening the vagina into the rectum.' He pulled the blood-clotted lips of the genitals apart with his thumbs. 'Had she lived, she would have suffered for the rest of her days from a fistula, her faeces passing freely into the vagina. A horrible condition. This cut is sometimes inflicted upon some woman of the lower classes, as a revenge for infidelity. Though I am glad to say it is a foul practice only by persons of foreign race. Eh, inspector?'

'That's right sir. Frogs, Jews and the like. Happens now and then among the greeners arriving in Whitechapel.'

'This woman Smith was carried into the receiving room on a shutter,' Tom continued. 'She must have jammed her shawl between her legs to staunch the blood. She was past speech, *in extremis.* Had she not died of haemorrhage, she would have succumbed in a day or so to traumatic peritonitis.'

While talking, Tom handed the long knife to Janet. With a pleasure as keen as its blade, he watched her soft white hand dig its point below the chin, then slit the corpse down to the bony girdle of the pelvis. Questioning, advising, he pressed close beside her as she cut the rib-cartilages as if the crackling on pork, lifted the narrow, flat breastbone like a coffin-lid on the dead heart. She plunged in her arm to the elbow, cut free squelching lungs and liver, slit the transparent fatty mesenteric membrane and drew the corpse of its guts, dropping all into successive earthenware receivers held by Hans, standing attentively at her elbow like a butler with the vegetables.

As neatly as a cook in a kitchen, Janet opened the organs on the chopping-block, blood dripping on a flagstoned floor spread with sawdust. The contents of the stomach – half-digested meat and onions – went into one pickle bottle, the contents of the intestines into another. She returned to the corpse. She slit the vault of scalp from ear to ear, masked the face by peeling back the forehead, and sawed through the skull to remove the brain like a giant, pale walnut. Hans turned the eviscerated body over, as gently as laying a baby in its cot. Janet opened the spine with bone-nippers and removed the spinal cord like an elongated soft roe. Their scrutiny of Emma Smith was over. They rinsed their hands in limewater and hung up their leather aprons. Tom noticed how Janet looked – flushed, pleased and excited at performing to his satisfaction. He had enjoyed only one woman in his life, the daughter of his former landlady in Parliament Hill, who feigned influenza one Sunday while her parents went to church. He remembered she had looked exactly the same. He had left the lodgings the next week, through guilt.

'Cause of death, haemorrhage from vaginal wounds,' Tom concluded to Inspector Abberline. 'Our work is done. Yours begins.'

'Just a matter of time, sir, a matter of time.'

It was approaching twelve when the police left. Hans sewed up the riven body with a long length of hempen thread on a thick needle, replacing the sliced organs higgledy-piggledy inside like the stuffing of a Christmas goose. Leaving the post-mortem room with Janet, Tom found Bertie Randolph smoking his cigar among the coffins outside.

'Hello, old fellow. Have you carved up my stiff 'un yet? Should have come earlier, but I'm a bit seedy this morning.'

'No, I haven't.' Tom disliked Bertie. His flippancy he found a disgrace to their profession and affront to himself. 'Yes, you look ghastly pale.' Seedy! Tom thought. The only contagion he's likely to catch is from the neck of a brandy-bottle.

'This is the stiff, isn't it?' Bertie unknotted the shroud from the face of a slightly-built corpse on the oilcloth-covered table. 'Can't understand why she croaked. Healthy girl of eighteen. Oliver was doing nothing more serious than amputation of the big toe – gangrenous from a rat-bite. One whiff of chloroform, and she was gone. Her people are cutting up rough. Sister Surgery is handling them, thank heaven. Don't the poor grow so insolent, when they take the charity we afford here as their right?'

'You know my views on chloroform, Randolph.' Tom's quiff seemed to bristle. 'We'll find distention of the right ventricle, I'll be bound. Death due to syncope. There are dangers in that drug,'

'There are dangers in every drug,' Bertie replied amiably. 'Including Eno's Fruit Salts and Carter's Little Liver Pills.' He tipped back his hat. 'How fares the Juno of this medical Olympus?' he asked Janet.

'I've just done my first post-mortem for the Whitechapel,' she replied, eyes shining. Tom fought to iron a scowl from his face.

'So, you have come out in pathological society? How much more estimable than being presented at Court. Were all our "new women" like you, Dr Veale, I should never trouble myself with the old.'

Hans appeared from inside with a handcart bearing an open coffin chalked EMMA SMITH.

'What did *she* die of?' Bertie asked Tom.

'Murder.'

Puffing his cigar, Bertie stared down at the naked corpse. 'How did it happen?'

'The poor soul had a knife thrust up her vagina,' Janet told him.

'How uncomfortable.' The flap of scalp had been re-placed, and sewn to its fellow. Bertie pulled up the woman's eyelids with thumb and forefinger. 'Did you know, Dal-house, that the vision of a murderer's face is left imprinted on the victim's eye?'

'That goes against all the logic of physiology.'

'Logic? But our profession is often as irrational as a poet's.'

'Now, that's an interesting wrinkle,' Janet agreed. 'The police could photograph it.'

'The click of the camera-shutter would lead to the snap of the hangman's trap,' Bertie reflected. 'I'll leave you to slice up my corpse, Dalhouse. I'm meeting some fellows in the West End for luncheon.'

5

THE MORNING POST has come, sir.'

'Ah! One with a French stamp? I'll read it directly. Open the newspaper and tell me the news, Freshings.'

Bertie Randolph was in his hip bath, of cast iron brown-enamelled outside, white within. It stood on a square of blue-checked American cloth spread over the Turkey carpet, beside his brass bedstead with crumpled linen sheets. A fire leapt in the well-blacked grate, under marble mantel and oval mirror. He rubbed himself with a sponge the size of a football, sent specially from the island of Rhodes, lathering himself with lavender soap sent specially from Trumpers' in Curzon Street.

It was the last Friday in February, a sunless morning of sleet and snow.

Freshings the valet was Bertie's own age, burly, dark hair in a cow-lick plastered to his forehead, his nose sharp and upturned like the pert beak of a Cockney sparrow. Reared in an orphanage, he faced the world with the envied talent of reading, though words over three syllables were his conundrums. He wore a tail coat, a high stiff collar with a white tie and well tailored trousers – Bertie thought the economy amusing, that his man could wear his own discarded garments. He paid him ten shillings a week, with keep and Saturday afternoons to himself.

Freshings laid his silver tray with *The Times* and the letters on the ormolu–inlaid walnut secretaire, beside lace-curtained windows facing Belgrave Square. He opened the paper in the middle.

The news is about the Crown Prince, sir.' Freshings

frowned at the print. 'There is no change in 'Is Royal 'Ighness's condition. Three bul-bulletins are being issued each day from San Remo.'

'Anything on the court page?'

Freshings turned over.

' 'Er Majesty travelled from London to Windsor, escorted to Paddington Station by a detachment of Life Guards. The Prince of Wales 'as arrived at Marlborough 'Ouse from Sandringham. Miss Emily Skinner during the evening 'ad the honour of playing the violin before 'Er Majesty.'

'Bravo for Miss Emily Skinner! That's all the news, Freshings? Does the world enjoy salutary tranquillity? Or does it suffer the symptoms of insidious languor?'

The valet spread a white Turkish towel on the oilcloth, holding another like a cape.

'By the by, Freshings, tell Mrs Anstey I've a gentleman coming for breakfast.'

Bertie vigorously rubbed his short, plump, hairy body. Freshings proffered a lilac dressing-gown of quilted silk, tying a hand towel round Bertie's neck like a bib. Bertie reached for an ivory-handled paper-knife on the secretaire, slitting open the envelope with the yellow 3-centime stamp. 'I'll shave myself this morning, Freshings.'

'Very well, sir.' The valet carried a steaming brass can under another fresh towel into the narrow dressing-room, a fire glowing in the grate, its smell bay-rum, Trumper's Eucris and *pomade Hongroise*.

The letter was headed only 'Paris'. It was in French, which Bertie read more easily than Freshings' English.

My dear,

It is so many months since you were here, you must have quite forgotten my little shop. I have just heard from friends in the country of two delightful statuettes, which will definitely be in my hands by March 20. They are exactly the sort to suit English tastes, I assure you. Should you wish to import them for sale in London, I can make a price like our

43

last bargain. Please tell me as soon as possible whether you can come and inspect them. Naturally, there will be others interested.

It would be a great pleasure to meet you again, dear Bertie. Remember – discretion! Our world of art is an increasingly suspicious one, eyes are everywhere, even in the post offices.

Always yours,
Colette

Bertie dropped the thick, mauve, wavy-edged paper with a satisfied look. From the dressing-room came the sound of Freshings stropping his razor.

'You might also tell Mrs Anstey I shall be going abroad for a week. From March the nineteenth. That's a Monday, I believe? And I want a telegram taken to the post office right away.' Bertie looked benign as his man reappeared. 'What price you going to Paris, too?'

'I'd like to see the world, sir, I must say. 'Aving bin no further afield than the five shilling excursion to Margate.'

'Not this visit, which is going to be dull and damn busy. I shall spend all my time walking the hospitals. But we'll see,' he promised. 'If you do your job always to my liking. I expect to be crossing the Channel fairly regularly.' In the dressing-room, he added to himself, 'Simple minded clod!' Bertie had an insuppressible contempt for ignorance, except embodied in a beautiful young woman.

The house was tall and narrow. The ground floor dining-room, looking across the area railings and tradesmen's steps down to the basement kitchen, doubled as the patients' waiting room. The doorbell rang while Bertie waited for his visitor politely beside the table, its shiny linen covered with silver jugs and lavish cutlery, on the sideboard a pair of chafing dishes with spirit-lamps flickering blue underneath.

Freshings showed in Oliver Wilberforce. 'Breakfast is simply a meal, not a social occasion,' Bertie greeted him. 'It's pretty informal here, I'm afraid. You must forgive a man who lives *en garçon*.'

'Informal the deuce.'

'On so rotten a morning, there's no need to sit in the dark.' Bertie reached for a china bulge like an inverted teacup, above the fireplace, and proudly turned an ebonite knob.

Oliver blinked. 'You have the electricity.'

'Oh, it's so much less smelly than gas.'

'How do you manage it?' Oliver gave his thin smile. 'At the Whitechapel, you're a mystery. No one can flatter you with the most lucrative practice in Belgravia. You must do handsomely in the City.'

'Come, old fellow! Would you have me trembling at the share prices every morning, like Ambrose? I'm resigned to being a mystery. Any man with his mother a Frenchwoman is a mystery in England. I can assure you that my father was respectably dull, and as short on words and temper as any other doctor desiccating in the Indian Medical Service. The English in India were dreadfully suspicious of his marrying out of his race. A French bride somehow suggested going native. We'll help ourselves,' he added to a pair of young, pink-cheeked maids appearing at the door in brown morning uniforms, round caps on their black curls. 'Though fetch some more coals for the fire.'

Bertie grinned as the door shut. 'You suspect that I make them lie with me sometimes, like the maidservants of Candide's noble Venetian? I see the Venetian's point. A man tires of the coquetry, jealousy, meanness, pride and folly of society ladies. He enjoys a bout with a working girl of no pretensions. Who better still, does not expect *him* to assume any.'

'I'm sure you are far too shrewd to play cuckoo in your own nest.'

Bertie laughed, serving fried eggs, bacon, kidneys and sliced potatoes. 'When's Morell Mackenzie back from Italy?'

'He's bringing his daughter Ethel home early next week. The German press is meanwhile inflamed at her playing lawn-tennis with the daughters of a Crown Prince. You'd imagine it a *casus belli*. Did you read Mackenzie's statement in the *Lancet* last week?'

'He is trying to convince the world that his patient hasn't got cancer, when he hasn't been able to convince himself.'

'Well, yes, *The Times* was perhaps right that he produced a universal feeling of profound uneasiness,' Oliver admitted. 'But there's never been any positive proof of cancer, you know.' The two sat at the table. 'The German doctors are so devious, that Bismarck accused them last year of plotting to chloroform the Prince and remove his larynx by stealth, like Shanghai-ing a sailor.'

'Chloroform! So powerful, so silent.' Bertie produced a small brown-tinted bottle with a beaked stopper from his top pocket. 'So sweet in its sickly mysteries.'

'I wish you'd use ether instead on my patients. Chloroform is also so dangerous.'

'Not in the right hands.' Bertie let a couple of drops fall into his palm. 'I inhale a little when I'm feeling blue. At breakfast, it sets a fellow up for the morning. Try some.' Oliver declined. Bertie sniffed, replacing the bottle. 'So gentle its touch, so insidious its grip, the stealthiest thug with the silkiest scarf in Bengal could not work as effectively.'

'Or even Mrs Adelaide Bartlett of Pimlico?' Oliver suggested. 'Whatever happened to her, I wonder?'

The Pimlico Mystery gave a tingle to 1886. Adelaide Blanche de la Tremoville, illegitimate daughter of an Englishman, born in Orleans but reared at Richmond, was married off aged nineteen to thirty-year-old Edwin Bartlett, with six grocer's shops in the south London suburb of Herne Hill. Deeply concerned for her education in Latin, history, geography and mathematics, he commissioned tutorials from George Dyson, a Wesleyan Minister of twenty-seven. George and Adelaide became lovers. She had him buy a bottleful of chloroform. On New Year's morning she woke with her husband dead, his last supper of oysters, mango chutney and cake found mixed internally with chloroform. Suicide or murder? Had she chloroformed him in his sleep? Then the grocer's widow had worked a scientific miracle, said Sir Edward Clarke in her defence. She was acquitted, cheers bursting from the Old Bailey. Across the road at St

Bartholomew's Hospital, Sir James Paget interrupted a surgical lecture to declare that the young woman should in the interests of medicine now say exactly how she did it.

'What happened to Adelaide Bartlet?' Bertie repeated. 'Whatever happens to any beautiful woman acquitted at the Old Bailey or the Palais de Justice? Oblivion. Did you know that using chloroform upon a person to commit any indictable offence is a felony?'

'I hope you do not think my surgery comes under that legal category?'

'Stupid ass.' Bertie laughed again. 'Are you breaking with Mrs Wilberforce?' he asked abruptly.

'No.'

'Why?'

'It would cost me five thousand a year. My career has advanced both too far and not far enough to withstand scandal.'

'So to the world, you're as lovey-dovey as a honeymoon couple?'

'Yes.' Oliver's thoughts seemed absorbed by his food.

'Though you wish she was dead?'

'How can you say a thing like that?' he demanded crossly.

'Because it's a thing you said yourself. In a hansom driving to the hospital a fortnight ago. Remember?'

'Very well. I hate the woman,'

'Why?'

'She's undutiful.'

'Doesn't give the cook proper orders? Invites disastrous social enemies to dinner-parties? Or is it her flower arrangement?'

'You know perfectly well,' Oliver told him impatiently. 'It's the one duty a wife must fulfil above all others. Mrs Wilberforce does not. She will not. Even when I am driven to implore her. It is entirely her fault that I am forced into the company of temptations I no more care for than that of pickpockets and cut-throats.'

They were interrupted by the maid with the coal.

'These kidneys are superb,' said Oliver.

47

'My housekeeper was in the service of Lord Rosebery. She was sacked for addiction to laudanum. A fitting servant for a man making his living from stupor.' When they were alone, Bertie said, 'To save you broaching the subject, you'd like to meet one of my lady friends?'

Oliver said nothing for a moment.

'I fear that I am suffering from spermatorrhoea,' he announced bleakly.

Bertie went on eating his breakfast.

'I have always felt the sex passion strongly. Possibly I was immoderate in my demands on Mrs Wilberforce,' Oliver admitted, staring down at the tablecloth. 'I sought relief two or three times a week, sometimes more than once a night. Now the pair of us live as strangers, my seminal animalcules burst from me, the fluid oozes from the penis. I suffer nocturnal pollutions, though I swear I correct my thoughts whenever I find them straying upon libidinous subjects, to spare the danger of sleep echoing them louder. Yet my mind at night is full of lascivious dreams,' he declared contritely.

Bertie placed knife and fork together, producing his gold-bound sharkskin cigar case.

'I have apathy, irritability, abeyance of concentration, loss of self-reliance,' Oliver continued miserably. 'Haven't you noticed how pale I'm getting? Look at my clammy palms! I've all the symptoms of a boy committing self-abuse. The sight of one eye is affected, I'm sure. Besides ...' He tightened his lips, but was unable to relinquish the comfort of narcissism. 'I have impulses, terrible impulses. You remember, we talked of such things? When we were younger, and used to walk together on Hampstead Heath. Now they have become impulses which I dare not put into words, lest my mind read them too clearly and my body be the instrument of their execution.'

'Try a cigar for once?' Bertie invited.

Oliver shook his head angrily. Bertie struck a match. ' "Sweet when the morn is grey," to quote the delightful Calverley. "Sweet, when they've cleared away lunch; and at close of day possibly sweetest. Here's to thee, Bacon!" Not

Cambridge's famed philosopher, but equally famed tobacconist.'

'Bertie!' Oliver jumped up. 'I confess with pain. You receive it with flippancy. You're the sort of man who'd play billiards on an altar.'

Bertie grabbed him. 'Sit down, you fat-headed chump. I'll find you the loveliest girl in London. You don't know what you're missing.'

'I'd be ashamed of myself.' Oliver wavered. 'I nearly told my hansom to drive on this morning, and leave an excuse with your man.'

'Ashamed?' Bertie was amazed 'Would you be ashamed, asking me to fix a week's first class shooting or fishing?'

'But this is immoral.'

'Morals are largely fashions, and moralizing largely self-indulgent intolerance. You're making a deal of money. Why shouldn't you enjoy the pleasure of a woman?' he asked persuasively.

Oliver swallowed. 'How much?'

'Five sovs.'

'That's a fair sum!'

'You don't expect me to sell my friends "seconds", surely?'

'Would she be healthy?'

'As Hygea.'

'No, let us forget this conversation.' Oliver's mood having changed from self-pity to remorse now touched panic. He rose again. 'My honour would not permit my doing such a thing in cold blood.'

'There's an old sailor's proverb – a standing prick has no conscience, and a drunken cunt keeps no watch.'

Oliver received this encouraging philosophy with a shrug and turned towards the door.

'I must show you something.' Bertie eagerly whisked back a narrow red curtain on a brass rail. A panel on the wall supported a Japanned box the size of a biscuit-tin, with two domed bells in front, an ebonite earpiece dangling from one side and a small revolving handle from the other, curly wires connecting it to a flat mouth-piece below.

'Not only the electricity, but the telephone,' Oliver said admiringly.

'It's dashed convenient. The Belgravia Telephone Company can connect me with every subscriber in London. Supposing I've a patient with apoplexy, needing urgent transfer to a nursing-home? I can talk instantly to Mr John Furley, manager of the Invalid Transport Corps in Clerkenwell, who advertises in the *Lancet* ambulances with skilled attendants and all proper apparatus, costs moderate.' He unhooked the ear-piece invitingly. 'Speak to someone.'

'I know no-one with the apparatus. If I did, I should hesitate to break upon their privacy unannounced.'

'It's the coming thing. A general will shortly be ordering "Charge!" from the comfort of his armchair. The Prime Minister can govern us while shooting grouse in Scotland. Why, it will preserve the unity of the Church – the Archbishop of Canterbury may preach from his study on Sunday mornings an identical sermon for every pulpit in the land. A curate on a modest stipend will do well enough to repeat the telephone message out loud for the congregations, and to perform the hack work of marrying, christening and burying. Shall Freshings get you a cab?'

Alone at the breakfast-table, Bertie poured more coffee and stretched out his feet with the air of a young man who at nine in the morning had no need to look at the clock. He opened the *Sporting Times*, the famous *Pink 'Un*, which baptised its shrewd, jocund contributors as 'The Shifter', 'The Stalled Ox' or 'The Dwarf of Blood'. The doorbell did not disturb his weighing the prospects for the Lincolnshire Handicap. Freshings announced, 'A person to see you, sir.'

'A patient?' asked Bertie over the pink pages.

Freshings looked lost. 'Can't say, sir. I sent 'er down to the tradesmen's. She's not of the front door class, sir'. Bertie nodded. The sharpest snobs were servants.

'She gave me this.' On his salver was Bertie's card, dirty and crumpled.

'Ah!' he exclaimed. 'Show her into the consulting room.'

He finished the paper. It would do even a countess good to wait.

The consulting room was behind the dining-room, overlooking a small walled garden with laurel, yew, berberis and box, shrubs beloved in Belgravia Square. It was small, with books, a flat desk, an armchair, water colours of Scottish scenery, like a gentleman's study. A divan with bright yellow brocade had a pair of organdie cushions. A dark green silk screen hid a many-drawered instrument cupboard, a marble-topped table and a washstand with rose-patterned pitcher and basin. A door beyond that led to a household improvement Bertie rated with the electricity and telephone. Sturdy porcelain, mahogany seated, ·the capacious tank above releasing with a jerk of the chain a sanitary waterfall to sweep through its wide gorge into the sewers, 'The Thunderer', latest model from the Staffordshire Potteries, which flushed the world.

Candy was standing with hands clasped, overawed. She wore the same dress and shawl, a broad-brimmed black straw with crimson ribbon pinned to her hair.

'How'd you get here?' Bertie greeted her off-handedly.

'The Metropolitan Railway, sir,' she whispered.

'More blood come up?'

'No, sir.'

'Good. Why aren't you at work?'

'I've lost my place, sir. They were frightened I might have something catching.'

'Then you'll starve?'

'I've a little put by, sir.'

Bertie leant against the desk and lit another cigar.

'You don't chirp like a Cockney.'

'I'm from Kent, sir,' she continued in a crushed voice.

'Then what are you doing in a beauty spot like Whitechapel?'

'My father murdered my mother and then himself, sir.'

The simplicity of her reply made Bertie choke. 'I suppose that's as good a cause as any for a girl leaving home. Take your clothes off, please.'

She looked aghast, 'All of them?'

He shrugged. 'I'm a doctor.'

She slowly drew the pin from her hat. Bertie watched until she was standing naked. 'And your boots,' he commanded. He took her chin. 'Open your mouth. Wider. You say you're eighteen? Well, you're not lying, your wisdom teeth aren't through. Doctors can't be bamboozled about ages, you know. There's always children trying to creep under the Factory Acts.'

He took a boot, holding it close to his face. 'Cracked, worn and dirty,' he murmured. He stroked the thin leather. 'Straight from stamping in the dust, dirt and dung of Whitechapel.' He abruptly threw it in the corner. He nodded to the divan.

'You're clean, for a Whitechapel girl.'

'I wash every morning in the bucket, sir.' She lay down obediently.

'Cleanliness is considered preferable to godliness for those in one's immediate vicinity. You've good hair. Can you sit on it?' From the desk drawer he took a small piece of glittering concave metal, shaped like a shallow M. 'Open your legs. Go on!' he insisted. 'This is only a Sims' speculum.'

Instrument in one hand, cigar in the other, he examined her. He gave a whistle. 'Five years past the age of consent, and you still have your hymen. A pearl of great price. Can you read and write?'

Candy sat up, scarlet-cheeked. 'You're mocking me, sir. You're mocking a poor gal. You've no right to talk about such things. I was brought up proper, among respectable people, sent to a Church school, I could get a living from my brother's farm, if I cared to.'

'You could get a living much better and more comfortably from your own pinfold,' Bertie told her calmly. 'Come! Don't play the humbug. You know a hundred women on the game in Whitechapel. Don't you?'

'There's Martha Turner, the gal I live with,' she confessed uneasily. 'She's good-hearted, I'll say nothing against her. She was coming with me today, but she was too poorly.'

Bertie gave a laugh. 'Too drunk, you mean? Human rat-bags! I'd touch them with nothing more intimate than the ferrule of my cane.'

His eyes raked her body, soft, smooth and white, except for hands rough as hogshide and the ring of old flea bites and scratch marks round each ankle. He sat close to her on the divan.

'Listen, Candy Farnaby. I could set you up, not a mile from here, living like a lady. Think of cambric chemises trimmed with Lyons lace. Silken petticoats, a maid to wait on you. Everything you wanted to eat. Roast fowls, beefsteak pie, custards, cheese cakes and French pastry, pineapples and preserved ginger, golden syrup,' he listed mouth-wateringly. 'Just for being kind to gentlemen, as carefully selected for your company as for the daughters of the most loving mothers in London society.'

Candy stared at him, lip trembling. She knew nothing of doctors, nor needed to. Old Dr Smallpiece at Blessington, in his black coat and black hat, came from Maidstone with his black gig and pony, watched silently by the assembled vil-lagers as he entered cottages with his little black bag, the reliable forerunner of the Angel of Death. Doctors were the croaking ravens of the old. The young were nursed through their fevers by their mothers, with gruel, goose-grease and brown paper, poultices and purges, until they recovered or raised a mound in the churchyard. Now doctors were laying their hands on her with the freedom of milkers upon cows' udders. This rich, learned gentleman was telling her the same as Sal and Lizzie and Martha. She decided there must be something in it.

'But I'm only a country gal, sir. How should I give myself to a gentleman?'

Bertie rolled her left nipple between finger and thumb, as though feeling a fresh cigar.

'Lust is an abolisher of class distinctions as instantly effective as the guillotine. Fucking is the only activity which a flowergirl can share with a prince without giving offence. Our cocks and cunts enjoy an egalitarian republic which should delight the Radicals and most of the Liberal Party.'

She cast down her eyes. 'It would be sinful, sir.'

'Only the lower classes suffer an *idée fixe* about sin. Because theirs are usually punished, while those of the upper classes are generally forgiven. Virtue!' He exclaimed derisively. 'What's the value of virtue when it brings poverty, degradation and phthisis? But how holy is vice, offering a life in which you'll be well cared for, infinitely amused, and most highly thought of by a large number of people. Get dressed.'

He stood up, puffing his cigar. 'Arrangements must be made. I shall seek you out in Star Place a week today, about noon. Look after that little curly parsley bed of yours.' He nodded towards her pubic hair. 'If you let some prick-louse of a tailor crack your Judy's teacup before then –'

Candy nodded back. She would guard her virginity like her brother Jethro guarded his bulldog bitch on heat.

'You can stay otherwise in Whitechapel until you're pickled in gin and rotten with syph, living off a pinch of tea and a ha'p'orth of milk, going round the streets after the coal-carts, taking workmen's stiff pegos with your back against a brick wall, until one day someone decides they'd like to cut your throat. Understand?'

He thought he had frightened her sufficiently. 'Remember, you wear a fortune in your cunny between your legs, as surely as the Queen a crown on her head,' he warned solemnly. 'My man will show you out.'

He left her alone in her shift.

6

THE PATIENT was drawn to the bottom end of the operating table, thighs up, knees bent, feet splayed in the lithotomy stirrups. Oliver Wilberforce sat between, rubber sheet over his knees, china receiver in his lap to catch the blood.

It was a week later, the Friday morning of March 2. Oliver's surgical 'firm' was taking-in, a week of 'full duty' for accidents and emergencies too serious for treatment in the receiving room beside the front entrance. There was always a surge of work. Over 4,000 people were killed or hurt a year by the London traffic. The ill-lit maze of Whitechapel invited injury, its inhabitants persistently attacked each other or ignored their afflictions until they were half-dead.

Oliver's patient was a drayman, pale and flabby, with a stone in his bladder. Through the passage of his penis ran Syme's shouldered steel staff, like a stout, curve-tipped bodkin. Oliver's scalpel, the size of a potato-knife with a heavy knurled handle, was cutting between the man's anus and scrotum – held out of harm's way by the ladylike fingers of the theatre nurse.

'The blood's a shade dark, Bertie,' Oliver murmured.

Bertie squeezed with his left hand a red-rubber, double-bulbed bellows, which blew air through a blue-glass vial hooked to the lapel on his frock coat. His right held a dome of black canvas over the patient's nose and mouth.

'Why are you using the Junker's apparatus today?' Oliver inquired.

'It's the latest modification, straight from Zürich. All the thing on the Continent for giving chloroform.'

Oliver felt his scalpel-tip meet the metal of the staff inside

55

the man's urethra, running from bladder to penis. 'The Clover's evacuator,' he ordered his house-surgeon pumping the carbolic spray at his elbow. 'I'm through to the bladder.'

'How's the blood now?' asked Bertie.

'Brighter.'

'You still think chloroform's dangerous?' Bertie asked. 'But all drugs are dangerous. A patient could kill himself with rhubarb mixture.'

'Only by falling into a vat of it, like the Duke of Clarence.' Bertie grinned. 'Oh, cheese it.'

Through his bloody incision Oliver pulled a jagged blue-grey stone. 'Size of a bantam's egg,' he announced, dropping it into the receiver. 'I'll sew up with round hempen ligatures, Mr Tomkins,' he told the house-surgeon. 'We'll insert a rubber catheter into the bladder, and pack the perineal wound in the hope of its healing by granulation. Then antiseptic dressings and a layer of waterproof gutta-percha tissue under the bandage.'

'What shall I do with the stone, sir?'

'Give it back to the patient. He'll pass it round in the public house, when he sees the inside of one again. In Mayfair, I've known them cut and polished for cufflinks.'

While they replaced their frock-coats in the corridor outside, Bertie said to Oliver, 'Have you half an hour? There's someone I'd like you to meet.'

'Ambrose wants to see me in the library.'

Bertie groaned. 'I'll tandem with you,' he volunteered his company. 'Ambrose anyway regards me as your sorcerer's apprentice.'

The library was at the far end of the long, straight stone corridor, past the medical wards. It was a square room with a good fire, its bays of books inhabited by busts of Hippocrates, Galen and Versalius, and the tawny portraits of past Whitechapel Hospital consultants in crusts of scrolled gilt. Its comfortable armchairs were sought by the doctors more for repose than erudition. It served as their clubroom, a silver tray on the table bearing cut-glass decanters of sherry and madeira, bequeathed for their daily refreshment

56

by a kindly and sagacious Whitechapel vintner. Ambrose Porter-Hartley was alone, standing before the hearth reading *The Times.*

'Appalling business, the illness of the Crown Prince,' he said at once.

Oliver nodded gravely.

'Totally upset the Stock Exchange. All the joint stock banks are down. Cotton is terrible. Coal and Bessemer steel don't bear thinking about. It's going to cost a lot of people a pretty penny, this imbroglio at San Remo. What's going on at the Villa Zirio, Oliver? For all the bulletins, the Crown Prince could be equally in rude health or *in articulo mortis.*'

'I gather there is some trouble with the silver cannula they passed through the tracheotomy hole into the windpipe,' said Oliver guardedly. He never cared to squander news won by closeness to Mackenzie, news which was sought, or speculated upon, by every chancellery in Europe. Particularly to Ambrose, who assayed the metal of any conversation for its value to himself.

'The Crown Prince is being treated like the Cambridge boat with eight strokes and no cox,' remarked Bertie, pouring three thin-stemmed glasses of madeira.

'Surely Virchow can inspect another specimen?' Ambrose took a glass. 'Then he could say whether it's cancer one way or another.'

'Virchow is digging up mummies in Egypt,' Oliver told him.

Ambrose frowned powerfully. 'Germany's getting too big for her boots. I was talking to my banker only yesterday. Do you know how industrial production in Germany has overtaken ours these past two decades?' He fixed Oliver with a bulging eye. 'Theirs is increasing by 60 per centum per annum, ours by a mere 16. That's food for thought. Germany's out to beggar us, mark my words. Her goods are ousting ours all over Europe. A shrewd man might well put his money into one of their big four banks.'

'Have you?' asked Bertie.

Ambrose ignored him.

57

'Surely, Germany will no longer be an awkward bedfellow in Europe, once the amiable Crown Prince with his English Princess ascends the throne,' said Oliver reassuringly.

'If,' was Ambrose's gloomy reply. He stood legs apart by the fire, staring deeply into his glass, moving slowly backwards and forwards on his heels. What an unfashionable creak his boots make, thought Bertie. Oliver fell into one of his taciturn silences. Ambrose is barely ten years older than me, he reflected, a full physician to the hospital while I am still an assistant surgeon. Shall I grow as fat, pompous and money-grubbing? Ambrose has over a thousand guineas a year as his share of the students' fees. I must content myself with ten shillings a head for each student who favours my teaching above my colleagues'. Yet Ambrose claims to walk through the valley of the shadow of penury. He is a Scrooge for all seasons.

'I wished to speak to you, Wilberforce, of other matters.' Ambrose glanced at Bertie, who demonstrated disinclination to be ousted by pouring another glass of madeira. 'How tragic is the dilemma of charitable relief! If we help a man exist without work, we demoralize the individual. We encourage the growth of a parasitic class. We save him only at the cost of those who compete with him. Nothing is achieved *pro bono publico.*'

'*La philanthropie, c'est un mensonge,*' Bertie sighed.

Ambrose ignored him. 'Much pauperism in England is the result of unthrifty marriages, which are encouraged by our system of out-door parish relief. The more the family, the more the relief. In addition, promiscuous intercourse lessens the natural expectation of life, its fruits are stillbirths, higher mortality among infants and lasting effects for a generation.'

Bertie sighed more deeply. '*Le funeste héritage du vice.*'

Ambrose glared at him. 'Worse still, it produces the class of *fallen woman.* I was inspired to meet recently Mrs Josephine Butler, in Winchester – her husband has lately become a canon there. We all know her agitation brought repeal of the Contagious Diseases Act. Mrs Butler saw it as an underhand method of installing the abhorrent Continental system of licensed brothels, by imposing compulsory inspection on unfortunates in troop towns.'

'It would never have been enacted in the first place, had the Queen not imagined it an agricultural measure applying to cattle,' Bertie informed him.

'The vile "white slave traffic".' Ambrose's cheeks puffed in a breeze of indignation. 'Which abducts young girls, some hardly free of their mothers' apron strings, even the mothers' arms.'

'Didn't we get all that in the *Pall Mall Gazette?*' asked Oliver uninterestedly.

'The editor, Mr Stead, is a man with a nose for the truth.'

'And his newspaper's circulation,' said Bertie.

'Rapacious men – worse, women – have their eyes everywhere. At the railway termini for innocent country girls seeking work. At the docks for pretty colleens from Ireland. Many are transhipped straight into the hands of *foreigners.*' Ambrose made the crime seem doubly wicked. 'Amsterdam alone has 186 houses of ill-repute imprisoning 1,064 women, Brussels has 20, Liege 29, and 33 of our own *Englishwomen* have been found in them.'

'How do you know?' Bertie asked.

Ambrose faced him. 'I interviewed Inspector Greenham from the Metropolitan Police. He volunteered to penetrate the brothels of Europe.'

'In that case, I should prefer to suspect his motives rather than his arithmetic,' Bertie conceded politely.

'We need but recall our Prime Minister of two years ago –'

Bertie guffawed. 'Gladstone? The harlots called him "Old Glad-Eye". He got a thrill from providing a girl with a lecture and a bowl of soup. He only rescued the pretty ones. Ugly East End whores didn't interest him. His idea of the Magdalen is an incomparable example of pulchritude with a superb figure and carriage.'

'I would have preferred you not to say that of so respected a public figure.'

'I didn't. His fellow-Liberal Henry Labouchere did.'

Oliver had a barely perceptible smile on his face.

Uneasily feeling Bertie was getting the better of the conversation, Ambrose decided to close it.

'I have walked the streets of Whitechapel. At night. Alone. Well, accompanied by a policeman. And I firmly believe in this hospital's responsibility to reclaim Whitechapel's fallen women. I am starting a small committee – there are many such reforming bodies in London.'

'I'd be delighted to join,' said Bertie.

'I didn't ask *you*,' Ambrose told him angrily.

'Then I'll persuade Wilberforce. Come along, we've work to do. You'll excuse us, I'm sure?' To Ambrose's vexation, Bertie pulled Oliver into the corridor. Like a cheeky schoolboy released from the headmaster's study, he exclaimed as they hurried towards the hospital entrance, 'Why was Ambrose acting as holy as an old whore at a christening?'

'There must be something for Ambrose in it.'

'Oh, he wouldn't fart unless it blew a banknote into his tail pocket.'

'A royal appointment, do you think? They're as dependent on politics as physic.'

'I suppose rescuing harlots is all the rage just now – General Booth's Army, Mr Wookey's Gospel Purity Association. But those are only out to cane the vices of the upper classes. The lower classes are allowed their lusts like their lice, and the Queen is more interested in fallen horses than fallen women.' They had reached the portico. 'An old growler!' Bertie exclaimed with delight. 'A four-wheeler's just the ticket. You don't mind iron tyres and straw on the floor? A hansom would be a squash.'

'Where are we going?' Oliver looked apprehensive. Bertie could be as full of pranks as Till Eulenspiegel.

'To see one of my patients. I'd value your opinion.' Bertie called to a bowler-hatted, raw-faced driver, a blanket and a sack warming his shoulders, 'Star Place, off Star Street. It leads from the Commercial Road. You can wait on the corner.'

The mist which had prowled the roof tops with the threat of fog by nightfall had swooped impatiently. It was hard to see across India Road. The gas threw yellow lagoons round the windows, the passers-by in comforters and turned-up collars hurried along blowing on their hands and coughing. Bertie removed his silk hat, flicking away delicately specks of soot which fell from the still clouds of chimney-smoke like Devil's snowflakes.

They ground along the narrow streets running behind the hospital. Oliver stared through the cracked cab window, its strap pulled tight against the fog. He could find much to disapprove in jolly, ruddy Bertie, but nothing to dislike. Oliver had to confess, there was much to covert. How he longed for so easygoing a way with the world, such cheerful disrespect for the pomposities of Ambrose or the mysteries of women! He could envy Bertie's shameless relish of comfort and luxury, even his blatant pursuit of them.

The fog seemed thicker every yard, but the journey was short. Bertie let down the window. 'Stay in the light of this cook-shop. We'll be only a jiff or two. There may be a box for the roof.'

Both climbed out. Grasping Oliver's arm, Bertie led him round the corner into a street so narrow that it seemed in the fog to meet over their heads like a tunnel.

'You know your way round the East End,' Oliver observed.

'Like the West End. I make it my business.'

'You are afflicted with *nostalgie de la boue*?'

'If I am, it is here in abundance.'

Bertie stopped at a slit in the brickwork under an archway. Oliver drew back. 'We can't go there. We'd be murdered.'

Bertie laughed. 'That's far too romantic a misfortune. You'll more likely put your foot on someone's turd.'

The door had a metal 4 screwed to it, almost invisible under dirt. There was no knocker. Bertie banged loudly and repeatedly. Almost a minute passed. It opened a crack.

' 'Oo is it?' croaked a female voice.

'Have no fear,' Bertie said cheerfully. 'We are medical men, come to perform deeds of charity. Where's Candy Farnaby?'

'She ain't 'ere.'

Bertie flipped a shilling at the woman. Nobody was there when you first asked in Whitechapel.

They went inside. Oliver stared round in wondering disgust. He had never entered such a hovel, even a labourer's cottage on his father's estate in the Norfolk fens. It seemed in the flickering gas batswing a repository for street refuse furnished with table and chair. Smoke blew from the grate, coals tumbled from a cupboard in the corner on to the bare floor. A metal plate on the table had a scrap of meat in congealed fat, some pickled cabbage occupied a teacup, in the broken-spouted pot Oliver suspected saturated tea leaves were reinforced by pinches of fresh during the week. On the chair crouched a second woman, as gaunt, pale and dirty as the one at the door, but some ten years older. His nose wrinkled.

'It's not worth opening the windows,' Bertie informed him, 'because the air in the court outside is equally foul.'

'I'd prefer to hotel it at the Black Hole of Calcutta,' Oliver muttered.

'There's fifteen funerals a day from this area,' Bertie said cheerfully. 'Sundays and Mondays are the busiest, when there's always a good crowd to enjoy the sight. You're Martha Turner?' he asked the woman with his shilling.

' 'Ow did yer know?' She glared with intense suspicion.

'Who's your friend?' Bertie enquired.

'That's Polly Nichols.'

'A good afternoon to you, Polly Nichols.' He noticed the gin bottle, as she rocked back and forth staring glazedly at the visitors and muttering.

'Where's Candy? We haven't all night. Hiding in the yard, I suspect.'

Bertie pulled open the back door. The yard was cramped, leading almost directly into the privy. Candy stood holding her shawl tightly with both fists.

'You'll catch your death,' Bertie warned her pleasantly.

'I'm all to pieces, sir,' she said timidly.

'Why?' Bertie was close against her, his breath a cloud before her frightened eyes. 'I'm your Fairy Godmother, whose delights shall not stop so ungenerously at midnight.'

'I dursn't go with you, sir.'

'What nonsense. Come on, don't keep me on hot coals.' He seized her arm, but she pulled back. 'Listen, you mad cat,' he said fiercely. 'If I wanted, I could have you taken from here by a pair of ruffians in half an hour. Tonight you'd be held down by a strong girl in a padded room with a mattress floor, while a man forcibly seduced you and paid someone else twenty-five sovereigns for your part of the bargain.' He tightened his grip so that she squeaked. 'You could scream your head off, and even if the policeman on the beat heard you, he wouldn't stir his arse to stop the fun. An unchaste woman can't complain. She can't be believed. God, I'm the soul of kindness. You deserve skinning alive.'

In panic, Candy said, 'I haven't my things packed.'

'Things! You don't need things. Soon you'll have everything.'

She let him draw her into the room. Bertie heard Oliver gasp. She must shine like a nugget in a shovel of Witwatersrand dirt, he reflected. Martha stood motionless, bewildered by the two gentlemen, clutching her shilling. Polly sat crooning. Another minute, and Candy had quit the house.

Bertie gallantly helped her into the growler first. How she trembled, he thought.

'You're a cool one, for a ponce,' Oliver said behind him.

Bertie spun round. Oliver was startled to see him angry. 'I'm rescuing her. And a damn sight more comfortably than Ambrose, with his soup-kitchen mentality. She's seen the last of these slums.'

'Bertie the moralist?' Oliver asked sarcastically. 'We'll hear your voice rising above the Salvation Army tambourines yet.'

Bertie seemed struggling to know what best to say. As often in such difficulty, he laughed. 'Do you object, sitting in the same cab as a frail?' he asked, using the genteel word for a whore.

'Only to her fleas.'

'Where can I leave you?' Bertie climbed in beside Candy. 'In the vicinity of Harley Street. I've an appointment with Sir Morell Mackenzie. I should prefer not arriving at his door in such colourful company.'

7

F OR EIGHTEEN YEARS Sir Morell Mackenzie had rented
No. 19 Harley Street. He spent £3,000 on renovations before
moving in. He had come round the corner from Weymouth
Street, into the street of the big doctors, and his house was
one of the biggest.

Portland stone and red brick, it was three broad windows
wide, five floors from area steps to the dormers under the
chimney-pots. The front waiting-room was vast, gilt pillars
supporting the ceiling, and exacted a two-hour inspection of
the decor unless the patient had Sir Morell's signed visiting-
card or tipped the butler.

The consulting-room at the back was packed like a furniture shop. There were two couches, squat Georgian chairs
on ball-and-claw feet, a tall, brass-handled mahogany filing
cabinet, paintings almost hiding the green brocade wallpaper. An immense Sèvres vase had come from a grateful, if
sadly testate, patient. Bric-à-brac and keepsakes lay thicker
than toys in a nursery. The wastepaper basket was pede-
stalled by two stuffed foxes. Silver-framed photographs
were scrawled with the ebullient gratitude of actors, more
mummers' signatures were engraved on the huge silver bowl.
Mackenzie drew his practice from Covent Garden, the
Houses of Lords and Commons, the stage, the Church, the
Law, and from others who spoke to live and lived to speak.

Behind a damask screen stood his operating chair, its high
oval back to arrest the squirming head. On a small table
gleamed the deadly cutlery of instruments. His examination
lamp, like Bertie Randolph's dining-room, was a flirtation
with electricity.

Beside the Adam fireplace, freshly banked with Welsh nuts,

65

Mackenzie was busy on proofs of his *Diseases of the Throat and Nose*. With his pamphlets *On the Treatment of Hoarseness and Loss of Voice* and *On Enlarged Tonsils and their Treatment Without Cutting*, autographed and thoughtfully distributed, his writings had chipped the granite face of established surgery for the foothold of a reputation. But the Golden Square Throat Hospital in Soho was still regarded by the Royal College of Surgeons in Lincoln's Inn Fields much as the Royal Mint viewed a den of counterfeiters.

He threw down his pen and rose eagerly as Oliver Wilberforce was shown in.

'The man in London I'm the most glad to see! How kind to call so soon. Four months is a long spell to be away from home and family. Particularly when it embraces the blessed season of Christmas.'

Mackenzie shook hands warmly, but did not smile. He never did. He did not see the necessity. His familiarity was surely a privilege which needed no embellishment. If anyone made a joke, it was clearly superfluous to demonstrate that he saw the point. He was rising fifty, a Scot born in Leytonstone, a village beyond the East End. He was dark-haired, bright-eyed, sharp-nosed, neatly side-whiskered, spare and self-satisfied.

'I interrupt literary work,' Oliver apologized.

'No, just snatching a few moments between patients. Forgive this stramonium cigarette.' He held one in his fingertips. 'My asthma is bad today. Can't you hear the sibilli from there? This fog throws a pall over the delight of my return.'

'Your return for good?' Oliver sat down.

Mackenzie sat at the desk, wheezing and puffing his cigarette. 'No, I don't think so. Were I superstitious, I shouldn't dare have Bowden unpack my bags.'

Oliver crossed one long leg over another. 'Was your life at San Remo tolerable?'

'As Hamlet's at Elsinore. It was trying for a man of principle.' Mackenzie was shaken by coughing. 'Oh, San Remo is agreeable enough, and the Villa Zirio new and clean, which is something for Italy. The Prince rents it from an Italian gentleman. His previous villa at Lake Maggiore – from which I moved him, the winter there is cold and damp – was owned by an Englishman. Which irritated the German press. The petty pride of these Prussians! I have spun in a maelstrom of malice, since Reid sat in that very chair almost a year ago, when all I knew of the Crown Prince's illness were fragmentary reports in *The Times*.'

Dr James Reid, the Queen's personal physician, was an undistinguished doctor who offered the irresistible combination of speaking her late husband's German with John Brown's Scots accent. A former pupil of humble Aberdeen grammar school and MD from Aberdeen University, practising with his father near Buchan Ness, he was summoned to Balmoral when the resident physician fell ill. By a stroke of luck, the old doctor died. With her sentimental fondness for everything at Balmoral, Queen Victoria carried young Dr Reid back to London and created him Physician-Extraordinary. Reid was balding and pince-nezed, his face as unremarkable as an egg cushioned on thick moustache and whiskers. He was whispered to advise his patient on more than medical affairs. The previous May he had hurried from Windsor, and dispatched Mackenzie to the Queen's son-in-law by next morning's Continental Express, in a snowstorm of telegrams cancelling consultations and social engagements.

'I have been bedevilled by malevolent colleagues and malevolent chance. I first arrived in Potsdam last year with no instruments save my patient mirror.' Mackenzie held up an angled mirror the size of a shilling on a metal stalk. 'I had to make do with unfamiliar French forceps for my specimen from the growth, like a split pea on the left vocal cord. It took *even me* two attempts. Did you know, Professor Gerhardt had quite foolishly attacked the tumour with the electro-cautery thirteen times! It did nothing but inflame the larynx, quite disgraceful treatment. Fortunately, the Crown Prince is a man of splendid constitution.'

'During the Jubilee he appeared a fine fellow with a full

67

greying beard, glittering with decorations. But can he still speak?'

'No. He always keeps pad and pencil by him.' There was a knock. 'Yes, Bowden?'

'The waiting room, Sir Morell, is crowded to overflowing. There'll soon be patients on the front steps.'

'You see, Oliver? I kept my return secret but the news has already gone round Town. That is surely a poke in the eye to English surgeons who can be as malicious as German ones. I'll see them directly.' He added as the door shut, 'Bowden's made himself a sovereign or two this afternoon.'

'Shall I go?' Oliver asked courteously. 'I know you always put your patients first.'

'I wish they did as much for me,' Mackenzie said bitterly. 'While my back was turned, my rivals slipped in as swiftly and treacherously as assassins.' He crushed the cigarette into a silver bowl. 'Stay. It's a relief to tell the true story to a true friend.'

'Doesn't the story lie in one question?'

Mackenzie shrugged slightly. 'Whether the growth is cancer or not? Well, it's not syphilis, I can tell you that. The story got about because we administered the cure for syphilis, potassium iodide, as a prudent aid to diagnosis, by exclusion. Had the condition cleared up, we should have known the cause.' He struck a match for another stramonium cigarette, coughing as he inhaled the pungent smoke. 'Your question is more crucial than you imagine.'

'Surely nothing is more crucial than the life of a man?'

'Yes. The life of a nation. Look at the Prussian situation. The old Emperor William has bad lungs and a bad heart, though his mind is clear.'

'Chancellor Bismarck's mind is clear enough, which serves as well.'

Mackenzie nodded energetically. 'Exactly. Did you see how Prince Bismarck had the Reichstag swallow his Military Organization Bill last month? Every young German now has seven years in the army, four in the reserve, service in the *Landwehr* until he's 30. Why, the army rules their lives. It was passed *en bloc*, with great enthusiasm. Such demand on the individual's liberty is neither asked nor given without a solid reward in prospect – if in distant prospect.'

'From the French?'

'General Boulanger?' asked Mackenzie sarcastically. 'The *brav' général?* His revenge politics are taken in Prussia as seriously as the music-hall song which puffed him to fame. The only people in Europe who are frightened of General Boulanger are the French Government. But Great Britain, Oliver – *we* are moving from the status of competitor to enemy. An easy transition in the eyes of the jealous and nervous Prussians.'

Oliver looked alarmed. 'But your noble patient will ascend the throne and dismiss Bismarck. He is well known to move among those Prussian junkers like a cultured Athenian amidst warlike Spartans.'

Mackenzie said nothing.

'*Is* the growth cancerous?'

'Yes.'

The two looked at each other.

'I was perfectly justified in diagnosing a non-cancerous condition at first,' protested Mackenzie. 'There was Virchow's clean bill of health ...' He paused, and continued less surely, 'I may have removed from the Prince's larynx a speck of normal tissue. I may have missed the tumour. I told you just now, I had unfamiliar instruments and the cauterization increased my difficulties.'

'What have you told the Prince?'

'I found when I arrived at San Remo on the fifth of November last that the tumour had suddenly increased in size. It had a distinctly malignant look. His Highness asked me outright, "Is it cancer?" I replied as optimistically as possible that it looked much like it. He shook my hand, and thanked me with a brave smile for being so frank. He quoted his favourite motto, *Lerne zu leiden ohne zu klagen* – We must learn to suffer without complaint. He added that he really must apologize for feeling so well in himself. Prince Fritz is a noble man in both senses.'

69

How self-satisfied is Mackenzie! Oliver thought. His patient might be on the road to recovery rather than faltering towards the tomb.

'Naturally, I sent an immediate cypher to the Queen and telegrams to my colleagues in Berlin and Vienna. But I was careful to avoid the word "cancer". These days, newspapers will not always accept a professional man's word unquestioned. Do you know, I had reporters by the score besiege me at the Hotel Mediterranée. They even *trained telescopes* on the Villa Zirio where the sick nobleman lay. Such people have neither manners nor morals.'

Mackenzie rose and stood by the fire.

'But if, there and then, you had totally removed the cancerous larynx – ' Oliver suggested.

'A most dangerous operation. How many survive? One in twenty. You can read that in my textbook.' Mackenzie indicated the proof-sheets on the desk. 'For a few painful voiceless years, when suicide is always contemplated and often accomplished. Surely it is sounder practice to hope that the condition will progress but slowly, as often the case?'

'But the truth you broke to the patient you hide from the world.' Oliver was beginning to feel Mackenzie guilty of both surgical incompetence and professional duplicity, to him equally reprehensible.

'Haven't I given you the answer? The world "cancer" is as potent as the name of some international incident. Were *I* – ' He tapped his breast. 'To declare outright it was cancer, I should at once trigger Bismarck's plot.'

Oliver's eyebrows rose.

Mackenzie clasped his long fingers tightly before him. After a moment's hesitation he confided, 'Listen – you know the ancient Salic Law, excluding females from the throne? Without it, our Queen would today be ruler of Hanover as well. Well, there is an analogous rule in the Hohenzollern family, excluding the weakling and the sickly from the throne of Prussia. Bismarck is itching to declare Frederick unfit to succeed, and if the ninety-year-old Emperor predeceases my patient, to establish a Regency under Frederick's son, William.'

Startled at the revelation, Oliver could only exclaim, 'But William has a paralysed left arm himself.'

'Oh, that's nothing, dislocation of his shoulder during birth, not recognized by the German medical fraternity until too late to repair the damage. But his mind is as twisted as his limb – unscrupulous, ambitious, violent and reactionary, everything which his father is not, the true product of Blood and Iron. Do you know, he has already made agreements on his future policies as Kaiser with *Reichskahzler* Bismarck? And has been empowered by his grandfather the Emperor to sign State papers over the head of his own father.'

'Our Queen dotes on him,' Oliver pointed out.

'Even a favourite grandson cannot have his way in everything. My orders are to keep open the chances of Prince Frederick ascending the German throne as long as possible, and then to keep him there as long as possible. Only so may our two great nations maintain the peace of Europe – we with our great fleet, they with their mighty army – and the warlike posturings of his son William may be disregarded like the ridiculous antics of an African tribesman.'

'Orders from whom?' Oliver asked.

'Dr Reid'.

'Who takes them from—?'

'Sir Henry Ponsonby, the Queen's secretary.'

Oliver gave a soft breath that was almost a low whistle. 'Then the policy is the Queen's?'

Mackenzie nodded. 'I am optimistic of its success. Though the German doctors insist on performing all the treatment. They are as rough as apes. Do you know why they hate me? Because I am free and independent, while they are all servants of the State, who can be dismissed for kicking against authority.' Red spots appeared on his cheeks. 'The German press hates me for the blackest of crimes, which I commit with the Crown Princess Vicky – being English. Though perhaps they have forgiven me?' he asked sarcastically. 'They now say that my real name is Mortiz Markovicz, that I am not an emigré Scot but an emigré Polish Jew. If I really did belong to the remarkable race which has produced so

71

many men of the highest distinction in every department of literature, art and science, so far from being ashamed of such an extraction I would be proud of it.'

'But the Rumplestiltskin nose of the press surely has a whiff of Bismarck's stratagem?'

'They are forbidden to print it. If they award me the accolade of Kaisermaker, it is only because Princess Vicky need occupy the German throne but one day, to draw the pension of an Empress for the rest of her life – which is considerably more substantial than that of a Crown Princess. They even say that Count Seckendorff, her Chamberlain, is waiting to marry her once she is possessed of her widowhood and her Empress's dowry. That was actually told Ponsonby during the Jubilee by Count Radolinsky, who is Marshal of the Prince's Household, and in an excellent position at San Remo to open all letters and telegrams, stick his nose in everywhere and pay the servants for gossip, which he passes daily to his master Bismarck. Oh, the villa is full of Claudius's "lawful espials". And the Crown Prince is a prisoner, his illness his bars.'

A knock came at the door, which was opened by Lady Mackenzie, large, full-bosomed, dark-haired, almost fifty, in tight-waisted dress of green silk. 'Mr Wilberforce, how delightful.' Oliver leapt to take her hand lightly. 'I must interrupt your male chat to say that Mr Henry Irving is downstairs.'

'So the voice which nightly fills the Lyceum Theatre is of your creation?' Oliver complimented Mackenzie.

'Henry Irving is more than my patient. He is an old and good friend, a useful companion in my present storm of calumny and insult.'

'Can you and Mrs Wilberforce join us soon for dinner?' Lady Mackenzie invited.

'*More* dinner parties?' Mackenzie complained. 'With the Channel salt not off my skin?'

'My wife has not been too well,' Oliver excused himself. 'Ambrose Porter-Hartley is attending her. She'll be right as rain shortly, there's no doubt.'

72

Preparing his instruments behind the screen, Mackenzie called over his shoulder, 'There are unfounded rumours in the press – particularly the Paris press, where all the news from Germany must be bad to be joyful – of deep differences of opinion between us physicians attending at San Remo. Utterly untrue! I signed a document to that effect before leaving, with my eminent colleagues Dr Schrader, Dr Krause, Professor van Bergmann, Dr Bramann, and of course Mark Hovell, my assistant from the Throat Hospital here. I'd be obliged if you'd put that information about, Oliver, among the medical profession of London. Such is the repute of your integrity, it would be accepted as enjoying unimpeachable veracity.'

Oliver politely agreed to propagate such paper quackery. The Crown Prince's doctors clearly distrusted each other like his courtiers. He followed Bowden downstairs. He had heard the secrets of Europe, and all the time thought of a girl in a London slum.

8

BERTIE RANDOLPH sat in a low yellow plush fireside chair, nibbling a ginger cake with a blanched almond in the middle and sipping a glass of madeira. He would have preferred brandy and soda. It was four o'clock that same day, the afternoon merging with foggy imperceptibility into dusk. The gas flared, the red plush, gold-laced curtains were drawn in a first-floor room with bright pink silk wallpaper and a gilt-rimmed mirror over the marble fireplace. There was a crimson plush sofa with snowy antimacassars, two large reproductions of Millais's little girls in mob caps, and in each corner tall bamboo tables bearing shiny, spiky dark green plants.

It was a comfortable room, but without the imprint of human personality. There were no books, no newspapers, no scraps of darning, no piano, no untidiness deposited by the daily tides of life. An angular maid with a noticeable grey moustache, but smart in black bombasine, a lace apron and cap with streamers, replaced the stopper of the decanter at Bertie's elbow.

'Mrs Floyd says she'll be down directly, sir.'

Bertie inclined his head. As she left him, he held up his glass, staring at the amber wine against the gas, and speculating how much better off he might be by dinnertime.

He was at No. 2 Garden Gate, south of the Park. It was a house well known to a few people. The men who rang at the brightly holystoned front steps – or unlatched the gate of the walled garden behind, or tapped the plain door of No. 6 Garden Mews, with which it freely communicated – stepped into Mrs Floyd's world from that of politics, the City, the aristocracy, the army, the moneyed arts, the bar and even the bench.

It was known to a few important officers at Scotland Yard, who were paid regularly to prevent its officially reaching the ears of the others. It was known vaguely to many as a sink of iniquity cruelly beyond their own pockets. It was known specifically by the few fervid men and women who in any age are frenzied by the hair-shirt of their indignation. So powerful were its patrons, so astute its manageress, they might as well have turned their fiery energies on trying to shut No. 10 Downing Street.

The *Lancet* a few years before had calculated there were 6,000 brothels and 80,000 prostitutes in London, on which some £5 million pounds were spent a year. There were 60 brothels and 10,000 prostitutes in Whitechapel alone. Mrs Floyd felt distaste at her house and her girls being included in this common lot. Any man seeking the casual romances of the kerbstones need only stroll from Piccadilly to the Strand, between the hours of a late lunch and a late supper or early breakfast. 'Are you good natured, Charlie, dear?' was the sentry-challenge of the 'gay' girls, as the sad, squalid street-walkers were known. Every afternoon they infiltrated the West End of London from the East, as far as the glass-roofed Aladdin's Cave of the Burlington Arcade, where the extravagant shops did better trade from their bedrooms than their counters.

The night houses of the Haymarket, where similar trysts might be made away from the weather and public inquisitiveness, were closing from the law which banned public drinking by half-past midnight. The girls paraded instead among the flowering shrubs and gilt pillars of the spacious promenade behind the balcony at the Empire Theatre of Varieties in Leicester Square – appropriately, prostitution being the continuance of theatrical enjoyment like war of Clausewitz's foreign policy.

Mrs Floyd saw hers as an 'introducing house'. Those who could afford such discernment might there be acquainted with severely-selected young ladies, and advised of their recruits by letters addressed to their club. Her girls were never seen at the windows, even dressed – in Maiden Lane, off the Strand, they fleetingly appeared naked. 'Good wine needs no bush,' Bertie had once told her, laughing loudly at his *double entendre*.

The door opened behind its crimson chenille curtain on a hinged brass rail. He needed not rise. They were old friends.

'How clever, Bertie,' Mrs Floyd congratulated him. 'She'll suit me very well.'

'Englishwomen make good whores. Especially country girls. Being an entirely practical job, it suits the temperament.'

'Clean, too. Not a flea on her.'

'And as intact as the vaults of the Bank of England.'

He handed her a glass of madeira. She sat in the matching pink chair across the fire. A pretty woman turned thirty, thick dark hair, cut short, worn in tight curls. Her face had an asymmetry which increased its interest – the right eyebrow was arched, the other flat, that eye narrower. Her nose was short, her mouth full, her figure as neat as a pair of nutcrackers. She had a lively boyishness, which Bertie found refreshing in a world furnished with women like sensuous upholstery. Her pinch-waisted dress was of watered magenta silk, a collar of cream Brussels lace covering the shoulders. She had a French accent as faint but assertive as the rub of garlic in a good omelette.

'*A votre santé*,' Bertie raised his glass.

'And yours.'

Her social status was hard to pin. She was not decorously dowdy enough to be lady of a middle-class household. She was certainly not an upper servant. Nor a self-consciously emancipated woman doing a job. She fitted easiest as governess in a well-to-do family, a mademoiselle trusted to assume professional self-effacement in the unavoidable company of her betters. She was genteel. It showed in her careful walk, her subdued speech, her restrained smile, the extended little finger as she raised her glass.

'I had a letter from Madame Landouzy a week ago,' Bertie told her. 'I can leave for Paris in a fortnight.'

She nodded gently, compressing her lips after a sip of madeira. 'How many?'

'A *colis* of two. You can take them, Angela? I don't expect two will attract attention at Dover.'

'Your appearance alone would save you from being suspected as a *placeur.*'

Bertie grinned. 'But what of theirs? Her last pair looked as though clothed by charity, and in the dark.'

'Call the evening before your journey,' she counselled. 'I can warn you of any danger in the air, My friends in the police will certainly have caught a sniff.'

'Why don't you take my advice and install the telephone? Then you could ask for Belgravia 12 and speak to me when you wish.'

'Electricity frightens me.'

'I should not have imagined that anything in the world could frighten you.'

'Is that quite the compliment to pay a lady?' She raised her arched eyebrow. 'Timidity is an allurement of our sex.'

'Why, you sound quite cross.'

'Oh, Bertie, no! I could never be cross with you. I owe you so much.'

He made a deprecatory gesture. 'When a lady I admire is obliged to start a new life, I am glad to put her in touch with friends who might make it a comfortable one. It suited everyone's convenience, didn't it? I'm *always* starting a new life. I'm always trying to make a living from something different. Otherwise, a fellow gets bored with himself.'

'And haven't you done well for yourself?'

He made a pout of half-hearted contradiction. 'I'd be telling stretchers to say that I walked on the sunny side of Queer Street. It's not the truth. I hope you can be generous over the girl?' he added, nodding upwards.

Mrs Floyd sipped madeira and squeezed her lips. 'Fifty sovereigns?'

'Oh, come,' he objected amiably but earnestly. 'She can make that in a night. I'd hoped for seventy-five.'

'How do I know she'll settle? The little baggage might run off tomorrow.'

They bargained, though Bertie knew he could strike little warmth from the flintiness of her mind. He took sixty, with another ten in a month if Candy fulfilled expectations.

'Your name came up the other morning.' Business completed, he resumed their bantering conversation. 'One of my colleagues at the Whitechapel wondered what had come of you.'

'Really? I thought the world had forgotten me, as it forgets last year's fashionable novel.'

'You were a name on everyone's lips.'

'So is the Derby winner. Who can recall it two seasons later?'

Bertie grinned. 'Doesn't anyone ask after *Mr* Floyd?'

'Never. Perhaps they assume I take the title "Mrs" by virtue of my occupation, like a gentleman's cook?'

'Nobody knows your real name?'

'Only my friends at Scotland Yard.'

Bertie laughed. 'That's ripe.'

'The girls are too stupid to put two and two together, of course. For the clients ... well, perhaps they are too gentlemanly to mention it.'

'Oh, only a rank cad would remind a woman of her age, her past or seeing her in the same dress.'

Mrs Floyd rose to fetch the money. Bertie puzzled where she secreted the takings of the house. And who owned it. He heard it was a Member of Parliament, but the man does not pry who has much to hide.

Saying that he wanted a word with Candy, Bertie lit a cigar and followed her from the room. He mounted two flights of thickly-carpeted stairs, then a narrow lino-covered staircase past a brown-stained door to the servants' bedrooms under the roof. He entered without knocking a clean, plain room with a sloping ceiling and a dormer window looking north over Kensington Gardens. Bertie had exaggerated to Candy the allurement of a room to herself – it contained four truckle-beds on castors, as might accommodate the maids in any gentleman's household, a washstand and a chest of ill-fitting drawers. Some black stockings and a camisole were drying on a clothes-horse before the fire. Candy sat on a bed, still in her hat. Talking animatedly on another bed was a small, pretty girl with dark ringlets, in a pink silk dress trimmed with white rabbit-fur, which reached just below her knees, like a child's.

'Hullo, doctor.' The girl jumped up. 'What a nice new china you've brought us.' Sharp Cockney tongues snipped their slang. A china was a china plate, who was a mate. 'We've been having a proper chin-wag,' she described their chat expressively.

'Rose could talk a dog's hind leg off,' Bertie observed amiably. 'Run along and play, there's a good girl.'

Rose pulled a face and left. Bertie strolled slowly round the room, puffing his cigar. Candy sat still, following him with frightened eyes. 'Is it to be now, sir?'

'Now? What's to be? Oh! My dear girl, no. Why, you'd have me like some Regent Street counter-jumper, pocketing his firm's goods. The event will be conducted by Mrs Floyd with the ceremony of leading a princess to her bridal chamber. How do you like the donah?' That was the lady of the house.

'She seems very nice, sir,' Candy pronounced timidly.

'There's no stinginess here, no turning down the gas when you're out of the room half a minute, no sticking old cakes of soap together, no outside ha'penny-bus mentality.' It was the meanest way to travel. 'The donah runs the place with style,' he complimented Mrs Floyd. 'Treat her fair, and you're on velvet.'

'I'm proper scared.' She shivered.

'You've no need. Though it might hurt a bit, the first few times,' he admitted casually. 'You know all about it, surely? You're a farm girl. You've seen the animals. It's the same with humans. We all of us live in God's farmyard. Personally, I've never understood why people become so excited

79

over so fleeting a pleasure, in so uncomfortable and ridiculous a position.' He dropped cigar ash into the plain, cracked pitcher on the wash-stand. 'But it's something which has moved whole worlds.'

He seized her chin with his free hand, staring fixedly into her eyes. 'Do you know what you have inside you? A womb. Like an unripe pear. It radiates femininity into your eyes, your limbs, your skirts, your boots, the atmosphere around you, like the vibrations of animal magnetism.'

He dropped her chin and clutched a handful of mud-edged petticoat, pressing it to his face like a nosegay. 'The hot, spicy smell of dirty petticoats,' he murmured. 'I have Karl Huysmans' nose for it.'

He let the material drop on the thighs beyond her black cotton stockings, one held above the knee with ribbon, the other with a piece of string. 'You'll learn that many men prefer the appurtenances of a woman to the woman herself. Because they are scared in their hearts of the creature whose pelt they fondle. By the by, don't call them "Sir". You're the mistress.'

With disbelief and anxiety she asked, 'But won't they be gentlemen?'

Bertie laughed. 'Noblemen, most likely. But they will be standing *not* on ceremony. You'll do well for yourself.' He stared at her assessively through the cigar smoke. 'Yes, I could make something of you. Were you mine, and not common property like an omnibus. Rose will tell you all that needs knowing. Don't fret over getting a baby. The donah's clever with the sponge on a ribbon, the baking-powder douche, and Mr Rendell's patent soluble quinine pessary, two shillings a dozen, very reliable. Not to mention Lambert's Paragon Sheath, the latest from America, fully vulcanized, four shillings a go, as long-lasting as the tyres on a hansom.'

He dropped his cigar-butt into the chamber-pot, where it sizzled in an inch of urine. From the pocket of his frock coat he took a flat, square box, no bigger than four postage stamps, inlaid with mother-of-pearl. He told Candy she might have it. Wonderingly, she opened the lid to find a sponge under a silver mesh.

'It's a vinaigrette, Candy. That a lady may inhale a mixture of vinegar and lavender should she feel faint.'

She sniffed gingerly. 'It don't smell like lavender.'

'It's chloroform. Go on, take a good noseful,' he urged. 'It's better than mountain air, when you've a fit of the blues. The sponge dries out quickly, but I'll bring you some more.' He drew out his watch, pressed the spring and heard the chimes. 'Time for your dinner. The bub and grub's good,' he commended the food.

'I'm ashamed, sir,' she announced.

'Why?' he demanded peevishly. 'When everything is lovely and the goose hangs high.' He deliberately chose a country phrase – the Christmas dinner hung safely out of foxes' reach.

'You make many a fair speech, sir,' Candy said firmly. 'But I'm doing wrong here, and I knows it. It gives me a sickening.'

'Gammon! You're providing a valuable service to the nation, by preventing the molestation, the very rape, of respectable women. You're just like our lady doctors. With whom gentlemen closet themselves alone, and willingly doff all their clothes. The professional lady attends to them expertly, and rings the bell for the next gentleman. Lady doctors are novelties. Ladies like you have been busy since the first page of the history book.'

Bertie put his arm round her shoulders and squeezed tightly. 'Every pretty girl in society knows her worth, and how to extract the last penny for it. Whether it's from one man or a thousand is only a matter of arithmetic. You'll soon stop feeling a guilty Gawd-'elp-us. Whores don't make hypocrites. That's a virtue lost to a good many women who change nothing in their beds but the sheets.'

Bertie found Rose was on the landing, he suspected listening. He drew from his pocket a shiny white box.

'A present from Jermyn Street.' She opened it, inhaling the smell, eyes glistening. Bertie smiled indulgently. 'They're Turkish cigarettes, quite the latest blend.'

'Oh, thank you, doctor! If I do have a vice, it's smoking.'

The evening was pitch. Deciding he had no hope of a cab, Bertie turned up the collar of his ulster, bag of sovereigns in the pocket, to walk a mile past the invisible Albert Memorial and Albert Hall. Not being home since leaving that morning for the hospital, he carried the Gladstone with his anaesthetic appliances. Outside his front door he met the yellow gaze of a hansom, the horse still, its breath a cloud, the driver with his whip hunched on his perch like a crow on a chimney-pot. Freshings took Bertie's top coat, with the news of a gentleman upstairs. In front of the drawing-room fire waited Oliver Wilberforce.

'I came to beg your pardon, Bertie. For the remark I made this afternoon.'

'Yes, you called me a ponce.' Bertie became angry again.

'I didn't think you'd resent it. You often use such expressions, grinning like a street knocker.'

Bertie thrust hands towards the flames. 'I resent it from you. Because everything you say, you mean.'

'But I'm your friend – '

'It's only friends who can wound, never enemies.'

'I spoke from embarrassment. The slums are *terra incognita* to me.'

'Oh, let's have a brandy and soda,' he said impatiently. Tempers were scudding clouds in Bertie's life.

'I imagined you took only chloroform?' Bertie noticed how relieved Oliver looked at this dismissal of the quarrel. Now, he would not think me worth an apology for anything, Bertie reflected. Certainly not worth making it by hansom on a choking night. He's cunt-struck on Candy.

He went to the tantalus. Freshings would have broken the conversation, perhaps scared Oliver into second thoughts. The drawing-room was small, with books, a brass microscope under a glass bell, a table under a green chenille cloth, a Japanese screen guarding the deep armchair from draughts.

On the mantel stood a box of cigars with a staghorn cutter and a round tasselled smoking-cap. Above it, the crest of Cambridge University and a photograph of some laughing undergraduates. Along the cornice, an oar with college colours on the blade. It was the room of an undergraduate with money.

'You're cunny-haunted, aren't you?' With this amiable accusation of lecherousness, Bertie handed Oliver a tumbler. 'You wouldn't mind shooting your roe into that girl from Whitechapel?'

'As you're being so blunt, yes,' said Oliver reluctantly.

'Where is she?'

'Mrs Floyd's, round the corner.'

Oliver frowned. 'What are you doing in that *galère*?'

'I perform the regular medical examinations, by which Mrs Floyd reassures her patrons and augments her income. They order this matter better in France, you know, where the public health doctor examines the ladies once a week, by law. You can often see gentlemen taking a *coup de rouge* in the café nearby, watching for the medical man to leave and knowing themselves assured of a safe ride. Typical of French prudence and hypochondria.' He gulped his brandy. 'I knew the former madame there, who suffered from palpitations. She was one of my first patients. When she retired to run a family hotel in Biarritz, I was able to recommend Mrs Floyd for the vacancy.'

'How much would that girl be?' Oliver asked hesitantly.

'Twenty pounds.'

Oliver gasped. 'But that's a vast sum.'

'She's *virgo intacta*, which is *rara avis*,' Bertie told him calmly.

'How do you know?'

'The hymen is untorn. The breasts are virgin. The vagina is rugose. Look for yourself, if you feel like it. I daresay I could persuade Mrs Floyd to knock off a sov or two.'

'You're haggling as though this girl's virginity were a piece of merchandise,' Oliver said severely.

'But it is. We live in a practical age. For a girl to empty

your slop-pail in the morning, you must pay her the going wage. Virgins are less available than housemaids, that's all.'

'I can't take a girl's virginity.'

'Oh, rats. Someone will before the sun rises. Regard it as a surgical operation for which you possess exactly the right instrument. Have another b and s.' Bertie returned to the tantalus. 'Be bloody, bold and resolute.'

'Macbeth is hardly an encouraging example.'

'You are bewitched by a more agreeable enchantress.'

'By God, I will!' Oliver decided.

'We'll use your cab,' said Bertie, immediately moving him towards the door. 'We'll be there in the catching up of a garter.' Nothing could be quicker. 'Are you short of the ready? I'll loan you. Mrs Floyd allows no credit, not to a duke nor even to a bishop, should one appear on her doorstep – and you never know.' He laughed loudly. 'You *are* a bally chump! You look just as if you were going to visit the five-shilling dentist.'

Oliver hardly spoke in the cab. In the gaslight of No. 2, he seemed paler than ever. Bertie introduced Mrs Floyd in the hall, money clinked and he immediately left through the front door.

After a wait in the silk-papered room, Oliver was admitted by Mrs Floyd to a bedroom with mirrors on two walls and the ceiling. The furniture was dominated by a square, silk-covered divan, reminding him of the one in Sir Morell Mackenzie's consulting-room. There was a marble wash-stand with a basin and ewer of blue-flowered china, a clean, neatly folded Turkish towel, a chamberpot decorated with entwined roses. No fire, but a porcelain German stove in the corner, the flue angling through the wall.

Candy wore a dress like Rose's but green, which Mrs Floyd thought better suited her colouring. Oliver hung his clothes carefully on the dumb-valet thoughtfully provided. Candy dropped hers on the carpet.

'It's like my wedding night.' Oliver's voice was strained, his body shaking. 'You're not frightened?'

84

'Not no more, sir. It's got to happen.'

'My Lavinia was terribly frightened,' Oliver confessed. 'She didn't come to me like you are. I've never once seen her naked.'

'Men don't, not their wives.'

He thought she was looking sorry for him. He felt he had better have his twenty-five pounds' worth. Candy's unrehearsed performance was not unusually dramatic. Oliver wondered afterwards why he expected otherwise.

He asked her to hold him tight. 'I don't love my wife.'

'No, sir?'

'I hate her.' He paused. 'I could kill her.'

Candy turned her eyes on him, not grasping what he said. His hands went round her throat.

'Give over – ' she pulled them away in panic.

He smiled. 'I'm only playing.'

She wondered if all the gentlemen acted like this. 'Is she wicked?'

'No more than any other woman who bilks her duty to her husband.'

He wondered why he was telling her. Mutual confidences are the offspring of mutual passions. And copulation makes strange bedfellows.

She shivered. 'I'm that cold.'

'It's a miserable day.' Oliver sat up. 'Did you spend?' he asked.

'I think so. I don't know much about it.'

He reached for his clothes. Behind a grille high in the wall, shaped like a ventilator, Bertie Randolph laughed silently and hugged himself. He had seen and heard everything. What Mrs Floyd called *divertissement détaché* was one of the infinite specialities of No. 2.

In barely a minute, Bertie emerged from a door with a different address, walking home through the fog for the second time that night. At Knightsbridge, he heard the strident newsboys. A ragged boy in a velvet cap, flaming torch in one hand, special edition of the *Echo* under his arm, appeared from the direction of Hyde Park Corner. Bertie paid a halfpenny, and saw there was something about the German Emperor.

Over a cigar in his drawing-room, he read that old William I was gravely ill. All places of amusement in Berlin were shut, all leave cancelled, all troops confined to barracks. A week later he died – the King of Prussia who became the first German Emperor, who had fought Napoleon, had ridden into Paris after Waterloo, had weathered the revolution of 1848 exiled in London, had founded the unity of Germany and saw its future in friendship with Russia. He died exhorting his son Frederick to cherish the friendship of the Tsar. Though the words went into the ear of his grandson William, the senile monarch confusing the generations.

'So Europe acclaims the accession of Frederick the Silent,' was Bertie's greeting to Oliver Wilberforce, when they next met ten days later. Though they were alone, sharing a hansom, Bertie talked exclusively about the new Emperor's larynx, for which Oliver felt an unusually warm gratitude towards him.

9

BERTIE ARRIVED at Charing Cross Station for the night boat-train. He wore a travelling-cap with ear-flaps buttoned on top, and a brand-new Harris tweed inverness with detachable cape. His portmanteau was registered through to the Gare du Nord. He had his tartan rug, his Gladstone and a wicker basket with cold chicken and brandy, because he did not fancy the fare on steamers. It was Monday, March 19. The weather was cold and snowy, though the 80-mile an hour Channel gales of the previous week had fortunately blown themselves out.

'I shall spend long days at the Salpêtrière Hospital,' Bertie explained on the platform to Freshings. The valet wore a black overcoat with velvet collar which Bertie had transferred to him, to mitigate the disappointment of staying behind. 'It is fitting that I should travel without a servant, and live with the simplicity of a student. As an English novelist has put it, "It is so difficult for a man to go back to the verdure and malleability of pupildom, who has once escaped from the necessary humility of its conditions." '

Freshings did not follow Trollope's argument. He knew more of his master than the master suspected. He surmised some shady transaction afoot, which he would be unwelcome to witness. He calculated he need but wait, to go everywhere with the doctor through the indispensability of his own silence.

Bertie arrived in Paris to the whiff of breakfast coffee from the station buffet. He smiled over a memory of *petits pains* with Normandy butter and apricot jam, dipped in the steamy, milky cup. He bought from the bookstall *Le Temps*, *Gil Blas* and *La Vie Parisienne*, which he opened for a glance at the pictures as he followed the blue-bloused porter with his luggage. He took a fiacre to a small hotel in the rue d'Uzés, off the boulevard Poissonnière, which was convenient for his business.

He had been three times to Paris in a year, the last time just before Christmas. He never advertised his absences, even to Oliver Wilberforce. Though Bertie had lived long in London, he always felt at home there. It was in the blood, he speculated. In the late 1850s, his father had come home from India, fashionably fast, from Bombay to Marseilles, then taking train to the Channel ports. He had broken the journey in Paris, gone to the Gaieté, fallen for an actress in the operetta, and at the age of 40, crisped with ten years in the Eastern sun, became a stage-door Johnny.

His father stayed, baffling his friends, alarming his family, his wooing subdued by total ignorance of French. She took to the attentive, formal, courteous, devoted Englishman, who seemed to have money. They married in London with privacy indistinguishable from secrecy. Dr Randolph left the Indian Medical Service, Bertie was born in Cheltenham. Love cooled. She went home to Paris. With Bertie at prep school, his father returned to India, developed malaria from the marshy miasmas, took quinine and died.

Like many children in an age when parental life was hazardous, Bertie was reared by aunts. Seeing his mother was a triple treat – the journey to Paris and always some new gentleman in her apartment to divert him. She grew fat, married a rich cotton-spinner from Lille and had choked to death two years before on a Chateaubriand in the Hôtel Marivaux.

Bertie remembered most powerfully her smell. The *profumo di donna*, as the Italians put it, had wildly excited him in childhood from her dresses, her underclothes, her body when taken close in the rumpled, warm morning bedsheets. Chloroform was a later substitute, and less delightfully heady.

The cab rattled over cobbles between pavements pierced with trees and lined with houses solid as cliffs. The traffic flowed straighter and easier than London's, and the omnibuses had three instead of two horses. Bertie looked affectionately at the cafés, the glass screens of winter enclosing their share of the public flagstones, customers warmed by iron stoves among the small round tables and served by waiters in floor-sweeping aprons with the dexterity of jugglers.

He dallied the morning in the *grands boulevards*. Madame Landouzy never rose before noon. When his watch chimed half-past twelve, he turned into the tangle of little streets between the boulevard des Italiens and the rue des Petits-Champs, to the tall house with well-painted shutters in the rue des Verres Dalles. Madame was breakfasting in her tiny parlour full of massive black furniture, its tall window hung with thick lace the colour of parchment.

Like nurses, policemen, engine-drivers and those who serve the world's needs while most of it sleeps, her mealtimes were unsociably out of step. She was old and scrawny, her grey hair piled high, her dress plain black with a fresh white lace collar, steel rimmed pince-nez on her beakish nose. She always struck Bertie – who like many Englishmen was bewitched by Gilbert and Sullivan – as the genius tutelary of a ladies' seminary.

Her welcome was warm. They spoke in French. She asked after Mrs Floyd, whom she had never met. They exchanged opinions about politics.

'Now the *brav' général* Boulanger has been sacked, he has fallen into the hands of a committee formed by a splinter of the Radical party,' she told him. 'Just ten deputies, who carry little weight. *I* certainly don't know them. We have deputies of all parties here, but never radicals. I don't know if they are all sea-green incorruptibles, or cannot afford my prices. Perhaps they prefer dirty establishments. Well, they are trying to present Boulanger as a great statesman, though he is nothing but an obscure soldier without a single brilliant action to his credit, or even a single heroic mistake.'

'But he satisfies your national characteristic of glorification,' Bertie suggested, sitting on a hard chair of black leather.

'Oh, the people must be able to cry "Vivre!" someone,' she agreed. 'He is a man without tact or frankness, and if next Sunday he finds himself elevated as deputy for L'Aisne, it is a fate the people deserve.' She drained her *café au lait,* holding the bowl in both hands. 'You wish to take the two?' Bertie nodded. 'They are pretty little things, with the bloom of youth on them. One from Normandy, one from Gironde. One thirteen, the other probably fourteen, though she does not know. That's why they're no use to me, our age of consent being twenty-one. It is still thirteen in England?'

'There was a fuss about raising it to fifteen, but it never got through Parliament.'

'The masters of these revels must be as powerful in London as in Paris,' Madame Landouzy said shrewdly. 'I can be comfortably deaf to the ranting of reformers, because I am more assured of a majority in the *Assemblée Nationale* than the prime minister. Anyway, young girls are more to English taste than French.'

'Are both unseduced?'

Madame looked shocked, as though accused of marketing faulty goods. 'Their treasure is intact.'

'A pure woman is highly esteemed in England,' Bertie said apologetically. 'We are vicious in a more complicated manner than you practical French.'

'Obviously, when Englishmen enjoy being strapped to a flogging horse.'

'Well, I was swished often enough at Rugby,' Bertie reflected. 'We were told that it formed our character. Perhaps it did, too well.'

'Would you still enjoy being whipped?'

'Only by an elegant woman with dignity of mien, with grace of attitude, elegance and good breeding.'

'I can arrange something, if you return tonight,' she said hospitably. Bertie declined smilingly. 'Then you must try the Nouveautés,' she suggested as an alternative diversion, ringing a handbell. 'They have a pleasant operetta, *Le Puits qui Parle.*'

A maid in black with white lace produced a pair of spindly

girls, one fair and one dark, their expressions a normal child-ish mixture of awe, fright, uncertainty and impishness.

'Would you like to go for a nice ride on a boat?' Madam Landouzy asked sternly. They nodded enthusiastically. 'This kind gentleman shall take you. That'll be lovely, won't it? Say "Thank you".' They giggled at Bertie. She opened a silver box. 'Now you have a bon-bon. Only one each.'

The maid took the children out, one in each hand.

'How much?' asked Bertie.

'A hundred Louis-d'or the pair.'

He nodded. Two thousand francs. About £80. A fair price. 'I'll take them on Sunday. I'm spending the week at the Salpêtrière.'

She shuddered. 'Why a gloomy, smelly place like that, when there is so much gay in Paris?'

Bertie laughed. 'I cannot forget my profession. I'm after the latest uses of mesmerism, whose mysteries excite me even more than those of chloroform.' He rose. 'Please see the urchins are dressed respectably.'

She kept him with a gesture. 'You would care to travel further afield? I have an old friend in the city of Belem, in the Brazils. At the mouth of the great River Amazon, grow-ing prosperous because rubber is sent in greater and greater quantities to America every year. There are plenty of women there eager to earn a living below the waist, but European girls are much esteemed, and would fetch a fine price.'

'Why not go yourself?' Bertie said politely.

'The French do not travel, doctor. We have no need to.'

The following morning, Bertie took the horse-omnibus along the boulevard du Temple, across the place de la Bas-tille and over the pont d'Austerlitz, to the vast Hospice de la Salpêtrière between the Seine and the Jardin des Plantes. He had no need to enter the buildings, Professor Charcot's lectures being so renowned, his audiences being so large, a pavilion within the high walls had been evacuated of patients and furnished as his lecture theatre.

Bertie bore a letter of introduction from the Clerk of the Whitechapel Hospital governors, which a sallow young man in a tail coat at the door inspected with disdain fitting the agent of so famous a physician. Inside, tiers of narrow benches rose steeply to the roof, separated by an iron rail on which the class could lean while scribbling notes on their knees. Bertie squeezed between two young Frenchmen smelling strongly of garlic. Immediately in front sat a stolid, dark-suited man of about thirty, with thick black hair, well-kept moustache and a short beard. He turned to stare at Bertie for some seconds and seemed about to address him, but Charcot entered.

Professor Jean-Martin Charcot was blazing in the noon of his fame. Simply to have sat as his pupil was any doctor's testimonial. He was tall, square-faced, clean shaven, long haired, in his early sixties, with thick straight eyebrows and a mouth seemingly turned down in permanent disdain. His right eye had a squint. He wore a frock coat, high collar and bow tie. He stepped into the constricted floor under the gas globes, followed by the tail-coated young man, escorting a pale, dark-haired girl of twenty or so, in a plain dress of plum-coloured velvet with a white shawl and a wide-brimmed red hat.

The professor was a nerve specialist. The girl's right arm was rigid to her flank, her right leg swung like one of wood. She sat. A case of right-sided paralysis of the spastic sort, Bertie assessed, from excess of muscular action. Though there was something false to the story her body told of its disease. He noticed small movements of the fingers and ankle, belying paralysis. Bertie's quick eyes and wits would have won his reputation as a diagnostician had he patience for the arduous and penurious training, rather than impatience for the luxuries and amusements of its distant success.

'Gentlemen,' Charcot began in French, hands clasped behind him, staring up the crammed benches. 'Mademoiselle Deneuve, *aet* 22, demonstrates hemiplegic paralysis, as you observe.'

92

He spun on his heel. He asked of her illness, his questions cold, rapid, not waiting for finished replies. Bertie imagined Napoleon interrogating some low-ranking messenger. She confessed her condition not painful. It was more a tiresome inconvenience.

'*La belle indifférence.*' Charcot turned to his audience. 'She suffers a most distressing complaint without the slightest emotional consequence.' He asked her, 'When this started last summer, did any other important event occur?'

'Yes, I was to be married. But because of my illness, the ceremony was postponed.'

'Postponed until you get better?'

'Yes.'

'You note how she stands to gain from her illness, gentlemen? She has an *idée fixe* that part of her body is diseased, when it is not. She does not wish to marry this suitor.'

Charcot's gaze held her. He raised a finger before her nose, ordered her to stare at it, told her she was feeling sleepy. His other hand slowly reached for her eyelids and gently shut them. Her mouth opened, she gave a snatched snore.

Bertie watched fascinated. His hero was Dr Franz Anton Mesmer of Vienna, who died in the year of Waterloo. Bertie believed in 'mesmerism', the transmission of animal magnetism, the subtle fluid which pervaded the universe and perfused human nerves, connecting one creature to another, woman's womb to woman's womb, and to the sun, the moon, the stars. In Mesmer's luxurious, ludicrous salon at Paris, his lilac suit flitting in the dim light of stained glass, amid incense and the murmuring of harpstrings, ladies squeezed round iron *bacquets* of magnetized water which emitted foul hydrogen sulphide like bad eggs, moaning in rising frenzy as young male magnetizers massaged their breasts. The Revolution did for Mesmer, though James Graham imported the idea to Soho, with his 'Temple of Health' and earth baths for naked ladies, including Lady Hamilton.

The girl remained asleep, once-stiff arm and leg now flaccid. '*Le grand hypnotisme,*' Charcot pronounced. He took her right arm, held it horizontal. It stayed, as he removed his grasp. He told her severely she had nothing wrong with her limbs, that she could walk, run, dance. A smile spread slowly over her face. He shook her roughly by the shoulders, commanding her to wake. He ordered as her eyes flickered open, 'You will walk out of that door, and return to your mother in the corridor.'

Silently, the girl rose. She stepped normally. She opened the door with her right hand. Unseemly applause broke out, but Charcot did nothing to quell it.

'I must be honest, gentlemen, that her paralysis will return. The cure is marriage – to another young man. I have simply demonstrated how unlimited is our power of hypnotic suggestion. No,' he corrected himself, 'not entirely so. A young assistant of mine quite disgracefully commanded an attractive lady, in the hypnotic state, to draw her skirts and petticoats to her hips. She instantly slapped his face.'

Charcot followed his patient.

The audience pushed out. At the door, Bertie lit a cigar. A voice at his side asked in English, with an accent, 'Excuse me, sir, but you would doubtless be an Englishman?' Bertie nodded. It was the bearded young man sitting in front of him. 'I imagined as much, from your excellent clothes. The cut of an English tailor is as obvious as the stitch of a Parisian dress-maker. And your cigar!' He sniffed. 'No cigars can touch those made in England.'

Bertie politely offered his sharkskin case. 'You often visit our shores?' he enquired.

'Only once, when I was nineteen. My half-brother Emmanuel has settled in Manchester.' Bertie struck a match, but his companion looked embarrassed. 'I should prefer not to smoke in the street. I suppose that is an inhibition from my native Vienna, where folk are more strait-laced than in Paris.'

'I noticed a café opposite the hospital. And I could do with a *fine à l'eau*. I have always found education so exhausting.' They strolled towards a gate leading into the boulevard de l'Hôpital. 'My name is Dr Bertram Randolph, of London.'

'And mine is Dr Sigmund Freud. I am a *Privatdozent* in neuropathology. I have been working at the General Hospital in Vienna, but I won a travelling scholarship, and clearly there is no better place in the world to spend it than at Charcot's feet. I have never met an Englishman here.' He sounded more puzzled than damning. 'But why need you cross the Channel, when the seas carry your ideas with your merchandise everywhere? I am a passionate admirer of England and the English. Particularly Oliver Cromwell.'

Bertie laughed. 'I'd admire more Sir John Falstaff. Puritans make poor company.'

The café at the corner of the boulevard St Marcel was warm behind its screens. Bertie ordered brandy and water, Dr Freud coffee.

'You speak excellent French, Dr Randolph.'

'Not my mother-tongue, but my mother's.'

'Do you practice hypnosis?'

'I should like to.'

'Hypnosis and hysteria – the condition of our young lady this morning – are two sides of the same coin. You cannot achieve hypnosis in those unlikely to suffer from hysteria. And those who have hysteria can always be hypnotized.'

Bertie thought him a solemn young man. He associated Vienna with *Apfel-Strudel* and *Sacher-Torte*, imagined its inhabitants as gay as an operetta. Of course, this fellow was Semitic, he reflected. What a strange passion for Cromwell! Then Bertie seemed to remember that Cromwell had done something decentish for the English Jews. Or perhaps Cromwell was the only English figure he knew? Who in London could add to Maria Theresa?

'Other doctors disagree with Professor Charcot. They say that hypnosis is nothing but the patient subconsciously obliging the hypnotist, by producing the effect expected of him. That it is no more than brow-beating.' Dr Freud savoured his English cigar. 'I am a neurologist. I study nerves as physical components of the body. But I find psychical illnesses, as this morning's, most fascinating. Some seven or eight years ago, Dr Joseph Breuer, who you will know – '

95

Bertie shook his head. Dr Freud looked disapproving. 'He is known very well in Vienna. He brought to my notice a most interesting case, "Anna O". Far worse than Charcot's patient. Paralysis of *all* her limbs, areas of numbness, contractures, disordered vision and speech, no appetite, a cough like the creak of a graveyard gate. Sometimes she was an attractive and intelligent young woman. Others, an unruly child. Then Dr Breuer found by chance that Anna's talking to him of each particular symptom caused its disappearance. She went through them one by one, chimney-sweeping them from her mind. So you see, Dr Randolph, how human speech can act as a powerful drug? Anna O's troubles were like Mademoiselle Deneuve's, seeded in the marriage-bed. Charcot agrees with me, there is *la chose genitale* in most nervous cases.'

Bertie looked more interested. 'I am always intrigued by ramifications of the endeavour to bring human genitals into contact with those of one from the other sex.'

'We must distinguish *genital* from *sexual*,' Dr Freud said seriously. 'Sexual satisfaction equates with self-preservation. From the moment the baby first sucks the nipple.'

Bertie frowned then smiled, as the waiter brought their drinks, the price in centimes glazed on each saucer. 'A baby? Sexual satisfaction? Any respectable London doctor would find that even more disgusting than the prospect of sexual satisfaction in a woman. Which they can tell you is dangerous, leading to cancer of the uterus and madness.'

'I always find difficulty in the acceptance of my ideas,' Dr Freud said simply. 'Anyone must who nudges the world awake from its comfortable doze. I have already assured an unpleasant welcome home, by writing that Charcot has demonstrated that hysteria can occur in a man – '

'My dear fellow!' Bertie interrupted. 'You *will* make yourself look a chump. Surely you know that "hysteria" comes from the Greek for "womb"? How can a man possibly be hysterical? He's not equipped for it.'

'You are more amiable in your criticism than the president of our *Gesellschaft der Ärzte*. He described my ideas as no matter for scientific discussion, but for the police.'

Bertie looked at him with schoolboyish admiration. 'A bit of a scorcher, aren't you? The way you stand up for your notions? I'm sure you're right about the genital thing. Fellows in London will tell you that a man enjoys a woman – whether she's his wife, or his fancy woman, or a Haymarket whore – in the way he enjoys his dinner, or his shooting, or riding, or getting drunk, or saying his prayers if that's his nature. *I* know there's more to it. The act of copulation is a dynamo. It creates a magic current which illuminates our lives.'

Dr Freud observed drily, 'Perhaps we have more in common than our taste in cigars.'

Bertie suddenly suspected the neurologist was mocking him. He decided to withdraw his toe from the currents of Viennese philosophy. 'I'd like to send you a box of Havanas from Fribourg and Treyer. May I have your card?'

Dr Freud thanked him with touching solemnity. 'I'm soon returning to Vienna. I shall be sorry to leave this magic city, though the people are arrogant and sharp. And have you noticed, Dr Randolph, how ugly all the women are?'

'Where are you living?'

'The Hôtel de Brésil, in the rue de Goff. A hundred and fifty francs a month for full board is not ruinous. I have won Professor Charcot's consent to my translating his *Lectures on the Nervous System* into German,' he revealed modestly. 'Which affords me the privilege of limited entrée to his house. Madam Charcot is of course worth millions and millions of francs. She is as ugly as any other Parisienne, but much fatter. When do you return to England?'

'On Sunday.'

'Even four or five days here can be profitable.'

'Oh, very,' Bertie agreed heartily.

10

THE CLOCK was touching midnight on April 3. It was the end of Easter Bank Holiday Monday. Bertie recollected that they had half-an-hour before the bottles and half-empty glasses were whisked from the tables by law.

They were in Romano's, in the Strand, London's Broadway of 1888. Both wore tails. Oliver Wilberforce was drunk, but Bertie was unable to calculate how much. Oliver was a man only amused when others roared their ribs out, who smiled when others sang, who grew amorous rather than passionate, and tipsy when his companions were riotous. He was that irritating sort who went abruptly from sobriety to insensibility, Bertie thought, calculating the chance of conveying Oliver in a cab to his own front door like a case of apoplexy.

They had opened four bottles of 'the widow', – Romano's jargon for champagne – followed by brandy-and-sodas and some sweet Barsac for the two girls. Bertie never drank deeply. He had no need to stimulate his cheerfulness. The pleasurable weakness of other men he found greater pleasure in despising.

'Sir Morell Mackenzie is an old friend of my family,' Oliver was boasting, chalky face pink-tinged. 'I hear more that goes on in the new Emperor's court than anyone in Europe. You know, he can't utter a word, since the doctors cut his throat – '

'Cut his throat? What did they want to cut his throat for?' asked Flo shrilly. She was the blonde one in the pink dress and white boots.

'If you ask me, all foreigners want their throats cutting,' giggled Mabs, who was dark and fat, in scarlet.

Oliver stared blankly over the cloth. It was cleared of dinner, swept of crumbs, bearing only glasses, coffee cups, a plate with a lace doily containing two unfavoured *petits fours*. They had a private room, just big enough for the round table, a pink satin-covered couch and the dumbwaiter. Crimson plush curtains were drawn across the window, a fern in a brass pot stood in one corner.

'It was an operation,' Oliver explained solemnly.

'Ug!' Flo shuddered.

'The Emperor had to take the train, seven hundred miles, across the Alps, from sunny Italy to the freezing blizzards of Berlin. Because Prince Bismarck says he must. Why? Because Prince Bismarck hoped the journey would *kill him*,' Oliver said impressively.

'Pardon,' said Flo. 'I've just done a raspberry tart.'

Oliver looked blank. Bertie grinned. He knew that in Cockney slang she had farted.

'You don't seem very interested,' Oliver complained crossly.

'Oh, ever so,' said Mabs. 'You can't trust these bleeding foreigners.'

'And I don't half want a piss, too,' said Flo.

'I wouldn't say no to a piddle myself,' Mabs agreed cheerfully.

They left, giggling. Oliver propped his elbows on the cloth and his face on his hands.

'What am I doing in this place?' he demanded self-pityingly.

Bertie started singing, '*Romano's, Italiano's, Paradise in the Strand*. Every man in London should go to Romano's once. It's a sign of nubility. Like girls being presented at court, but a dashed sight more amusing.'

Romano's was one of the world's lucky few restaurants whose extravagant and extroverted patrons create a club. Starting as a fish-and-sauce shop, it was enjoying the fame of Magny's in Paris during the 1860s. The building was as unsuggestive of convivial feeding as a station buffet. Narrow, yellow-painted, with a big gas globe in front, one door led

99

into a long bar crammed with men in their top hats. This was overseen by a chubby, big-eyed barmaid with high-piled blonde curls, in black dress and severely starched collar, known only as 'the Brown Mouse'. The long restaurant lay beyond, so narrow it held a single row of tables, and was known only as 'the shooting gallery.'

The private dining-rooms upstairs were reached through a second entrance, past the window containing a decorative tank of goldfish in which patrons often tried to bathe. Plovers' eggs, chops, even whole chickens, were sometimes playfully flying about the dining-room. Romano's was the haunt of mashers. Of topers and spoofers. Of journalists down the road in Fleet Street, actors from the West End, gamblers, bookies, crooks, raffish aristocrats and aristocratic roughs. Sir Arthur Sullivan often dined there, Mr W.S. Gilbert rarely. Oliver had stepped inside with the bewilderment of the fictitious Revd Joseph Slapkins, regularly depicted in Romano's by Phil May in *Punch*.

'What am I supposed to do with the girl?' Oliver asked despairingly.

Bertie upended a bottle of champagne into Oliver's glass. 'I should imagine that – for sufficient money – either of them would permit anything short of hanging, drawing and quartering.'

'But where do I take her?' he implored miserably.

'She'll conduct you to an accommodation house, probably round the corner in Covent Garden. Surely you've noticed the signs, "Beds Within"? You pay for the room, by the by. You'll have a good time, now her belly's full of grub and wine,' Bertie said knowingly. 'A woman always feels the warmth of a good dinner in her cunt.'

He put his feet on the tablecloth and drew a cigar from his case. 'Oh, yes, now they've let slip a fart or two and had a piss, they'll be ready for work. Take your pick, or both if you like. I'm going home. Just talk a little quiet smut to her first, to put her in the right frame of mind. Then show her your prick as soon as you've the chance. It's a great persuader with any woman, even the most respectable schoolmistress.'

'Why must you be so crude?' Oliver complained bitterly.

Bertie struck a match on the sole of his boot. 'It's a crude activity.'

Oliver slapped the table-cloth. 'I wish you'd never got me into this.'

Bertie arched an eyebrow. 'Me? That's ripe. I put myself out, introducing you to a pair of nice lady-friends, because you're dead nuts on doing the chaws with some woman or other.'

'Chaws?' Oliver was mystified.

'Fucking.'

'Oh. I see.'

'Why couldn't you take your stiff pego back to fair Candy? She wouldn't have cost so much, now you've cracked her pipkin.'

Oliver supposed he meant taken her virginity, and looked more miserable than ever.

'I don't care to visit such places.'

'I say, you *are* dashed fastidious,' Bertie mocked him. 'It's the only occasion you're likely to shoot 'twixt wind and water over the same covert as noblemen.'

Oliver sensed a low pun, which he could not be troubled to unravel. 'Why should I be reduced to this squalor at all?' he complained pathetically. 'It's all the fault of my wife.'

'Oh, rats. You can't blame your cook because you go out and overeat in a restaurant.'

'The food here's filthy.'

'Well, it's expensive. A man has the compensation of knowing the prices will dazzle his lady-friend.'

'How can I rid myself of this girl?'

'You'll have to pay her.'

'How much?' Oliver asked gloomily.

'She might let you get away with half a sov.' There was a knock. 'Ah, the Roman himself,' Bertie exclaimed cheerfully, feet still on the table.

'Hey, Mister Doctor, everything a' right?' Alfonso Nicolino Romano came in. The thick Italian accent, being expected of him, was never lost. He was dark, curly-haired, thick-moustached, lively and voluble. Oliver stared, as if Bertie had conjured a spirit from the hell he inhabited so comfortably.

'Everything's ripping, Romano. Were you on Veracity for the Lincoln?'

'Oh, the poor old Roman!' he exclaimed tragically. 'Looka, he goin' to putta monkey on Veracity, but Mister Shiff – ' Romano referred to 'The Shifter' of the *Pink 'Un*. 'He say, six stone ten pound, too much for the bloomin' animal to carry all that way round the racecourse. So the Roman, he loose.'

Bertie knew that Romano would bet on everything from the Derby to pitch-and-toss with his customers. He nearly always lost. This instinct for misfortune was another expected joke, as much part of the restaurant's personality as the goldfish in the window.

'Well, I've heard Fullerton's a good thing for the City and Suburban.'

'Thank you, Mister Doctor. Romano remembers. If it wins, next Saturday Romano stand you a free dinner. And your friend.' His gesture generously embraced Oliver.

'Oh, God, no,' Oliver exclaimed.

The two girls returned, chattering and laughing. They gathered hats and wraps. On the stairs, Bertie remarked to Flo, 'Did you know, you can tell the time on the new Law Courts' clock from outside the Roman's front door?'

'Betcher can't. There's them two churches in the way.'

'An Abraham's willing on it?' He held up the shilling. She nodded. On the pavement under the gas globe, Bertie pointed. The clock jutted from the building, and by the angle of the streets could be glimpsed a quarter of a mile away beyond St Mary-le-Strand and St Clement Danes, lying like battleships in line astern.

'Well, I never!'

'Many a masher's made a case of champagne on that,' he told her proudly.

'Oh, you're a real heavy swell, you are.'

They were interrupted by a scream behind them. 'You

fucking mean bastard!' Mabs shouted to Oliver. 'Look what he gimme! A tusheroon.' Her indignant palm quivered with a half-crown.

Oliver seemed puzzled at his ill-taken liberality. 'But I don't want anything more to do with you,' he explained.

'Nor shall you,' she told him warmly. 'I wish I may die first. I wouldn't give a knee-trembler to a mingey bugger like you.' Her biting scorn over ambulatory copulation amused a bunch of swells, hats tipped, leaving the restaurant.

'Here's a sovereign,' Oliver hissed desperately. 'Now be off with you. Or I'll call a policeman.'

'Pliceman? I'd like to see you,' she mocked him stridently, grabbing the gold coin while retaining the half-crown. 'You dursn't! Too lardy-dah, you are.'

Bertie took charge. 'Pike it,' he commanded, jerking his head down the Strand.

'I'll go when I feel like it,' Mabs told him defiantly. The swells were laughing. Others were emerging from the long bar, to find what the noise was about. Mabs stuck out her lower lip and glared at Oliver. She felt the power of her position. The shameful trumpeting its attachment to the respectable.

Bertie seized her arm. 'Listen, you trull,' he said quietly, close to her face. 'If you're not back in your whorehouse in a pig's whisper, I'll see to it that someone skins you alive before morning. I know how to set about it – and *you* know that, don't you?'

Her mouth opened at this threat, the anger in her eyes chilled to fright. 'Don't you?' Bertie repeated, squeezing her arm tighter.

'I ain't a common slut,' she said defensively. 'I only goes with a gentleman.'

'I'd make her go down on her marrowbones and beg pardon, if I had my way,' suggested Flo piercingly, adhering to the winning side.

Bertie held out his hand. 'The sovereign. You can keep the silver.'

She snarled, throwing the gold coin on the pavement.

Bertie slapped his foot on it. A rolling sovereign in the Strand had a life of short liberty. The girl turned, and stalked in the direction of Trafalgar Square.

'Common tit,' Flo shouted after her.

Oliver took back his sovereign, trembling with fright and indignation. 'You've made me a laughing-stock,' he complained.

'They're only threepenny mashers,' Bertie said scornfully towards the top-hatted onlookers drifting after other amusements.

'I'm off.'

'Where?' Bertie enquired.

'I don't know. Anywhere. If this story gets out, it'll ruin me.' He started, then turned back to Bertie. 'The whole class of loose women is loathsome. Had I my way, I'd exterminate the lot.'

'How dreadfully unfriendly.'

Oliver strode in the opposite direction to the girl, hands hidden under his long cape, top hat hard over eyes, shoulders hunched, instantly lost among the midnight crowds. He walked unseeing, at every kerb in danger of being run down. 'That swine Bertie Randolph,' he kept muttering. Bertie was a wicked Jack O'Lantern, leading a man of intelligence and character into street brawls with common whores.

He found himself in the massive shadow of St Paul's. His mind flashed with the notion of taking a cab to the hospital. A consultant in evening dress was not unknown, summoned from a banquet or family evening for some special case. There would be people he might talk to, his yawning house-surgeon dancing attendance, the night nurses, a dozen patients in the wards to encourage in their wavering between life and death. He did not care to return home, though his wife had not for some months stayed up for him. He resented bitterly that his marriage was not as happy as the marriages of his colleagues, or as theirs appeared to be. The marriage-bed held its secrets as securely as the tomb, he reflected. He kept thinking about Candy, which made him angrier still.

Outside Romano's, Bertie held up his hand for a hansom.

'Do you want to come home with me, dearie?' Flo mounted the iron step.

He called up to the driver. 'Take us towards the Bank of England. No hurry. I'll pay by the hour.'

'It's a tusheroon minimum fare,' the man said surlily.

'What's that to me?' asked Bertie, flipping him the coin with millionaire airiness.

'Where are we going?' Flo settled on the velvet cushions, excited rather than nervous.

'I haven't made up my mind.'

'Mine's a nice clean place.' Bertie was staring through the cab window as they clopped past the Law Courts, searching for Oliver but hoping to miss the inconvenience of spotting him.

'Want a bit of firkytoodle?' Flo invited, putting his hand between her legs. He drew it away. 'You ain't exactly dead nuts on me, are you, Charlie?' she complained.

'Not at the risk of getting a dose of crabs.' Bertie was feeling in the pocket of his velvet-collared overcoat.

'I likes that! It's a bloomin' lie. I'm as clean as the Queen of England.'

'Mabs has got them. I saw her scratching her cunny, when she thought no one was looking.'

'Oh, her,' said Flo dismissively. 'She can go and eat coke and shit cinders.'

Something she took as a silver tobacco-box glittered on Bertie's palm in the faint lamplight. He opened the lid, pouring drops from a small bottle concealed in his hand. 'Take a sniff,' he invited.

Flo wrinkled her nose. The smell was strong, sweet, new to her nostrils.

'Go on,' Bertie encouraged, holding the box closer. 'It'll make you feel spiffing. It's better than a yard of satin.' Her expression reflected intimate familiarity with a glass of gin.

'Lawks! It makes me quite swimmy.' She looked pleased at this discovery.

'Sniff some more. The feeling gets better.'

Flo giggled. 'You'll 'ave me proper foxed, you will.'

'You won't get drunk. Sniff, sniff!' Bertie's voice was low and urgent.

Suddenly she pushed the *vinaigrette* away. 'I don't like it,' she said thickly.

'Don't be silly,' he told her crossly. 'It's as good as a tonic.'

She was suddenly frightened. 'It's making me sleepy.'

'That'll pass,' he said impatiently. 'In a minute, you'll be soaring like an angel.'

'No, I don't want none.' Bertie grabbed her head and pressed the box against her nose. She struggled. 'Let over! I can't breathe – '

'Don't be a silly little cunt – '

She screamed.

The cab-driver reined his horse. He had been listening ill-temperedly to the thumping under his nose. He had started work at nine that morning – a day which kept him sixteen hours on his perch, and left his legs so numb that he needed to haul himself upstairs to bed in Islington grasping the handrail, one step at a time, like a paralysed beggar. He threw open the knee-doors and Flo stumbled on to the cobbles.

'Come back,' Bertie shouted angrily. 'You're missing a treat.'

'I've 'ad enough. You're doing me a mischief, that's what you're doing.' She started to weep, standing on the kerb-stone. They had reached Cheapside in the City, as deserted at midnight as crowded at midday.

'Control yourself,' Bertie commanded from the cab. He saw a policeman's bullseye flash across the street. Flo started crying hysterically. He ordered the cabman, 'Drive on.'

'No, I ain't,' he said defiantly. 'I don't like what you're up to.'

Bertie was furious. 'I gave you a half-crown.'

The man pointed into the darkness with his whip. 'Want ter take it up with the copper?'

Bertie swore, turned up his velvet collar, leapt from the cab and hurried into the cats-cradle of lanes between black-windowed office buildings. Flo's noise stopped with his departure. Bertie supposed she had encountered the police-man, and as a common prostitute the trouble she created would rebound on herself. He hurried away, not caring where he went, though a gentleman alone at night east of Charing Cross walked with his watch and his throat at peril. His anger subsided, as he calculated his chances of screwing the cost of the evening from Oliver Wilberforce.

Freshings had a room hardly bigger than a cupboard over Bertie's dressing-room. He was squeezed into his rough-blanketed truckle bed with Maud, the fat new housemaid, snoring naked in his arms. He woke to hear his master shuffling below, opening and closing doors, pouring water, pissing in the pot. Freshings had no notion of the hour, a watch being as far beyond his means as a carriage. Bertie was often home nearer his breakfast than his dinner.

The valet dozed again. He was woken by a crash below. As Maud jerked up, he clapped a hand over her mouth. The house was still. Mrs Anstey was full of laudanum. Under Maud's frightened eyes, Freshings scrambled from the bed, reached for his new overcoat behind a curtain, and crept downstairs in the darkness.

He tapped the bedroom door. No answer. He went in. The dressing-room door was ajar, the gas lit within. On the floor appeared to be a pig in dress clothes. Bertie's nose, mouth and chin were in a wickerwork snout, secured by an india-rubber strap buckled round his neck. The small room reeked of chloroform, to which Freshings' nose was no stranger. A blue bottle of ridged glass lay unstoppered on the carpet. Bertie's eyes were shut, his complexion dusky. Freshings knelt, ripped off the appliance, held Bertie's head on his bare thigh, slapped his cheeks.

Bertie took a deep, sighing breath, his colour turned pink, he sluggishly stirred an arm. Freshings cradled his head for some minutes, wondering if to rouse Mrs Anstey, even to send across the square for Dr Greville, who Bertie consulted when off-colour. Bertie groaned. Freshings decided his master's condition best treated as drunkenness.

He raised Bertie to his feet, pulled an arm around his own

neck, dragged him to the bed, undressed him, bundled him between the chilly sheets. Bertie was moving his head slowly from side to side and groaning louder. He retched violently. Freshings brought a towel from the dressing-room, wiping the green vomit from chin and pillow. Bertie started breathing regularly, as though in a normal deep sleep. Freshings crept away. The more he knew of Bertie's abnormalities, the easier his life would be.

The fanlight at the top of the servants' stairs shone grey. He shook Maud awake, despatching her silently to her own room on the far side of Mrs Anstey's. The church clocks struck quarter-to. It was approaching six, when they must all be up and about and to work.

11

ON THE FRIDAY of June 15, Sir Morell Mackenzie's patient, now the German Emperor Frederick III, died at eleven in the morning. He was succeeded by his son William II, twenty-nine, of the swept-up moustaches and businesslike views on foreign policy.

Two days before, Mackenzie had sent a cypher telegram from Potsdam to Queen Victoria at Balmoral expressing no hope. Pieces of free cartilage were appearing through the incision made four months before. The Emperor was coughing up his own windpipe. The crowd outside the Schloss Friedrichskron knew before the lowering of the royal standard to half-mast. They recognized among the hurriedly arriving officials Anton von Werner, the artist everyone had heard was to sketch the Emperor immediately after death.

After six hours at his patient's bed, Mackenzie stumbled into his own. He was shortly routed out by the new Emperor, demanding an immediate report on the fatal illness. Mackenzie wrote, 'It is my opinion that the disease from which the Emperor Frederick III died was cancer.' Humble pie is often the doctor's portion at the funeral breakfast.

Profesor von Bergmann, sharing the case with Mackenzie, pressed for a post-mortem. The widow Empress Victoria, grief-stricken, heavily veiled, weeping, begged that her husband's body be spared the cruel indignity. The new Emperor William had businesslike views on post-mortems as well. It was squeezed into an hour before the lying-in-state, conducted by ten doctors and the Minister of the Household.

Armed guards were already at every entrance of the Schloss Friedrichskron, which Frederick had renamed in honour of Frederick the Great, and his son William immediately resorted to its ancient title of the Neue Palais. The grounds were alive with marching patrols and galloping officers. No one might leave without an aide-de-camp's exeat, nor dispatch a telegram without his visa. The widowed Empress implored an interview with Prince Bismarck. Her son the new Emperor refused her. He had businesslike views on family relations.

A secret letter of constitutional advice by Frederick-William IV, written before he went mad in the 1850s, was presented to his great-nephew William II. He tore it up. His first duty was taking the oath of allegiance from his armed forces.

'We belong to each other, I and the army,' he declared with a lover's passion. 'We were born for each other and will cleave indissolubly to each other, whether it be the will of God to send us calm or storm. From the world above, the eyes of my forefathers look down on me, that I shall one day have to stand accountable to them for the glory and honour of the army.'

The funeral was private. The new Kaiser complained to his grandmother in England of the cold reception she afforded the Prussian general sent officially to inform her of his succession. 'The Queen intended it to be cold,' said the Queen.

The generation of Frederick III vanished in ninety-nine days, grandson in effect succeeding grandfather. The Foreign Minister – Bismarck's son – expressed widespread sorrow that the dead Emperor would have lived many years had he not consulted Sir Morell Mackenzie. The Kaiser quickly doffed the shroud of mourning. He was off to review the fleet. To meet the Czar in St Petersburg, the Emperor Franz-Josef in Vienna. Queen Victoria told him that such disregard of etiquette was vulgar. William replied that we Emperors were above such affectation. It was clear to Europe that he had businesslike views on everything.

In London, it was the season. The lords and ladies left their broad acres in May, bringing to Town their families, their family plate and their family servants, who opened the shuttered houses, stripped the dust-sheets, freed the chandeliers and fireirons of their holland bags, blackened the grates and scrubbed the floors, and threw open the windows to exhale camphor into Mayfair and Belgravia.

For three months, the seeds of England's nobility, extruded from her country core, drove in the Park, heard the opera and saw the Academy, and took their pick of a dozen balls a night. The gentlemen went out for lunch, the ladies invited them in for tea, the daughters were mated and the gossip exhausted. At the end of July, everyone left except miserable persons like members of Parliament, who had to close their drawing-rooms because there was no one worth inviting to fill them.

The weather that season was sunless and stormy. The hansom-cabs went without their white linen roof-covers, the horses stayed bare of their straw-hats with ear-holes. Snow fell in mid-July. It poured for Goodwood Races at the end of the month. The wet afternoon of Tuesday, July 30, found Bertie sitting in his drawing-room after tea, at a loose end. That was unusual, in a young man with a brain as restless as an over-indulgent diner sleeping through a nightmare.

He had drawn from his bookcase *Esoteric Anthropology or the Mysteries of Man*, by Dr Thomas Low Nichols, of New York. Opening the cover, he found a forgotten leader page torn from the *Lancet* of April 24, 1886.

By the verdict of the jury at the Central Criminal Court on Saturday last another celebrated case has been, legally speaking, removed from the catalogue of crimes, though left by that verdict in an atmosphere of suspicion. However strong was the suspicion, there was certainly not sufficient evidence to prove beyond all reasonable doubt that a murder had been committed. The whole course of the Bartletts' married life seems to have run in such peculiar grooves, and to have been directed by influences so unnatural . . .

Bertie skipped half a column.

When the principles of Esoteric Anthropology *are made the guide of wedded life, the instincts and craving of human*

*nature find no fitting opportunity for their normal mani-
festation and satisfaction. We are glad to read the condemnation passed by the learned judge who presided at the
trial upon literature which, whatever the intentions of the
author, is fit only to be burned by the public hangman.*

Bertie smiled. *Esoteric Anthropology* was a manual on
birth control. Its American author claimed it as pure in
morals as true in science, its inspiration the welfare of man
and society. The awkward link between copulation and con-
ception, tempered afresh in the blaze of the *Lancet's* indignation, seemed to Bertie an unnecessary shackle.
Pornography lies in the eye of the beholder, he reflected.
The condemnation of sin varies with the delights of its temptation. The heady wine of righteous indignation produces
the drunkard of intolerance, what shocks one generation
bores the next.

There was a knock. Freshings had a letter and a visiting-
card on his salver. The card drew from Bertie a whistle.
Ambrose Porter-Hartley had never called on him before. He
wondered that the man knew his address. A visit unexpected
and inexplicable. The brown envelope bore a stamp with the
spreadeagle arms of Austria.

'He may stay in the waiting-room for a while.' Bertie
reached for a paper-knife. If he let Ambrose cool his heels,
the pomposity might drain from his brain. 'By the by, Freshings, it seems I shall *not* be going to Paris next week.' A *colis*
from Madame Landouzy had escaped its dispatch to
London. 'It'll probably be another month or two.'

'Perhaps I can come with you then, sir?' he asked eagerly.

'Perhaps,' Bertie opened the letter.

'You need someone to look after you, sir. Like that night
last Easter.'

'All right, I was as drunk as a besom,' Bertie said mildly.
'That's more common in the gentleman's household than the
curate calling for tea. I was fooling with an old chloroform
mask, which are strapped on hospital patients every day.
There's no need for you to mention the incident again,

Freshings. I'll ring when I want the visitor.' He added to himself, as the door closed, 'I *must* be careful. Or one morning he'll find me a goner.'

The letter was in English, addressed from the Kaiser Josefstrasse in Vienna.

Dear Dr Randolph!

Thank you for your gift of cigars, which arrived in perfect condition. It is typical of English courtesy for so slight a desire from a stranger to be remembered und acted upon.

Your letter raises many interesting points. You are right that the disorder of hysteria has been regarded until our own days as beneath the dignity, or even attention of any physician jealous of his reputation. It has been ascribed often to specific disorder of the womb. But Professor Charcot specified hysteria as a disease of the nervous system. He made the womb respectable.

As you say, hysteria has been treated by the inhalation of valerian, the unpleasant smell of this volatile oil being genuinely believed to force a wandering, unstable womb back to its proper place between the bladder and rectum. Possibly, valerian contains some active principle, yet unknown, which depresses the nervous system. I consider that its effect is simply that of any physic, which the patient feels must do good if it is unpleasant enough. This medical treatment of hysteria is as lastingly ineffective as its surgical treatment by amputation of the clitoris.

I cannot agree with you that the womb has any function in the body except bearing children.

I do agree on the importance of sexuality in the psychology of everyday life. According to William James, a doctor I admire who is Professor of Philosophy at Harvard, 'Habit is the enormous flywheel of society.' I should say instead, 'sexuality' is our flywheel.

But I know from the silence which greets my communications to medical societies, the hints dropped by my friendlier colleagues, and the asperations by my more hostile

113

ones, that postulating sexuality as the cause of neurosis cannot be made, even in scientific circles, like suggesting the cause of any other disease.

A prime example of hysteria in the male is 'railway spine' after minor accidents, if likely to gain the sympathy of the courts. Unhappily, many doctors do well financially from advising these cases upon litigation.

Sincerely yours,

Freud

Bertie replaced *Esoteric Anthropology* and rang for Freshings to show up Ambrose Porter-Hartley.

'I hope I'm not an inconvenient visitor?' The physician entered looking uncomfortable, his pale, flabby cheeks flushed. 'I should have sent a hansom with a letter first.'

'I'm delighted to have company. I'm going to dine at the club, but it's dull before the fellows start assembling.'

'Which is your club?' Ambrose was bafflingly polite.

'The Odeum.'

'Very theatrical. I'm at the Athenaeum.'

'Very erudite. A glass of wine?'

'Thank you.'

Bertie pressed the bell. 'The Bual, Freshings. I'll have a b and s.'

'The electricity,' said Ambrose in amazement, sitting by the fireplace. 'You must do pretty well? You've the good sense to choose an area where people don't begrudge a guinea to find if they're ill or well. Did you know, Sir Morell Mackenzie charges *two guineas* for just shining a light down the throat? Even for administering a puff of powder? He performs with the speed of a machine, while one patient is removing his wrapper, Sir Morell is administering a gargle to another, and while that one is clearing his throat he's whipping out his instruments and removing the tonsils of the first. He tells every new patient his fee, and if the sufferer can't afford it, that's the end of the consultation there and then. According to Wilberforce, the man works fourteen hours a day, which must bring him the region of *twenty thousand pounds* per annum! Honestly, I think Mackenzie would practise on Sunday if he could.'

Why such flattering freedom of opinion? Bertie wondered. Ambrose regarded him as but the imp on Oliver's coat-tails. Over their glasses, Ambrose asked solemnly, 'I do not know if you are a religious man, Randolph?'

'Well, I accept the Church of England, from gaitered bishop to pale curate, as a reliable social reservoir, and repository of variable erudition. Nonconformists, not being gentlemen, are beyond my reckoning. And Catholics are unhealthily preoccupied with chastity.'

Ambrose seemed unsure of his response. 'As you know, I live my life in the light of Our Lord, which I attempt to direct into dark places with good works. The unfortunate class in Whitechapel, for instance.'

Bertie nodded gravely. He glimpsed another light in which Ambrose might lead his life. Bertie had inherited his mother's sharp actress' eye for human peculiarities, her sharp assessment of hidden temperament in friends or enemies, the more important discernment of who was which from the two. Ambrose would always be his enemy. But the destructive devil which man called his soul could pitchfork him into perilous imprudence.

'They demand our attention in Whitechapel like the reeking sewers which run open in the street. In the fashionable quarters of this, the greatest metropolis in the world, the sewers run underground, unknown to the populace going about its daily business, but running their foul way just the same.' Ambrose wagged a pudgy finger. 'Even here in Belgravia this hellish trade continues.'

'Really?' said Bertie.

'Yes, Randolph, it does.' Ambrose spoke with the emphasis of the pulpit. 'Every day, girls with the early sunshine of life on their fresh faces are vilely seduced. We need not be medical men to specify the consequences. Degradation, destitution, disease.'

Ambrose knows that Oliver had been regularly to Mrs Floyd's all summer, Bertie calculated. Possibly Oliver himself hinted it. The pair were old acquaintances, and a man will often reckon that cutting a dash is worth an indiscretion.

Ambrose sipped his madeira. 'I should like to make a public example of some fashionable house of ill-fame.'

'Admirable.'

'But the prosecution of a brothel is more difficult than that of a fraudulent shopkeeper.'

'Yes, it needs the complaints of two ratepayers from the same parish.'

'Exactly. Armed with evidence so incriminating that the police must be forced into action. Clearly, difficult for a respectable man to obtain.'

'It is your duty to penetrate one of these foul dens.'

'I might be blackmailed,' Ambrose objected practically.

'I give you my word you shall not. The proprietress has her good name to think of.'

'You are acquainted with such a place?' Ambrose exclaimed.

You know I am, Bertie thought. Had he not been named as Oliver's cicerone, it would have been simple for Ambrose to deduce it.

'Or I might be arrested,' Ambrose suggested, more horrified.

'The vigilant eyes of the police are dazzled with gold. Here – '

Bertie scribbled on the back of Ambrose's visiting card. 'There's the address. I'll tell them to expect you. Saturday at midnight? That's a lively time.'

'You seem remarkably familiar with the establishment.' He sounded more curious than shocked.

'I attend as their medical man. The girls get quite ordinary things, you know. Coughs and colds and the measles. It's a most respectable disreputable house. If you try to prosecute it, I shall be dreadfully cross. Though for your chances of success, you could as well try prosecuting for immorality the dean and chapter of Westminster Abbey.'

'It is merely a matter of investigation.' Ambrose stared doubtfully at the visiting card. 'A doctor cannot prescribe for a case without examining it. We must gaze on many things which are disgusting to the world in general.' He hesitated. 'Sometimes I walk the pestiferous streets round the hospital by night, you know, completely alone.'

'How brave.'

'Should anyone threaten me, I say that I am a doctor. The Whitechapel is held in affection by everyone in the district. Apart from the necessity of seeking our attention, the uneaten nourishment from the wards is sent out to feed the poor.'

'Stale bread, pork grease, burnt skin and bones from the joints,' said Bertie contemptuously. 'The leavings of the sick.'

'They are hungry,' Ambrose pointed out reprovingly. 'They would eat pig-swill.' He rose. 'It will be confidential?'

'I'm not a sneak.'

'There's another thing – ' He stopped. Bertie fixed his eye. 'That woman Smith, who was murdererd. I believe I spoke to her within the last hour of her life.'

'You did?' Bertie looked unaccustomedly startled.

'The creature was drunk. I requested her name. I asked if she was a common prostitute, as I wished to help her. She was so fuddled, she seemed to think that I wished instead to avail myself of her services.'

'How much did she ask?' Bertie enquired with interest.

'Tuppence, the price of a loaf of bread. I gave her this money.' Ambrose shivered. 'Dalhouse found the coins in her ragged clothing. It was mentioned at the inquest. Shortly afterwards, I was seen by a policeman in the India Road. He flashed his bullseye at me, curious at a gentleman being abroad at that hour in that area. I volunteered that I was a medical man. I am concerned that the policeman might remember me, and as they have still failed to apprehend the murderer I might be subjected to the shame of questioning.'

Bertie laughed. 'A policeman on that beat would no more connect a gentleman with a murdered whore than the governor of the Bank of England with a street-corner card game of find-the-lady.'

Ambrose looked relieved. 'I'm glad of your opinion. I know nothing of the seamier side of life, of course.'

Freshings showed Ambrose out. Bertie grinned. 'I know what he wants. He shall get it. Oh, this is going to be capital fun!'

He rang for another brandy and soda, lit a cigar and drew out *Esoteric Anthropology*. He grew bored with it, and remembered that he had not read the week's instalment of *The Diary of a Nobody* in *Punch*.

'I wonder why he told me about Emma Smith?' he murmured. He blew a smoke ring. 'Is he frightened the police suspect him? Surely not. Cannot he tolerate a guilty secret echoing in his own breast? Well, *that's* a failing which has brought a good many men to the gallows.'

12

THERE WERE gentlemen's clubs aplenty in the London of 1888. The newly-moneyed middle-classes intruded into the delights of club life, like those of foreign travel, hunting, public school education and mistresses. White's, Boodle's and Brooks's clubs had faced each other across St James's Street for over a century, their coronet-speckled membership lists not despising, simply ignoring, all the newcomers. Forty of London's sixty-odd surviving clubs were founded under Victoria, including those for farmers, who might be gentlemen, for fly-fishers, who could be, and for American women, who outrageously were not.

At ten guineas a year, the Odeum Club in St Martin's Lane, amid the West End theatres, was an extravagance even for a prodigal like Bertie. Once or twice a week he took the club dinner, served from four in the afternoon until nine. He preferred the supper until two, because he enjoyed meeting actors, who could not take the earlier dinner when they were working, and dared not display the fact when they were not. Like most London clubs, the Odeum shut at three in the morning, but on Saturdays at four.

On the Saturday of August 4, Bertie had arranged to meet George Bracegirdle for supper after the curtain fell on his farce at the Vaudeville. Bertie was waiting in the smoking-room with a brandy and soda, reading the *Illustrated London News*, when another member in evening dress approached him. He was heavily built, in his mid-forties, square-faced and exemplifying what Dickens called 'all that pleasing and extensive variety of nose and whisker for which the bar of England is so justly celebrated.' They had not met for two years, but Bertie carefully followed the fortunes of important people to whom he could claim acquaintance.

'I must congratulate you on your appointment as Solicitor general. And on your knighthood,' Bertie said.

Sir Edward Clarke accepted the compliment staidly. Bertie knew him as strait-laced, a powerfully-tongued Conservative MP, spending a fortune from practice at the Bar on the austere enjoyment of building a church beside the Thames at Staines. He wondered why the man had joined so easygoing a club as the Odeum, but reflected that lawyers feel a passionate affinity with actors, from whom they differ only by having scripts in their hands.

'I'm glad to encounter you this evening, Randolph. I have been anxious to show you a letter I received from Mrs Bartlett, shortly after her acquittal. I have been showing it at a dinner in the Temple.'

He handed Bertie a double-folded sheet of writing-paper, the front page heavily bordered in black. Bertie frowned, puzzled. Then he remembered she was still in mourning for the husband she had been accused of killing.

It was addressed from 66 Glasshouse Street on April 24, 1886, exactly a week after her freeing. The handwriting had an elegant flow.

Dear Sir, it started.

Forgive me for not earlier expressing my heartfelt gratitude to you. I feel that I owe my life to your earnest effort. Though I cannot put into words the feelings that fill my heart, you will understand all my pen fails to express to you.

Your kind looks towards me cheered me very much, for I felt that you believed me innocent. I have heard many eloquent Jesuits preach, but I never listened to anything finer than your speech. My story was a very painful one, but sadly true, my consent to my marriage was not asked, I only saw my husband once before my wedding day.

Assuring you that I shall ever remember you with feelings of deepest gratitude.

> *I am*
> *Sincerely yours*
> *Adelaide Bartlett*

'Very touching,' said Bertie. He wondered how so massive a buttress of the Church of England felt at comparison with Jesuits.

'Very. But I thought in due fairness that similar gratitude was due to you. Had you not insisted on seeing me in my chambers, had you not expounded on the medical unlikelihood of Mrs Bartlett chloroforming her husband to death in his sleep, had you not lectured me upon the qualities of chloroform, had you not incited my interest in the drug, I should not have pored over the medical books night upon night, equipping myself to shatter the prosecution's case in a single speech, without calling any evidence, medical or otherwise.'

'I felt sorry for the woman.' He handed back the letter. Sir Edward was still standing as Bertie lolled in his plush armchair with the antimacassar. In a club, all men are equal, and he revelled in it.

'Her husband was a pig,' Bertie said firmly. 'He threw his wife and this miserable Methodist clergyman together, that he might derive strange enjoyment from the knowledge of their coupling, in his absence from home at his grocers' shops.'

'That is perhaps going far. The husband certainly treated her as a child.'

'Well, some men prefer children, they find grown women too frightening.'

'I had no doubt about the verdict when it was pronounced. But I have spoken to many medical men since, who suspect that the scientific miracle I mentioned might well have been wrought.'

'But surely only by a most exceptional woman?'

'Isn't Mrs Bartlett? I am a quick and sure judge of men and women, Randolph, I think I may claim. I should not have the honour of my present post otherwise. But some can spin a cocoon of innocence with such delicacy that an angel in Heaven might be deceived. I have a growing belief that such was Mrs Bartlett.'

'Why?'

'That Mrs Bartlett induced the Reverend George Dyson to buy the chloroform, that he secured the considerable quantity of five ounces by cock-and-bull stories in three separate chemists' shops, that he threw the bottles away in panic on Wandsworth Common after the death . . . had Mrs Bartlett wished to solace her indisposed husband with chloroform, their Dr Leach would have readily prescribed a safe dose . . . I am glad that these points did not rest more heavily upon the minds of the jury.'

'We all make professional misjudgements,' said Bertie cheerfully. 'Mine, mean someone croaks. Yours are life-saving.' This clearly was not to Sir Edward's liking. Bertie stood up. 'Will you excuse me? There's a fellow I've to meet.'

George Bracegirdle was tall, lean, stooping, hollow-cheeked, his fair hair reinforced against invasive greyness, his large eyes constantly moving, which gave him the look of suffering subdued frenzy. The pearl studs of his stiff shirt, the buttons of his white waistcoat, the extent of his tails down his calf, were all slightly more extravagant than a gentleman might allow himself. His clothes fitted him so fashionably tightly, Bertie wondered if he allowed himself the indulgence of carrying loose change or a latch key.

'Dear boy! How good we should be meeting tonight,' he greeted Bertie exuberantly. 'I've had some absolutely topping news.'

Bertie knew that, to an actor, this might range from inheriting a fortune to discovering a new tailor.

'I have been offered the lead next autumn in an entirely new production of *Jekyll and Hyde*,' he explained proudly. 'The book's by Richard Mansfield. Damn clever young man. Protégé of Irving. Cast of ten. Great chance to show my talent for quick changes. I want to get the medical mannerisms for Dr Jekyll.' Drawing himself up, hands clasped behind, George Bracegirdle assumed the expression Bertie saw so often on the faces of complacent consultants. 'We must make more fat and blood,' he pronounced gravely to the invisible recumbent patient. 'Ah, yes! There exist two varieties of fat. That creating firm tissue. And the very unstable.'

Bertie laughed. 'You've been reading the medical papers.'

'Pain? Arthritis in the joints? I recommend kava-kava. Efficacious in every case. If that fails to cure, we shall try the patent electropathic belt, excellent also for indigestion, kidney disease, torpid liver, general debility and the ovaries – in the female, naturally. Otherwise, I advise a brisk rub with Ellerman's Embrocation for Horses and Humans. My fee will be two guineas. You see how I take my art seriously? I am relying on you to instruct me in the further subtleties of a medical consultation.'

'I can pass you off as Dr Jekyll. Mr Hyde you shall have to concoct for yourself. Shall we sup? I have to be away early-ish.'

'There are devilled brains tonight. Heavenly.'

The club porter hailed Bertie a hansom shortly past eleven o'clock. He gave the address of No. 2 Garden Gate. He did not doubt the man knew the nature of his destination.

A fat middle-aged woman took his hat, cape and stick. Mrs Floyd always employed ugly maids, to make her girls look better. He mounted the thick red stair carpet, reflecting he was possibly the only male in the house. The scattered doors of No. 2 opened frequently in the late afternoon, until the time a gentleman needed to dress for dinner. The house grew busy again when the clubs, supper-rooms and banqueting halls thinned. Mrs Floyd always had a girl dressed and perfumed ready in the morning, for customers who saw no rule for such delights to be tasted only after luncheon. Often she had Scottish noblemen impatient from the overnight express, their luggage still on the waiting hansom.

'Did you take my tip last Wednesday? Stourhead for Goodwood?' Bertie entered the pink-papered drawing-room. Mrs Floyd was alone, in a gown of grey and crimson silk, hands clasped, fan dangling from wrist, standing before the empty grate. Her poise suggested a governess assured in the affection of the family she so usefully served.

'Indeed. We shall have a bottle of Clicquot on it.'

Bertie lit a cigar, heels on the highly polished brass fender. Another maid appeared with a bottle, which she opened with the efficiency of a wine-steward. The domestic service was skilled at Mrs Floyd's.

'A sniff?' Bertie offered Mrs Floyd a silver box from his pocket.

'Chloroform?' she exclaimed in horror. 'Oh, no, never.'

Bertie grinned. 'How's Candy?' The promised extra ten sovereigns had already changed hands.

'A real find,' Mrs Floyd told him appreciatively. 'Not just a strong country girl, but *extrèmement gentille et caressante*. The men go nuts on her. That Mr Wilberforce –'

'My fellow lint-scraper from the India Road,' murmured Bertie, amused.

'Mind, I think he's a streak of misery. He always wants Candy, won't look at other girls if she's busy. He'll wait, which none of the men like doing.'

'I suppose it is rather like waiting for someone else to finish their dinner before you can use their dirty plate,' Bertie reflected. He raised his glass. '*A vôtre santé, Angela.*'

'*A la vôtre.* While those two girls you brought from Paris were useless, just *gamines*.'

'They must have been worth a bit, just to lose their rings?'

'They did good business because they were young,' she conceded. 'I've several customers not looking for anything over thirteen or fourteen. But they weren't very interested in their work. They were impolite and difficult to control. I sold them to Mrs Hambury down at Dock Street in Poplar. She specializes in kids.'

'Oh, she'll keep them in order,' said Bertie knowingly. 'Skin them alive for answering back. They fetched a fair price?'

Mrs Floyd, sipping with little finger extended, compressed her lips, 'I've never had so much gold through my hands as this season,' she confided. 'Well, I keep a good house, and my reputation runs in the right channels.'

'You are a woman I admire.'

'You do not admire me for anything particularly admirable.'

'You are too severe with both of us, Angela. I admire you as a soldier who's prepared to risk his life. Particularly if he gets away with it. That's the important qualification, to my mind. A posthumous medal is only a lost bet.' He gave a sly smile. 'You'd be interested in an encounter I had earlier this evening at the club. A mutual friend, to say the least –'

There was a knock. Rose's dark curls appeared. 'Mrs Floyd – can we show the doctor our new frocks?'

She came in with Candy. Bertie had medically examined Candy regularly, but now she was powdered and dressed ready for work, he reflected how beautiful she had become. She vindicated the scientific theory, of a woman's radiance being fuelled by the animalculae of semen, penetrating the delicate mucous membrane of the vaginal wall. A spinster grew dry in skin and spirit, as a plant without humus.

Both girls proudly displayed *décolleté* dresses of bright tartan taffeta, a green silk band at the waist streaming from the bow behind, their knees exposed in black lisle stockings above shining kid boots.

'They did make Lord Killiekrankie laugh so,' Mrs Floyd explained amusedly to Bertie. 'It's the tartan of his neighbour the Laird of Glenshee, whom he hates.'

'Pooh, Lord Killiekrankie is always too drunk to do anything,' Rose dismissed him. 'Oh, ta, ever so,' she said, eagerly taking a cigarette from Mrs Floyd's silver box. Bertie lit it politely. 'Candy and me is real china plates.' Rose put an arm fondly round her companion, head on one side in admiration. 'Lovely gal, ain't she? She's got such beautiful dairies. The men go mad.'

'Some of the things I've found about men!' Candy told Bertie smiling. 'You wouldn't believe. What they get up to with their hands and their mouths and their tallywags don't signify, it's like the animals on the farm, just as you said. But never in my born days did I think they'd want to dress up in bustle and bonnet, tight-laced stays and all.'

Rose laughed, puffing her cigarette held between tip of

finger and thumb. 'Or they wants to be cuddled and put to the breast like a baby, beard, whiskers and everything.'

'I'm sure it's a better education for the "new woman" than Oxford or Cambridge,' Bertie suggested.

'Well, you certainly meet the upper crust,' Candy agreed. 'All them lords, and that, members of Parliament –'

Rose interrupted, giggling, 'I've had more members in my box than Mr Gladstone could count.'

'And belted earls –'

'I've belted an earl.' Rose giggled the louder.

'Candy, do you remember the day you went to the hospital?' Bertie asked. Her face fell at the recollection. 'Do you remember the doctor, the fat one in the frock coat? He'll be showing himself here tonight.'

'Bless us and save us,' Candy cried. 'He's going to swallow me.'

'I'll bet you a bob to a yellow boy he doesn't even recognize you.'

A shilling to a sovereign was a confident bet. 'A face is like a line of poetry, meaningless out of context.' He turned to Mrs Floyd. 'The good Dr Ambrose Porter-Hartley has the intention of releasing your canaries from the cage.'

'I'll have no gospel-gabbing.' Mrs Floyd frowned. 'He shan't pass the doorstep.'

'Bet you another sov he'll end up doing the chaws.' Bertie grinned at Candy, emphasizing the word for copulation by rubbing index finger in fist. 'He's got a spring in his cock like a bear-trap,' he assured her. 'His wife's as fat as a lard tub, and I should think as pleasant to poke as a pack-saddle. A fellow never pays through the nose so much as marrying for money. Middle class money,' he emphasized. 'Your aristocratic lady knows a man must race and gamble, drink and fight, pursue foxes and whores, like he did in days of King George. It's his nature, as much as it's a monkey's to climb trees. It's only bourgeoise women who faint at the thought of their husband dipping his wick in a knocking shop. And that's only because they're too selfish to see men's fundamental desires, too frightened even to imagine them.'

The doorbell rang as he spoke. The maid announced the Marquess of Sherwood. 'Sherwood the tireless,' murmured Bertie approvingly. 'They say there's half a dozen women in London with nightdresses made in his racing colours.'

Mrs Floyd declared that she must receive the nobleman herself. She dispatched Rose upstairs. Alone with Candy, Bertie took her chin in his fingers like the afternoon of her arrival. 'You're a cool hand, aren't you?'

She looked at him puzzled. She could no longer be frightened of him.

'You're not like a lot of girls, so thick-skulled they don't know how many holes they've got in their tails. According to the sermonizers of the *Pall Mall Gazette*, you should be hurtling to perdition with the speed of an express train. Instead, you look like any other sharp and pretty chit, who makes her living type writing in a city office. It's the same with the Gaiety girls – good, honest Cockneys, polished and sharpened in the grinder. There's nothing like mixing with lecherous gentlemen for waking up a girl's wits and giving her a good line in back-chat.'

'I haven't done no harm to myself, nor to anyone,' Candy said defensively. She esteemed and trusted Bertie even more than the donah.

'You've done nothing but good,' he assured her heartily. 'Think of the family life you've preserved, in all its splendour of dullness. Your customers become a hundred times more amiable to their wives, who only get fucked at all because their men are inflamed with your vision while they're doing it.'

'I know it's wicked, really,' she said doubtfully.

'No more wicked than enjoying your breakfast. The middle-class always confuse purity with discomfort.' He tightened his grip on her chin. 'You have astute self-awareness of your value, and unlimited self-confidence in realizing it. The necessary instincts of the successful courtesan. But perhaps you'll be married one day, Candy? Perhaps you'll be a respectable grocer's wife?'

The movement of her big eyes told Bertie he had spoken

her thoughts. 'I could pass you off as a grocer's wife,' he said thoughtfully. 'You'd have to mind your ps and qs. Not say "ain't", which is only for Cockneys and aristocrats. You're learning already – you don't drop your "hs" and spit on the floor. Perhaps I'd ask you to marry *me?*' he suggested lightly. 'That would be a compliment. There's no sharper judge of woman-flesh in London.'

'You're making a fool of me.'

'No need to be snappish. Don't you like me?'

'You're my only friend, apart from Rose.'

'By the by, don't get too cosy in bed with Rose. I've seen plenty of these *affaires de coeur*. You start as innocently as schoolgirls, and end scratching each other's eyes out, or worse.'

They were interrupted by Mrs Floyd, bearing the card with Ambrose Porter-Hartley's name on one side and Bertie's scribble on the other.

13

CANDY WAS SCARED. Ambrose Porter-Hartley might recognize her. His eye might instantly pronounce her the victim of some dread disease. He might have her forcibly transported to the horrifying hospital. How dare she venture her gifts upon a man of such learning, who might be cold to feminine charms and wise to their wiles?

'You go and join giblets with him,' urged Bertie, slapping Candy on the seat of her tartan dress to dispatch her upstairs. 'Remember this – the wisest man in the world with the urge for a woman becomes a monkey. And if it's built to scale, he's got a prick like a pillar-box.'

Alone with Mrs Floyd at the door of the drawing-room, Bertie warned, with a nod downstairs, 'You'll get a dose of psalm-singing from him. But you know men well enough – they like to meet temptation half-way. Don't you agree, the most respectable manner of achieving your lowest desires is succumbing to a wild moment of weakness?'

She smiled in agreement.

'I'll make myself scarce,' he said.

Beside the grate of the pink-papered room bulged an old-fashioned porcelain bell-handle – big London houses without electric light mostly had electric bells, powered by Leclanché wet batteries. Bertie tugged it, then pushed against a shallow alcove under an arch beside the fire. The disguised door led him to a narrow staircase, windowless, lit by a thin, flickering gas jet. In Mrs Floyd's house were many mansions.

'Please be seated, sir.' Mrs Floyd led Ambrose into the empty drawing-room, like a fashionable milliner or other capable business-woman receiving a new customer. He was in evening dress, with tail coat and stiff shirt, standing frightened and indecisive, his cheeks flapping like yacht sails caught in cross breezes. She repeated the invitation, adding, 'A glass of champagne, sir?'

Ambrose held up his hand with a feeble smile of disapproval.

'On the house,' said Mrs Floyd.

He acquiesced.

'Are you French, madam? I thought I detected the Gallic "r".'

'I have lived here most of my life. I was married to an Englishman – I *am* married to an Englishman,' she corrected herself. She stood with hands clasped demurely. Ambrose regained some self-confidence by scowling at her from the armchair as though she were Countess Elizabeth Báthory of sixteenth-century Hungary, who murdered 650 young girls to enjoy a bath in their blood.

'The address of this — er, establishment was passed me by a professional colleague,' he said sternly, 'who specializes in sanitary matters. I need not mention his name.'

'You will find nothing in the least insanitary in this house, sir.'

Ambrose looked round. It struck him as resembling a prosperous Mayfair tea-room. He drained his champagne. Mrs Floyd poured some more.

'I am here as a matter of professional duty. I'm sure I need not labour the fact, that one of my standing would never penetrate such a den from mere idle, or morbid, curiosity.'

'I assure you, sir, that I am glad to meet so fine and agreeable a gentleman as yourself in any circumstances.'

Ambrose could find no reply. He swallowed the champagne. It was excellent.

'I am aware,' he pronounced warningly, 'men come here knowing that women of the unfortunate class are available any hour of the night.'

'Our doors do not shut, and I am always prepared to serve a good breakfast.'

'May I continue to question you, madam?'

Ambrose was puzzled. The miserable woman should have

been overcome in his presence with silent shame. Was she making a fool of him?

'How much,' Ambrose speculated, 'might a man be obliged to pay for his depravity?'

'Three pounds,' said Mrs Floyd, having judged the strength of his pocket and desires.

Ambrose sat bolt upright. 'That is a very considerable sum of money.'

'My girls are capable of very considerable delights. They are all superb beauties. There is one waiting at this moment . . . oh, so charming! Only eighteen years old.'

Mrs Floyd had been moving closer with imperceptible gentleness. Her silk skirt touched his cuff. He could smell the Cassie perfume which Bertie had brought her from Paris. 'She is a girl with lovely fair hair, soft as silk,' continued Mrs Floyd, dropping her voice. 'Her complexion is wholesome and perfect, her figure would draw every eye in London were it displayed on the walls of the Royal Academy. Yet she is of such a friendly, such a laughing nature, like a playful and affectionate child. She raises the spirits of every gentleman she meets, as though he had won a substantial bet on the races. Might I refill your glass?'

Ambrose tried to look shocked rather than interested. 'But surely, a woman engaged in this degrading trade can do nothing but infect others with the misery she feels at it?'

'Why not see her yourself, sir?' Mrs Floyd paused. 'She is upstairs.' She nodded gently towards the door. 'She is waiting,' she said in a lower voice still.

Ambrose puffed his cheeks, trying to regain steerage-way.

'She has until recently been a virgin,' Mrs Floyd murmured.

'I should certainly be interested to observe this woman who seems to wear her misfortune so lightly.'

'Then it must be this minute,' she told him with soft persuasiveness. 'I have many gentlemen arriving at this hour of the night.' The doorbell had been ringing shortly and repeatedly during their conversation.

Ambrose recovered his frown. 'You understand that I

shall do everything in my power to indicate the error of her ways?'

'You may do exactly as you like with her, sir.' Mrs Floyd emptied the bottle into his glass. 'It will still be three pounds.'

Ambrose did look shocked. 'But I wish only to remonstrate.'

'Her company is valuable, and many of my customers call for a little more than a chat.'

Ambrose took a small round leather purse from his pocket and handed her three sovereigns, scowling more fiercely than ever. He followed her up another flight of stairs, heart racing, wondering if the person inside his dress-clothes was still himself. He entered a room walled with glass. Candy sat on the bed, showing her knees, smiling pleasantly. She saw Bertie was right. He did not recognize her.

'I am a person of some importance,' Ambrose announced.

Those men in tails in the mirrors were staring at him accusingly. He shivered.

'Cold for the time of year, ain't it?' said Candy.

'I was invited by the madame of this establishment to address you.'

'Bet she charged for the pleasure.'

'How did you reach Hell?'

'I hope never to, of that I'm sure.' Candy let the hem of her tartan dress ride over the top of her stockings, secured at mid-thigh with white lace garters.

'You are kept here by force, I take it?'

'Go on! I could walk out tomorrow morning, if I fancied.'

'But your clothes are locked away? You have no money?' Ambrose persisted fiercely, sitting on the bed beside her. 'What would happen if you escaped? Followed by bully boys, no doubt? Your head and bones broken?'

'By the donah?' Candy looked amazed. 'Likely!' She protested. 'She's as nice as a ha'pennyworth of silver spoons.'

'Then fly, I implore you, before health and mind are broken on the wheel of vice,' said Ambrose earnestly, staring closely into her eyes.

'Why leave a good crib like this? You're as mad as May butter.'

132

'You receive money?'

'I don't do it for love,' Candy told him scornfully. 'The donah keeps it for me. I'd trust her like the Bank of England.'

Ambrose looked thoughtful. 'If the lady invested the sum, then you would be receiving dividends instead of letting it stay idle. Ebbw Vale Steel is a snip at four and a quarter. My banker recommended it.'

'Clever one, ain't you?' Candy took his hand.

Such simple admiration so affected Ambrose, he replied with unusual modesty, 'A man must make the most of the world as he finds it.'

'Now ain't that funny? It's exactly what I says myself. Want your bit of fun?'

'Fun!' He was appalled.

'You've paid for it. I ain't got all night.' Candy stood up impatiently.

'Are your dear mother and father alive, to know of your shameful life?' Ambrose asked in panic to divert her – hoping he would not.

'Come on! You're as slow as a wet week.' Her swift, practised tug loosened his white bow tie, her fingers slipped lightly through his starched shirt-front.

Ambrose sat motionless. The girl was having the effect of wine and brandy – he drank at home more than he let people imagine, it was the only sunray to brighten his domestic world. He was growing intoxicated, unable to control his galloping thoughts with their customary tight reins.

'Stop that,' he ordered feebly.

She slipped off his tail coat, waistcoat, broad yellow felt braces, like a nursemaid undressing her charge. With a gesture which surprised him in its deftness, she was out of her tartan dress and cambric petticoats, naked but for stockings and boots. She undid his trousers in a business-like way. She noted his drawers and undershift were of expensive spun merino. Ambrose sat unresisting, motionless, eyes bulging, cheeks becalmed.

133

'Naughty boy', murmured Candy, swiftly assessing her customer. 'He needs a good spanking.'

Ambrose gave a soft moan.

'You've a good cock on you.'

'I feared it rather small,' he confessed in a murmur. Examination of his male patients at the Whitechapel often left him with a sense of inadequacy.

'It's got a lovely nut on it,' she encouraged him. 'Want a bit of a wank?'

The blasts of the trumpet of strumpetry were overpowering. The walls of Ambrose's personality collapsed. He fell on his knees, embracing her ankles, slobbering over her boots, groaning. Candy stood hands on hips, with the everyday detachment he afforded his patients.

'Rub your nose in my twat-rug if you like,' she invited, offering her pubic hair.

'Delicious orbs,' he croaked, clawing her buttocks. 'I must embrace them.'

'Kiss my arse.' She stuck her behind in his face. She remembered his indifference towards her body in the hospital, his indifference to the terror she felt at her illness. She was beginning to enjoy herself.

'I must be scourged, scourged ... that is all I deserve ... I am a wicked, wicked boy ... flog my botty.'

Behind the couch was a large brown Gladstone. It contained racing silks, cap, breeches and spurred boots. 'Want me to dress as a jockey?'

Sitting on the floor, Ambrose asked blankly, 'Why?'

'To ride you like an 'oss.'

'No, I don't think that will be necessary.'

Candy produced a riding-crop. 'Bend over, you naughty lad.'

She struck him hard. 'Cruel governess!' he cried.

'You can yell as hard as you like for mama, but I've got you now.' She hit him again. Ambrose exclaimed in pain. His pale skin took an excited flush of scarlet streaks. Candy lashed harder. She beat gentlemen who required it as a matter of course, thinking no more of it than the parlourmaid serving their luncheon. Now she saw the lecherous hospital students, the bullying porters, the insulting sisters and nurses, the filthy patients, the cold rooms and hard benches. His skin turned the colour of a ripe plum. She noticed it had burst, she was smearing him with his blood. She thought it time to stop.

Ambrose rolled on his back. 'Void your bladder on me.' She was lost. 'Do pee-pee.'

'The idea! Ruin the carpet? What would the donah say?' Candy carefully replaced the whip, closed the Gladstone, lay on the bed and invited, 'Come on, boyo! Let's have a goose and duck.'

It was a rhyme plain even to Ambrose. Intoxicated with sexual stimulus, his body as uncontrollable as a Saturday night drunk's, Ambrose climbed upon her, still sobbing. Candy looked over his fat shoulders towards the ventilator grille in the wall and winked. Next door in *la chambre de divertissement détaché*, Bertie had been tightly hugging himself to stop laughing like a yokel at the music hall. He went softly down the hidden stairs, letting himself into the mews. He chuckled all the way home. 'Screwing one of his hospital patients! There's a merry jape!' He handed hat, cane and cape to Freshings, with the expression of a schoolboy who had played an uproariously successful practical joke on one of the prefects.

14

'THIRTY-FOUR, thirty-five, thirty-six . . .' counted Dr Thomas Dalhouse.

He was interrupted by Dr Janet Veale. 'You've missed one.'

'Thirty-seven, thirty-eight . . .' His finger wandered.

'In the left axilla.'

'Ah! Thirty-nine. You counted them too, Inspector?'

Inspector Abberline nodded. He stood in his gingery short overcoat and brown bowler. It was the morning of the following Wednesday, August 8. The weather was still sunless and cold. The Whitechapel Hospital mortuary contained the scrawny body of a woman. In his leather apron, Hans was stitching the rent down its front with hempen thread, in the pattern of lacing a boot.

'Thirty-nine puncture wounds,' the inspector summarized, writing in his note-book. 'On various portions of the torso. Cause of death, slit throat.'

Tom washed his hands in the same pail of chlorate of lime as Janet. Any activity which brought their fingers together – passing a test-tube of microbes, slicing a corpse – gave him a tingle along his spine. 'Where did you find her?' he asked the inspector.

'On the first floor landing of the common staircase at George Yard Buildings, at three this morning. Usual working-class dwelling house. Brick-built, four storeys, cracked drainpipes. About a dozen families there, with lodgers and hangers-on. Perhaps you know it, sir? Off Postern Row, in the middle of Whitechapel High Street, behind the new Toynbee Hall.'

'Now, that's dreadfully odd.' Janet gave a frown which

Tom thought more delicious than any other woman's smile. 'Why did no one hear her scream?'

'Hadn't the chance to, ma'am. Her throat was cut.'

'But I'm certain I'd let out a peep before my own jugulars were divided, however neatly.'

'Screams are the birdsong of Whitechapel,' the inspector dismissed the anomaly. 'I'm confident the murderer was seen by someone. He'd be dripping with blood.'

'So would anyone at that hour of the morning from the abattoirs,' Janet pointed out. 'That's when the slaughtermen are busy, killing before the next herd is driven into Whitechapel from the country.'

'The murderers were two soldiers,' said inspector Abberline firmly, disregarding this second objection. 'The deceased was observed keeping company with them earlier in the evening. My men are at the Tower, questioning rankers at the garrison this very moment. An arrest is only a matter of time.'

'So the murder weapon might be a bayonet?' Janet nodded towards the body, which Hans had nearly sewn to the chin. The inspector nodded.

'Two men? That would explain an interesting point about the wounds.' Tom started drying his hands with a towel on a hook in the wall. 'Look at the pattern. Through the breasts, in the armpits, into the belly, three low ones into the pelvic basin. Made equally on the right and left of the body. Were the murderer but one man, he would have to be ambidextrous.'

The door of the post-mortem room opened. To Tom's annoyance, Bertie entered, in his frock coat, smoking a cigar. 'Heard you'd got another murder,' he greeted them cheerfully.

'Not unusual in Whitechapel,' Tom replied shortly.

'Unusual that somebody tried to make her a human pepper-pot,' said Janet.

Bertie stared at the expressionless face with closed eyes, sagging mouth, hair wet with blood. 'My word! I could swear I know her. Though I suppose a lady does not look at her best in such circumstances. Perhaps she was a patient? Most people who live round the hospital end up at some time inside it. What was her name?'

'She passed as Martha Turner,' the inspector told him. 'Though her real one was Martha Tabram. Aged thirty-five. A common prostitute, of course.'

'Been doing the naughty, had she?' murmured Bertie amiably.

'In Whitechapel, that's almost the same as saying she wore petticoats,' observed Janet.

'The deceased had been all evening with another of the unfortunate class.' Inspector Abberline flicked the pages of his notebook. 'A Mary Ann Nichols – one 'l' – lodging at 18 Thrawl Street, Spitalfields. That's next to Flower and Dean Street.'

'I once went to Thrawl Street as a student, delivering a baby on a midwifery card,' Bertie recalled. 'Our medical school teaches thoroughly the anatomy of Whitechapel.'

'Nichols is an important witness,' the inspector continued. 'She shall be able to identify the two soldiers. They are the key to the cypher. Solving it is merely a matter of time.'

'A hateful trade.' Tom glared at the corpse. 'In no other country is prostitution so undisguised as in England. The effect upon the virtuous female population is very serious. Surely you agree, Dr Veale? Young and unwary servants see the fine clothes, hear about the idle and luxurious lives led by women of the town. What a temptation to abandon the honest hard work of service.'

'Well, now, Dr Dalhouse –' Janet eyed him. 'If a means of gratifying the male sexual instinct is imperative – and if marriage is not economically possible – these unfortunate women may be regarded only as the victims of male licentiousness.'

Tom's pasty complexion heightened. The straits she had quoted were his own.

'To my mind, Dr Dalhouse,' she continued assertively, 'such women should be properly registered, domiciled and placed under organized medical inspection.'

'That is a *questio vexata*.' Tom sounded sharp towards her, because he was annoyed with Bertie. He felt annoyed with himself, and went pinker.

Clearly and firmly, Janet told him, 'Might I remind you what happened in Prussia, Dr Dalhouse? When the brothels of Berlin were shut by law in 1845, illegal prostitution simply *flourished*. And so did disease. Public morals became so *utterly* dreadful, that after six years prostitution was again legalized. Our own Contagious Diseases Act, now repealed through the opposition of philanthropists – whom I regard as completely misguided, Dr Dalhouse – lessened primary syphilis by nearly one half. What's vexed about that?'

'Bravo!' said Bertie, clapping.

Tom turned on him. 'This is a mortuary, not a music hall.'

A brass-buttoned porter opened the door, to Tom's relief announcing breathlessly, 'Dr Randolph? Wanted at once, sir, in the receiving room. Party with fits.'

Bertie followed him hurriedly across the small courtyard, and down the flagstoned corridor which ran the length of the hospital. The receiving room looked on to the forecourt, at the opposite side of the portico from the out-patients' surgery where he had encountered Candy. It was smaller than the surgery, painted the same ochre, furnished with similar stained and splintered benches, its high porter's desk with the same ledger and sheaves of certificates, the same hopeful brass-bound collecting box. Its only decoration was a framed notice with disembodied arms, legs and heads, illustrating the methods of bandaging, and another with line drawings of a sprightly man in a striped bathing-suit and vast moustache, illustrating the methods of restoring life to the seemingly drowned.

There was always something going on in the receiving room. Bertie hurried past an ashen-faced navvy, holding a right arm broken at the wrist. Men and women waited with bloody cuts and black eyes. A girl about ten with an old face tripped among them, brandishing one of the red hospital cards sent by a mother to summon the midwife. Another the same age was screaming, while her mother thumped hard on her back – probably swallowed a farthing or a marble, Bertie thought, the children of Whitechapel ingesting small inedible objects with as puzzling regularity as they jammed them up their noses, ears or genitalia.

Two dressing-rooms led off the receiving room, for men and women. Here treatment was given by the nurses and the student 'dressers', overseen by the house-surgeon. Though the true skill, experience and authority lay in the tiny, sinewy receiving-room sister with the muslin bow under her chin. She had so long been the stage manager of medical drama, that a drunk docker or dead baby left her equally unmoved. Each room had a big square sink, some pails and metal bowls in the corner, a mop in a bucket and a narrow couch of black leather, indelibly stained with all fluids emitted by the human body.

In the male dressing-room, Bertie found two tousled dressers struggling to apply the receiving-room strait-jacket to a thin, gingery young man with windmilling arms and foaming lips. Half on the couch, half on the scrubbed and sanded floor, the patient's shrieks reached the ears of new arrivals beyond the open windows. He caught one student on the ear, stimulating him to twist so fiercely the arm being forced into the continuous single sleeve of the brass-buckled canvas jacket, that Bertie foresaw the student having the added trouble of reducing a dislocated elbow. Small brown bottle of chloroform already in one hand, square of lint in the other, Bertie stopped, startling the two students with a laugh.

'Well, if it isn't Soapy Sam,' he exclaimed. 'Come off it! What's the use of giving a performance here? There's no one to pass the hat round.'

The cure was instant. Soapy Sam opened his eyes. 'Just my bloomin' luck! I never in my born days thought you came to these parts, Dr Randolph.'

'I once attended this gentleman for an epileptic fit, when going to dine in the West End,' Bertie explained to the students. 'A man having a fit always draws a good crowd, including a few Good Samaritans prepared to put their half-crowns where their heart is. Those who do not, make involuntary contributions by his friend, the pickpocket. Oh, Sam's a consummate actor, the Henry Irving of the kerbstones,' he said admiringly. 'But performing here, Sam, will only land you in a padded cell.'

'Sorry to give you gents trouble.' Sam wriggled from the strait-jacket, spitting a square of soap into a scrap of rag for further use. 'Bin 'avin' a bit of bovver wiv the rozzers, y'see. The law,' he explained politely to the students. 'Thought if I could come to the 'orspital and get a sustificate, saying I was proper poorly, with the fits – I could do with a tot o'rum,' he broke off.

'Get along with you,' said Bertie. 'Go and do your act outside the nearest rub-a-dub.' He meant pub. 'Some kind soul usually appears with a reviving stimulant, don't they? Now, you'd better hook it, before these two gentlemen deservedly throw you into the India Road.'

They were interrupted by the scream of, 'My baby! My baby!' A young woman in a black shawl burst past the porter into the receiving-room, carrying a golden-curled child of one or two, chalky white, limp as a sock, clothes soaked through. Scalded from an overturned kettle, Bertie supposed, or the copper if the mother took in washing, a common occupation in the cramped rooms of Whitechapel. As it looked a more interesting case, the dressers abandoned Soapy Sam.

The mother was still screaming when the door from the forecourt was pushed open by a policeman, each hand grasping the arm of a shouting woman. The trio instantly amused Bertie. The policeman was barely twenty-one, the women old enough to be his mother. Both were drunk, their faces smeared with blood, which matted their hair like red lead and spattered their bodices. They swore violently at each other, one shouting 'Thief!' the other 'Whore!', which Bertie felt applied equally to both.

Suddenly they broke from the policeman, one clawed the other's face, one grabbed a handful of hair, both screamed. Bertie perceived through the frenzy that one had a deep gash from ear to chin and a puncture pumping blood in her neck, the other a slashed nose. Probably been fighting with broken bottles, perhaps carving knives, he thought. A noisy crowd of supporters for both tried pushing inside, but were evicted by the porter with practised autocracy.

One woman collapsed on the bench and began to weep loudly, mouth sagging, legs stuck out, arms dangling. The tiny receiving-room sister bustled up. The other woman took from the pocket of her skirt a six-inch sliver of broken glass and turned on her savagely. Bertie moved quickly. His left hand was round her neck from behind, the lint pad over her bloody face, as he poured chloroform from the bottle in his palm. She struggled to wrench free, to jab his own face with the glass dagger. Bertie dexterously switched bottle and mask from one hand to the other. Her upraised arm wavered and fell, the glass clattered to the floor, she sagged in his arms and surrendered with a snore.

'Put her on the dressing-room couch,' he ordered the students. He replaced bottle and lint in the tail pocket of his frock coat. 'She'll be round in a minute or two. How harlotry, gin and savagery always go together,' he reflected disapprovingly.

The policeman was showing the admirable imperturbability of the Metropolitan force by asking the sobbing woman on the bench her name and address.

'Elizabeth Stride,' she replied surlily.

'Age?' The policeman held notebook against blood-smeared tunic.

'Forty-five. I don't care who knows.'

'What's your friend's name?'

'She ain't no friend. Name of Catherine Eddowes. Same age as me, I know that for a fact.'

'Address?'

She held against her gashed cheek the pad of lint applied by the receiving-room sister. 'Fashion Street, Spitalfields. Same as 'er.' She threw a contemptuous look towards the dressing-room. 'Anyone in Fashion Street will vouch for me. I'm called "Long Liz" generally.'

'You're foreign, aren't you?' said the policeman suspiciously.

She looked at him resentfully. 'I'm from Gothenburg. That's in Sweden. I married an Englishman, wot was a carpenter at Sheerness. I used to be Elizabeth Gustaafsdotter.'

'How do you spell it?'

He tried writing the name, but after two attempts gave up. 'Where is your husband?'

'Drowned. In the great Thames disaster, ten years ago. You're too young to remember,' she said despisingly. 'When the *Princess Alice* sank, with five hundred poor souls out for a day's pleasure. With two of our dear, lovely children.' She started to weep loudly again.

Bertie had followed the dialogue closely. He had a keen interest in the grotesque and macabre. The Swedish woman seemed too respectable for either her bloody rags or gin-soaked body. He reflected that degradation was a disease for which many harboured the susceptibility. Sister reappeared with a pewter bowl and sponge to wash her wound with permanganate solution. Through the open window, Bertie saw approaching across the forecourt a knot of men and women, slow and subdued as mourners, small boys their outriders, bearing the still figure of a man on a window-shutter. It was the common way of a bad casualty reaching hospital.

'A docker fallen off a ship, or a builder off a roof,' he observed to sister. 'Doesn't look much life left in him. I enjoyed my days as a dresser in the receiving-room,' he recalled. 'I'm a fellow who needs plenty of action – or life hangs as heavy as a wet Sunday.'

He felt for his watch and pressed the spring. It was past one o'clock. He was shortly expecting some patients in Belgrave Square. His hat was in the consultants' library, which he found empty save for Oliver Wilberforce reading the *Lancet*. He rose as Bertie entered.

'Just off?' Bertie knew how desperate Oliver had grown to avoid him. They stood close in the middle of the book-bound room. 'So you've been back?'

'I am perfectly aware you know the comings and goings of everybody at that place,'

'Quite the Court correspondent of *The Times*, old man,' Bertie admitted readily. 'But I assure you, my information isn't read over breakfast even by the Recording Angel. She's a lovely canary, isn't she?'

'Why must you mock me?'

'I'm congratulating you. Why, you're the one who docked her.' Oliver winced. Why must Bertie tediously harp on that defloration? 'I expect the other slices of the pie taste as sweet as the first.'

'Please save your flattery,' said Oliver bitterly. 'I hate myself for going there. When thoughts of it come into my mind, I throw them out, as I'd throw a diseased beggar from my drawing-room.'

'That's a guilt most men feel the morning after,' Bertie told him easily. 'It generally evaporates with a good luncheon.'

'That part of my life is like the dark side of the moon,' Oliver told him miserably. 'It must never, never be exposed.'

'I need no telescope to aver there're other bodies with the same astronomical peculiarity. I'm off home. Will you share a hansom?'

'No, thank you.'

How disagreeable the man has become, Bertie thought, rattling his way home. He couldn't even ask to pass the mustard without sounding forbidding.

In his drawing-room, before it was time to change for dinner, Bertie sat in the fireside chair, lit a cigar, and reached into his bookcase for a leather-bound volume blocked in gold, *The Decline and Fall of the Roman Empire, By Edward Gibbon*. His fingers flicked over pages as worn with familiarity as his own hearthrug. He began reading,

Mrs Cole, in the course of the constant confidence we lived in, acquainted me that there was one Mr Barville, who used her house, just come to town, whom she was not a little perplexed about providing a suitable companion for. Which was indeed a point of difficulty, as he was under the tyranny

*of a cruel taste: that of an ardent desire, not only of being
unmercifully whipp'd himself, but of whipping others . . .*

'Come in!'

Freshings appeared, the evening paper on his salver.
Bertie continued his book,

*But, what yet increased the oddity of this strange fancy
was the gentleman being young. Whereas it generally
attacks, it seems, such as are, through age, obliged to have
recourse to this experiment, for quickening the circulation of
their sluggish juices, and determining a conflux of the spirits
of pleasure towards those flagging, shrivelly parts, that rise
to life only by virtue of those titillating ardours created by
the discipline of their opposites, with which they have so
surprising a consent.*

Bertie took the *Echo*. 'By the way, Freshings, my white tie
is becoming frayed. Get me another in Jermyn Street
tomorrow, there's a good fellow.'

He found a heading at the foot of the front page saying,
WHITECHAPEL MURDER. There was only a paragraph
underneath.

*No arrest has yet been made at the Tower garrison, where
the troops were paraded before a witness of the murder, in
George Yard last night, of a common prostitute. The deceased woman's companion, one of the same class, was either
unable or unwilling to identify the men keeping company
with the victim earlier in the night. Inspector Abberline of
Scotland Yard said that the apprehension of the culprit was
a matter of time.*

'A matter of time,' Bertie murmured, as Freshings left. He
tossed the paper to the floor, and returned to *Fanny Hill* in
1750.

*Seizing now one of the rods, I stood over him, and accord-
ing to his directions, gave him in one breath, ten lashes with
much good-will, and the utmost nerve and vigour of arm
that I could put into them . . .*

'*Plus ça change, plus c'est la même* chaws,' punned Bertie
with a yawn.

15

'HE WAS DRUNK, as drunk as a peasant,' said Sir Morell Mackenzie indignantly. 'Professor Bergmann's a Slav, you know, for all the "von" in front of his name. He hails from Riga. He's wedded to the bottle, they all are. It was back in early April, at the Schloss Friedrichskron, as it was then. The late Emperor developed difficulty in breathing, there was some inflammation, I judged the cannula we had inserted into the throat be best changed for one with a different curve. A simple manoeuvre. But I felt that Bergmann should be informed, as a matter of courtesy, he having joint responsibility for the patient with myself. I had a courier ride to Berlin, with a note desiring him at the Schloss as soon as possible – the last few words I underlined. Bergmann was not at home. He was in a hotel, at five in the afternoon. He interpreted my note as some dire emergency He was, in the language I am obliged to use in public, over-excited. From causes of a more personal nature than agitation at the Emperor's condition.'

Oliver Wilberforce nodded sympathetically. The patient was dead, the controversy flourished.

The two were alone in Mackenzie's consulting-room. A cloth had been spread on a small square table, they were eating a chop with a glass of sherry and water. Mackenzie breakfasted at seven, and took lunch hastily between patients, who still filled the waiting-room downstairs, sustained by Bowden the butler's sandwiches.

'Without more ado Bergmann thrust into the Emperor's neck another cannula of his own. Unfortunately, he entirely missed the windpipe. He jammed it into the solid tissues. The Emperor understandably turned blue. Our professor then rudely jabbed his forefinger into the hole in the patient's neck. I eventually passed another cannula, the Emperor escaping suffocation but afflicted by terrible coughing and bleeding for several hours after the drunken doctor's departure.'

Mackenzie placed knife and fork together on his half-finished plate. It was Friday, the last day of August, the first time they had met since Mackenzie's return. He had gone with his daughter Ethel to restore his spirits in Venice, travelling as 'John Morell'.

In August, all the foremost surgeons were out of London at their country houses. No big operations were performed until October. Oliver needed to stay, to nourish a growing practice with crumbs from richer men's operating tables. Mackenzie to remuster the thousand patients he needed a year for his living, after a single one in the year past.

'Naturally, Bergmann put out an entirely different version,' Mackenzie continued. 'That he arrived to find the Emperor blue in the face, that he saved his life by snatching the case from my hands and opening the trachea with a pair of hooks. This of course was published in the *Kreuz-Zeitung*. I can assure you, Bergmann was not at the time in a condition to observe anything.'

'Do I understand from your letter to *The Times*, you're suing the *Kreuz-Zeitung* for libel? Not that *The Times* seems more on your side than the organs of the Prussian Court and officer corps.'

'The paper is most unworthily represented in Berlin,' Mackenzie said angrily. 'Mr Charles Lowe writes viciously about me, because he imagines my earlier opinion that the Emperor had *not* cancer to have misled him. Newspaper correspondents should not question matters which are technical and beyond their comprehension. If justification of my treatment is needed, here it is.'

He tossed on the table a slip of yellowish, glazed paper, about six inches by three. Oliver deciphered an uncertain scrawl,

The serene Morell just tried, before Bergmann ill-treated me.
'In the Emperor's own hand,' Mackenzie said smugly. 'He wrote a similar note, asking me, "Why did Professor von Bergmann put his finger into my throat?" To which I could only reply, "I do not know, sir. I beg most respectfully to say that I can no longer have the honour of continuing in attendance on Your Majesty if Professor von Bergmann is to be permitted to touch your throat again." Nor did he. It's all to be in my book.'

He nodded towards a pile of paper on the desk at his elbow. *'The Fatal Illness of Frederick the Noble* will be published this autumn. My amanuensis has set it all out by the type writer. It's the only use for that American instrument – the patients dislike receiving letters with so cold, impersonal appearance.'

Mackenzie lit a stramonium cigarette. The high-pitched wheeze from his chest had intruded throughout the meal. 'After that, everything started going badly. Swallowed liquids began to appear through the larynx, indicating a fistula. We fed the Emperor by a tube. We thanked God he suffered no pain.'

'What did he die of?'

'Septic pneumonia.'

'At least Vicky got her Empress's pension.'

'And all I have for thirteen months of anguish and physical trial is a fee from the Prussians of £12,000, which has done no more than save me from ruin. Once my back was turned, the very men I trained at the Throat Hospital fell upon my patients like wolves on sick sheep. Greville Macdonald, left in charge of my private patients for the customary two-thirds of their fees, has set up shop in Harley Street with a brougham and pair, with the effrontery to claim such success comes from his own hands, and not from mine. My only joy is that bounder Felix Semon – another throat specialist, a German Jew – has been going round declaiming, "Mackenzie killed my Emperor", for which my good friend Henry Irving got him blackballed at the fashionable Garrick Club.'

The mantelpiece clock struck half-past one. 'I've a ward round at the Whitechapel.'

'In the afternoon?'

'Oh, we're very go-ahead. Do you know how many operations the hospital performs a year? Well over a thousand,' Oliver told him proudly. 'Fifteen years ago, it was under four hundred. More importantly, mortality for primary amputation has fallen from forty to only four in a hundred cases. This of course comes from my employing the Listerian method of antisepsis.'

'I hope you stay a minute more, because I have something of importance to tell you.' The irate red spots had faded from Mackenzie's cheeks. 'Which could affect your whole life to come.'

Oliver looked puzzled. Mackenzie was not a man to exaggerate the importance of anything, except himself.

'Your advocacy of Lister's carbolic spray is famous in London.'

'I am hoping it will shortly be adopted universally at the Whitechapel.'

'Other hospitals are less enlightened. It is the fate of the Scot in London to be ignored or misinterpreted, and always suspected. I honestly think there is no more parochial place in the world than London. Look at Sir James Paget and his cronies at St Bartholomew's. They would as soon be seen dead using the spray, though that is unfortunately the fate of their patients.'

'Antisepsis has killed germs, as anaesthetics have killed pain,' Oliver said forcefully. 'We may operate with impunity even on joints and bones, without the melancholy and almost invariable sequel of pus, gangrene and amputation.'

'Luckily, my fellow-countryman Lister enjoys support in the highest quarters. You'll remember, he opened an abscess in the Queen's armpit, back in 1871?' Oliver nodded. 'The royal physician, Sir William Jenner, himself worked the bellows of the magic spray at Balmoral. He has remained enthusiastic towards the method and its inventor. More importantly, so has the patient. Surgery is advancing with

149

great rapidity.' Oliver nodded again. 'It needs to be matched by young men with new ideas.' Mackenzie paused. 'Her Majesty is shortly to appoint another Surgeon-Extraordinary. My own influence at Windsor is at present unassailable.'

Oliver stared at him. 'I am not worthy.'

'Of course you are. And no man disobeys the Queen's command.'

The honour which Mackenzie thrust towards him, which glittered enviously in every surgeon's eye, was the badge of a lifetime's prosperity. Oliver could not see it for the face of Candy. He was already a man depraved, as unfit for noble society as an urchin crossing-sweeper. Even if the powerful hand of ambition silenced the tormenting tongue of guilt – a scuffle which Oliver reflected occurred often in the minds of famous men – his terrible secrets might seep out, his disgrace would be doubly shameful. He had never hated Bertie more.

'Why should Her Majesty not appoint Lister himself?' he asked.

'Because the Queen desired him to make a public stand against vivisection, and his Quaker conscience would not allow him dissemble. He *believes* in dissecting animals for medical knowledge. This angered the Queen. More I understand than any utterance of Mr Gladstone.' Mackenzie rose and touched the bell. 'I must resume the treadmill. I try to see fifty or sixty patients a day, and finish with time for a rest before taking tea with my family at four o'clock. That is a sacred feast.'

Oliver's own brand-new carriage and pair was waiting outside in Harley Street. It was the conventional symbol of his success. At least, he need never share another cab with Bertie Randolph.

At the Whitechapel Hospital, the smell of soot was in the air. A huge fire had blazed that night at the docks, its glow like a midnight sunrise to the rollickers of Romano's, five miles away in the Strand. Oliver had charge of twin wards, freshly painted and newly equipped. The female ward held twenty beds, their white counterpanes tucked with the identical smartness of guardsmen's collars. A well-polished table ran down the middle with large bottles, pewter bowls, a handbasin for the doctor with folded starched handtowel, inkpot and blotter. The hospital now allowed flowers, and a few small pictures. The ward was lit with gas, night-lights in small glass jars standing on most of the patients' bedside lockers. There was even a new bathroom, the tubs with deal covers, on which the patients' dinners were carved.

The nurses were stepping from the gin-tippling world of Sarah Gamp to the crisp-aproned one of Miss Nightingale. There had been a training school for lady nurses at the Whitechapel Hospital almost ten years. They started immediately in the wards as probationers, unprivileged with a bow to their white caps, risking illness and death from erysipelas, diphtheria, typhoid, typhus, even from a septic finger. They worked from seven in the morning until ten at night, with two hours off a couple of afternoons a week, an evening once a fortnight. The day nurses slept in beds still warm from the night nurses. They educated themselves, or learned from the housemen and students, the other nurses and Albert the bathman.

Oliver slowly circulated round the beds with his ward sister in butcher blue. She was one of the old nurses, who had risen by observation, dexterity, shrewdness, labour and character. These were esteemed more reliable than the ladies, who were as addicted to flirting as their predecessors to tippling. Sister was shadowed by her staff nurse in striped merino, the house-surgeon and his 'firm' of a dozen students. Oliver changed the dressings, swabbing the wounds with carbolic solution. He lifted the poultices – kaolin on a cloth, applied wet and scalding. When he enquired a temperature, a student took it with a thermometer a foot long, which cost him twelve-and-sixpence if he broke it.

'Who is responsible for the seton and issue on this case?' Oliver asked.

One of the students pushed forward. The patient was a grossly fat woman, pale but for the pink of fever, her leg exposed, dripping and stinking, a jagged wound in her calf reaching with scarlet fingers towards her trunk.

'Well, Mr Fergusson, tell me exactly what you are doing.'

'I pull the strip of silk seton through the flesh, twice daily, to emit the pus, sir.' Oliver nodded approval. 'And I thrust into the slough the issue pea of ivy wood to keep the sore open.'

'What types of pus are there, Mr Fergusson?'

'Laudable, sir,' the student enumerated. 'Which we are pleased to see, as an indication of the healing process in the wound. Sanious, which is more offensive. And ichorous, which is foul, and tells us that the wound will never heal.'

'Quite correct. Though we regard wounds which heal by suppuration as normal, we overlook that ideal healing is by . . .?'

'By first intention, sir. By granulation, with no pus at all.'

'Exactly. With my use of Professor Lister's carbolic spray, I am able to achieve that result with an increasing number of cases.' Oliver broke off. Bertie Randolph had appeared in the ward, bottle of chloroform and lint in his hand. They had a rendezvous which Oliver had forgotten, at the bedside of a woman needing the simple but painful operation of avulsing the great toenail.

The patient was in the corner, a gaunt woman of forty-seven, her greying hair in two short plaits, shivering in her shift as the bed-clothes were withdrawn, a rubber sheet laid under her left leg. Mr Fergusson had been given the excitement of performing the operation, under Oliver's eye. Bertie sat beside the pillow, comforting her with trivial conversation.

'My name's Annie Chapman, sir,' she replied to him timidly. 'I lives in a lodging house, 35 Dorset Street, against Spitalfields Market.'

'Your husband's in work?' Bertie was already soaking the lint with choloroform, out of her sight.

'He went off, sir.'

'Well, are *you* in work?' She said nothing. Bertie already

suspected she was on the game – of prostitution. 'Just breathe this.'

'Will it hurt?' She was suddenly terrfied.

'You'll have a delightful sleep. And by Sunday morning, you'll be up and walking about.'

The operation was done in a minute, a carbolic dressing was applied.

'She needed a hefty dose.' Bertie folded the soaked lint. 'She's more used to the taste of gin than tapwater. How are those two Amazons the Missus Stride and Eddows, Mr Fergusson? Who gave battle in the receiving-room earlier this month.'

Replacing his jacket, the student looked surprised. 'You have a good memory for names, sir.'

'And faces. It's essential for private practice. If you cannot remember a patient's exterior, he'll not trust you to remember his interior.'

'Recovered, sir. Their injuries looked worse than they were.'

'I'm nipping down to the mortuary,' Bertie told Oliver, as they walked between the rows of beds to the door. 'A jolly interesting murder has come in. Most spectacular.'

'It surely makes no difference to the unfortunate victim whether his murder is spectacular or deadly dull?'

'Who cares about the victim? The principal actor leaves the stage before the curtain rises. Fleet Street is agog, I understand.'

Oliver declined to accompany him, though he was an assiduous attender of the post-mortem room. Bertie found it crowded. Inspector Abberline was accompanied by two more men in bowler hats and three constables. Tom, Janet and Hans stood in their leather aprons. On the floor was a scratched, battered black-lacquered coffin, its interior brown-stained with blood, the 'shell' in which so many unexpected recipients of death in Whitechapel were removed under a shabby pall by the police.

On the zinc-topped table lay the body of a woman in her forties. Her throat had been cut right across, slicing through

153

windpipe and gullet, back to the bones of the neck. A wide, jagged cut made a half-moon from the bottom of her breast-bone across her abdomen to the brim of the bony pelvic basin, ending half-way up the other side. The greater omentum, the fat-speckled, blood-pulsating membrane which hung like an apron from the curve of the stomach, extruded from the wound and itself bore three or four cuts. Bertie noticed that the face staring at the lantern piercing the roof had a bruise on each cheek.

Tom Dalhouse stood with his knife, about to start work. 'There are two further wounds inside the vagina,' he was explaining to inspector Abberline, glaring as Bertie pushed his way in.

'By quite a coincidence,' said Inspector Abberline, when Bertie inquired the corpse's identity, 'she's the Polly Nichols – one "I" – who couldn't identify the soldiers in the Turner murder. A couple of market porters going to work in Spital-fields found her at four o'clock this morning in Buck's Row. That's just across the India Road by the Metropolitan Rail-way line. She was on her back by a stable door, skirts round her waist. They summoned the assistance of PC Neil here.'.

'I felt the body,' said a middle-aged, heavily-moustached policeman solemnly. 'It was as warm as a toasted crumpet.'

'Any clues?' asked Bertie.

'The deceased was wearing two flannel petticoats sten-cilled "Lambeth Workhouse",' the Inspector told him. 'She was known there, they'd sent her into domestic service but she was dismissed without a character for stealing. What was her property, Sergeant Eccles?' he asked a plain-clothes man.

'Only a broken mirror, sir, and a comb. No money, not even a pawn ticket. Her apparel was a black straw bonnet, old boots, a brown ulster, a worn frock of brown linsey and stays.'

'The cause of death was of course severance of the carotid arteries.' Tom indicated the neck with the point of his knife.

'Now, it's a funny thing,' remarked Janet. 'There was little blood, when you'd have expected a fountain. A wee patch only six inches across on the pavement, didn't you say,

Inspector? Nor was a sound heard, not so much as the squeak of a tim'rous beastie. And Buck's Row's a busy sort of place.'

'She was drunk when she went to meet her Maker,' said Inspector Abberline in explanation. 'She'd been at the Frying Pan in Brick Lane, trying to raise her fourpence doss money, but she spent it on more gin. She was seen in India Road about three this morning, as drunk as a rolling fart, if you'll forgive the expression,' he added hastily.

'Any idea who did it?' Bertie inquired.

'Some bully-boys, sir. They make these unfortunates part with half their takings. And if they don't . . .' He indicated the savaged corpse.

'I assume an arrest will be merely a matter of time?' Bertie said, as the sweep of Tom's knife from chin to pubis eclipsed the murderous cuts.

'You took the words right out of my mouth, sir.'

16

'Look ... look ... *look* ...' Bertie's voice had a rising intensity.

He held as a pendulum his glittering watch on its fine gold chain. His face was six inches from Nellie the new housemaid, who was fifteen, fresh-faced, willing, lazy and stupid. Her full-lipped mouth was open, her brown eyes squinted at the watch. The breakfast dishes were still on the dining-room table, she was in her morning uniform of brown holland, a round dusting-cap over her dark hair. It was Friday, September 7. The London weather had turned bright and warm with the new month, but the heavy curtains were drawn, the only light a gleam through the chink. Nellie was in the velvet fireside chair. Bertie leant across the wooden back of a chair from the table.

'You are growing sleepy, Nellie.'

'Oh, no, sir! I'm not.'

He continued the watch's pendulations.

'Let your body go loose,' he commanded.

'Please sir, I wants to sneeze.'

'No! Don't! Look hard at the watch.'

'I can't help myself, sir—'

'You are dropping to sleep.'

'Aaaa-tishoooo!'

'Great God,' muttered Bertie. He stood up, replacing the watch in his pocket and drawing back the curtains. He had thought Nellie the passive, simple sort of female so susceptible to hypnosis. He seemed to lack Charcot's touch.

Freshings appeared with two letters, both with foreign stamps. Bertie dismissed his servants, sitting in the armchair. He wore a brown tweed suit with a high-buttoned cutaway jacket, a high white collar with a Cambridge blue bow, Russian leather shoes and a red handkerchief flowing from his top pocket. With his penknife, he opened first the one post-marked Vienna.

Dear Dr Randolph! it said.

May I thank you most heartily for the totally unexpected second box from Fribourg and Treyer. The Havana 'Legitimas' which your country imports are so superior to any found in my own. They give the most pleasant reminder that much of the terrestrial globe and the Seven Seas lie under the sway of your Sovereign.

I can best reply to your questions on the value of hypnotism by confessing that I am abandoning it as treatment. I believe that hypnosis, and the bodily phenomena of hysteria, are produced by auto-suggestion, arising from the nervous excitability of the patient. But I must not lay myself open to common charges of originating my patients' symptoms – such as lameness and blindness – by my own unconscious suggestion.

I prefer to sit out of sight, behind the head of a couch. I ask patients to say out loud any thought entering their heads, however apparently disconnected from those preceding. This free association of ideas will, I believe, display the mind as links of different shapes and sizes are seen joined in an intricate chain.

I shall take your enquiries about the phenomena of sadism and masochism together, because neither is present in any individual without the other. Sadism expresses the aggressiveness and mental dominance of the male, masochism the dependence and submissiveness normal in the female. I am sure you will be neither shocked nor surprised at my indicating that these qualities may both be present in any male or female. Yet masochism is the more powerful of the two forces, an expression of man's eternal tendency to self-injury, an indication of the death wish.

These conditions in your patient 'A' are best considered in the narrower sexual context. Clearly, the lady 'C' enjoys

157

inflicting pain, and such females are never short of partners eager to receive it. The behaviour of both is only a variant of the sexual drive. Sex is the explosive charge in every projectile from the human mind, which burst into shrapnel of many strange pieces.

I think of your serene country, Dr Randolph, in the soothing haze of cigar smoke.

Sincerely yours,
Freud

The letter from Paris was in French. It inquired when he might pay a visit, Paris being so charming between the heat of August and the frosts of November. Madame Colette was pleased to announce that later in the month she would have for sale two interesting precious objects, of the same age but more beautiful than before. She would be happy to see them exported to England, where the market for such things was brisker. She was sure he found her terms advantageous.

The first letter Bertie folded and slipped into his pocket with his watch. The second he lit with a vesta, watching paper and envelope blacken to ashes in the grate. The face of the mantelpiece clock, between two pairs of miniature Ionic columns, told him it was time to leave. Freshings was waiting in the hall with a wicker picnic basket, a tartan rug and a boater with a black ribbon. The hansom was already at the steps. Bertie mounted, directing the driver to Garden Gate. Candy came hurrying at once from Mrs Floyd's front door, as excited as a schoolgirl on a day's outing.

'Where are we going?' She squeezed breathlessly beside him.

'Paddington. We'll take a train to Windsor, and hire a skiff. There's fewer 'Arrys and 'Arriets splashing about further up river, than if we started from Hampton Court. Then we'll row gently in the direction of Marlow. I doubt if we'll get there, but that matters less than finding a delightful spot for lunch.'

'How do I look?' She twisted towards him, both hands extended, one with a bright yellow silk parasol. She wore a primrose tight-waisted dress, brand new, broad scarlet ribbon edging her neck, circling her wrists, running along the four flounces of her skirt.

'Scarlet is vulgar,' Bertie told her. 'Crimson would have been better. You shouldn't be showing the uppers of those nice white kid boots. The hat's a millinery catastrophe.' It was orange-dyed straw decorated with thick bunches of bright cherries. 'I'll use my pocket-knife, for a spot of fruit-picking. Don't wear scent for a day in the open air. It's too suggestive of the place you've come from.'

She stared, mouth open. He might have struck her.

'You can't expect to look like a lady, the very first morning in your life that you've tried to,' he consoled her. 'Think of the Birmingham ironmongers' daughters, resolutely "finished" by Englishwomen of unassailable breeding – and barely assailable fee – that they might be daily exhibited in society. They never advance further than looking like the daughters of curates, while speaking like those of pawn-brokers, and behaving like the ones of Jewish millionaires.'

'But I took such care.' Candy's eyes shone with tears.

'That's the trouble. The result would have been better had you kept the gown you milked your cows in.'

The 'Lawn' at Paddington Station, the asphalted concourse, was as busy as a regatta day. Clerks got up as dudes, Bertie thought contemptuously. Raucous young men in striped blazers and caps, many with hampers, one with a banjo like a Margate nigger, City men in cutaways and tall hats, plenty of women in gay bonnets and bright frocks with the sensuality which eagerness gives the female face. With the sudden bright weather, all who could command a day away from their desks took it. The others invented illnesses and dead grandmothers. Bertie pushed to the first class ticket office. If he could not afford to travel *en prince*, he stayed at home.

They had a compartment to themselves. Candy had never been in a train, except the Metropolitan Line at White-chapel. She sat stiffly on the beige, lace-trimmed upholstery, frowning over the *Morning Post* which Bertie had bought her. Candy was prouder of her ability to read than her more utilized attributes. Rose could hardly spell, and puzzled over the advertisement for Cherry Blossom boot polish, with the coifed lady proclaiming 'Nun Nicer.' She ran her finger slowly along the column, mouth moving, reconstructing the appeal by Mr Labouchere, of whom she had never heard, for the abolition of the House of Lords, some of whose members she knew intimately.

'No need to swot like a schoolboy.' Bertie lolled in the corner, boater tipped over brow, as they steamed past Wormwood Scrubs. 'Aristrocratic ladies regard reading as an activity beneath them. Those of the bourgeoisie are unable to form an intelligent opinion on anything, so it does not matter whether they read or not. The only English females who gain any personal advantage from the knack of de-ciphering print are governesses. And whoever is allowed the chance for an intelligent conversation with someone's governess?'

Finger still on the last word she interpreted, Candy asked eagerly across the swaying carriage, 'Bertie, will you really make me sound like a lady?'

'I'll fill in your aspirates like the gaps in an old whore's teeth.'

'I've already stopped saying "ain't." Though I'm blowed if I know what I should talk about in society. There's thoughts in my head, but they just come out squawking, like chickens from the roost in the morning.'

'Say nothing at all. Then you'll be esteemed as a serene, agreeable woman of profound wisdom. Nod your head, smile, and murmur, "How clever," if you like. No man cares in the slightest if he is understood so long as he is admired. You'll win the reputation of a brilliant conversationalist, with every man in the drawing-room eager to address you and to hang breathlessly on your every silence.'

'I've tried ever so to be better mannered with the gentle-men at No. 2. But I don't fancy they like it.'

'Of course they don't. When they descend to a whore-house to have a good fuck, they want an unabashed slut like you. Otherwise, they feel it wears the dignification of adultery, which makes them guilty towards their wives. Don't say "ever so," by the by. Try "awfully." '

'But it must be ever so much nicer with their wives,' Candy speculated. 'When they love them.'

'Lust and love are two different articles on a man's shopping list. Love means only the duty of a middle-class woman to lie on her back and receive her husband's thrusts, like the piano. Admitting she enjoys it would be like admitting she wonders in church about the size of the curate's prick, which I've no doubt she does every Sunday.'

Candy giggled. 'But the larks they get up to! Do you suppose their wives spank them with the carpet-beater?'

Bertie looked shocked. 'Oh, dear me, no. What do we keep housemaids for? Though I daresay a good many respectable wives would enjoy having their bums made to blush with a besom. A woman revels in a beating, you know. It's deep in her nature.'

'Yes, I reckon some of them in Whitechapel haven't much minded a black eye,' Candy said thoughtfully. 'When they earn it by deliberately working their husbands into a fury.'

'Oh, lust lies much closer to fury than to love. Both are uncontrollable and exciting. Both express themselves in many strange ways. People fuck or fight, or for that matter make money or make friends, or suffer, or face death according to character. We're the same grain all the way through. Why don't you get on with your *Morning Post*?'

Candy's conversation was like the music-hall, best enjoyed in short turns.

She gasped when Windsor Castle appeared through the carriage window. 'It's awfully like a fairy tale,' she exclaimed. 'Is the Queen really there?'

'She may be. One fat little black slug, curled somewhere in that huge wedding-cake.'

'Bertie! You mustn't talk like that. It's ever so awfully rude.'

'Try "quite too awfully",' he suggested helpfully.

They walked along the river bank, Bertie with hamper

and rug, Candy twirling her open parasol on her shoulder, face upturned, full lips parted, eyes glowing like a bride's.

'What's that?' Her white-gloved finger pointed across the river.

'A school.'

She gasped again. 'It's big enough for all the boys and girls in London.'

'Common children would never tolerate Eton's cleverly refined hardships. They're for tempering the ruling class. Don't point, by the way. It's rude. Except at servants, of course.'

They hired a light skiff from a red-faced, matted-bearded waterman. Bertie had chosen the first boatyard above Romney Lock – locks on fine days he thought boxes of brightly coloured human scum, with a long wait to get in and the locals gawping down with their dogs to pass the time. Bertie abhorred locks, as he abhorred omnibuses.

'I'll row.' Candy stepped into the narrow, bouncing boat with perilous enthusiasm.

'You shall not.' Bertie took the oars. 'A *lady* is not expected to exert herself upon the rowlocks any more than upon the bedsprings.'

She sat in the stern, framed by her parasol, as he started pulling upstream. The river was full after the wet summer, the current toilsome.

'Why don't you take your hat and jacket off, Bertie? All the others have. You'll come out in a muck-sweat.'

'Removing one's jacket, even for saving a female from a fire, is the emblem of the lower class. Will you please remember that a navvy sweats, a gentleman perspires and a young lady glows?'

Bertie noticed his rebuffs furrowed her brow. She took her beatification as a lady earnestly.

Candy stared intensely at everything they passed, the swans with their customary look of implacable hostility, a floating dead dog, urchins fishing with bent pins, loungers smoking clays on the bank. They had a moment of excitement when a steam-launch passed too close, whistle shrieking, men in straw hats and girls in bright dresses staring sneeringly from the rail.

'We might have been drowned!' complained Candy, parasol quivering.

'Can't you swim?'

'Bless us and save us! I've never so much as seen the sea.'

'Perhaps a lady's function is not to swim but to be rescued,' Bertie mused at the oars. 'You're showing your knees. The next steam-launch will be able to assess your working capital.'

As she hastily pulled down her skirt, Bertie rowed for the bank. 'The coolth under that willow is inviting.'

'The sign says, "No Mooring",' Candy exclaimed. 'By order of somebody.'

'That only applies to the public,' he dismissed it.

He tied the prow to a branch overhanging the grassy bank. Freshings had packed a bottle of claret and a chicken, carved and wrapped in cheesecloth. They had mustard pickles, ginger cakes, grapes, aerated water and a flask of brandy. The afternoon was golden but sultry. After their picnic, Bertie stretched full length with a languour that seldom lay so voluptuously on a frame always so briskly busy in so varied occupations. As Candy packed up the basket, he carefully cut the cherries from her hat, tossing them one after the other into the water, leaving a single shiny red blob.

'I'm giving you back your cherry.'

Candy laughed, pinning the hat on her piled golden hair. 'I'd be the only girl in the world.'

'The loss of virginity and of life are the only two entirely irreversible experiences of our existence,' he agreed. 'Those, and posting a letter.'

She smiled at him sentimentally. 'I owe you a debt as big as a gold mine, Bertie.'

He agreed readily. 'The graduations of harlotry are more savage than those of society. *Les grandes horizontales* are surely as respectable as public buildings? Had I left you in Whitechapel, you'd have ended being knocked for fourpence and getting your throat cut. Did I mention it – that woman you knew in Star Place has gone to grass with her teeth upwards. Martha Turner.'

Candy was aghast. 'What happened?'

'Got run through by a bayonet – an honourable end, like many of the Queen's enemies. They never found the soldier who did it.' Bertie felt for his cigar case. 'By an odd co-incidence, the other one there the afternoon I rescued you was done for, rather later. Or was it a coincidence in White-chapel? No more than two women both developing bad colds in the head. What was her name—? Polly Nichols.'

Candy gasped. Bertie looked surprised. 'They meant nothing to you, did they?'

'It's dreadful to hear of someone you know dead. And murdered, cut up. Like my own mother was.'

'I'm sorry, your parental estrangement had rather slipped my memory.' Bertie saw she was about to cry. 'Don't pipe your eye for those two in Whitechapel. No more than for a couple of alley cats squashed by the carts.'

'Polly Nichols was a nice old thing.' Candy had turned white as milk.

'Was she? The woman struck me as a disgrace to this planet who was better pushed off it.'

'You didn't know her, Bertie.'

He cut a cigar with his pen-knife. 'I did. More intimately than you. I saw her stretched naked on the post-mortem table. Where the doctors dismantled her, setting eyes on her innermost organs, of whose nature and existence she had not the faintest notion herself. Her throat was cut right to the bone,' he added informatively. 'Dr Guillotin's machine could hardly have done better. For good measure, her sto-mach was ripped open and her tripes spilled on the pave-ment.'

Candy suppressed a shriek. 'Don't tell me this! You'll be giving me nightmares.' She drew a lacy handkerchief from the reticule at her wrist and dabbed her lids. 'Poor Martha! Poor Polly!'

Bertie struck a vesta. 'I was introduced to yet another of your profession in the post-mortem room, a little earlier.

164

Somebody had stuck a knife up her twat and ripped her insides.'

'Have they hung the man?' she asked fearfully.

'The police are far too busy to puzzle themselves more than half an hour over matters as commonplace in Whitechapel as speculating in the City. The very same day as your friend Polly was disembowelled, the Duke of Berkshire's town house was burgled. *There's* heinous crime for you.'

She inquired, 'Were Martha and Polly in the papers?'

'Yes. Fame is the democratic compensation of slaughter. Though neither life was worth a line of print.' He lay smoking, looking into the leaves of the willow. 'I don't suppose they cared much dying. Only substantial possessions and effective power punish us with fear of death.'

'But them what did it! They must be devils hot from Hell.'

'Oh, I should imagine they're much like any other bloke on a penny omnibus. I'm strongly against murder, particularly among the working classes. It's generally a perfectly respectable labourer who finds he's done it. Which can start him on a life of crime, if he's not careful.

She said with a mixture of wonder and resentment, 'I don't ever understand half of what you're getting at, Bertie.'

'Neither do educated women. But they laugh, because I speak with a pleasant look on my face and have a reputation for joking.'

'You're a queer card.' He said nothing. She asked with touching timidity, 'Don't you never want to fuck me?'

'No.'

'But you don't mind other men what you know doing it. The one with the fat bum, and the other what gives me the cold creeps.'

'The delights of the pimp are under-rated.'

Candy dangled her fingers in the water. 'Will you really make me a lady?'

Bertie noticed how she returned repeatedly to the question. 'Why not? You've a quick ear, and imitation saves much drudgery in the way of learning. I'll get you out of the lupanar.' She looked lost. 'That's a Latin word meaning "whorehouse". Like I'd say "uterus" for "womb", to distinguish anatomy from butchery. Oh, you'll soon have everyone "Missing" you.'

'But no man would ever take me for a wife.' He wondered if this impelled her pathetic scratching at the enclosing walls of infamy.

'I don't know,' he told her easily. 'Marrying a reformed whore has advantages. It's less noticeable than marrying your own cook, and of greater value to domestic bliss. With such a pair of prize faggots under your bodice—' He nodded towards her bosom. 'Half the young aristocrats in London could be itching to take you up the aisle.'

She sighed romantically. 'I'd take to that, like a tom-tit on a horse turd,' she agreed.

Bertie touched the spring of his watch. 'Time is God's shameful waste. He allows those to indulge in it who are old, or sick, or rich, and get no proper pleasure from it.'

He bought her a sixpenny tea at Windsor. In the station refreshment room he stopped for a half-a-crown's worth of brandy, which he swigged neat. They sat silent on the journey home. As their hansom from Paddington neared Garden Gate, he noticed she was quietly crying. He briefly clasped her hand. It was the first time he had touched her all day, apart from helping her out of the boat.

'It was lovely,' she said.

'Next week, I'll take you to the races.'

'Really?' A smile burst on her face.

'Only if you're a good girl,' he told her, grinning.

'As you won't fuck me, will you kiss me?'

He removed his boater and met her lips.

'You're a regular brick, Bertie. I've never felt spoony like this with any man, you know. That's my Bible oath.'

'You're being sentimental. But I suppose that many more women have given themselves to men for sentimentality, than for either curiosity or cash.'

He left her at the door. She'll give full value to her customers tonight, he reflected as he clattered away alone in the hansom.

166

17

ON SATURDAY MORNINGS, when the India Road was blocked by herds of cows and sheep, country wains, carts, wagonettes and jostling humans marketing or idling, Bertie would direct his hansom from the City along Ropewalk Lane. The long, narrow, twisted cobbled street ended at the green-painted double door in the back wall of the hospital by the mortuary. He had often seen the 'fever gate' admitting smallpox suspects to the isolation ward. The sufferer would be carried on a stretcher like a coffin, but with more serviceable handles, followed by the public disinfectors – two men in white calico suits with a closed, two-wheeled handcart like a baker's, in which all the patients' household goods were packed for transference with tongs into an oven, for baking at a regulation 280 degrees.

The medical staff shunned the fever gate. Everyone was uneasy about smallpox. The law submitted every Briton within three months of birth to the public vaccinator, at the cost of 1s. 6d. But continued epidemics had shaken faith in Dr William Jenner's ingenious reasoning from the Gloucester milkmaids who suffered cowpox and never smallpox. And vaccination was rumoured to risk giving you syphilis. The Whitechapel Hospital doctors avoided smallpox patients, their bedding, their dead bodies, even crossing their paths. Bertie was more concerned at a convenient short cut, and a way of avoiding boring colleagues in the front hall.

The gate was always unlocked, being also employed for the traffic of corpses. Bertie used it in the morning after his excursion with Candy. In the middle of the cobbled yard, between the isolation block with its tall stovepipe and the mortuary, was the short, black-suited form of Tom Dalhouse. He was alone. At his feet lay the displaced manhole cover, and he peered as though directly into the fires of Hades.

He looked up with a start. 'Drains,' he said savagely. 'It's a disgrace, Randolph. Worse, it's an insult. This sewer runs under the very foundations of my post-mortem room, which I strive to keep sanitary, unlike many of the hovels where you're expected to perform such scientific work in London.'

'There is a bit of a pong,' Bertie agreed. 'Makes you want to light a piece of brown paper under your nostrils.'

'Thundering blazes,' Tom continued angrily. 'Don't you know the law?'

'You are more lettered in the jurisprudence of sewage than I am.'

'The Public Health Act of 1848 compelled the emptying of sewers into rivers. That of 1875 prohibited it,' specified Tom forcefully. 'Yet this law is observed in Whitechapel no more than any other. Under this yard runs a brick sewer – egg-shaped, big enough for the rat-catchers in their thigh boots. It empties the filth of the India Road directly into the Thames at Wapping. Do you know when they last caught a salmon in the Thames? 1833! It was the summer they had to hang disinfected sheets over the House of Commons' windows to keep out the stink. It'll be 1933 before another's taken,' he ended glumly.

'It does rather strike the nose as an essence of shit and dead babies.'

'I have written to the secretary of our new London County Council. I have written to Sir Charles Warren, the commissioner of police. I have written to the Lord Mayor. I have given them my opinion that the exhalations of this sewer can be the source of enteric fever, cholera, relapsing fever and tapeworm. All have been too haughty, or too ignorant, to heed my advice.'

Bertie was relieved he replaced the manhole cover. 'Sewers are a science in themselves, Randolph. Did you know that the recommended velocity in large ones is 176 feet per second when running three-quarters full, but 146 feet when running one-third full?'

'No!' exclaimed Bertie.

'It is of course perfectly straightforward to calculate the discharge from sewers. The velocity in cubic feet per minute equals 55 times the square root of the hydraulic mean depth, times twice the fall in feet per mile, multiplied by the section area.'

'You amaze me.'

'I could give you other formulae to calculate the velocity due to different heads of water, the discharge of water from orifices and sluices, and the inclination of house drains,' Tom told him enthusiastically. 'Did you know that the modern flushing of stagnant sewers has saved London £30,000 per annum? Water with the velocity of 180 feet per second will disturb angular stones one and three-quarter inches in diameter ...'

'Dr Dalhouse!' To Bertie's increased relief, Janet Veale came urgently through the door leading into the main hospital corridor. '*There* you are! I've been searching high and low. This message has just been delivered from Mr Wynne Baxter, the coroner.' Tom took a sheet of paper covered with copper-plate. 'There's been yet *another* murder. Would you believe it? The body was found at six o'clock this morning, outside a lodging house in Hanbury Street, off Brick Lane. The corpse should be arriving any minute,' she said, as comfortably as though expecting friends for tea. 'Another of those woman of the fallen class, it seems. Good morning to you, Dr Randolph.'

'Dr Dalhouse finds not only books in running brooks, but sermons in sewers,' Bertie complimented him.

'I do declare, you look quite peaky.' Her concern jerked Tom's eyes from the coroner's letter.

'Perhaps I had a bad night.'

'Ah! You're a masher.' She wagged her finger playfully. 'Everyone in the hospital says so.'

Bertie disclaimed the reputation. 'I live in Dull Street, and my amusements would not excite a curate.'

'But you speak *French*, Dr Randolph,' she accused him, as though he could speak the name of every devil in Hell.

All three were aware of a rising hubbub outside the fever gate. The green doors were thrown open by two policemen propelling a handcart, which bore a long box covered by a familiar black cloth. Outside were more policemen, pushing back a shouting mob which filled the street. The doors were shut in the agitators' faces. The policemen removed the pall, revealing the same battered shell in which Polly Nichols arrived at the same place a month earlier.

The fever door again opened briefly, admitting Inspector Abberline in his brown bowler, his two plain-clothes assistants, two more policemen and a sergeant. The noise outside increased in volume and anger. How ludicrous, thought Bertie, that the mortality of Whitechapel harlots should be a matter of public concern. The door reopened a crack for a rat-faced man with a ragged moustache, in black serge and a black bowler, carrying a square camera on a tripod under a baize cloth. The policemen took the shell into the mortuary. Everyone followed, tailed by Bertie, lighting a cigar.

The woman's body lay still clothed on the post-mortem table, rigor mortis capturing her limbs in the position which was their last. Her skirts were above her waist, her knees bent and turned out, her hands palm-outwards defending her face. Arms, legs, features were painted with blood. Her neck had been almost severed, the flesh of her abdomen ripped into three flaps, the one bearing her navel averted to the right, two drawn up towards her chest. Over her right shoulder was draped the bloody epaulette of her guts, sliced clean from the filmy folds of the mesenteric membrane which gathered them to the body's inside.

'Name of Mary Anne Chapman,' Inspector Abberline announced. 'Aged forty-seven. She was an unfortunate.' Bertie savoured the understatement. 'Residing in a Dorset Street lodging-house against Spitalfields Church – though she'd gone missing a week. Last seen alive at half past five this morning, by a woman making for Spitalfields Market. Must have been drunk. She'd been in and out of the Queen's Head and the Ringers all night. She was seen talking to a man,' he revealed with satisfaction, 'who said, "Will you?" To which the deceased was heard to reply, "Yes." He was a middle-aged man. A man of foreign appearance.' This seemed to explain the crime. 'The body was found in a yard behind a catsmeat shop, often employed by these women for their immoral purposes.'

Leather-aproned Hans began slitting the clothes with a long knife. Janet asked, 'Many people sleeping over the shop?' Inspector Abberline nodded. 'Seventeen.'

'That *is* a wee bit strange, I must say.' Janet clasped her hands thoughtfully. 'At the inquest on that last woman, Nichols, I recall she was found on that landing between the doors of a Mrs Green and a Mrs Perkins, neither of whom lost a wink of sleep. But surely, having one's throat cut *must* be a noisy process.'

'The murderer approached her like a Judas, ma'am. No sign of struggle, you will observe. No cuts on the hands. He seized her from behind, preventing any cry. Insensibility was caused by suffocation.'

'The operation was a success, anyway,' remarked Bertie, as Hans drew boot and black cotton stocking from the corpse's left foot. They stared at him. He nodded towards the great toe. 'One of Mr Wilberforce's dressers avulsed the nail, up in Martha ward a week ago. I gave her a whiff of chloroform. If the wound hadn't healed, it could have saved her life.'

Inspector Abberline was opening an oilskin pouch, taken from a brown Gladstone held by Sergeant Eccles. 'We found these two rings at the deceased's feet. Also these three pennies and two new farthings. A twist of paper with some pills, an envelope with a London postmark dated August 28, and her comb. They were laid round the body, as if some sort of pagan ritual.'

'Look for a Zulu,' said Bertie. Everyone stared at him again. 'Don't you remember the Matabele War, inspector, nine years ago? I'd just gone up to Cambridge. There was no end of fuss about the Prince Imperial of France—' He flourished his cigar. 'Who lived within our shores, because the

Emperor Napoleon, who was his father, unlike the Emperor Napoleon who was his great-uncle, wisely preferred exile in leafy Chislehurst to remote St Helena.'

Tom expressed his lack of interest in this recital by turning his attention to the body. Janet stood gazing at Bertie.

'The Prince Imperial was killed in Matabeleland while in the care of the unfortunate Lieutenant J B Carey – a dull vicar's son from Devon, who was sent to Coventry by the Army ever after. The point lies in the Matabele method of killing. Surely you recall the disaster at Isandhlwana?' Inspector Abberline nodded. 'When King Cetywayo and his Zulu warriors called upon Lord Chelmsford's camp without invitation? Ritually disembowelled, the lot of them. Even the drummer boys, sliced open like sheep. With assegais sharp as razors.'

'If I may say, Dr Dalhouse,' murmured Janet, 'an Impi in a grass skirt and a necklace of skulls might be obvious even in so mixed a community as Whitechapel.'

'Then look for a sportsman with a deerstalker hat and a telescope,' he suggested breezily. 'He'd be a dab at gralloching a dead stag.'

'I say –' Tom had his hand deep in the pelvis, through the murderer's oozy red slit. 'The uterus has gone.' He pulled the squelching organs aside. 'By jove! Yes, he's taken out the uterus, the upper end of her vagina and a chunk of bladder. You didn't see a womb on the pavement or anywhere, did you?' The inspector shook his head decisively. 'Then the murderer's made off with it.'

'If you ask me, sir, he's touched.'

'It seems he was intending her head as a souvenir, too,' observed Janet. 'Now, there's another funny thing. The face is livid, as in asphyxia. Not blanched, as with haemorrhage. There was little blood about, I believe, Inspector? No more than you'd expect when the blood pressure is low during a surgical operation performed under a general anaesthetic.'

'Don't look for a Zulu in a deerstalker, but a surgeon,' Bertie instructed him.

'The man must have *some* anatomical knowledge,' Tom declared. 'A uterus is a difficult article to find. It doesn't stare you in the face like a spleen or even a kidney, it's tucked out of sight. Particularly difficult in a backyard, on a dark night in a hurry.'

'I'm ready, sir,' said the photographer, who had been adjusting his tripod while nervously eyeing the corpse.

'The eyes first, Larkins,' Inspector Abberline directed. 'Did you know, sir,' he asked Tom, 'that the murderer's features may be imprinted on the victim's eyeball? The image is frozen by death.'

'I've heard of it, and don't believe it.'

'It's a well known fact in police work,' the Inspector assured him.

Bertie watched while Tom and Hans took the corpse by the armpits, holding it against the brick wall. A camera could not be tilted, even the dead must pose standing. Tom's two fingers raised the eyelids. The photographer disappeared under his hood, still in his bowler. One emerging hand squeezed the bulb of his shutter, the other triggered the flash of his magnesium light, filling the room with white smoke. Bertie pressed the spring of his watch. He had chloroform to give for Oliver Wilberforce – the reduction of a dislocated shoulder, with ropes and pulleys tugged by hefty dressers.

The post-mortem took two hours. Afterwards, Inspector Abberline accompanied Tom and Janet to the small triangular room with the microscopes and test-tubes. Tom had something to divulge.

'The importance of a letter I had last March is suddenly apparent,' said Tom excitedly. He shut the door, opened it to ensure no one was listening outside, and shut it again. 'It was from an American, addressed from Gresham's Hotel in Dover Street. He was unknown there, I discovered, but had written asking them to hold his mail. The letter requested my assistance in obtaining numerous specimens of the human uterus.'

Tom looked smug. The Inspector looked curious. 'The

American had an explanation for this odd request. He had written a book on the uterus, and desired to issue an actual specimen with each copy. He offered me as much as £1 apiece. He particularly wanted the organ preserved in glycerine, which would keep it supple, unlike the hardening effect of the usual formalin.'

'And what did you make of that, sir?' asked the inspector.

'Fishy. Dashed fishy. Supposing he'd written a book on amputation of the limbs? He wouldn't give a leg free with each copy.'

'To my mind, he was a crackpot,' decided Janet. 'Setting a plot to discredit all anatomical research. That happened in Edinburgh, you know. After the *most* unfortunate incident of Burke and Hare.'

The Inspector was opening the Gladstone taken from Sergeant Eccles. 'First of all, sir, what about this?'

He laid on the laboratory bench a folded leather apron.

'Found at the scene of the crime,' he said solemnly. 'It's exactly as you use in the course of your painful duties.'

'And by cobblers or stonemasons,' Tom told him.

Inspector Abberline looked sly. 'What do we know of this fiend so far? First, it's a sound bet he did the other two, Turner and Nichols. Both with their throat cut. Perhaps he did Emma Smith? All were submitted to mutilations not seen in your everyday murder. Second, he's a local man, knowing his way round Whitechapel. He's possessed of a knowledge of human anatomy, as you said just now, sir.'

Tom nodded. 'And he has – or has access to – a knife like you use in your professional work.' Tom nodded again. 'Lastly, he's a man probably known to the police as a molester, an annoyer of women from the unfortunate class. Well, sir! I ask you.' He gave a satisfied smile. 'Who is it? Your mortuary porter.'

'Hans?' exclaimed Janet. 'But he's as gentle as a nurse.'

The Inspector nodded gravely. '*And* he is foreign. From Hamburg, I believe? You will not know, he has been reported three times to Commercial Road police station, for threatening unfortunates who won't give what he wants without paying.'

'But I can't believe Hans—' Tom glanced at Janet. How terrible, he thought, if the murderer were his own factotum. The doctors at the Whitechapel would be horrified. They would jeer at him in Bart's. They would gloat at Guy's. He might be told to resign. 'Any man could buy such an article in any outfitters,' he pointed out. 'There's no blood on it, it's almost brand-new.'

'I shall keep the suspect under close observation.' Inspector Abberline replaced the leather apron in his Gladstone. 'Not a word to him, if you please.' Tom and Janet nodded obediently. 'Men become strange creatures under the influence of women. It's like lunatics and the full moon. Inquest ten o'clock Monday. Working Lads' Institute, Mr Wynne Baxter presiding. He's just come back from his holidays in Sweden. Expect it did him the power of good. The poor gentleman has to work hard in a district like Whitechapel.' He snapped the bag shut. 'Rest assured, sir, apprehending the perpetrator of these diabolical crimes is only a matter of time.'

18

THEIR DEPARTURE from St Pancras was as ceremonious as if they were royalty, rather than three doctors hastening to attend on it. Each day he was in residence at Sandringham, 'The Prince of Wales' Special' waited steaming for his guests, with their tweeds and furs, their well-polished luggage, their guns and dogs. It was nine o'clock on the morning of Friday, September 14. The weather was bright, with an early snap. The station was filled with busy noises, engines hissing and puffing, jingling cabs and rattling porters' barrows, the scuffle of jostling travellers. The top-hatted, frock-coated stationmaster gravely opened the carriage door. Brass-buttoned, gold-braided Midland Railway employees in shakos, their boots polished, even their trousers pressed, Bertie noticed, were deployed along the platform like a guard of honour. Barely were they seated than the green flag waved, the whistle shrieked and they slid from the iron and glass cavern.

'Well, this is a bit of a lark,' said Bertie. Oliver Wilberforce made no reply.

'We must hope an operation upon the eventual heir to the throne remains a secret until it is successfully completed.' Sir Morell Mackenzie in the other corner lit one of his stramonium cigarettes. He had met Bertie for the first time on the platform. 'The very word is as terrifying to the well-educated as among the lower classes. Unfortunately, our visit itself could never pass unnoticed. Even royal servants talk. But it would have caused greater alarm, had Sandringham been evacuated of guests on the eve of the pheasant season. The Prince of Wales is an expert shot,' he added, indicating their intimacy. 'They bag over fifteen thousand head of game there in a season.'

'Oh, I'm sure he's an expert turning his weapon on any bird,' Bertie responded.

Puzzling what to make of him, Mackenzie said solemnly, 'There is a stone in the grounds where the late Prince Consort shot his last pheasant. I have seen another at Balmoral to mark his final stag. The Queen is deeply concerned with his memory.'

'I hear the Blue Room at Windsor has been left exactly the same since Albert croaked in it.' Bertie produced his sharkskin cigar case. 'Evening clothes laid out fresh every day, shaving tackle awaiting the royal chin, even medicine bottle and spoon. An unhealthy attachment to putrefied matter, I call it. They replace his favourite soap in the dish, his pisspot is scoured daily, and put from the commode every night under the bed. Wouldn't it be a lark, if one morning they found piss in it?'

Mackenzie grew uneasy.

'Of course, Albert would never have caught enteric at all, if the drains at Windsor hadn't been so bad as in Whitechapel.' Bertie struck a match. 'Used to stink so much, the Queen couldn't go near parts of her own home, you know. Shouldn't think they're much better where we're going. Didn't the Prince of Wales catch enteric at Sandringham? Luckily he didn't snuff, despite having papa's same doctor. I gather the Queen is similarly planting memorials to that whisky-sodden serf, John Brown.'

Mackenzie now felt alarm. 'Her Majesty perhaps unwisely allowed Brown a certain intimacy. But that was only to keep in touch with the feelings of her subjects during the seclusion of widowhood.' He disliked Bertie's mocking eye. Blowing plumes of smoke through flared nostrils, he said, 'Lord Beaconsfield told me shortly before he died, that he never proposed a new measure to the Queen unless sure it had the approval of the two JB's – John Bull and John Brown.'

Bertie laughed loudly. 'Mentioning Disraeli reminds me

of a capital story I heard at the club. You know how Jews make such efforts to shake off their Jewish names? Le Voy for the obvious Levi, Abinger for Abraham? One lawyer of that persuasion was referred to as "the learned counsel Mr Abinger, *nez* Abraham".' He laughed again, spelling the joke out.

'Shut up, Bertie,' said Oliver.

'Don't you think it funny?' Bertie looked surprised.

'I am in the same mood to be amused as a man mounting the scaffold.'

Bertie stuck his cigar in his mouth and sulked. Mackenzie sat in silent embarrassment. Why must I make the most important journey of my life in Bertie's company? Oliver thought angrily. But he could no more have left Bertie behind than a singer his usual accompanist for a royal performance. Colleagues would have raised eyebrows, asked questions. Bertie himself would have been furious. His reckless impulsiveness might have spread tales along the hospital corridors ... Besides, Bertie was the most skilful and the safest anaesthetist in London.

Sharing a jolting railway carriage soon rubs off the prickles of vexation. Feeling he had made his point of equality with the other two, Bertie prepared to amuse rather than to outrage. They had a journey of almost three hours to lighten. As they rattled through the harvested fields and plucked orchards of Essex, he said as a diversion, 'Wasn't it a jape about Hans our mortuary porter? "Leather Apron", as the papers called him. Dragged from his house and almost lynched, just for exciting himself by talking to whores – being too timid, or too mean, or too frightened of the pox, for any intercourse with them beyond the social. But he spoke with a guttural accent.' Bertie sighed hopelessly. 'No man who wants to save his neck when the English are thirsting for a culprit should allow himself a Teutonic inflexion.'

'Abberline was a fool, hinting to the papers he might be the culprit.' Oliver was as eager to resume trifling conversation as Bertie.

'But the man was arrested, surely?' asked Mackenzie.

'For his own protection,' Oliver said. 'Which allowed the newspapers to let loose "Ghastly Murder, Dreadful Mutilation, Capture of Leather Apron", and so on.'

'How distressing for the fellow.'

'Distressing my foot,' said Bertie. 'Hans is suing all the editors for libel. Playing dead ringer for the Whitechapel murderer was a stroke of luck just short of winning the Derby.'

'Dead ringer?' Mackenzie asked him, mystified.

'Double. Racing term. Not a corpse in a belfry.'

'Did you see this week's *BMJ* on the murders?' Oliver passed the *British Medical Journal* from a Gladstone like Bertie's. Mackenzie had a portmanteau in the van, the honour paid him being extended to staying at Sandringham overnight.

When any serious and unusually bloody deed is done, Bertie read the leading article, *the public, still possessed by the idea that the insane are all more or less fiendish, look for an insane agent. It is pretty certain that where a modern miracle takes place, or where any strange and uncanny performance occurs in a country village, a hysterical girl is at the bottom of it, and so there is some foundation for the belief in the unusual often being connected with insanity.*

Bertie skipped across the rest of the page. 'The *BMJ* seems to think the answer in Whitechapel is evening classes, organized athletics and flowers in the windows.' He handed it back to Oliver. 'I'd never have imagined dead whores to cause such a rumpus. Every vicarage in the country must have sent a letter to *The Times*. Clergymen have an interest in unfortunates which I find dashed suspicious.'

'Every respectable person in London must surely be concerned at such obscene, such violent murders occurring within a cab-ride of their own homes,' said Mackenzie severely.

'Only because every respectable person in London prefers staying blind to the rat-hole conditions of Whitechapel, and deaf to the scum who dare complain they are starving,' Bertie told him.

'I'm afraid it would need a duchess decoyed there and ripped up for that,' suggested Oliver.

'You sound like Mr Bernard Shaw in the *Star*,' said Bertie.

'Who's Mr Bernard Shaw?' asked Mackenzie.

'A man described by Frederick Engels as a paradoxical *belletrist*, very talented and witty but absolutely useless as an economist and politician.'

'Who's Frederick Engels?' asked Oliver.

'A Rhinelander who wisely combined being very revolutionary with being very rich. He went to study the poor of Manchester, and hunted twice a week with the Cheshire.'

The special whistled its way non-stop. When they reached the tiny Norfolk station of Wolferton, they were on easy terms. Mackenzie reconciled himself that professional collaboration with Bertie could be no worse than with the Prussians.

A carriage and four was waiting. They drove a mile through the low-lying village and Dersingham Wood, to the Norwich Gates of the estate. As they crunched on royal gravel, Mackenzie showed an ease which was practised while the others' was affected. A long, low, many-gabled red-brick and stone house appeared through the carriage windows.

'The Queen bought this place for the Prince of Wales only to keep him out of mischief in London, you know,' Bertie gossiped. 'He has an allowance of a hundred thousand a year, and gets through it like a prairie fire. Everyone knows he's in the hands of the Jews. That's how the Rothschilds got into society. Not that I object to a Prince who would stand a champagne supper round his own death-bed.'

Mackenzie responded by coolly pointing out the Royal pigeon lofts.

Two frock-coated whiskered equerries waited under the gas globe of the stone porch, behind them the butler, three footmen, a pair of maids in black with lace caps and streamers. The Gladstones were seized, the hats and canes, Sir Morell Mackenzie's portmanteau instantly manhandled towards the Bachelors' Cottage beyond the lakes. Oliver gasped at the hall clock. 'We're half an hour late.'

'That's Sandringham time,' Mackenzie assured him com-placently. 'The clocks here are always kept thirty minutes fast.'

'Why?' demanded Bertie.

'Don't ask questions,' Oliver scolded him.

'Oliver, you are behaving like a nervous nursemaid. I shan't be sick on the carpet.'

Oliver muttered urgently, 'I hope you'll show proper re-spect in our patient's presence.'

'Surely you know you can rely on me to butter up abso-lutely anybody, whenever needed? Anyway, I gather our patient is such a simpleton that it was noticeable even when he was serving in the navy.'

They were shown to a cloakroom with hand-basins and a water-closet, which Bertie approved for mahogany-seated comfort. The equerries took them to a small panelled room on the far side of the hall, its table set with mineral water, a decanter of sherry, a silver basket of biscuits. Four other medical men were already waiting.

Reid of the bushy whiskers and rimless pince-nez, who almost daily had his finger on the Queen's pulse and his notions in her ears, introduced the pair of distinguished doctors thirty-five years his senior. Sir William Jenner had large eyebrows and a moustache drooping at the ends, his slit eyes giving him the look of a squat Mandarin. He found professional renown in 1850 by differentiating typhoid from typhus fever – which did not prevent the Prince Consort dying of it under his care a decade later. He was a teetotaller who swilled tea and nibbled raisins. He wore a high old-fashioned collar with a black cravat, and hobbled on a stick from a stroke the year before. He was touchy, curt and intol-erant, and Bertie knew he was the son of a Chatham inn-keeper.

Oliver and Bertie recognized Sir William Gull from the 'Ape' cartoon in *Vanity Fair*. Square-faced, heavy-featured, double-chinned, balding, head cocked sapiently forward, hands clasped over stomach, short and fat, the medical Nap-oleon. Witty, opinionated, overbearing, short-tempered, he was flippantly dismissive of any medical practice he disliked – including anaesthesia. He was rankly unpopular in the profession, and Bertie knew he was the son of an Essex wharfinger, who got an education by becoming usher at a school amid the Bermondsey docks.

The fourth was Dr Laking, about forty, the Prince of Wales's personal physician, who stood in the corner as irrelevant as a curate.

'Sir Morell has doubtless appraised you of the case, Mr Wilberforce,' Sir William Jenner started. All seven stood as solemnly as a clump of graveyard yews. 'The eldest son of the Prince of Wales has a lump in the neck, which we must explain as soon as possible.'

'Savages explain.' Gull corrected him waggishly. 'Science investigates.'

Jenner glared at his colleague. 'His Royal Highness Prince Edward first noticed the affliction on the eighth of June last, when at Cambridge to receive a Doctorate of Law, *honoris causa*. He travelled thence to York, to take command of his troop in the 10th Hussars. The nodule irked under the high collar of his uniform. He put it from his mind, having various civic ceremonies at York, until the end of the month. When I was called into consultation, I believed that the lump would disappear with the appropriate medicaments. My colleague, Sir William, was not of that mind.' He nodded at Gull disagreeably.

'I think everyone is aware of my opinion that the road to medical education lies through the pathology museum and not the apothecary's shop,' said Gull briskly. 'Clearly, Mr Wilberforce, there is a likelihood this painless lump – which has grown from the size of a hazel nut to that of a pigeon's egg – might be scrofula.'

'Then he's as good as cured,' Bertie interrupted. 'Scrofula being the King's Evil. It should be convenient enough, submitting it to the royal touch.'

Jenner and Gull looked startled. Gull continued to Oliver, 'But there is another possibility – the disease described in 1832 by Dr Hodgkin, the Quaker of Guy's. I can feel the tip of Prince Edward's spleen, indicating a preference for Hodgkin's disease.'

'I entirely fail to,' Jenner responded haughtily.

'That's because Sir William Gull was at Guy's,' suggested Bertie. 'They stick together. What do we say—? You can always tell a Guy's man, even if you can't tell him anything.'

The two royal physicians looked dumfounded. A man they had never heard of, a rag-and-bottle merchant, was daring to join their clinical discussion, and embellish it with medical student jokes. Practised at embarrassments in royal antechambers, Mackenzie snatched the trailing reins of conversation. 'Should it be a scrofulous lymph gland, it will suppurate and heal in time. Don't we see the scars of scrofula on the neck quite as commonly as those of smallpox on the cheeks? But Hodgkin's disease being invariably fatal within a year, I suggested from my experience with the late Emperor Frederick of Prussia that the gland be removed, and the correct diagnosis established by examination under the microscope.'

The door was opened by one of the frock-coated equerries 'We must go at once,' said Reid.

The party was led down a corridor into a large drawing-room furnished for comfort more than style. There were heads of stags round the walls, the fire was paled by sun through mullioned bow windows. The Prince of Wales sat in a crimson plush armchair, in Norfolk jacket and knickerbockers, smoking a cigar which Bertie's nose recognized as superior to any sniffed at Romano's. Princess Alexandra sat stiffly in a chair shaped like a scallop – pale, distressed, hands clasped tightly on a lace handkerchief in the lap of her brown silk morning dress.

'So you are the doctor-r-rs.' How often had Bertie heard that accent imitated!

All bowed. Oliver prayed Bertie would keep his lips shut. The audience extended barely beyond the newcomers' introductions. Bertie assumed the Prince only wanted to see if he liked the look of them. A clock struck one, indicating that it was half past twelve. Princess Alexandra led them to the room upstairs, quietly weeping, supported by two ladies-in-waiting. Laking trailed behind. The Prince of Wales stayed downstairs with his cigar.

The bedroom was large, containing a four-poster with embroidered hangings and much furniture. A space had been cleared by the window for a brand-new operating table on stout deal legs. The marble-topped washstand was filled with pewter basins, bottles and dressings. There were two nursing sisters in butcher-blue, their white caps as crisp as fresh rolls. The patient lay in bed in a cream silk nightshirt, clutching as a talisman a small wooden replica of a fearsomely antlered stag.

'Eddy darling, you must be brave,' directed Princess Alexandra timorously.

'Yes, Motherdear.'

The two royal doctors and Mackenzie flanked the bed. Oliver and Bertie prepared for the operation. Laking found a corner and stood in it. Jenner and Gull had charge of the case, decided the diagnosis, dictated the operation and would bring the patient through it. Oliver and Bertie had been summoned as a trapper and his ferrets by the gamekeeper to clear the Sandringham rabbits.

Prince was led from his bed by Princess, clasping his hand tightly. Leaving with her ladies-in-waiting, she addressed Oliver for the first time. 'He will stand the operation, I am sure. He has been built up for it.'

Oliver bowed.

Prince Albert Victor Christian Edward of Wales was twenty-four, thin, willowy, brown hair parted just left of centre, large-eyed with an upturned soft moustache and a vacant look. He mounted a chair placed by the nurses and calmly climbed on the table.

'Your Royal Highness, this smell will make you feel quite delightful, and you will float into a refreshing sleep,' Bertie assured him.

The operation was uncomplicated. Sir William Jenner again pumped the carbolic spray. Oliver made his incision along the edge of the diagonal neck-muscle, extracting the gland like a slimy red new potato, dropping it into Gull's jar of formalin. The blood was staunched, the wound stitched with carbolized catgut, a short rubber drainage tube inserted – as by Lister into the Queen's armpit.

'It may well heal by first intention,' Oliver gave his opinion. 'Our patient is of sound constitution and temperate habits.'

Lint and bandages were applied. It had taken under an hour. The Prince was still unconscious, breathing heavily. Reid and the sisters carried him back to bed. The Princess reappeared, clearly having wept throughout.

'The operation has been a complete success, ma'am.' Jenner announced proudly.

The equerry took Laking, Oliver and Bertie down to a small room with a luncheon of cold partridge and hock. They had seen the last of their patient. 'At least the royal hairdresser is allowed the satisfaction of observing his subject admire his handiwork in the glass,' Bertie grumbled.

As the footmen were serving the fruit, the equerry reappeared. 'His Royal Highness is recovering consciousness. Dr Reid presents his compliments, and requests your presence immediately. Not you, Dr Randolph.'

Bertie stared, fixed half out of his chair. The equerry smiled pleasantly. 'You may stay and enjoy your port in tranquillity.' Oliver said nothing. He threw a glance at Bertie's thunderous face and followed Laking to the room of their first meeting. The atmosphere was different. Reid was smiling, Gull had his hands in his pockets, Mackenzie smoked his stramonium cigarette, Jenner sat in an armchair munching some raisins.

'A good job of work, Wilberforce.' Reid seemed firmly in command. 'He'll be taking nourishment by and by, calves-foot jelly, blancmange and suchlike. In a week to a fortnight he'll be as right as rain, ready to get up and convalesce in the mild breezes of Osborne with his Grangran. Though first he'll have to show his face for a day or two in London, just to tell the population he's alive. Has Laking told you what lies behind all this?'

'I did not want to mention it in front of—' Laking nodded to where they had left Bertie eating a banana.

'This must by no account meet that young man's ears,' said Jenner angrily. 'We all have an impression of his utter untrustfulness.'

'Well, I gathered from Sir Morell a sad similarity between the case of this Prince and that of the Crown Prince of Prussia,' said Oliver.

Reid nodded briskly. 'If Prince Eddy suffers from scrofula he will recover with nothing worse than a scarred neck. If from Hodgkin's disease, he will be dead in twelve months.'

Gull held up the pot with the specimen. 'This leaves by courier within the hour to the Royal College of Physicians in Trafalgar Square. To be examined in secret by an expert in morbid anatomy.'

'Exactly as Virchow in Berlin,' said Mackenzie.

'If the microscope discloses fatal Hodgkin's,' continued Reid. 'Or if the report is indeterminate – then the way is open for Parliament to exclude Prince Eddy from the succession.'

Oliver gasped. He was unprepared for this forecast of a constitutional thunderbolt.

'Even if the report shows scrofula,' added Gull sombrely 'we doctors must lie for the good of our country, like diplomatists.'

'Let me explain,' Reid continued. 'The Queen is in her seventieth year, remarkably sound in physique—'

'If they're old they're tough,' quipped Gull. 'If they weren't tough, they wouldn't be old.'

'But her son the Prince of Wales is far from that. Eh, Laking? He admittedly enjoys a healthy corpulence, but cigars, champagne, banquets, *chemin de fer*, Mrs Langtry, Miss Margot Tennant, Miss Chamberlayne ...' Oliver had heard these names from Bertie. 'Enough to sap the strength of Hercules. And he is chesty, with a tendency to sugar diabetes. He may therefore undergo his funeral before his coronation.'

Oliver was lost. 'But why shouldn't Prince Eddy, even in

those melancholy circumstances, succeed his grandmother?'
Laking tapped his forehead.

'Prince Eddy is subject to mental unsoundness,' said Reid
bluntly. 'He suffers periodic attacks of moral mania.'

'He has a morbid perversion of the natural feelings,' added
Jenner pessimistically. 'Of the affections, inclinations,
temper, habits and moral disposition.'

'Though without any notable lesion of the intellect, or the
knowing and reasoning facilities,' qualified Gull, sagely
shaking his head.

'And without any maniacal hallucinations,' said Reid
more encouragingly.

Gull revealed darkly, 'He suffers erotomania.'

'He is subject to attacks of uncontrollable desire for sexual
intercourse,' said Jenner, more gloomily than when contemplating Hodgkin's disease. 'Though like all unfortunate
victims of the condition, he later expresses the greatest disgust and repugnance at his conduct.'

'How did this come to light?' Oliver asked wonderingly.

'While in the Navy,' Reid told him. 'On a cruise with
HMS *Bacchante*, in 1879. He went ashore at a Caribbean
island and tried to murder a native woman.'

'His tutor was J K Stephen, a most eccentric man,' explained Jenner. 'Wrote comic verses.'

'The Queen is of course devoted to her grandson Eddy,'
Reid continued. 'But that would not stop her forestalling a
disaster to the throne of England.'

'The Queen was devoted to her grandson William of
Prussia,' said Mackenzie. 'Since becoming the Kaiser, he has
rubbed *that* in the Queen's face until her eyes smart.'

'Prince Eddy anyway has no stomach for the throne,' said
Reid comfortably. 'He told a young American lady, he dis-
likes royal pomp, he prizes country life, he would gladly give
everything up for £3,000 a year and a decent house. His
brother George, who would then succeed, is of strong
character and constitition. Of quick wits – well, com-
paratively – brave and bluff, all that the English love in a
man.'

'John Bull in crown and ermine,' concurred Gull.

'The matter has become complicated through Prince Eddy falling in love with Princess Hélène of Orleans,' Reid disclosed. 'Even a completely sane prince of the royal blood cannot marry a Catholic.'

'Has not an alternative bride already been found?' inquired Gull. 'Princess May of Teck? But twenty-one years old, born here in England, in Kensington Palace and in the very same room as our Queen.'

'It is surely sad if so worthy a lady as Princess May were excluded from the throne through our prognostications,' said Oliver feelingly.

'We medical men cannot afford to be sentimental like circulating lady novelists,' Gull asserted.

'When shall we hear the result of the microscopical examination of the gland?' Oliver asked him.

'A week.'

'Virchow took only two days,' said Mackenzie.

Reid began polishing his pince-nez briskly with a silk handkerchief. 'I suggest, gentlemen, we play down the operation in the bulletin. No mention of Hodgkin's, naturally, even of scrofula.' The other five nodded. 'Nor do I think our colleague the anaesthetist need be troubled to sign it.' He raised an eyebrow at Oliver.

'As you wish,' Oliver said after a moment.

19

THE DECANTER of port stood untouched at Bertie's right elbow. A banana lay uneaten on his plate. As Oliver returned, he rose, threw down his napkin, and snapped, 'We must catch our train.'

'It's a special,' said Laking, behind. 'They wait for you.'

'I'm suffocated,' he said irately. 'Can a fellow walk on the terrace?'

Their Gladstones and hats shortly appeared, Mackenzie alone bade farewell. They clopped through the woods, Bertie saying nothing. The train was short, two first-class coaches, engine steaming hoarsely. There seemed no other passengers. The whistle brought a brace of pheasant from cover beside the track, they began chuffing along the coast towards Kings Lynn Junction.

'Why did you exclude me from that consultation?' demanded Bertie, scowling.

'*I* did not.' Oliver was cool, prepared for the attack. 'It was Reid.'

'What right had the man? He and I are both doctors, attending the same case.'

'My dear boy, you are getting yourself into a tremendous lather about this. You know how gossip comes from you as song from a bird? You revel in spreading stories at the Whitechapel. I admit, quite as much as we revel in hearing them. The small misfortunes of others always warm the ear more than their greatest achievements.'

'You told Reid that was my reputation?'

'I did not,' Oliver said calmly. 'I did not need to. Your reputation is all round medical London.'

He noticed Bertie accept the justice of the remark, and trim the flame of his anger.

'You are rather young to be the repository of State secrets,' Oliver continued consolingly.

'Secrets? What secrets?' asked Bertie at once.

'The illness of an heir to the throne is always a State secret,' said Oliver uneasily, annoyed by his own remark.

'Yes, a secret between the State and the newspapers,' Bertie said sarcastically. 'There's something fishy.'

'Of course there isn't,' said Oliver impatiently. 'Any royal illness attracts political overtones.'

'Like the balls Mackenzie made of Prince Fritz?' Bertie unexpectedly laughed. 'Great Caesar, Oliver! You lie like a housemaid who's broken a teacup. They'd never have commanded you to excise a fairly obvious scrofulous gland had they not *hoped* to find Hodgkin's. They want to see the last of Eddy. Who? Come on! I know my Hippocratic oath. Why shouldn't I be trusted with a prince's secrets any more than a pedlar's?'

'I gave my solemn word not to divulge our consultation after luncheon.'

Bertie laughed again. 'Not to me, you didn't.'

Oliver had left Sandringham resignedly knowing he might be letting Bertie into the conspiracy before they reached London. If Bertie wanted to know, Oliver had to tell. Now he had operated on royalty and been flattered with royal confidences, he felt more in Bertie's satanic power than on leaving St Pancras.

'If you so much as breathe a word, Bertie, I'll cut you for life.' Oliver added with a shrug, 'He's mad.'

Bertie looked disappointed. 'Everyone knows the Prince is backward. Does it matter? The most learned monarch has others to make up his mind for him.'

'He suffers moral mania.'

Bertie sat up. 'What type? Homicidal? I was reading it up only last week in Husband's *Forensic Medicine.*'

190

'No. Erotomania.'

Bertie slapped his thigh. 'I've a corking notion. Supposing he did the Whitechapel murders?'

'Bertie! You won't even show reverence when one day you find yourself in the presence of God. Or of the Devil, who I venture to suggest you venerate more.'

The train whistled past a level crossing on the table-flat countryside. The remark seemed to please Bertie. 'Don't look at me so sternly, old fellow. Have you ever had reason to mistrust me?' Oliver nodded agreement reluctantly. 'You're on your way to becoming tripe-butcher, By Appointment. I'll still be your butcher's boy, surely?'

'I wish I had your confidence in my own destiny. My bosom hides two traitors to my cause. One . . . is what you know about me. You may carry it unuttered to the grave, but nothing mocks a man like his own stupidity.' Bertie's expression did not change. 'The other is my wife.'

'She's easily scratched from the contest. Put on a show,' Bertie advised. 'Like your new carriage and pair. Give a soirée. She'll surely play lovey-dovey for an evening?'

'Will she?' Oliver asked bleakly.

'No woman acts disloyal to a man when her practical, feminine sense sees it puts money in both their pockets. Particularly if you have spoony music.'

'No, no, that would only be a satirical charade.'

'Why not? So is all society.'

Oliver fell silent. He wondered why he was so frightened of Bertie. They had once been close, if never enjoying the precious unrestraint of true friendship. Bertie was the man friendly to everyone and the friend of no one. 'Why don't we go out walking on Hampstead Heath?' Oliver suggested impulsively. 'Like we used to, when you were still a student? How about the last Sunday in the month? It should still be fine weather.'

'That's the day I'm travelling to Paris.'

'Again? Quite the English milord, aren't you?'

'I have family business to transact.' Bertie took the *Lancet* from his Gladstone. Oliver brought out that morning's *Times*. Both read for a while, but silence clothed Bertie like a hair shirt.

'Look at this!' Grinning, he pointed to the correspondence column. 'Letter from some Dr Winslow, apropos the Whitechapel murders. Patient sat in his consulting room with the remark, "I have a desire to kill everyone I meet." Doctor didn't believe him. So patient produced carving-knife, attempted to perform practical demonstration upon doctor.'

'You seem unhealthily preoccupied with the Whitechapel murders.'

'Do you remember telling me, Oliver, on those Hampstead walks, that *you* sometimes had an overpowering desire to kill someone?'

'We talked a lot of flummery in those days. Don't we all suppress an urge to push some solitary walker over a cliff? It's no more dangerous a disablement than clergyman's sore throat.'

Bertie closed the *Lancet* and replaced it in his bag. 'It was enough to make you wonder whether to give up your career,' he reminded Oliver. 'Perhaps to turn monk, or somehow put yourself out of harm's way for others.'

Oliver smiled. 'Well, I've killed no one yet, have I? Except in the way of business.'

They were lighting the gas-lamps as the train snorted into St Pancras. The rest of their conversation was amiable mockery of their colleagues at the Whitechapel.

The next morning, Bertie, pink and soapy, opened *The Times* in his hip-bath.

The bulletin headed the main page.

Sandringham
Friday, September 14 1888

His Royal Highness Prince Albert of Wales was this afternoon submitted to the surgical incision of an abscess under the left arm, incurred on duty with his regiment. The Prince

bore the operation excellently, and is expected to be conval-
escent within a week.

(*Signed*) *William Jenner*
William Gull
James Reid
Francis Laking
Oliver Wilberforce

Bertie hurled the newspaper across the bedroom, scat-
tering its pages against the towel-horse. 'Eradicated! As if
they'd taken me out and cut my throat,' he exclaimed to
Freshings, who stood startled beside him. 'No mention of
me. No mention of the anaesthetic. I'm treated as a servant
of servants. A skivvy not worth a name.'

Bertie sat back in the bath, squeezing his sponge fiercely.

'Bad news about someone what you know, sir?'

Bertie washed himself in silence. He shook his head, rising
from the water while Freshings held out the fresh Turkish
towel. 'I'm off to Paris on the thirtieth. Tell Mrs Anstey,' he
said shortly.

'Ain't I coming too?' Freshings asked eagerly.

His mind still afire from the insult, Bertie said off-handedly, 'I shan't need a man. I'm there barely long enough to
unpack.'

Togaing himself in the towel, Bertie advanced to his dressing-room. Freshings started stropping the razor. 'Shall I be
coming one day soon to Paris, sir?'

Controlling his words, Bertie told him, 'You're a scamp,
Freshings. You know too much about the can-can and the
ladies of easy virtue displaying themselves in the pavement
cafés.'

'Not so much about them as you, sir,' Freshings replied
with a grin.

Bertie's anger blazed. 'Hold your tongue! What do you
mean? A man of my position consorting with fancy pieces?'

Freshings looked alarmed. To defend himself, he said,
'Them's only the things I 'ear, sir.'

'What things?' Bertie seized him.

'Below stairs, sir . . .' Freshings stared at him, terrified. He said in a low voice, 'There's talk sometimes of the young women what you 'as come here.'

'How dare the servants gossip about my patients! *How dare they*! Any doing so again will be instantly dismissed, without a character. Tell them. And it includes Mrs Anstey. Why isn't my shaving tackle laid out properly? I've no tooth-powder. I'll shave myself this morning. Get out!'

As Bertie shaved he decided that he must rid himself of Freshings. Which could be awkward, the valet having a hold upon him somewhat like his own on Oliver Wilberforce. He should never have brought Mrs Floyd's recruits to Belgrave Square. Servants were not always the simpletons everyone assumed. Their gossip rose from below like the stink of drains, and likely to catch the nose of their betters. Besides, Bertie reflected, drawing the razor up his chubby cheek, economy if not prudence must soon give Freshings his quittance. Mr Ravin in Chancery Lane was growing restless over his little loans. Mr Ravin could puncture the festive balloon of his existence with the tip of a pen-nib.

Bertie did nothing to dislodge Freshings in the next fortnight. It was not his nature to embark readily on any activity likely to be paining, or tedious or socially complicated. The moment in the dressing-room, like the earlier one with the chloroform-mask became in the common interest of master and man forgotten.

After breakfast on Sunday, September 30, Bertie took the train from Charing Cross for the Folkestone boat. The weather had deteriorated overnight, the sea was surly, but he was a practised Channel passenger. He strode the deck amid emetic misery, cigar smoke snatched from his lips by the gale. He arrived in Paris in time for dinner. The bustle, noise and gaiety of a Continental Sunday immediately raised his spirits.

Bertie strolled the boulevard Poissonière towards Madame Landouzy's. His London clothes, his new overcoat with astrakhan collar, his gleaming hat, attracted the admiration of the café patrons as earlier in the year from Dr Sigmund Freud. Some of the cafés already had their winter's glass screens, at the corners white-aproned vendors with braziers sold paper cones of chestnuts. A fellow could live so unfussed in Paris, he thought. London was jolly, with plenty of men in whose company he felt at ease, and plenty of women who felt so in his. But London could be damnably stuffy. A Parisian doctor flaunting a mistress would be thought only enviably fashionable. Oliver walked in terror of society discovering he was a normal man. How could people grow concerned about morality, Bertie thought, when it was only a matter of geography?

Madame Landouzy received him in her tiny room with a glass of her best cognac. They talked about General Boulanger again. 'Boulangism is not a party,' she told Bertie in French. 'It is only a personal ambition. But he will nevertheless triumph. The masses have little confidence in parliamentary government. But crying *Vive Boulanger!* does not mean *Vive* Philip VII, or Napoleon IV. It means only *Vive* something new. The *brav' général* is anyway impelled by moments of political crisis to disappear in the arms of his mistress, Madame de Bonnemains.'

She tinkled the handbell. 'I have a special package for you this time, Simone and Claudia. Simone is a cherub, pink with golden curls, she will send a man mad. Just twelve. Claudia you shall see for yourself. Both unseduced, that goes without saying.'

A maid brought the pair. The cherubic child was about to climb on Bertie's lap, when Madame Landouzy rebuked her. She had no right to such familiarity with a visiting gentleman. Claudia was a little older, a hunchback.

'Deformity is an attraction to many men,' Madame Landouzy remarked. Bertie nodded. The girl had Pott's disease, scrofula of the spine, first named by a London surgeon. 'They are difficult to get hold of, but I have had girls here with limbs twisted by rickets, who have done very well for themselves. And for their families, usually so poor they have appreciated it. I had a simple-minded girl once. Thirteen, but she looked five or six, and proved most popular. There are some men who would satisfy themselves with the gargoyles at the Notre Dame. There are other men who cannot satisfy themselves with anything less grotesque. I still have Lucienne here – you remember, a dwarf with tiny arms and legs and a big head, she is always busy. I once had a girl with both legs off, removed by the surgeons after an accident at Les Halles. She could have made a fortune, but the life did not suit her.'

Madame Landouzy rang the bell again. The girls were removed. Bertie handed her a bag of sovereigns. 'I shall take them tomorrow, by the night boat.'

'You will find little to amuse you in Paris,' she said apologetically. 'The new theatrical season is starting with revivals of the last one. By the way, the prefect of police is arresting rather freely the men and women who he claims to infest the boulevards.'

'An attack of morality?' Bertie inquired.

'Morals? Oh, no, we have a great exhibition approaching. Morals in Paris are directed by politics, like everything else.'

Bertie collected the girls the next afternoon in a fiacre, and drove to the Gare du Nord. They were excited and frightened, but from experience he knew that a pocketful of expensive sweets calmed their minds. They sat silent in the second-class carriage, overawed by a train. The three shared their compartment with a heavily built middle-aged lady in black, who could not prevent a whispered inquiry about '*La pauvre petite*'.

Bertie explained she had a curious affliction of which only a famous English doctor knew the cure. The other girl was her sister. The lady opened her purse and gave Claudia a Louis d'or. Bertie noted to take it from the child once they reached Boulogne.

The sea had hardly a white horse to break the darkness. The Channel packet was hissing steam, moving gently against the jetty, ropes creaking like a gate in the wind. The crowd of passengers picked their way across the railway tracks, blue-bloused porters shouldering their luggage. Bertie gathered the two against his coat. They stared wide-eyed at the ship. It was an object they had never seen before, even in a picture. At the foot of the steep gangway, a sailor was scrutinizing the tickets in the circle of a naptha flare. The usual pair of gendarmes stood in the darkness, hands on sword-hilts.

To Bertie's terror, they moved towards him.

'*Pardon, monsieur—*' The man asked for his papers.

'I need no papers,' Bertie replied in French, with arrogant simplicity. 'I am an Englishman.'

'Come with us, please.'

'I shall miss the boat,' he complained urgently.

'The boat cannot leave without our permission.'

One gendarme gripped his arm. The other took the hands of the two girls. The hunchback started to cry. Thought lay paralysed in Bertie's head. They reached a dockside shed, gaslight streaming through the small window. Inside at a trestle table a moustached man of military look in plain clothes was sitting on the only chair. Before him lay papers and a ledger. The rest of the space contained a prosperous looking man with an imperial in a black overcoat, and two nuns.

The man at the table brusquely asked Bertie in French to identify himself. Bertie slowly produced his card case. He was recovering his composure, he saw. His hand did not tremble.

'Why are you taking those little ones to England?' The children were big-eyed and thumb-biting, close to the gendarme's striped breeches.

'For treatment. I am a doctor. I know where the hunchback can be cured. The other child is to keep her company. It is unpleasant to be ill and alone in a strange land, you will agree?'

'You speak good French, doctor.'

'It is my privilege that my mother was French.'

The questioner jerked his head towards the children. 'Their parents know of this?'

'Of course.'

The man's mouth twitched disagreeably. 'For the same

197

reason, you brought two other children through this port six months ago?'

'Yes. Both were patients. All illness does not sit so obviously as upon that misshapen one.'

'Why take them to English doctors? Are French ones imbeciles?'

'English doctors specialize in different diseases.'

'Let us stop this comedy. The *Sûreté Générale* know you collected these females from the rue des Verres Dalles in Paris this afternoon. Look, here is the telegram. Are you a doctor? Or are you a quack from a fair? Your practice seems restricted to taking young girls from a well known brothel in Paris, assumedly to one equally well known in London.'

Bertie saw the man with the imperial looking as though at the Devil. The policemen and the nuns had an air of detached interest. Bertie supposed he was just another of the malefactors who came regularly to the attention of all four. He declared, 'I am a British subject, and refuse to submit to this insolent interrogation. If I am not released immediately, I demand you summon the British consul.'

'What do you want doing with him?' the man at the desk asked the other casually.

'Why, he must be arrested and punished severely,' the man with the imperial replied furiously.

'That wouldn't be easy,' said the plain-clothes policeman, to Bertie's immense relief. 'We cannot check this story without involving the British police, who regard us as inferior beings. One cannot deal logically with people who have not forgotten the Battle of Waterloo.' He glared at Bertie.

'We must save these poor children from his evil clutches,' the bearded man persevered excitedly.

The plain-clothes policeman continued glaring. 'They are French subjects and present no problem.' He motioned to the nuns, who gathered the children. 'Monsieur here is a patron of the Society of St Ursula, devoted to the reclamation of fallen women. You may catch your boat, doctor.' He nodded sneeringly towards the door. 'Your description has been circulated to the ports of France. If you are seen again up to your tricks, you will be arrested, I assure you. Scotland Yard may take as long as they like to answer our inquiries, but you shall not be seeing daylight meanwhile.'

'I assume the gentleman is motivated by political considerations,' Bertie said in the direction of the philanthropist. 'I have never known a man perform an altruistic deed in this country unless sure of a substantial reward.'

'Good evening, monsieur,' said the policeman.

'As for you, I assume your usual bribe has been either delayed or thought inadequate.'

'Good evening, monsieur.'

'You have infringed the liberty of one of Her Majesty's subjects,' said Bertie thunderously. 'The Foreign Office shall hear of it in the morning.'

The detective nodded to a gendarme. Bertie found himself outside the hut. He heard through the window the children crying that he was the nice gentleman who gave them sweets.

On deck, portmanteau at his feet, Bertie watched the fading harbour lights bobbing with the motion of the ship.

'A close shave,' he muttered. 'A close shave, indeed.'

He sweated in the cold mid-Channel night.

20

'I DO DECLARE, there's nowhere like this in Edinburgh,' said Janet Veale. 'What's it called?'

'The Café Vaudeville, but never anything but Romano's,' Bertie told her.

She looked round with the level-headed assessment of a thoroughly educated Scotswoman. 'What sort of persons would take their meals here?'

'The *demi-monde,* sprinkled with respectability by the *haut.*'

They were at one of the tiny tables towards the inner end of the 'shooting gallery'. It was ten o'clock on the next night, Tuesday, October 2. Outside was cold, wet and gusty. Inside was smoky, noisy with the clatter of dishes, the loud conversation and louder laughter. No one had yet started throwing hard-boiled eggs.

'All the waiters are foreign,' Janet noticed.

'A lot of young Frenchmen slip over to London, to avoid conscription.'

She carefully unfolded her coned napkin, tucking one corner into the belt of her crimson silk dress, smoothing it purposefully over her knees. 'It must be *very* expensive. And I'm *dreadfully* hungry. I usually have my tea at six. Why did you ask me here?'

'A man always likes to be seen with a pretty woman.'

'Go on with you,' she said in a sensible voice.

'May I call you Janet?'

'Naturally you can, I'm a modern woman. Away from the hospital, of course. And you shall be Bertie. Didn't you miss all the fun?' she consoled him. '*Two* murders in the wee hours of Sunday. We performed the post-mortems yesterday afternoon.'

A black-moustached young waiter, white apron to his boot-tips, handed them the menu.

'My, it's in French,' she exclaimed. 'What's *bisque d'homard?*'

'Lobster soup. I strongly recommend it. Then, if I may suggest, an entrée of *cerveau vinaigrette*, which is stewed brains with capers. Afterwards, you must try *filet à Romano*. A heavenly beefsteak.'

Her eyes shone. Bertie wondered if from admiration at his casual worldliness, or the prospect of food after missing her usual six o'clock high tea. Taking Janet Veale – as wholesome as an oatcake – to a raffish resort like Romano's he thought a spiffing jape, though knowledgeable men said the Scots were a sensuous race, particularly the red-headed, sweaty ones. 'My usual champagne,' he told the waiter, handing back the menu. 'The Roman knows which *marque*.'

'We had a *most* interesting case today. A mother had been treating her baby's septic ophthalmia with *cold tea* – would you believe it? She brought it to the receiving-room with eyes nothing but pits of pus, and only then because the lens had popped out like a little clear jujube, and was sticking to its cheek. It died almost at once.'

'I'm more interested in the murders.'

'Well, the first body was found at one o'clock on Sunday morning, near the Socialist Working Men's Club in Berner Street. Which is between the hospital and the Tilbury railway line. Still warm. An unfortunate, like the others. We found cheese and potatoes in her stomach, partly digested. She had a little packet of cachous in her hand, so she'd not struggled in self-defence. Her throat was cut, right across, severing carotid and jugular, cutting the windpipe in two. It was as if the murderer wanted her head, like the other woman. But he must have been disturbed, there were no mutilations.'

The waiter served from a tureen the pink, aromatic soup laced with brandy. The somelier poured champagne.

'I've never tasted wine before,' Janet confessed, as Bertie raised his glass. 'My father allows whisky in the house *strictly* for medicinal purposes, though fortunately with a large family someone is always ill. Mmmm! Such a lovely tingle going down.'

'It was described by its inventor as swallowing stars.'

'*Shooting* stars,' she agreed enthusiastically. 'I should like to drink it every day of my life.'

'And so you shall, if you sup every day with me.'

'You would find that *dreadfully* boring.'

'No, I shouldn't,' he told her, serious-faced. 'Modesty in itself is a powerful allurement. And I have a flair for transforming women by patient tuition. I could make you turn men's minds with desire, as belladona causes delirium.'

From her uncertain smile, he saw she wondered whether he was bantering, or uttering some exciting fragment of truth. Bertie was not sure himself. Such eager simplicity he found fascinating. It was like Candy's.

'Now the *other* murder,' Janet continued, wriggling back into the comfortable shell of her profession, 'was found within the half hour. At Mitre Square on the edge of the City, fifteen minutes walk away from the first. Throat cut, sterno cleido mastoid muscle sliced like a boiled kipper. The knife went with such a force, it nicked the vertebral bone behind. This soup is *delicious!*'

They looked up, laughter and cheers busting from the tables nearest the door. Two rolls sailed through the cigar-misted air, someone started singing *Never Introduce Your Donah to a Pal* – a donah was also a sweetheart. From the Strand came a short fat man in opera cape and top hat, and a striking dark young woman with nipped waist, trailing skirts of pink silk, bulging corsage and vast hat.

'Who's that?' asked Janet.

'Bessie Bellwood. There's a first night at the Adephi.'

'Who's Bessie Bellwood?'

'An actress, a singer, a music hall turn, an Irish slut called Katharine Mahoney and an intimate friend of the Duke of Manchester.'

'My, I am seeing life. There was a great jagged cut from her pudendum muliebre to her breastbone, swerving right to avoid the umbilicus. The liver was an awful mess, cut in three places, the intestines were severed at the root of the mesentery and laid over the right shoulder like the last case. A length of small gut had been chopped off completely, and put between the left arm and the body. The uterus had gone, with the adjacent tissues from the bladder and vagina. So had the left kidney. To find those organs by touch in the dark *must* mean he's a medical man.'

Bertie laughed. 'If a doctor feels like killing somebody, he can do it any day in his life with far less trouble.' The waiter removed their soup plates. 'He could have been a *shochet* from the Whitechapel slaughterhouses. That's one of the Jews' ritual butchers. They make a great song and dance about killing their dinners, roping the animals and cutting their throats with tremendous politeness.'

'There were snicks in the middle of both her lower eyelids,' Janet said thoughtfully. 'Which could have been ritualistic. Her nose had been nearly cut off, by the by, and her right ear lobe. There's another thing. A bloodstained rag was found during the night, in the open staircase of some flats near Mitre Square. High on the wall was chalked in writing like a schoolboy's, "The Juwes are the men that will not be blamed for nothing". He spelt Jews "Juwes", and started some of the words with capitals.'

'A valuable clue,' agreed Bertie.

'It *could* have been. But we heard from Inspector Abberline that Sir Charles Warren – the police commissioner himself – ordered it sponged out. That very night, before it could even be photographed. He was afraid of anti-Jewish riots. That house could have been wrecked before sun-up. Oh, the East End was like Paris in the Revolution last Sunday.'

'People always want someone's blood, when they are angry only at their own terror.'

The waiter served the soft yellowish calves' brains, speckled with parsley and dotted with capers. 'And do you know,' Janet said forcefully, 'that female with her guts all over her bodice had been locked up at nine o'clock that very night, as drunk and disorderly in Bishopsgate Police station. Yes! They let her loose after midnight, when she'd sobered up. Why, they remember she walked out saying, 'Night, old cock,' to the sergeant, and disappeared towards Mitre Square. It's disgraceful. In Edinburgh, they'd have kept her for the sheriff's court in the morning.'

'How do you like your brains?'

'Scrumptious.'

'Wasn't there some confusion between the police forces? The first body being in the Metropolitan Police area, the more elaborate murder being under the independent City Police?'

'If you ask me, there's more red tape in the police than the army. By the time they've written their reports to one another, the murderer's on his way to China. He's got a name now, hasn't he? "Jack the Ripper." Did you see that letter he sent to the news agency? It was in Monday's papers?'

Bertie shook his head. 'I was travelling on Monday.'

Janet set down knife and fork, producing a strip of newsprint from her handbag. 'I'm collecting every scrap about the murders and sending them home to Scotland, where they're much appreciated. Though they can't give the full mutilations, nor even mention the uterus. You have to read the *Lancet* for that.'

'The residents of Belgravia are trying to get the newsboys' shouts stopped, as too trying on gentlefolk's nerves.'

Bertie read the reproduced letter.

25 Sept 1888

Dear Boss

I keep on hearing the police have caught me but they won't fix me just yet. I have laughed when they look so clever and talk about being on the right track. That joke about Leather Apron gave me real fits. I am down on whores and I shant quit ripping them till I do get buckled. Grand work the last job was. I gave the lady no time to squeal. How can they catch me now. I love my work and want to start again. You will soon hear of me with my funny little games. I saved some of the proper red stuff in a ginger beer bottle over the last job to write with but it went thick like glue and I can't use it. Red ink is fit enough I hope ha ha. The next job I do I shall clip the ladys ears off and send to the police officers just for jolly wouldnt you. Keep this letter back till I do a bit more work then give it out straight. My knife is nice and sharp I want to get to work right away if I get a chance. Good luck.

Yours truly,
Jack the Ripper

Don't mind me giving the trade name wasnt good enough to post this before I got all the red ink off my hands curse it. No luck yet they say I am a doctor now ha ha.

'Now, there's another funny thing,' she told Bertie, as he handed the clipping back. 'Both those women, like the last one with the toenail, had been treated at the Whitechapel. They'd been having a fight, and ended in the receiving-room. One of Mr Wilberforce's students remembered the names, because you chloroformed one and asked afterwards how they'd got on.'

'Evre'ting all right, Mister Doctor Randolph?' The Roman was at their table. Bertie introduced Janet. He bowed deeply. 'A great pleasure, Missus Doctor. Soon there will be missus doctors everywhere, eh? You marka my words. The Roman, he take to a missus doctor. More sympathy than a man doctor, eh? Soft hands, not so cold. There's a gentleman like to see you,' he told Bertie. 'An American. A detective. He arrive specially to catch Jacka the Ripper. I tell him you famous doctor at the Whitechapel Hospital, just right for the Ripper. He may be one of your patients?'

The Roman found this possibility amusing. Bertie noticed a man his own age with a pale, drawn face, a black moustache drooping towards a bony jaw, and eyebrows so close he had a look of constant anxiety. He wore a good quality brown suit braided with silk, buttoned high on his chest, a turned-down collar and a brown satin tie. He said at once, 'Cyrus B Scutter, Pinkerton's National Detective Agency, 191 and 193 Fifth Avenue Chicago, motto *We Never Sleep*, the greatest in the world.'

'Charmed,' said Bertie. The Roman produced an extra chair. 'Champagne?' Bertie invited.

'Whisky.'

Bertie introduced Janet. 'Was not your agency founded by this lady's compatriot, one Allan Pinkerton from the Gorbals of Glasgow?'

Scutter nodded. Bertie assessed his face worth ten dollars a game at the poker table. 'Forty years back. Still runs on the same principles. We never operate for reward contingent on success. We never compromise with thieves,' he recited. 'We do not investigate public officials in the performance of their duties, nor trade union officers. We do not accept employment from one political party against another, nor from crusaders against vice. We do not investigate cases of divorce, or others of a scandalous nature. We never investigate the morals of a woman, unless in connection with another crime.'

'And you've a good line in strike-breaking, too,' said Bertie blandly.

'A lie, sir,' Scutter told him evenly. 'Our uniformed guard service protects mines, plants, transportation systems, race tracks, any private property. The railroad strikers at Clinton last June were wrecking the locomotives and dynamiting the tracks. You'd expect some blood and thunder. And I guess Scotland Yard has its own methods,' he added slyly.

'Bloody Sunday, last year in Trafalgar Square?' Bertie looked unaccustomedly chastened. Sir Charles Warren, brought from commanding the army in Africa to commanding the police in London, had called out the Life Guards against the East End mob. As the Home Secretary had picked Warren to organize the Metropolitan Police like a regiment, to stiffen it with military men, Bertie never expected such a commander to chase nimbly a ghoul who flitted round the Whitechapel kitchen-midden after shiftless old whores.

The waiter brought Scutter's whisky. In a single movement, the American raised the glass, emptied it, and replaced it on the cloth. Janet looked alarmed, as if he were next to spit on the floor.

'And you're going to capture Jack the Ripper?' she asked.

'Reckon I've a good chance, lady. Pinkerton's caught the Texas train robbers last winter. We saved Mr Lincoln from the Baltimore plot in 1861. We broke up the Mollie Maguires in Pennsylvania. Your Mr Gladstone called us in to apprehend the Fenian assassins in 1882, but Scotland Yard kept us out. As they're keeping me out right now.'

'They're rather embarrassed with help,' Janet excused the Yard. 'Mostly daft. People suggest policemen shave off their moustaches and dress in skirts. Or put all Whitechapel harlots in chain-mail wired to electric batteries, to give the Ripper a nasty shock through his knife.'

'Dummies with spring arms, to grab the Ripper like an octopus.' Bertie laughed. 'Read the letters in *The Times*, and you'll know why England produced *Alice in Wonderland*. I notice that respectable ladies in large numbers are offering to walk the Whitechapel streets as decoys. I suspected all women are harlots at heart.'

'Dr Randolph!' exclaimed Janet, wagging her finger playfully.

'And bloodhounds.' Scutter pulled out a large, noisy watch. 'Week today, Hyde Park, before breakfast, dog trials. They reckon it's the only way they'll catch the Ripper. Got to be moving along. I've a party to see in Whitechapel. If there's anything you want to tell me, I'm at Brown's.'

'Bloodhounds?' murmured Bertie, when they were alone. 'My only new information is of that dreadful fellow Mr Lusk from Alderney Road in Mile End recruiting a Whitechapel Vigilance Committee. A terrible busybody, always sticking his nose into hospital affairs. Not even a gentleman, but a tradesman.'

As the waiter served their steak, Janet sighed, 'How can I

tolerate my lodgings again in Crouch End? To be regaled, as they light the gas in the evening, with cold ham and mustard pickles?'

'The peaches in kirsch – a Hungarian liqueur – are delicious,' Bertie remarked. 'Does Dr Dalhouse mean anything to you?'

'Not a thing.'

'Nor to me, nor to anyone at the Whitechapel. An unseemly fellow. Most enlightened doctors want to *kill* germs. He nurtures them, like a sow her piglets.'

She shivered. 'I do wish he'd leave me alone. He follows me *everywhere*.'

'You are far too valuable and delicate an article of femininity to be wasted on Tom Dalhouse.'

She gave the same uncertain smile. 'You know, he really does frighten me sometimes. He looks at me . . . as though he wanted to kill me, cook me and eat me, like a cannibal. He could be Jack the Ripper!'

Bertie laughed. 'Only one thing's certain about the Ripper. If he's killing prostitutes today, it'll be peeresses tomorrow. You in Scotland wouldn't understand it. But every successful man of enterprise in England is an incorrigible social climber.'

IT WAS a week later, eight-thirty in the morning. Despite the hour and hard frost, a crowd big enough for a prize fight had collected on the open grass beyond the Serpentine, north of the gallopers in Rotten Row. The news of the bloodhound trials had escaped, and any event connected with Jack the Ripper brought Londoners from their doors. In Mitre Square, the inhabitants had the best earnings of their lives, hiring their windows as a peepshow upon the bloodstained corner.

Beside a knot of carriages was gathered a blue mass of policemen, in the middle the commissioner Sir Charles Warren on a brown, finely-groomed horse. He was tall, straight-backed, droopy-moustached, in a flat-topped brown bowler, wearing a monocle. Bertie recognized him from cartoons in the papers, their virulence rising with the public anger. He was addressing from the saddle a group of men busy with notebooks. Policemen kept onlookers at their distance, but Bertie's clothes and air of assurance brought him within earshot.

'The objective,' Warren told the reporters,' is to trace the criminal by means of dogs. There are the dogs.'

His riding-crop indicated a squat man in a black bowler, a long white calico coat and a heavy muffler. On his forked leash, two dogs groomed as handsomely as the commissioner's horse, their leather collars gleaming with brass, sat obediently staring ahead, tongues dangling.

'The dogs' names are Barnaby and Burgho,' Warren explained. 'The breeder is Mr Brough, of Scarborough. I will demonstrate how the pursuit of criminals is effected by means of dogs by volunteering myself as the quarry. The plan is simple. They smell my clothing. I proceed some distance away, possibly taking cover behind a tree. The dogs will follow my scent. The ability of bloodhounds to trace people is, I believe, uncanny. We shall patrol Whitechapel with several couple of these animals. Should another murder be committed, they will be unleashed within minutes to track the assassin, wherever he may be. Any questions?'

There were no questions. Sir Charles Warren dismounted. The dogs sniffed him. He departed among the trees at a run. The dogs were cast off, stuck their muzzles to the ground and tails in the air and trotted after the commissioner, who was visible only as a brown hat poked round a distant elm. Bertie became aware of the American from Romano's beside him. He wore a brown bowler with a well-curled rim, and carried a carpet bag.

'Do Pinkerton's employ bloodhounds?' Bertie asked.

'Pinkerton's don't need no help from dawgs.'

'I say,' exclaimed Bertie delightedly. 'There's a decoy.'

A small boy in a bowler hat which might have been his big brother's and a jacket which might have been his father's, carrying a basket almost as big as himself, had plodded unconcernedly into the circus. The London pavements were full of boys with baskets – baker's boys, greengrocer's, chandler's, cheesemonger's, all ambling, leaning, cheeking cooks, cadging ha'pence at the bottom of area steps. From everyday experience with dogs, the boy patted Barnaby's flat head while it sniffed his basket and Burgho licked his spotty face. He produced from under the oilcloth cover someone's Sally Lunn, and divided it in two. He then became aware of as many policemen pounding upon him as though he were Jack the Ripper.

The dogs sped from the blue-uniformed charge in opposite directions. The onlookers cheered as at the finish of a close Boat Race. The man in the calico coat shouted oaths, and told everyone the dogs were worth five pounds apiece. Sir Charles Warren shouted for his horse as urgently as Richard III. Once in the saddle, he searched for the dogs more desperately than for any fugitives from justice. The crowd was laughing like Dan Leno's audience at the Surrey music hall. The confectioner's boy had vanished like the dogs. 'Why can't you bring some reliable hounds, and not a pair of boudoir lapdogs?' Sir Charles Warren demanded furiously, riding pink-faced to the breeder.

'I'll have you know, both of them are champions,' thundered the Yorkshireman. 'And I want them back before I leave London. Call yourselves policemen! Oop in Yorkshire, you wouldn't get a job as a stray cat catcher.'

'Inspector Abberline!'

'Sir?'

'Dispatch a telegram to all police stations in London. To keep a sharp look-out for a couple of bloodhounds, answering to Burgho and Barnaby.' Sir Charles Warren removed his hat, mopping his sweat-plastered short black hair. 'Ah, dear me! Now *this* is bound to get in the newspapers, I suppose.'

'Care for a drink?' Bertie asked Scutter.

'Sure.'

They strolled towards the Running Footman behind Park Lane, Scutter expounding on the way about the cream of American criminals flowing to London.

'Why are we so honoured?' asked Bertie. 'Do they find, like Mr Henry James, company to match their particular intellect only in our country?'

'Fatter pickings, fewer pickers. No extradition law. And no Pinkerton's. Adam Worth, who did the big bank job in Boston, came to live over here in Piccadilly, right next to the house of Lord Palmerston. How about that? Pinkerton's reckon it was Worth who stole your Gainsborough painting of the Duchess of Devonshire in '76. We'll get it back for you some day. Jod Capman, counterfeiter and forger, was quite a man about London town. Yes, sir. Heard of Charles Bullard? Broke banks. Arrived in Liverpool, stole twenty thousand pounds from a pawnshop, married a pretty Irish barmaid called Kitty Flynn, started an American bar in Paris. Rue Scribe, if you're travelling.'

The pub was busy with early-rising servants from the

great Mayfair houses, tradesmen making their morning deliveries, and the threadbare-suited, shiny-bowlered, brass-watchchained men to be found in London bars at any hour, intensely transacting business, mostly illegal. Bertie led Scutter to the snuggery, with plush benches and bar separated by crimson curtain on brass rail above the counter.

'Whisky,' said Scutter.

Bertie ordered himself a glass of champagne. It was the only possible refreshment for a gentleman before luncheon.

Scutter unfolded from his carpet bag a sheet the size of a theatre poster, headed in large type METROPOLITAN POLICE. It carried the facsimile of the letter Bertie had read in Janet Veale's newspaper cutting. Below was a postcard, similarly posted in London to the Central News Agency in the City. Help was implored from anyone recognizing the handwriting. The disjointed, childish script said,

I was not codding dear old Boss when I gave you the tip. Youll hear about Saucy Jacks work tomorrow. Double event this time. Number one squealed a bit. Couldnt finish straight off. Had not time to get ears for police. Thanks for keeping last letter back till I got to work again.

Jack the Ripper.

'What gross flattery,' remarked Bertie. 'In Spain, the bull's ears are awarded the matador only for exceptional skill and a clean kill. They're hardly merited by our top bloodhound at Scotland Yard.'

'Those "rs" and "ns" are the form used by an educated man,' Scutter observed, finger tracing the level lines.

'Another American, perhaps? "Boss" is a word in your language, not ours. Those sort of letters are emptied into Scotland Yard by the sackful,' Bertie dismissed it. 'From pranksters, medical students, lunatics. The police had to print a special form of acknowledgement, with thanks.'

'This card was posted Sunday,' Scutter persisted. 'Nobody knew a "double event" had been perpetrated until they read

Monday's paper. Right? Only the murderer knew the police had kept back his first letter. Right again? Only the murderer knew he hadn't time to cut up the first victim. Sure, it's genuine.'

'How did you get your hands on the poster?'

'Same way I got this.'

He took from the bag a long sheet of buff lined foolscap, headed in print, METROPOLITAN POLICE, CRIMINAL INVESTIGATION DEPARTMENT, SCOTLAND YARD. The broad margin was marked *Central Officer's Special Report*, with lines below for subject and reference. It was covered with close writing in pencil, progressive untidiness indicating pressure to finish. The first line read *Whitechapel Murders. Suspects.*

'Copied for a bribe?' Bertie asked.

'Oh, sure. See – the Yard think any of seven could have done it. Hans Breugel, otherwise known as "Leather Apron—"'

'Mortuary porter at the Whitechapel Hospital,' said Bertie derisively. 'He sewed up the bodies, but hardly deserved a near-lynching for doing the murders.'

'Montague John Druitt—' Scutter's nail went along the page. 'A lawyer. From Oxford College. Now down in his luck, teaching school some place. Travels the country playing cricket. That's a kids' game?'

'No species is more inoffensive than the cricketer,' Bertie eliminated him.

'The police have special family information that he's mad. Number three, James Kenneth Stephen, Cambridge College, seems to be a poet. He's mad, too. Once tutor to Prince Albert, who's described here as feeble minded and a sexual degenerate. Maybe the two could be in it together?'

'My dear Pinkertonian,' Bertie exclaimed. 'Exactly the same just occurred to me. After all, the royals of English history murdered their subjects with more casualness than I'd cut my undesirable acquaintances. If the impulse to kill still circulates in the blue blood, how thoughtful of them to express it upon those who never would be missed, and would prefer the happy ease of Heaven as soon as possible.'

Scutter gulped his whisky.

'Sir William Withey Gull. Who's he?'

'The Queen's doctor. I expect he's as mad as a March leech.'

'Maybe the whole thing's a big royal hunting expedition, which the Yard is busy covering up?'

'Well it's happened before,' Bertie told him excitedly. 'In the 1560's, in Edinburgh. The Italian Rizzio, dragged from the skirts of Mary Queen of Scots, stabbed by a gang of noble murderers in the next room, all planned by her ghastly husband Darnley, who held the screaming Queen back, and her six months' pregnant . . .'

He sipped his champagne, savouring the vision like a robustly bloody Delacroix canvas.

'And within the year, Scutter, the Queen went to a midnight masque – alone. Darnley was getting over smallpox, abed in his mansion at Kirk o'Field. He was blown to bits by gunpowder. By the Earl of Bothwell, who the Queen was at that moment in bed with, and married within three months. There's always as many toadies eager to cover up a royal murder as to nose out a duchess's adultery. Any more?'

'Two. Klosowski. A Pole. A Whitechapel barber.'

'Mad as Sweeny Todd, I suppose?'

'And Dr Mikhail Ostrog. A Russian. Practises in Whitechapel. Maybe planted by the Okhrana, the Czar's secret police. They want to put the socialist Russian exiles in London in a poor light.'

Bertie sighed. 'The Russians! Overdoing it, as usual. Do you know, at the Albert Hall this week, they are giving concerts of forty-eight females playing twenty-four pianos, all at once. Remarkable, if not pleasing.'

The detective replaced paper and poster in his carpet bag, extracting an object like a metal T. 'It's a razor,' he explained. 'A safety razor. See – it unscrews. You fit in this piece of steel strip. There's a guard, to stop you cutting your chin. It's the latest.'

Bertie was fascinated with novelties. He twisted the heavy razor in his fingers. 'How do you strop the blade?'

'You don't. Throw it away, buy another. That's how we think in the States. The edge comes ready-whetted, by a secret process. Say, you're the smart fellow. You could do with one of these. Apart from a sm-o-oth shave like the hide of an Alabama water melon, think of the social uplift.' Bertie asked the price. 'Half-a-crown, same as Beecham's pills, and worth far more than a guinea a box.' He produced a small canvas sack. 'Why not give presents to your patients? They'll see you're a real go-ahead man. Yes, sir!' He dropped his voice. 'I can let you have a dozen for one pound.'

'I thought you worked for Pinkerton's?'

'Sure I do. But enterprise, my friend, need not be confined to the criminal classes.'

'I'll take the lot,' said Bertie admiringly.

Bertie gave the publican's boy threepence for delivering the sack to Freshings. He touched the spring of his watch. The morning was evaporating. He bid farewell to the American. It had clouded over and was cold enough for a flurry of snow, but he decided to walk. What a rum field of starters in the Ripper Stakes, he reflected as he passed the Iron Duke's Apsley House at Hyde Park Corner. The Prince Eddy-Stephen-Gull conspiracy had probably been put about by the republicans. Scotland Yard swallowed hungrily the bait of socialists, emigrés, Fenians, radicals, Catholics and others with mischievous ideas about the Empire. He was convinced Prince Eddy had not the inclination to swat a fly, nor the brains to know how.

Bertie had heard from Oliver, who he supposed had it from Mackenzie, that the Queen had urged the Marquis of Salisbury to make every prime ministerial effort in arresting the perpetrator of dreadful murders of unfortunate women of a bad class. The Ripper was being scorched by the high noon of domestic politics as Mackenzie himself by those of Europe. Bertie wondered what the Royal College of Physicians was making of Prince Eddy's lymph gland. Oliver had said yesterday the expert was baffled. Perhaps the maligned Prince was of use in revealing some disease hitherto unknown to science.

A German band was marching through the busy traffic from the direction of Kensington Gore, a dozen strong, in bright green, black-frogged short tunics and soft round hats, ponderously pumping out airs from *The Mikado*. There were fewer children in all the airy streets of Kensington than one single twisting alley in Whitechapel. Rosy faced and warmly clad, they were hurrying to bowl their hoops in the park, or obstructing him in their 'prams', pushed three abreast on the pavement by gossiping nursemaids. Off the main road, a group of tradesmen's or servants' offspring were skipping about the mews cobbles, singing to *Here We Go Round the Mulberry Bush—*

Hold your hat and hold your skirt,
Jack the Ripper wants a flirt.
He likes the girls all fat and ripe,
Turns them into butcher's tripe.

Two piping voices had mastered the second verse –

He may be a Yid or a sailor lad,
He may be a doctor ever so mad,
He plays with his knife, he plays with his chopper,
He'll never be caught by a London copper.

Passing into street-arabs' song, Bertie thought, was flattery awarded to Napoleon, Good King Wenceslas and the Grand Old Duke of York.

The back door of No. 2 Garden Gate was wide open, a one-horse closed van outside lettered in gold *The Belgravia Telephone Company*. Two men in waistcoats and bowlers were drawing into the house a length of thick lead-covered cable, instructed by a brisk, gingery young man in ulster and deerstalker.

'So you have taken my advice? You are installing the telephone.' Bertie was alone with Mrs Floyd in the pink drawing-room.

'Yes! A marvellous machine, isn't it? Most of my clients

know where to lay their hands on one these days. They can speak to me right across London – right across England – engaging whatever girl they fancy. I can offer a unique service. I think it quite justifies the cost.'

She wore a morning dress of coffee-coloured taffeta. Bertie stood before the fire, smoking a cigar.

'Why did you let them take those girls away from you so easily?' she asked. He had not seen her since returning from Paris, preferring to send by Freshings a letter of half-dozen sheets. 'Couldn't you have stuck to your story? The French police don't care to meddle with Englishmen.'

'Possibly. But I don't care to meddle with the police of any nationality.'

'Perhaps you had better let a few months pass until next time.'

'There won't be a next time.'

'Bertie! Wash the milk off your liver.' She enjoined courage.

'You're hard on me, Angela.'

He looked so despondent, she patted his cheek and said, 'Dear Bertie! I'm sorry. I'm sure the fuss'll soon blow over. Whole nations suffer attacks of remorse like men and women, but in time slip back to their pleasantly wicked ways. Or we'll find you another route, perhaps through Marseilles. I know they're very easy down there.' She added abruptly, 'Mary Kelly was here this morning.'

'Oh? What was she after?' he asked sharply.

'What do you suppose? Money.'

'What happened to the man she went to live with in Camberwell?'

'What happens to any of the men my girls go to live with? After six months he got tired, and threw her out. She threw herself out, more likely. Opening her legs to all and sundry.'

'I suppose whoredom's a habit as difficult to break as any other. Did she want to come back here?'

'You should have seen her! Dirty, frumpish, only twenty-four but her teeth going and her complexion's like raw beef. It's the satin. She was groggy, even at breakfast time. I wouldn't have her back, if she looked like Marie Lloyd at the Oxford. Always putting on airs and graces, saying she'd been kept by a French nobleman, when she couldn't recognize a word of French,' Mrs Floyd asserted contemptuously. 'She was from Welsh Wales, married at sixteen to a man killed down the pit.' .

'She could make trouble for you,' Bertie warned.

'Any girl I row with could make trouble for me. It doesn't give me wrinkles. The word of a canary isn't worth that of a costermonger. If anyone listened to Mary Kelly, I've plenty of friends in the right places to hush them up.'

'I found her for you in the hospital. She might go back there and spin tales.' He flicked cigar ash into the fire. 'How's Candy?'

'You're putting ideas in her head,' Mrs Floyd complained. 'You'd think she was going to marry an earl next Saturday.'

'Isn't it a kindness, giving these girls something to look forward to, even the end of the rainbow?'

Mrs Floyd shook her head firmly. 'Much better they don't think further than the next pair of gooseberries coming at them.' Her genteel speech allowed no mention of testicles.

'I wanted her to help me with a joke, that's all,' he protested.

'You *are* blue today, Bertie.'

'My affairs aren't going well. I'm getting damned short of money.'

'Retrenchment and reform,' she suggested.

'I haven't your resolve, nor your way of organizing things,' he said despondently.

'I could lend you a little. Though it was a severe loss you incurred me with Madame Landouzy,' she reminded him in a businesslike way.

He slowly shook his head. Reaching for her fingers, he pressed them to his lips. 'It is as hard for me to have ambitions, as for a man up to his neck in quicksand – apart from the ambition of getting out of it. But you and I could make a future and a fortune together.'

'You would badly tolerate a wife, Bertie.'

'I should badly tolerate playing the husband, which is not quite the same thing.'

She looked up at him, smiling. 'Would you be flattered if I said you were the only man in London I could take as one?'

'Not flattered. Frightened.'

She laughed. 'When they hang you, Bertie, you'll drop with a joke on your lips.'

'As I cannot discern the fortune, and prefer to avert my eyes from the future, perhaps I shall set up shop as a country surgeon, and you can assist me.'

'How?'

'Giving the choloroform.'

She laughed again. 'Well, I'd have no reputation to make.'

Bertie kissed her, taking her in his arms as she pressed tight against him. So unusual an excursion into sentimentality at No. 2 was broken by the front-door bell. Mrs Floyd tore away, to see that a girl was dressed and ready. Frosty mornings always brought a glow to gentlemen's genitals.

22

THERE WERE always loiterers outside the front railings of the Whitechapel Hospital. The chance was never far of someone arriving on a shutter, or sagging between two policemen, or fighting drunk. Accompanying relatives and friends were always emerging to be quizzed closely on sufferers' progress. Twice a day, a blue-uniformed porter would leave the portico with authoritative step to amend the names written against those of the wards in a frame on the main gate. This was the 'dangerous list', whose relatives might visit any hour, instead of the prescribed single one on Sunday and Wednesday afternoons. Once 'gated' recovery was almost unknown. 'On the gate and dying nicely', sisters would report cosily to the doctors.

The crowd outside in the autumn of 1888 would have fitted a horse-race. The railings became a more powerful magnet from the wide belief Jack the Ripper was a doctor, the necessary instruments of his frenzy carried in the familiar little black bag. Any well-dressed man with a serious air and a Gladstone was likely to be suspected, sometimes arrested, occasionally mobbed. A senior City clerk, bringing home his supper liver in such stateliness, spent an anguished night in the cells.

At nine on the morning of Monday, October 15, Tom Dalhouse walked with usual jauntiness from the Metropolitan Railway Station across India Road to the hospital. He wore bowler and overcoat and carried his bag. His mind was lost on the problems of growing diptheria bacilli in nutritive broth. His ears unheeded cries of, 'That's 'im!' quickly amplified as, 'That's the Ripper!' He was instantly in the middle of a pointing, yelling crowd, hostile – and worse – insanitary.

'What the devil – !'

'That's Jack! Fetch a copper!'

' 'Oo's Jack?'

'That young 'un. Look at 'is bag.'

' 'Anging's too good for 'im.'

'You can tell, can't yer, by that shifty look?'

'Let me through at once,' Tom demanded, frightened. 'I'm a doctor at this hospital.'

This remark increased the surrounding excitement. Men waved fists under his nose, there was no blue helmet within his frantic glance. A strong, black-coated arm was suddenly thrust protectively in front of him, and a voice with a thick accent commanded, 'Stand back, my brothers. I know this gentleman. He is no more the Ripper than I am.'

These words silenced the mob as easily as the bag had aroused it. Tom found himself facing a sturdy, cheerful, red-bearded man in an astrakhan hat. 'Dr Dalhouse, I believe?' he asked courteously. Tom nodded, escaping quickly into the forecourt. His rescuer strode closely beside him. 'I have been following the inquests on these drab creatures. I have the honour to share the same profession as you, sir.'

'What hospital are you from?' asked Tom automatically, still shaking.

'St Petersburg. I thank God every morning that the hospitality of England matches the unsociability of the Czar. I practise our art here in a narrow way. I am well-known in Whitechapel for giving advice, if not medicine, which is beyond the pockets of these poor people. But this work means nothing, nothing, to one who has in his possession the elixir of life.'

'I beg your pardon?' said Tom.

'It is a secret which I brought to my exile.' The Russian stopped, taking Tom's lapel, looking closely in his face. Tom inhaled the stench of garlic. 'A mixture of strange herbs, rare metals, infusions of little-known plants. It is a compound known only to Russians of the Caucassian basin, who may not succeed in shunning God's company for ever, but delay their introduction considerably.'

'I – I must be getting along.' Tom tried to detach his fingers. The Russian grasped the other lapel, and drew him closer.

'I have the prescription, all the directions for manufacture, locked in a safe place,' he continued in a fierce whisper. 'It needs but one item for me to bestow upon the world its greatest blessing since the birth of Christ.'

'What?' asked Tom weakly, aware his heels were being lifted from the cobbles.

'Money,' he hissed.

'I haven't got very much,' Tom apologized hastily.

The Russian chuckled 'We shall grow richer than all the rulers of the earth put together. Just find me a little money, Dr Dalhouse,' he wheedled.

Tom tried to struggle free. 'If you give me your card – '

'I have no cards, nor my patients silver salvers. My name is Dr Mikhail Ostrog.'

A porter appeared to amend the names on the gate. The Russian vanished into the crowd. Tom smoothed his lapels. His was a sheltered, scholarly vocation, and he had suffered more threatened assault in ten minutes than in a lifetime. 'Mad!' he muttered. 'The man's mad. Absolutely certifiable.' He hurried towards his little triangular laboratory, a haven from a world which seemed always indifferent and often unfriendly. Still in his mittens, Tom set a match to the fire and blew on his fingers. The door opened without a knock, and Bertie entered.

'Deuced cold in here, old chap.'

'I don't notice the temperature when I'm busy,' Tom told him curtly.

'Then you should go as Nansen's medical officer in Greenland. Still messing about with bugs?'

'The future of medicine is in those test-tubes.' Tom told him defiantly. Never patient with Bertie, that harrowing morning Tom found him intolerable.

'Not so long ago, its future lay in bleeding patients white. And before that in casting out devils. Medicine is as much subject to fashion, dear boy, as millinery.' Bertie drew his cigar case from the pocket of his frock-coat.

'Typhoid and cholera are caused by micro-organisms, exactly as broken legs by runaway carts in the street,' Tom declared in exasperation.

Bertie took one of the newspaper spills on the narrow cast-iron mantelpiece, which Tom kept to light his Bunsen burner, and dug it into the infant fire. Tom felt hate of Bertie like pain. He hated his sleek look, his slick manners, his insulting fashionable airs, his damnable condescension. And his flagrant prosperity. How it galled a conscientious demonstrator of morbid anatomy, living in lodgings in Holloway Road, on £2 a year from each student who thought it worth troubling with his lectures, with no solace but a bottle of ale with his supper and a pipeful of tobacco after it, and feminine intimacy a fantasy. 'What do you want of me, Randolph?'

Bertie lit his cigar. 'Of you? Nothing. I'm looking for Dr Veale.'

Tom's anger burned white as steel in a crucible.

'She's a corker, isn't she?' Bertie gave his opinion. 'Good biz for you, enjoying her company exclusively.'

'The relationship of Dr Veale and myself is strictly professional.'

'Gammon! Everyone knows you're as thick as two Jews on payday.'

'Randolph, you will withdraw your insinuation of the slightest impropriety between myself and Dr Veale,' Tom demanded furiously. 'Or take the consequences.'

'What consequences?'

Tom wondered.

Bertie was unable to hate, but he thought Tom a deucedly dreary fellow. He despised his reachmedown clothes, his foul tobacco, his patched boots, his stained fingers, his aggressive poverty.

'I shall give you a bloody nose, sir.' Tom believed from his reading this was how to put it.

'That is hardly the way for one doctor to address another,' Bertie said wearily. 'Or even one gentleman another.'

Tom stood silent, clenched fists at his sides.

'Did Dr Veale mention our supper at Romano's?' Bertie asked casually.

'Romano's!' spat Tom. 'You took her there? A lady? It's nothing but an antechamber of Hell.'

'Possibly, but it serves excellent lobster soup.'

'Please leave my laboratory.'

Bertie sighed. 'How inhospitable you pathologists are. Honestly, I don't believe you love your fellow man until he's dead. Tell Dr Veale to telephone me, there's a good chap. The number is Belgravia 12. I really don't know how I should exist without the machine.'

Bertie left. Tom slumped on the hard, round, spoke-backed chair, head bowed, hands clasped knuckle-white between his knees. His life was made bearable only through germs and Dr Veale. Without these living organisms – one so simple to be only a single cell, the other so complex he could not conceive how to understand it – he might as well cast himself into the Thames.

In his narrow Holloway bed, chilled like the grave with loneliness, he saw himself one day as famous as Koch and Pasteur, applauded by scientists, admired by kings, fawned upon by head waiters in places like Romano's. At his side was the delicious Janet, no longer his post-mortem assistant but his wife. It now occurred to Tom that he had made no start on the complicated diplomacy inducing her to make this change of status. He had felt there was plenty of time. The last few minutes indicated it a matter of extreme urgency.

Tom rubbed his strawlike hair with his knuckles. He had no sure notion of how to court a lady, particularly one so self-assured as Janet. He pulled out the thick, loud-ticking silver-plated watch which Bertie called a turnip. As she was never late, he decided that she had gone directly to the post-mortem room. He crossed the courtyard with the manhole, and found her in leather apron, post-mortem knife in hand.

Hans still worked there, while counting his expectations from the Queen's Bench. He had no reason to quit the employment he so enjoyed. He was sponging the body of a girl about sixteen, emaciated, breasts as flat as saucers, hair of gold hanging three feet over the head of the table to the floor.

'Good morning, Dr Dalhouse,' Janet greeted him. 'A horse fell on my omnibus, breaking a shaft. There was no end of a fuss.'

'What's the case?'

'Phthisis.'

Janet stuck the bayonet-point of the knife through the faint fuzz of pubic hair. With a steady, continuous stroke she cut upwards through the wall of the abdomen, the skin of the chest, and the neck to the point of the chin.

'Whose?'

'Dr Porter-Hartley's.'

'When did she die?'

'In the small hours. That's when most do, don't they? After midnight comes the period of minimum vital energy, and the dying cannot respond to the rallying of vital energies for a new day. Did you know, Dr Dalhouse, that the great majority of seizures by cholera are between midnight and six in the morning? In bad epidemics, people are afraid to go to bed.'

Tom was not listening.

Hans passed her a two-bladed saw with the outline of a drawn champagne cork. 'No, I shan't be needing the Hey's. The rib cartilages are young enough to slit with a knife. We're going to find some pretty commodious cavities by all accounts, Dr Dalhouse. She's been bringing up sputum by the cupful, and there's ulcers in the larynx.'

'Hans, leave the room,' Tom directed. The German made obediently for the door, wiping his hands on a bloody rag.

Janet blinked at him. 'And why are we to be alone?'

'I have something confidential to tell you, Dr Veale.'

'Oh? Ah! I know. About Jack the Ripper?' She nodded

after Hans. 'You heard the latest shave round the hospital? It's Jill the Ripper.'

'No?'

Janet drew out the pale, small heart, the glistening windpipe with its rings of cartilage like the whalebone stiffening a muslin dress. 'Yes, they say she's a midwife, a body who wouldn't be suspected out at night, even with blood on her apron. Though for a midwife to take a woman's uterus is like a blacksmith stealing shoes from a horse.'

The neck was open like a gutted fish, the two muscles wasted to a pair of ribbons, the voice-box poking forward like the fore of Nelson's hat.

'Why did you consent to pass an evening with Dr Randolph?' Tom snapped.

Janet paused, looked at him, and continued pulling windpipe, gullet and tongue through the neck.

'Everyone in the hospital knows that Randolph is nothing but a spiv,' he continued angrily.

'I shall go with whom I like, thank you, Dr Dalhouse,' she told him calmly. 'And that is not a very nice way to describe a colleague dedicated to cheering us all up.'

Tom felt a snap in his head, like the flying asunder of a driving-chain. He clutched Janet violently, pressing his dry, bristly lips on hers. Her cry was stifled, her knife clattered to the floor, the organs slipped back into the chest with a slither and glug.

'I love you, Janet, I adore you, I cannot live another day without you.' His breath panted like the bellows on a feeble fire.

'Let me go!' She was frightened.

His hand went under her skirt, leather apron and all. He felt lisle stockings, garters at the knee, smooth hot flesh – He became aware that she was screaming. He slapped his hand over her mouth. She bit it.

'God –!' He leapt back, holding the ball of his thumb.

'What *has* come over you, Dr Dalhouse?' she asked with curiosity.

'I'm sorry, I'm dreadfully sorry, horribly, terribly sorry,' he muttered. Head bowed, he clasped handkerchief to wound. 'I don't know what possessed me. Oh, heavens! Can you forgive me? What have I done?'

She assessed him for some seconds. 'You are not yourself this morning, Dr Dalhouse.'

'I had a brainstorm.'

'You had best go and rest in a darkened room,' she advised.

He nodded silently. He crept miserably from the mortuary. Hans had vanished. He crossed the courtyard, wondering if he and the Russian in the forecourt should be confined together as lunatics. How horrifyingly easily, he thought bitterly, a man can be torn from the favourable state of a regular life, one with unexcited passions, by morally disturbing influences. He stopped to inspect the wound. It was less severe than it felt. Viewing the four punctures of her teeth upon his body gave him a delicious tingling.

He found a young woman outside his laboratory. She had the appearance of being lost. She was pretty, but pinched, with an unhealthy raw flush. Her red dress was unkempt, her bonnet tied with frayed ribbon, over her shoulders lay a stained black shawl, which she fingered nervously.

'Oh, sir –'

Tom paused, handkerchief still held to ball of thumb. 'What is it?' he asked hastily. 'Are you a patient?'

'No, sir. Leastways, I'm not no longer. I'm looking for Dr Randolph, sir. One of the nurses said he'd gone this way.' She added timorously, 'I know I shouldn't be here, sir.'

Tom turned. He had intended to hide in the laboratory, dress his wound and salve his feelings, assess the damage to his reputation, perhaps his career. This was more interesting. Such a tatty young woman was not what one expected in Bertie's acquaintance.

'Why should you want to see Dr Randolph?' She looked more frightened. 'Come, my good girl. You can tell me. I am very close with Dr Randolph.'

'I need some money, sir.'

'Money? From him?' She nodded. Tom saw a sister and nurse approaching down the long corridor. He opened his laboratory door. 'Through here, and look sharp.' Inside, he demanded, 'What's the game, between you and Dr Randolph?'

'I don't want to get into no trouble,' she replied sullenly.

'I can promise you won't.'

'I used to be one of the girls at No. 2.'

'No. 2 what?'

'Garden Gate, sir. By the Albert Hall.' Tom frowned. She was surprised at any gentleman in London ignorant of the address. 'It's well known.'

'What is it?'

'A house, sir.'

'Doubtless.'

'A bawdy house, sir. Dr Randolph's always there, seeing that we haven't the pox.'

'Great Caesar!'

She turned towards the door in alarm.

'Stay!' commanded Tom. '*Why* are you in a position to demand money from Dr Randolph?'

As she said nothing, he felt with his unbitten hand for a coin in his waistcoat pocket. It was to last him a fortnight, to be distributed in pence, ha'pennies and farthings for tobacco, beer and newspapers. He would eagerly spend it on something smelling nasty for Bertie.

'A bright pound,' she muttered reverently.

He closed his fingers on it.

'He did me a wrong, sir. He ruined a gal's life. He brought me to work there. He often does, with gals what take his fancy. He found me sitting in the surgery hall. I'd come to the 'orspital with pain in my side, but the doctors said it was only the cramps.'

'By God! Or are you a wicked woman, making up a string of lies?' he demanded ferociously. 'What's your name? Where do you come from?'

'Mary Kelly, sir. I'm living at Miller's Court, No. 13. It's off Dorset Street, across Commercial Road from the church.'

She felt in the velvet bag hanging from her wrist. 'Here, sir, you'll see I speak the truth.'

Tom took a folded square of white paper, recognizing Bertie's handwriting and his address embossed at the head.

'I found it at No. 2,' she explained, adding like a respectable servant girl, 'the day what I gave in my notice.'

The letter was dated February 10, 1888. Tom read,

Dearest Angela,

Today I have found a real stunner at the hospital. A country girl, by her talk. Corn haired, apple cheeked, teats like ripe pumpkins. Too much to hope she is virgo intacta! But she'll make a fine fuck if she does her lessons at your school of Venus. I think I've enticed her to call on me. If not, I shall find her name in the surgery book, and trace her in the Whitechapel rat holes. Once you see her, I know you'll feel terribly generous towards me. More about her soon, I hope.

Your devoted,

Bertie

Tom whistled. 'But this is utterly scandalous. May I keep it?'

Her lips trembled. 'I dursn't –'

'I must,' he insisted. 'You're getting a sovereign, aren't you?'

He was interrupted by violent knocking on the laboratory door. A six-foot policeman stood outside. 'Dr Dalhouse, sir? Come at once. A terrible thing 'as 'appened. In the mortuary, sir.'

'My God!' cried Tom. His frenzied brain saw Janet on the floor in a lake of blood, having cut her throat with the postmortem knife, either from shame or remorse. 'Is she dead?'

'Dead?' The policeman looked puzzled. 'And buried.'

Tom stuffed the letter in his pocket, hastily telling the policeman he would follow. He grabbed Mary Kelly's arm.

'Go straight down that corridor and leave the hospital at once. If you're questioned, say your mother's on the danger-ous list.'

'My couter, sir!' she cried, palm stretched imploringly for the sovereign.

Tom pressed the coin into it. The pair separated in op-posite directions. In the courtyard, the policeman was talking to another outside the mortuary. The fever gate was open. Janet was inside among the coffins. There was another policeman and Inspector Abberline. Tom recognized a slight, ferret-faced man in deerstalker and inverness as Mr George Lusk, often seen about the hospital and depicted in the *Illus-trated London News* as chairman of the Whitechapel Vigil-ance Committee. He was pale, leaning against the pitch-pine wall, hand to brow.

'Ah, Dr Dalhouse,' Inspector Abberline greeted him. 'This was delivered to Mr Lusk this morning, sir. By the mail, to Leman Street police station.'

Janet looked up from the sodden scrap of paper in her hand. 'It's a human kidney, Dr Dalhouse. Or rather, half a kidney. A *ginny* kidney. Just as you'd expect to find in a drunken creature like Eddows. You'll remember, she was the one with the kidney gone.'

Janet kneaded the organ with her finger-tips. 'It's from a body I'd say about forty years old, and Eddows was forty-three by all accounts. It's afflicted with advanced Bright's disease – and so was the one left behind. Look, there's an inch of kidney pedicle attached, with the renal artery and vein. I *distinctly* recall, the other two inches were present in the body. It fits like a Chinese puzzle, doesn't it?'

She sniffed the kidney close to her nose. '*Definitely* re-moved post-mortem, within the past two or three weeks, and preserved in spirit a few hours after its extraction. A speci-men in very good condition,' she ended approvingly. 'Fit for any pathological museum.'

'Read this, sir.' Inspector Abberline thrust a crumpled sheet of yellowish cheap paper to Tom. He deciphered the scrawl.

Mr Lusk
Sir
I send you half the Kidne I took from one women pra-
sarved it for you the other piece I fried and ate it was very
nise I may send you the bloody knif that I took it out if you
only wate a whil longer
        signed
                    Catch me when you can Mishter Lusk

Tom's eyes went back to the address. It said,

From hell.

The eventful morning was already too much for his mind.
Now it overcame his stomach. He retched, and vomited his
breakfast into the empty shell which had borne the eviscerated young girl's body next door.

'Dr Dalhouse is not *at all* himself today,' Janet explained
to the others. 'I diagnose that he is suffering from over-
heating of the blood. He needs to go straight home, for a
long lie-down under an ice-bag.'

23

THE LONG-CASE CLOCK in Bertie's drawing-room tinged
nine. It was the evening of Thursday, November 8. The fire
was lit but low. It was the mildest November since 1771, the
first week's fog had cleared to the residual mist which sof-
tened the outline of London rooftops all winter. He sat in an
armchair in tail-coat and starched shirt and white tie, ready
to go out. He was reading a letter just delivered.

Dear Dr Randolph!
    I cannot express through the cold steel of a pen-nib my
warmth of gratitude for yet another box of delightful cigars.
And an English briar pipe, of impeccable straight grain. I
am the envy of colleagues obliged to puff the grotesque con-
traptions sold in the shadow of St Stephen's.
    Your letter did not break to me news of the White-
chapel murders, which had already excited the Viennese
press. I find an interesting comparison with the ritual mur-
ders in Hungary of 1883. These were similarly blamed
on the Jews. Anti-semitism, of course, flows through Vienna
like the Danube. The cause of this phenomenon, to which
mankind is either unthinkingly accustomed, or impotently
resigned, lies deeper than the Crucifixion, even deeper
than the circumstance of Jews forever being immi-
grants.
    Much resentment is caused by these immigrants main-
taining tight, aloof, communities with their own customs,
religion, even foods. Less consciously, Jews are resented as
the harbingers of Christianity. What is Christianity, but a
layer as brittle as hardened sugar on the primitive religions
deep in the storehouse of the mind? The Gospels are stories

about Jews, propagated by Jews. And circumcision does not help, reminding those left uncut of castration.

Mr Jack the Ripper I should diagnose as a case of necrophilia. That is, sexual love of the dead. This is related to lycanthropy – strictly, the transformation of man into wolf. The clinical condition of lycanthropy is manifested by a perverted appetite, a violent desire for raw flesh, preferably human. It is quite often seen in pregnant women. Clearly it is a form of hysteria, which deserves treatment like every other form, by hypnosis or suggestion.

Lycanthropy is mingled in the public mind with super-stitions about wer-wolves, witches, and the tiger-spirits which possess beings in the eastern lands of your Empire, who enter a state of automatism called latah. *Mr Ripper offers similiarities with the vampire, a popular demon of the Slavs. These innocent chiroptera are trapped, beheaded, and buried impaled on a stake in the grave of anyone dying from a wasting or bleeding illness. There is clearly a sexual ele-ment in a man becoming a bat and sucking a woman blood-less through her jugular vein. Hence the frisson Mr Ripper affords the respectable population.*

But for your letter I should have stayed ignorant about removal of the uterus, such organs not mentioned in our newspapers. I see this as a form of fetishism, preoccupation with inessential and secondary items for sexual satisfaction. Such as female underclothing (particularly if just worn), boots, furs, articles often associated with first sexual experi-ences, masturbation occurring with their aid.

In some cases, men must dress in the entire outfit of the female to achieve orgasm. Such patients are seldom of the antisocial type, and respond well to suggestion, particularly from a sympathetic sexual partner. Other men transvest as a ruse for voyeurism, *by which satisfaction comes from the secret observance of females* en déshabillé *or couples* in fla-grante delicto.

The perversions you mention – a liking for dwarfs, hunch-backs and the like – have much in common with necrophilia. But seeking intercourse with children or with animals are

233

examples of arrested sexuality, in which the symbol replaces the more intimidating normal. Mr Ripper may be wreaking revenge for the threat felt subconsciously in males that the female organ might bite off the male one during coitus, like a hungry monkey a banana – the vagina dentata. *This might indicate that Mr Ripper is like Plato and Michaelangelo a 'homosexual', a barbarously hybrid word for which I claim no responsibility.*

That people so often put their sexual urge and sexual organs to improper use may seem as illogical as milking a railway engine. But logical behavior is a fiction of those ignorant of the human mind.

The psychology of the thick-skinned, easygoing poor is different from ours. They suppress neither their natural instincts nor impulses, they endure privation wilh a feeling of community which we lack, they see Heaven as a more easeful and agreeable place than we who have pre-empted many of its comforts and lassitudes. Murder is thus hardly less familiar among them than their flea bites. Do not fear, Mr Ripper will soon be caught. Scotland Yard is the cleverest police department in the world.

Sincerely yours,

Freud

Bertie looked up. Freshings was at the door, a card on his salver. 'Shall I show the gentleman into the consulting-room, sir?'

Bertie laughed, reading the name. 'Why, he would catch a hundred diseases and die a thousand deaths before the night was out. Like all actors, Mr Bracegirdle is sensitive to the scenery. Show him up.'

George Bracegirdle apologized lavishly for appearing in street clothes. He had a black cutaway with black-and-white check trousers, a high wing collar, a lilac bow tie with crimson spots, and a dove-grey waistcoat which matched his spats.

'Straight from rehearsal, dear boy. No end of a rush.

234

Almost impossible to find a hansom. London's invaded by provincials and continentals. Can't complain, I suppose, they're our audiences.' He sat down briskly, drawing coattails over thighs. 'Utter disaster has struck.'

Bertie knew this might be any event from the demise of his whole family to being served a bad oyster.

'You've seen the bible this week?' George referred to the stage newspaper, *Era*. '*Another* version of *Jekyll and Hyde* has opened in London. Daniel Bandmann's, last night at the Opera Comique in the Strand. I expect you read all the notices? Luckily, it was terrible. He's an American, he played Jekyll with Buffalo Bill curls. The critics called the show crude and gruesome,' he continued with satisfaction. The world of George Bracegirdle, like that of all actors, was bounded by entrance, exit and the footlights.

'When the cast *shivered* in terror –' George demonstrated extravagantly. 'They brought the house down. It was far better than the pantomime. Then Bandmann presented every first-nighter with a free copy of his book on travelling the world, so the gods shouted, "Go back to Fiji!" '

He leant forward, tapping Bertie's knee, looking like Cassius. 'I'm going to play Mr Hyde as Jack the Ripper.'

'Property guts all over the stage?'

'I shall *suggest* all that. But I want to know what the Ripper looks like.'

'So does Sir Charles Warren.'

'I mean, I can form an idea from his haunts, his fellow denizens of Whitechapel. I got brilliant notices for my revival of Forbes-Robertson's *Dan'l Druce, Blacksmith* after spending twenty minutes in a village smithy when it came on to rain. Taking the tuppenny bus to the Bank would be quite enough for the lead in the Bancrofts' *Money*. I could do *The Corsican Brothers* like Irving himself, by passing Thomas Cook's ticket office. Whitechapel's your practice. Where should I go?'

'If you really want to wet your shoe-leather in blood, take the Metropolitan Railway to Whitechapel Station. Then try to find your way through the maze north of India Road, to

235

Brick Lane and Spitalfields Market. I'd advise you to dress plainly, and leave your valuables at home.'

'Thank you, dear boy. I've plenty of old clo', I assure you. And my valuables are already in safe keeping with uncle. It's been a poor summer. You're dining at the club?'

'I've a soirée in Wimpole Street.'

'I abhor "swarrying",' said George Bracegirdle, using the smart term. 'All talk and nothing to eat.'

'I hope the one tonight might be amusing.'

The actor left, gesticulating goodbyes from the steps as though acknowledging a tumultuous audience. Bertie followed when the London clocks were striking ten, an untidy succession of chimes lasting a minute or two. Oliver Wilberforce heard them in his shirt sleeves, tying his white tie before the pier glass in his dressing-room. As his wife appeared from the bedroom, he turned in surprise. The dressing-room was large enough for a bed, which he had first used when reaching home late. Now he slept there every night. She had not stepped into the room for months.

'The carriages will be arriving any minute, Oliver.'

'I see you've been painting.'

She made a slight irritated noise. 'It's all cant to be against painting.'

He turned back to the mirror. 'I daresay. It's not the paint that makes the Jezebel, no more than the spots the smallpox.'

Lavinia was tall like her husband, clear skinned, her light auburn hair piled and held by tortoiseshell combs. Her features had the severe regularity of a statue's. She wore a dark green silk gown, a wide matching band round the waist drawn behind in a bulky bow over her bustle, the neck edged with cream lace and cut square at the tops of her breasts. She displayed a double string of pearls and a brooch of tiny diamonds, all the jewellery she possessed. She carried a long Japanese fan. 'I can't go through with this evening.'

'A little late now, surely?' He was still adjusting his tie.

'This soirée was Bertie Randolph's idea, wasn't it?'

'Randolph's a scamp, but he knows the ways of society.'

'He's as many faces as a churchyard clock.' She pulled the

236

wrist of her white glove. 'Do you suppose for one moment, our putting on a show of connubial bliss among salvers of cold meat will convince a soul? Everyone in London knows we're estranged.'

'What's to stop a couple who are walking their own ways to retrace their steps?' He took his tail coat from the dumb-valet. 'Flaunting our sharing the same household is a chance to snuff the flame of scandal. Surely it's worth it? Mackenzie confides that I could be Surgeon-Extraordinary to the Queen with the New Year. That's as definite as a letter from Downing Street offering an alderman a knighthood. Then I've my eye on £15,000 a year, like Mackenzie.'

'Then I'm to live in this house to my dying day as your wife, yet be your housekeeper?'

Her unaccustomed finery, the wafted powder and scent, the rarity of intimacy in their conversation, made him feel that a strange woman had come to share his bedroom. 'Why should you not be my wife again?'

'How can you ask that?' she said sharply. 'Having our second child near killed me.'

'That's a future risk I have the knowledge to eliminate.'

'How disgusting! It was the sort of thing Adelaide Bartlett did, who murdered her husband. It all came out at the trial. A policeman found the ... articles in the dead man's trouser pocket.'

'That's only an excuse for your revulsion towards me.'

'I feel no revulsion towards you, Oliver. That's not fair. Should I otherwise humiliate myself this evening, by pretending affection before disbelievers, to help your own advancement?'

'Perhaps I should say your revulsion towards the act of love.'

'That's normal in a woman.' She was still playing with the edge of her glove. 'She must submit herself to the man's desires. I've done my duty enough.'

'That's a myth engendered by a conspiracy not to ask – or to admit – what any working girl would tell you in the street. The dissimulation of the middle-class is perfectly immoral.'

'How do you know about working girls?'

'From my profession.' He started stroking his sleeves with the clothes-brush. 'You equate gentility with purity, Lavinia, like everyone else we know. All agree that no passion is so enobling as love. All quake that it is a rosy mist hiding the danger of sexual activity. I cannot myself see anything dangerous even in unmarried couples behaving like normal humans. Yet many men – many eminent medical men – would be shocked at the prospect. Just as gravely, they warn schoolboys who play with themselves that their eyes will drop out. Is such enjoyment so dangerous? The mashers seem to have the best of health and spirits. No, Lavinia, what we middle-class really fear is slipping back to the free-and-easy promiscuity which marks the lower orders. We cherish the chastity and monogomy which distinguish ourselves from them, as the speech and walking on two legs which distinguishes us from the animals.'

'You're talking more like Bertie Randolph every week.'

He put down the clothes-brush, as a coach stopped on the cobbles. He took her arm. 'The performance as advertised shall now begin.'

A girl of three and a boy of four in their nightclothes waved delightedly through the banisters of the fourth-floor landing above. They were indulged by the smiling nursemaid to glimpse their parents descending to the splendour which had disrupted the house for a week. Oliver turned, blowing kisses. Lavinia gave a quick glance and stepped resolutely downstairs, flicking open her fan.

The chairs and sofas of the drawing-room which ran across the first floor had been swept round the walls. In the corner by the fireplace, four pinched-looking men in dress clothes surrounded the grand piano, tuning violin, cello and flute. In a smaller room overlooking the back garden, trestle tables with crisp white cloths bore beef, ham, game pies and lobsters, glasses, champagne and claret, a silver punchbowl. A room even smaller had been kept for gentlemen wishing to smoke. Oliver's eight domestic servants were supplemented for the night by four middle-aged maids in streamers, and a pair of footmen in mulberry tail coats and striped waistcoats, with the shifty air of footpads.

Oliver and Lavinia waited at the head of the stairs. Neither spoke. Lavinia was the daughter of a Gray's Inn solicitor. Though the wives of medical men surveyed the world from higher storeys each generation, their social sky shone through a smallish window. She could introduce to one another many doctors, a cleric and a don or two, a civil servant, a baronet with a sick wife and several men of affairs revealed on deeper acquaintance to be in trade. However indifferent she felt towards Oliver, Lavinia could not remain entirely so towards his possible journeys to Windsor and Osborne.

First came Ambrose Porter-Hartley and his ugly fat wife.

'I say, Oliver, what a grand show.' Ambrose's cheeks shook expressively. He lowered his voice. 'Must have cost you a pretty penny, eh?'

'Surely, providing for a man's friends is no more an extravagance than providing for his family?'

'I suppose not.' Ambrose's voice dropped further. 'Denver and Rio Grande Railroad. A snip at twenty-one and three-quarters. I was at my bankers this very afternoon.'

He took a glass of champagne from the footman's tray.

The guests arrived in a rush, announced raucously by the other footman. The drawing-room filled. Like every genteel gathering in London, they talked about Jack the Ripper.

'I would have the sensational placards banned, the newspapers censored,' Ambrose declared to a respectful circle. 'In the words of Horace, *Imberbus juvenis cereus in vitium flecti* – the beardless youth is wax for swaying to vice. I would add, *Segnius irritant animos demissa per aurem quam quae sunt oculis subjecta fidelibus et quae ipse sibi tradit spectator*. What enters by the ear influences minds more slowly than what is thrust before trusting eyes, or what the spectator seeks for himself,' he added for the benefit of those less lettered.

'God has ordained there must be poverty in the world,'

remarked a thin pale clergyman. 'But it is our duty to guard the sufferers of poverty from the taint of evil.'

'A most disgraceful peepshow was staged recently near the hospital in Whitechapel.' Ambrose extended his glass towards the footman's bottle. 'In which a demented curate was portrayed brandishing a revolver in a churchyard. And would you believe it? A week later, the local curate cut his rector's throat in bed!'

Horror was expressed at this deadly sequence.

'Never has wholesome family life been so precious to our country as today,' Ambrose continued. 'We must produce a plentitude of children, strong in body, quick in mind, and of high moral principles. Only thus may we counter the threat, growing every week, from Kaiser William and Prince Bismarck. We have but two hundred thousand men in our army. They have half a million.'

'Fortunately, our steel shield – the navy – requires fewer men than an army,' observed a belligerent-looking man with pockmarks on his face.

Ambrose wagged a finger. 'A keel for a keel, sir! That must be our policy. Kaiser William has *his* Imperial navy close at heart.'

'Yes, he dons his Grand Admiral's uniform to attend a performance of *The Flying Dutchman*,' the man said.

Heads were turned. Sir Morell and Lady Mackenzie were shaking hands with the Wilberforces. Everyone in London knew Mackenzie. He had even the prestige of an 'Ape' cartoon in *Vanity Fair*.

'How goes your book?' Oliver asked him. *The Fatal Illness of Frederick the Noble* had been out a month. He fancied Mackenzie winced.

'I cannot understand it. I expected to be praised to the skies, and it was reviewed with nothing but condemnation. You heard I was summoned like a schoolboy to appear before the Royal College of Physicians?' Oliver nodded. 'That was Sir James Paget's doing, of course. The surgical Czars are still after me with the knout. It is quite ridiculous to claim that I have violated professional etiquette. If I gave details of professional consultation, they are of historical importance. If I criticized my German colleagues, I was paying them back in their own coin. I shall *not* appear. I have instead removed my name from the College roll and returned my diploma. The book has meanwhile sold a hundred thousand copies,' he ended with satisfaction. 'If it has also been burned in public, I accept the compliment.'

Oliver asked quietly, 'Any news of Prince Eddy?'

'Only news which is no news. The pathologist has finally abandoned trying to diagnose the gland. It is not Hodgkin's. It could possibly be scrofula. It could be anything. Even syphilis. When he was sailing to such places as Teneriffe and the West Indies, it would have been no more difficult for the Prince to escape supervision for an hour than any other hot-blooded midshipman. Another means of achieving the aim of Court and Government must be found, though I shall not be party to it,' he said wearily. 'I have had my fill of royal intrigue. Did you hear that Sir Charles Warren has resigned as commissioner of police?'

'No!'

'It is to be announced in the House of Commons on Monday.'

'The seventh victim of the Ripper?'

'I hope the Ripper agrees. Seven being a mystic number might finally satisfy the fanatic.'

'Dr Bertram Randolph,' shouted the mulberry-coated footman on the stairs. 'And Miss Candace Farnaby.'

Oliver's mouth opened. Pale, over-painted, in a bright pink gown with gold sequins, Candy stood before him. Bertie beside her was bubbling with suppressed laughter, a schoolboy playing the best practical joke of the term. The whole house seem to have gone silent. Oliver could hear the quartet grinding out *Tales from the Vienna Woods.*

'I don't think we've met?' said Lavinia.

'No, ma'am, not that I knows – know of.'

Lavinia was puzzled. Why had Bertie brought a servant-girl? But no one could predict his behaviour. She wondered whether to feel insulted or pitying.

'Ullo.' Candy was smiling pertly at Oliver. 'Ever such a nice house you've got.'

'Do you *know* this young lady?' Lavinia asked him, frowning.

Oliver heard himself saying 'I know several of Bertie's friends from the theatre. Don't I, Bertie? Find her some champagne, there's a good chap.'

Bertie responded by singing softly in Oliver's ear, *'Two lovely black eyes. Oh! What a surprise!'* He seized Candy's elbow, and to Oliver's relief drew her into the crowd.

'Was I proper and right?' she whispered nervously.

'Proper? As proper as a novice new-shorn in a nunnery.' Bertie pinched her arm.

'I was scared out of my drawers that the gentleman might make a fuss and throw me downstairs.'

'Of course he wouldn't. I told you so. Any man has probably a hundred secrets he keeps from his wife. To be faced with them only one at a time is perfectly manageable.'

Bertie handed her a glass of champagne. She did not sip it. Champagne was something she had often seen but never tasted. 'Everyone's looking at me.'

'Why not? They don't see many pretty girls.'

'Do they think I'm a lady?'

'Of course. At the least, a type writer.'

She looked happier. She always believed Bertie.

Ambrose had moved from European politics to consulting-room sneak-thieves. 'These nuisances attend the houses of well-known consultants – I suffered from one only last month – pretending that a relative is ill, asking for notepaper to write an account of the imaginary patient in the waiting-room. Left alone by the servant, they proceed to snap up unconsidered trifles. One arrested recently for purloining a salver protested it was only plate, and not worth the trouble of his apprehension! Needless to say, that excuse could not have been made about *my* rooms.'

He was as usual addressing the picture-rail. 'Many steal visiting-cards. A doctor's name removes distrust from a housemaid's eyes, like an aristocratic one, or a military rank.

A greater pest is the medical beggar, who claims the kinship of medical school and reminds one touchingly of mutual help in hour of need. I was gratified to read a strong leader about it in the *Lancet* last week.'

'They were equally strong on the dangers of tight lacing,' said Bertie.

Ambrose's gaze came down. Candy stood smiling in front of him.

'Ullo, doctor. You're looking in the pink.'

His cheeks flapped like the wings of a trapped bird.

'*Who* are you?' barked his wife.

'A patient, Heloise' said Ambrose quickly.

'At the Whitechapel,' Candy agreed. 'Though I'm as right as a trivet now.'

'Good God!' gasped Ambrose, horrorstruck, matching Candy's two roles.

Heloise frowned, baffled. 'A *hospital* patient? Here?'

'Not a serious illness, I hope?' ventured the cleric.

'I'd blood in my spit. Better than having it in some other things, I suppose.'

'Are you from the Colonies?' asked the pockmarked man with curiosity. 'Australia?'

'Laws no, sir! I'm from Kent.'

' "Everybody knows Kent," ' he quoted, looking pleased with himself. ' "Apples, cherries, hops, and women." Mr Jingle, you know. Dickens, you know.'

'I should have guessed you were from the country,' the clergyman complimented her. 'By the wholesomeness of your complexion.'

'Wholesome? Me?' Candy laughed incredulously. 'Go on! I've been bang through the elephant.'

'The *Lancet* believes tight-lacing to make girls conspicuous but not attractive,' Ambrose continued in a distracted voice, eyes still on Candy. 'Incapable of taking sufficient exercise or food ... liable to become weak, pallid and chlorotic ... *De gustibus non est disputandum* – '

'Really, Ambrose,' said Bertie. 'Should we be discussing ladies' stays in the drawing-room?'

'Dr Randolph!' Heloise drew herself up. 'Your young lady is hungry. Kindly take her and feed her.'

Candy's eyes glistened as he obediently guided her into the supper-room. 'Lord sakes! What a spread! Enough for an army.'

Bertie filled a plate with pie, ham, beef, and mixed pickles. He introduced her to a man with a long white beard, who gratifyingly appeared to be stone deaf. He went to find Oliver and Ambrose. He had business to do, and time ran short.

Bertie tried motioning them into the smoking apartment. Oliver shook his head, and led them in silence down a flight of back stairs into his consulting-room.

'You swine,' he began furiously. 'Or lunatic. I don't know which. Fancy bringing that girl here. Your conduct is unbelievable.'

'You deserve a horsewhipping,' added Ambrose.

Bertie was aghast. 'You didn't take the joke seriously, surely?'

'Joke!' spat Oliver.

'Not so loud! My wife may have followed us down,' said Ambrose agitatedly.

'I thought it a capital wheeze,' Bertie said, mystified. 'There seems a lapse in your sense of humour.'

'You could have ruined us both,' said Ambrose angrily.

'You may still, unless you get that girl through the front door in a couple of shakes.' Oliver pointed a quivering finger.

'Oh, you're altogether too nervous.' Bertie lit a cigar, spinning the match with a flick into the banked fire. 'The respectable bourgeoisie upstairs wouldn't spot she's a trugmoldy warm from the whorehouse. Your wife will believe I'm playing some joke. I've the reputation for it. Women believe anything, if it saves them pain. Anyway, you've only yourself to blame.'

'I went to that loathsome place only as an unpleasant duty,' Ambrose said hotly. 'I did nothing to that girl except remonstrate on the evil of her ways.'

'Did you?' There was silence. The toreador's song from *Carmen* started over their heads. Bertie puffed his cigar. 'I know exactly what went on with both of you. There's a spy-hole in the room. It looked like a ventilator, if you'll recall.' He turned to Ambrose contemptuously. 'I've seen you naked as a worm, up to tricks your wife wouldn't credit, but might possibly appreciate.'

Ambrose's head jerked back. 'If . . . if you dared make that public, I should deny it utterly and sue you for libel. By God, I would! I'd take every penny you had. What jury would prefer the word of a rascal like you to mine?'

Oliver suggested more practically, 'You would ruin your-self, Bertie. You're in it as much as we are.'

'The difference is that I don't give a tinker's damn if I *am* ruined. Rather, there is nothing to ruin. Or pay in damages. I'm in the faeces, up to here.' He indicated his neck. 'I had a little visit earlier from Mr Ravin. A useful, even invaluable functionary, I'd not say otherwise. But a damn impatient one. "Just you be prompt, Dr Randolph, just you be prompt, and we'll be as brothers." '

Bertie imitated the Whitechapel accent. 'We've been having an argolbargol about it for weeks. By prompt, he now means Monday morning. Oh, the fellow has the right to everything I possess,' he said casually. 'And a good deal I don't. I'd be locked up in a pig's whisper. Can't say I blame the chappie, really. "The Jews are the men that will not be blamed for nothing," ' he quoted the words which had got round all London.

'What do you want?' asked Oliver briefly.

'A thousand pounds.'

'Impossible!'

'I've nothing like that,' cried Ambrose, as though Bertie had injured him physically.

'Listen, Bertie,' Oliver pleaded. 'This is no way to repay friendship – '

'Friendship? What friendship?' Bertie asked with unusual venom. 'I'm the man you snubbed tremendously at Sandringham. Now *I'm* in charge. That gives me more satisfaction than screwing money from you.'

'A loan?' suggested Ambrose weakly.

'Of course. I'm no cadger. Though on indefinite terms.' Bertie picked a human ulna from Oliver's desk, tapping the skull next to it in time with *Carmen.*

'You haven't thought very carefully.' Oliver had recovered the quicker of the two victims. 'Ambrose is perfectly right. Supposing you took this story to the newspapers, or the governors of Whitechapel Hospital, or a Member of Parliament? Who would believe it? The very day you faced bankruptcy and imprisonment for fraud?'

'Oh, it wouldn't be *my* feeble word, old chap. I have an account of all the times you came and left, all the money you spent, the girls you used, both of you. Mrs Floyd is a woman of business, and knows the importance of accurate records. They'd fit with the notes the policemen made.'

Oliver looked frightened. 'Policemen? What policemen?'

'There's one watching the house every night and most afternoons. It's a matter of courtesy to those excitable people so eager to stop such amusements, which divide pleasure and profit so admirably among its participants. The police reports are not heeded because someone is bribed for benign inactivity. He can equally easily be bribed into doing his duty. Your squalid little doings are neatly stored away in Scotland Yard, I can assure you, along with the latest news on Jack the Ripper.'

Ambrose and Oliver exchanged glances. Bertie continued beating time on the skull.

'It would take some days to raise such a sum,' muttered Ambrose miserably.

Bertie threw down the bone. 'I'd like the filthy delivered on Sunday night, please.'

'How do we know your silence will be permanent?' demanded Oliver, controlling his fury.

Bertie looked pained. 'Have you ever had cause to doubt my word as a gentleman?' He took out his watch. The chimes filled the consulting-room. 'Near midnight. I must take my lady home. She is allowed to the ball with the strictness applied to Cinderella. Besides, she's a night's work to do yet.'

24

A WOMAN'S SCREAM split the air like an express train whistle.

Bertie threw down the newspaper. It was teatime the following afternoon, Friday November 9, Lord Mayor's Day, when the new ruler of the City of London rode his golden coach through streets briefly given to merrymaking instead of moneymaking.

Bertie leapt for the drawing-room door, knocking over the 'curate's delight', the collapsible three-tiered cake-stand. 'Murder! Murder!' came frenziedly from the kitchen. He threw open the baize-covered hall door, and clattered down the flight of stone steps.

The stone-flagged basement was part of the house he visited only at Christmas and Mrs Anstey's birthday. There was a well-blacked range, a fire glowing, the kettle steaming, a Welsh dresser as heavy with cups as an autumn tree with apples, a deal table scrubbed near white. On a kitchen chair sat Nellie the housemaid, pale, weeping, blood gushing from her forearm. Tess the other maid was in the corner by the pots and pans, apron to face, howling. Mrs Anstey stood by the knife-grinder, looking dazed. On another chair sat Freshings, in his tail-coat and stiff collar, head bowed in hands, at his feet a bloody kitchen knife.

'Great God!' cried Bertie. 'Quick, a dishcloth! Or she'll bleed to death.'

He grabbed the housemaid's arm. Staring as though in the spell of laudanum, Mrs Anstey handed him a cloth. He twisted it into a tourniquet and pulled it tight above Nellie's elbow. She threw back her head and started screaming hysterically.

'Shut your face! he commanded. He shook her shoulders. 'Shut up!' He slapped her hard. She stopped. She stared dazedly across the kitchen towards the tradesmen's entrance, and the high-up arched, barred window next to the coal-hole, the proscenium for an endless show of boots and shoes. Tess went on sobbing. Mrs Anstey said quietly, 'Honest, sir, I don't know who he thinks he is, Jack the Ripper most likely.'

'Something queer came over me,' muttered Freshings, still staring at the floor.

'You damn near murdered this girl,' said Bertie ferociously.

'Murderin's too good for her,' he said sullenly. 'Faithless bitch.'

'I ain't!' screeched Nellie. 'There weren't nuffink between that feller and me. I wish I may die, if I said a word to 'im what I shouldn't. That's my Bible oath, Mr Freshings.'

'She's been making sheep's eyes at the postman,' Mrs Anstey exclaimed. She nodded towards the valet. 'Mind, sir, Mr Freshings is a man of hot blood.'

'Hold this tourniquet, and stop blubbing,' Bertie commanded Tess. He stared down at Freshings with arms folded and the expression of an Old Bailey judge in his black cap.

'I've suspected for some months, Freshings, that you've been helping yourself to a bit of whelk under my roof. That's right, isn't it? I shut my eyes to it, only because I have no wife, no dear children, to be corrupted by your disgusting behaviour. Now what do you do?'

His arm swept towards Nellie, bestower of the bit of whelk, now staring at Bertie with more terror than she had afforded to Freshings. 'You attack an innocent girl, because you are as much a prey to insane jealousy as an idiot epileptic to fits. Supposing you had struck truer? Supposing you had pierced the poor girl's heart –'

Nellie started screaming again.

'Had you thought of that? You'd have gone to dance the Paddington frisk, wouldn't you?' Bertie suggested hanging menacingly. 'Oh, do cork it, for God's sake,' he commanded the victim. 'You'd die of the hempen fever, Freshings, never thinking of the disgrace you brought on the house of your master, who took you in from the gutter and made you fit to black a gentleman's boots.' Bertie tossed a sovereign on the flagstones. 'There's the balance of a month's wages. Get out within the hour, or I'll turn you over to the police.'

The two women helped Nellie to the consulting-room door. Bertie inspected her arm on a white Turkish towel spread over the marble-topped table. She's lucky, he decided, no artery severed.

'I do feel queer, sir,' she murmured.

He soaked his handkerchief from a small brown bottle. 'This'll make you right as rain.'

She inhaled the chloroform. Her head sagged, a snore caught her throat, he let her sprawl over the table. He stitched the wound with fashionable catgut thread. Bertie always favoured the latest thing, professionally and socially. It would probably heal by secondary intention, he calculated. If it did not, someone would have to cut her arm off.

He waited with Nellie until she came round. Freshings had vanished. Bandaged and in a sling, Nellie still refused to spend the night in the house, lest her attacker return by the drainpipe. Bertie agreed on her going to mother in Lambeth, giving her five shillings for the hansom. Tess being obstinate about facing the murderer alone was freed to accompany her. While this domestic diplomacy was being conducted between them in the consulting-room, Bertie was aware of the doorbell ringing insistently. 'There's a Dr Dalhouse called to see you, sir,' said Mrs Anstey.

Bertie frowned. 'What the devil can *he* want?' Wiping a spot of blood from the sleeve of his frock coat with a sponge, he went into the hall.

'So, you at last give me the pleasure of receiving you in my own home?' Bertie tried to look agreeable.

Tom stared at him stonily. 'Where can we talk? Alone.'

'In this part of the world, it is customary to receive visitors in the drawing-room. Mrs Anstey, take Dr Dalhouse's coat. I must apologize for some household disturbance. There has been an accident in the kitchen. Luckily, not so serious as it might have been.'

Tom looked round the comfortable drawing-room up-stairs. Like all visitors from the Whitechapel, he wondered how Bertie managed. And *he* existed in two poky rooms with leaky windows and oilcloth floors within the shadow of Holloway Gaol.

'Take a pew.' Bertie replaced the overturned cake-stand.

'I'd prefer not.'

Bertie sat comfortably himself. 'Why am I honoured?'

'There's been another murder in Whitechapel.'

'So I saw.' Bertie picked up the evening paper he was reading. The headlines ran, *Another Whitechapel Horror. More Revolting Mutilation Than Ever.* The editor regretted underneath that he was yet unable to supply the details. Tom could.

'I have just come from Miller's Court,' he said. 'The police broke open the door with a pick-axe. The dead woman was lying on the bed, which almost filled the hovel. Her legs were apart, as though ... as though in the act of copulation. Her throat was cut, so that she was nearly de-capitated. Like the other cases. The nose was cut off. She had been scalped like a Red Indian. Both breasts had been sliced from the body, exposing the rib-cage beneath. They were lying on a table beside the bed. The left arm hung only by its skin. The muscles of her thighs had been cut and stripped, like a man picking the leg of a chicken. Their flesh had been arranged, with the nose, between the breasts on the table.'

Bertie offered his cigar case. Tom shook his head angrily. 'The abdominal wall was slashed in a crucifix. Other bits of her were hanging from picture-nails on the walls. The intes-tines and the liver had been cut from their peritoneal attach-ments and deposited between the legs. The left hand was thrust into the abdominal cavity, as though searching for the eviscerated organs. The uterus was missing. Perhaps that goes without saying? She was still wearing her chemise. The bedclothes had been drawn back neatly, her clothes folded carefully on a chair. She had been going to bed, for her own purposes. She was an unfortunate, that goes without saying, too. She had clearly no reason to feel an atom of fear about the foul murderer who shared the ghastly room. There was a fire in the grate. The embers were still warm. The man had been burning her skirt and hat.'

Tom stopped, breathless with horror, quivering to the tip of his quiff. Cutting a cigar, Bertie remarked, 'So the lady's room was decorated with her hinge and pluck, as the pork butchers call the entrails? No wonder she stole the thunder from Sir James Whitehead.'

'Who's Sir James Whitehead?' Tom asked impatiently.

'Our new Lord Mayor,' Bertie told him blandly.

Tom leant over him, eyes fierce. 'Can't you see the seriousness of all I'm telling you?'

'No more than anyone else who reads the papers. It's Grand Guignol, enjoying one of the longest runs in London. My friends in the theatre say the box-office is suffering, because they can't compete. Personally, I despise the common people smacking their lips over the antics of a violent lunatic. They're no better than the crowds who roared their ribs out at the antics of poor madmen in Bedlam a century ago.'

'Perhaps I can induce you to show more interest.' Tom straightened up. 'The police have the woman's name. She was Marie – or Mary Jane – Kelly. She was twenty-four. She was said by a fellow-unfortunate to be three months pregnant.'

Bertie struck a match. 'Well?'

'Well!' Tom hissed at him. 'You knew her, didn't you?'

'Certainly a girl called Mary Kelly came to the door here one night. About a week ago. She wanted an abortion. She was a maidservant, at one of the houses on the Park where I sometimes dine. I suppose she'd heard my name from her mistress, and thinking me the nearest medical man threw herself on my mercy. She offered me money, quite a considerable sum. Which I have not the slightest doubt was stolen from her employers. Need I say that I turned her away with a flea in her ear? Or whatever part of her anatomy would be more appropriate. I have only scorn for these wretches who try tempting us medical men from our cherished and honourable principles by bribery. It is as reprehensible as offering a *douceur* to a judge.'

'This was the same Mary Kelly.'

'From what you've just told me, I should hardly recognize her.'

'I too knew her.'

'Really?' For the first time in the lurid conversation, Bertie seemed surprised.

'She came to my laboratory one morning, over three weeks ago. She was looking for you. She had a letter you'd written to some woman who runs a bawdy house at Kensington Gore, where Kelly plied her infamous trade herself. You're connected to her as securely as by a pair of handcuffs,' he ended furiously.

'I really must object to your choice of similes,' Bertie said mildly. 'Are you implying that I'm Jack the Ripper?'

'No, no, of course not! But . . . but . . .' Tom's rage fizzed into exasperation. 'Damn it, Randolph. There's something fishy about all this.'

'My story is perfectly correct, dear boy. Except that she worked in a bawdy house, not a gentleman's one. Which made me even keener to be rid of her.'

'There's your letter.' He threw the folded paper into Bertie's lap. Bertie read it without change of expression.

'In fact, Randolph, I decided to say nothing about that letter. However much I felt it my duty, bringing it to the notice of the hospital governors. We've never made any bones about it, have we, that you and I aren't exactly chums?' he continued awkwardly. 'But there's a world of difference between personal antipathy and ruining of a man's career.'

'Your charity is appreciated.'

Bertie handed the letter back. His indifference confused Tom. The quality of his mercy was anyway strained by fright at his own possible disgrace over Janet. 'I don't think I want it.'

With a swift movement, Bertie crushed it and threw it into the fire. 'What do you expect me to do about it?'

'Cease contaminating us. Resign honourably from the Whitechapel. You need give no reason.'

Bertie stuck his legs on the fender, puffing his cigar for some moments. 'I suppose you are right in your view, the out-patients' surgery at the Whitechapel Hospital should not be be the province of the *procureur*. Like – for example – the Kapalicarsi Bazaar at Constantinople.' Bertie would invoke even geography to impress. 'But you condemn me only because your opinions on prostitution are more conventional than your opinions on microbes. I offer these young women from Whitechapel not degradation, but salvation. Whoring's a performance, like playing the flute. Much better doing it in style with an Albert Hall orchestra, than alone in a Whitechapel gutter.'

'Randolph, you do talk such rot.' To Bertie's relief, the doorbell rang. 'I shall *insist* you resign,' Tom said stoutly.

'I'll think about it.' Bertie was damned if he would. Quit the Whitechapel, and every doctor in the West End would wonder why. It would destroy the respectable armour of his life as a torpedo an ironclad. The bell rang again.

'I should advise you to think most carefully. Your connection with this infamous house is bound to come out, isn't it? Scotland Yard have got a little list.' Like everyone in London, Tom could not help quoting the Lord High Executioner.

Bertie rose. 'If you wish to pursue this further, Dalhouse, you can reach me by the telephone. Belgravia 12.' The bell rang again. 'I seem to have an unexpected and insistent visitor. Domestic turmoil forces me to answer my own front door. If observed, I may never dare show my face at anyone else's in Belgravia.'

'Very well, Randolph. But remember – I'm someone to be reckoned with now.'

Bertie inclined his head. It was exactly his attitude to Oliver Wilberforce.

Tom left, still struggling into his overcoat. On the front

steps was George Bracegirdle in flowing cape, hat cocked over eye, cane atwirl, hansom waiting.

'Ah, dear laddie –' He radiated high spirits, as though entering to loud applause. He thrust two slips of paper at Bertie. 'Must dash for the theatre. First night. Get all the papers tomorrow morning. Here's two stalls for Monday. Immense gratitude. Prowled Whitechapel till the small hours, been there all day. Immense crowd round Miller's Court, spilling into all the streets, would fill the Lyceum ten times over. *I saw the body carried away!* In a shell, like a box of sheeps' heads, under a dirty old cloth. Tipped the policeman, heard about the entrails decorating the picture-rail. I *absorbed* the atmosphere like seaside ozone. That murder was a magnificent stroke of luck! Tonight I shall give an inspired performance. One of a lifetime. Thank you so much, dear boy, for telling me where to see the show.'

He leapt into his hansom and clattered off. Bertie shut the door. He went upstairs slowly, hands in pockets of his frock coat, cigar between his teeth, frowning, his second visitor already out of mind.

Half an hour later, he left. He found a hansom at the corner of Belgrave Square, and drove to the back door of No. 2. He threw his ulster to the maid, striding straight up to the pink drawing-room. When Mrs Floyd appeared, she crossed without a word to the window, pulling back the heavy cream lace an inch.

'You see?' She pointed in the direction of Kensington Gore. '*Two* plain-clothes men today.' She dropped the curtain. 'There may be trouble brewing, Bertie. The man I grease at the Yard got the sack. I met him in the Park this afternoon as usual, to pay the hush-money. He says there's no end of coming and going there.'

'Warren's been sacked, too, that's why.' She looked surprised. 'The public's angry, and want blood as thirstily as the Ripper. James Monro is taking over as commissioner. He was head of the CID till August, when Warren booted him out. There's no love lost among our policemen.'

'I suppose Monro wants to show he's a new broom with stiff bristles,' she said, nodding towards the street.

'Closing down whorehouses is an easy way of looking clever, when they can't stop seven of their practitioners spewing their guts on the pavement,' Bertie said bitterly. 'But that's only the half of it. You saw about Mary?' She nodded. 'They'll know she once worked here.'

'What of it? That's no fault of mine, if she trusts herself with a man in Whitechapel until he's got a knife in her belly. She was drunk, for certain.'

'Jack made a salami sausage of her. I've been talking to one of the doctors.'

'She deserved it.' Mrs Floyd linked hands decisively in front of her skirt.

Bertie shrugged his shoulders. 'Things are getting hot in London. The duns are on me.'

She seldom saw him unlit with good humour. The eye which stared the world in brazen assurance wandered nervously from her own, the mouth so often pursed for a saucy quip fell slack in despair.

'For how much?' she asked.

'A thou. Perhaps a monkey would buy the man off. I'm trying to extract it from a couple of fellows, but I daren't tighten the thumbscrews too hard. They might find a way of turning the tables. They're intelligent. Only thick-witted people are easy game for blackmail. Unfortunately, they seldom do anything to make it worth while.'

She stood before the fire, hands still clasped. 'I have money concealed in the house. A large sum, all the takings for weeks. Only I know how much. The man should have called, but I expect the owners are as informed as you about goings on within the police.'

His eye came back to hers. 'I wouldn't ask you to steal for me.'

'I'm leaving, Bertie.'

He stared at her for a silent moment.

'I'm leaving in only the clothes I stand up in, and taking every sovereign. If I don't, who's going to get it? The police, most likely. It's due to me, for the risks I've run here. I'm not going to hazard facing the inside of a cell again. I've cheated them once, I'm giving no second chances.'

'*Autrefois acquit*,' Bertie murmured. He added more cheerfully, 'Your innocence *has* been established by a British jury. A body of such fair-mindedness and level-headedness it would have satisfied Pontius Pilate, and saved all that vulgar business at Golgotha.'

She laid her hand against his cheek. 'Dear Bertie! We would be across the Channel tomorrow.' He took her fingers. 'The end of both our troubles, wouldn't it? Listen – do you remember what Madame Landouzy said about the Brazils? I'm sure I could do well for myself out there. And there's a regular steam service from Marseilles these days. You could practise as a doctor, Bertie. A doctor from England in Para! You'd be like the greatest specialist in London.'

He kissed her knuckles. 'The idea has attractions.'

'Is that all you can say?' She smiled chidingly. 'The only man in the world I trust and admire, and you've never given me any encouragement.'

'It is not my nature to play the gallant.'

'What you have done for me speaks more persuasively than a lifetime of gallantries. I owe you my very life. You and I enjoy a strange connection between man and woman.'

'So did you and your husband, in the end.'

'You'd make a joke of anything, wouldn't you, Bertie?' she asked despairingly. 'Perhaps they should make you the public hangman, and let you tickle everyone to death.'

'The result would be the same for the unfortunate convict. You can't split tragedy and comedy. Women blub like fountains at weddings, and there isn't a man of importance who dies in London without smug grins as thick as May daisies.'

'Mind, I'm older than you.' She thought she interpreted his hesitation. 'The whole world knows I'm thirty-two.'

'I think the only woman I really loved in my life was my mother.'

They were interrupted by a tap. Candy's head appeared. 'I heard the doctor was here – '

Mrs Floyd stamped her foot. 'Go away!'

Candy advanced boldly into the room. 'I've come to say I'm going. Dr Randolph promised to find me a position as a type writer.'

'There's only one position you'll ever occupy,' Mrs Floyd told her angrily. 'On your back.'

Candy glanced at Bertie, and turned back to her defiantly. 'Oh? You ask the doctor. I can pass for a proper lady.'

The unbecoming cloak of gloom fell from Bertie's shoulders. He laughed. 'Lady of the bedchamber, and mistress of the unrobed! Last night was a great, glorious leg-pull, don't you understand? Confronting those pompous asses with their whore at their own fireside.'

Candy stared at him, unbelieving. She frowned and said softly, 'Why did you make a fool of a gal, sir?'

'You enjoyed yourself heartily, as I remember. You made an excellent supper.'

Candy turned to Mrs Floyd. 'I want my money.'

'What money?'

'The money what's due to me, o'course. What you've been keeping. I'm not like the other gals here, you know. I can find myself honest work. I'd as lief be a milkmaid on my brother's farm and sleep in the straw as be made sport of by my betters.'

'How dare you ask me for money?' Mrs Floyd was furious. 'You've been living here off the fat of the land, dressed in silk and satins, waited on as if you were a duchess. Got some funny ideas in your head, haven't you? You're a strumpet, and you'll go on having pintles pushed up you, till your teeth fall out and your dugs shrivel or you catch the pox.'

She grabbed Candy's blue silk dress and half-ripped it off her. Candy leapt back with a shriek. 'All right go, go back to Whitechapel. I can get on perfectly nicely without you.' Mrs Floyd clasped her hands again, continuing bad-temperedly, 'Very well, you shall have a bright pound or two. You'll have to take a dress, because I burnt the rags you came in. I'm not a hard woman, you see. Now get out, you pert baggage.'

Candy began to cry. 'Get out!' screamed Mrs Floyd, advancing on her. 'Before I scratch your eyes out.'

The door slammed. 'I really *do* feel some responsibility for that girl,' murmured Bertie.

'For a stray cat, turned back into its alley?'

'She took my joke seriously, Angela. Everyone seemed to take me seriously yesterday evening. How tedious the world is becoming. Perhaps we used up our supplies of fun for the Jubilee?'

'She can find a job sewing shirts at twelve shillings a week,' said Mrs Floyd contemptuously.

'Oh, she'll go on the game again, and be pissing out of a dozen holes in no time. Perhaps I can find something better for her. Let's see – there's a good licensed lodging-house for single women at No. 26 Finch Street in Whitechapel, opposite the free schools. It's well known at the hospital. Send her there tonight in a hansom. I'll pay.'

'Well! You seem to be playing Santa Claus all of a sudden.'

'I hate having anything on my conscience,' said Bertie.

25

'WATCH OUT, LOVEY! Jack will have them nice cambric drawers of yours full of your own guts,' cackled one hag in the basement kitchen.

A dozen women sat between the smoky, brick walls, a roaring fire at one end with a kettle, a dozen metal teapots on the mantel, cobwebs in the corners. The lodgers were mostly in their aprons, separated in stalls like a chop-house's, drinking tea, the solace which mingled with gin and beer in the veins of the poor.

' 'E'll take quite a fancy to them lovely curls o' yourn,' called another across the room. ' 'Ead an' all.'

'I'm not frightened of Jack the Ripper,' said Candy defiantly.

'Oo, listen to 'er,' said a middle-aged woman with a squint. 'Them nice diddies of yourn, me darlin', will be lying on yer bedroom table, just like Mary Kelly's, if you don't watch out.'

'What's it matter if the Ripper gets me anyway?' grumbled a hatchet-faced woman who had been at Candy's trade before she was born. 'Life ain't worth living for the likes of us.'

Candy's arrival at the lodging house was met with derision. She wore an old dress, stained and with the stitching going, but it was a ball gown to the clothing of the others. She was well nourished, her hair tended, she was clean. She had arrived in a hansom. And she was a whore. Candy was mystified how the women's eyes picked this as quickly as if she advertised it on a sandwich-board.

It was eleven at night, the same Friday. She had been there barely long enough to claim her bed. The derision was as intolerable as the hoots of the mob to Marie Antoinette. She abruptly gathered her shawl and climbed the stone steps towards the street door, jibes following her like rotten eggs.

She had decided on a return to Blessington. No one in the village would know of her life in London. She could forget it herself, once among the wholesome fields, the sturdy trees, the virtuous cows. She would marry. She already ran through her mind the unattached men left behind. She would make someone a good wife. It did not occur to her for exceptional reasons.

She had three sovereigns in a purse round her neck under her dress, some shillings and threepenny bits in her skirt pocket. She remembered the nearby Three Tuns public house in Lolesworth Street, which she had frequented with Sal and Lizzie. Finch Street was only a long twisting alley, the houses turning their backs upon the night, dark save for a hidden lamp gleaming yellow round the distant corner. Candy felt unaccustomed cobbles through her thin boots. It was cold and foggy, but not dense enough to stop the traffic, which she could hear rumbling in the India Road. There were no voices. Not even a cat about. She heard a soft footstep behind her.

Candy grasped her shawl, knuckles whitening. The step was heavy and quick, a man's. She dared not turn. She walked faster, her breath becoming a cloud. The light at the corner was her haven. Beyond would be people, perhaps a policeman. The footsteps came close. They were upon her. She turned with a gasp. It was Bertie.

'Oh! Dr Randolph. Well, I never did.'

He smiled. 'I couldn't abandon you, could I?'

She dropped her eyes. 'I was insolent to Mrs Floyd today. A proper saucebox.'

'Mrs Floyd deserved it. I've something for you. Come here.'

Curious, she let him lead her through a crack between two houses into a small courtyard. 'Something to cheer you up. On my handkerchief. Take a good breath.'

She could hardly see the white square in his hand. 'What is it?'

'Something better than gin or brandy. Go on. Sniff.'

She put her nose to the handkerchief. Instantly she thrust it aside. 'It's what you gave me in that little silver box.' She was suddenly suspicious. 'It's chloroform.'

'No, of course it isn't! Just smell it. Then it's my turn.'

'I ain't going to.' She moved away from him. 'You said that it put gals to sleep.'

'You *are* being tedious,' he complained. 'Smell.'

He thrust the soaked handkerchief over her face, but she pulled fiercely at his hands, choking. Bertie grabbed her waist. She was stronger than he imagined. She twisted violently, hitting him hard between the legs with her knee. A long piece of metal fell from Bertie's sleeve on to the flagstones.

He loosed her, snatching up the knife. They stared at each other. Since Bertie had first murdered Emma Smith in February, he knew he could afford not one mistake. An instant later, he knew he had made it. He hesitated. Candy's face held no terror, only the look of puzzlement she wore when he said something outrageous, her expression that summer afternoon on the Thames, or when he initially addressed her in the out-patients' surgery. She faced death with the same modest simplicity as life. *He could not kill her.* But with three words, now she could kill him.

'You're – ?' she said.

'Yes,' he hissed.

A window opened, a head appeared with a candle. 'What's a-goin' on out there?' a gruff voice demanded suspiciously.

Candy screamed.

Bertie turned and ran.

He made for Brick Lane. Controlling his pace, he strode round the corner into India Road. He heard no hue and cry. A shout of 'Jack the Ripper!' had anyway become as commonplace in Whitechapel as 'Murder!' from a woman getting on the wrong side of her husband. He looked anxiously through the fog for the yellow eyes of a hansom. He found one by the Aldgate pump, and directed to be dropped in Knightsbridge. He hurried down Wilton Place to Belgrave Square. His house was dark to the roof. Mrs Anstey was asleep. The clocks began to chime eleven.

He went to the telephone.

'Connect me with Belgravia 30.' He waited. 'Angela? Come at once,' he commanded. 'At once! It's imperative. Bring the money. All of it. Tomorrow may be too late.'

She asked nervously if he had heard something.

'You'll soon know.' he replied. 'Don't fail me. Leave the hansom on the corner of the square.'

Bertie took a deep breath. He could do nothing until she arrived. He went back to the hall. A letter with an Austrian stamp lay on the ledge of the hatstand. He tore it open.

Dear Dr Randolph!

A propos the murders committed by this pervert in White-chapel, still unknown at my moment of writing. You may be interested in the views of Dr Freiherr von Krafft-Ebbing, specialist in nervous diseases who next year will occupy the professorial chair here in Vienna.

Dr Krafft-Ebbing believes that murder performed for pleasure – as distinct from that incurred in a brawl, or through jealousy, for example – is nothing but a ghastly imitation of the act of defloration. Thus murder for pleasure must be performed with a sharp cutting instrument. A knife is a symbol of the penis, in the insubstantial pageant of our dreams. The victim must be slit, or ripped, or even cut to pieces. The similarity with defloration is emphasized by the wounds being inflicted upon the abdomen, and often in the vagina itself. Where no vagina is present, when the victim is a young man or boy, an artificial vagina may be created by the murderer's knife.

The killing itself is generally by strangulation. Causing the victim death is unsatisfying for the murderer, whose enjoyment starts with possession of the corpse. The internal genital organs of women are frequently removed in such pleasure-murders, indicating a strong element of fetishism.

If one man will steal a woman's boot for his sexual satisfaction, why should not another steal her uterus?

Bertie crammed the letter in his pocket. For once he could not draw comfort from the emotionless authority of Freud's mind.

He opened the front door a crack, that Mrs Floyd need not use the bell. He waited in the hall, hands in pockets. Suddenly, he covered his face, and quoted to himself Baudelaire –

> *Tu marches sur des morts, Beauté, dont*
> *   tu te moques;*
> *De tes bijoux l'Horreur n'est pas le*
> *   moins charmant,*
> *Et le Meurtre, parmi tes plus chères*
> *   breloques,*
> *Sur ton ventre orgueilleux danse*
> *   amoureusement.*

She arrived within the quarter-hour. The sight of her immediately steadied him. She was in plain black bonnet and black shawl, a Gladstone weighty in her hand. The sovereigns restored some of Bertie's usual confidence.

'Come into the consulting-room. We'll be quietest there. Though my housekeeper so drugs herself with laudanum, she'd sleep through a battle.'

Mrs Floyd removed her bonnet. 'Well, Bertie?' she asked calmly. 'What's turned up?'

'I've been rumbled.'

'What at?'

'Jack the Ripper. Didn't you suspect?'

She gasped. 'No!'

'That girl Candy did for me. I had my eye on her since I first saw her. I tried my usual trick with chloroform in Whitechapel, but she recognized the smell. Then she saw my little toy.'

Like a conjurer, he slipped from his sleeve and opened in

one movement a spring-loaded knife, its steel handle concealing a six-inch blade. 'Prussian and military,' he explained proudly. 'For amputations in the field. I bought it last winter in Paris.'

'You did all these murders?' she asked wonderingly.

He leant against the desk, motioning her to a chair. 'All seven. Oh, it was easy, I traced most of them from the hospital admissions book. It's a wonder nobody spotted chloroform in the bodies. But I didn't use much, and I suppose they took the smell for drink. I had to train myself to be ambidextrous, for doing the job properly. There was always so little time. I invented a disguised mask, but it wasn't handy and I burnt it in Mary Kelly's grate when I'd finished with her last night.'

'Bertie!' She shook her head in confusion. 'I just don't understand why you needed do such things.'

He unlocked a narrow cupboard in the corner. 'For these.' He had a large pickle jar filled with red, rounded objects. 'Three wombs. Preserved nice and soft in glycerine. Candy's would have made a fine addition. And half a kidney, by the way, which I shared with Mr Lusk. Mary Kelly wasn't pregnant, whatever they say. That's hers, at the top.' He placed the jar reverently on the desk. 'The womb! Glorious organ. The nucleus of femininity. Like the tiny brilliant nucleus of a comet trailing fire across the universe.'

'But needed you go to such lengths to possess them?' she asked reprovingly.

'I tried to buy some at a guinea a go in a roundabout way from the hospital, but they weren't interested. I had to find my own. It wasn't easy, I had to get the hang of it. First I went up the cunt, but that was a mistake. I started on old whores, whose lives weren't worth a candle-end. Women no use to anyone, apart from giving a fourpenny grind to some drunk navvy. Better off dead. But I got the itch for something younger. Are you frightened of me?'

'How could *I* be?' She rose, smiling, putting her arms round his neck tenderly. 'Haven't we now so much in common?'

'But it's going to be devilish difficult for us. I must fly this night. That girl will squeak, sure as the Creed. Half the harlots in Whitechapel say they've seen Jack the Ripper, the police are going to take time before asking questions of a respectable doctor in Belgrave Square. But come they will.'

'There's a boat train at eight in the morning.'

He linked his arms round her waist. 'What happens when they find I've vanished? A confession of guilt, isn't it? They'll look for me all over London, all over England, all over Europe. Even the French police will be as hot as hounds when they realize I've slipped them once.'

'Never in the Brazils.'

'If we get there,' he said dubiously. 'I'm big game. There's reputations to be restored and made. Why, I could create a couple of knights by walking into the police commissioner's office at breakfast time. I'd prefer to cover my tracks. I always did after my work in Whitechapel.'

'Did you write those letters?'

'The ones on the police poster, yes. It was a bit of fun. I used to concoct ghoulish notes at Rugby, and post them to the masters. I sent the postcard from Charing Cross, the morning I left for Paris after doing a job. I didn't write about the Jews, though. The world is full of scribblers and scrawlers on paper and on walls, who just want to show off. If you ask me, they're barmy.'

She kissed him softly on the lips. 'Isn't your conscience troubled with seven murders?'

'No more than one. Murder is surely qualitative, not quantitative? You know, for all the fuss in the newspapers, the murders were a very small part of my life. I went out, did them, and was back here within an hour or so. I thought no more of it than going to the theatre.'

They froze. The noise of a falling chair came from the kitchen.

'A cat?' suggested Mrs Floyd.

'Haven't one.' He picked up the knife, snapped it shut, and restored it to his sleeve. He lit the oil lamp on his desk – the ostentatious electricity often failed.

266

Mrs Floyd smiled. 'At least, it can't be Jack the Ripper.'

Bertie went down to the basement. Cowering in the circle of lamp-light was Freshings.

'Oh, sir!' he cried piteously. 'I've nowhere to go.'

Bertie scowled at him, holding the lamp high. Then a smile spread over his face. 'My dear Freshings! How delighted I am that you returned. My conscience has been troubling me sorely.'

He extended an arm, drawing the valet to his feet. 'I was hasty. Far, far too hasty. That girl was a good-for-nothing. You were perfectly right to feel yourself betrayed.'

'Oh, sir!'

Arm round Freshings' shoulders, Bertie piloted him upstairs. 'I've sent her packing, bag and baggage. And without a character. Of course, you may come back to your position.'

'You're very good to me, sir.' He rubbed his eye with his knuckle.

'I honestly don't know how I could go on living without you, Freshings.'

'Your couter, sir – ' He felt in his pocket for Bertie's sovereign.

'Keep it. As a mark of my affection. And next time I travel to Paris, you shall certainly accompany me. I promise it. You shall see the delights of the *Folies Bergère*, the *Moulin Rouge*, and places of even more intimate entertainment. It was just my valet,' he introduced Freshings to Mrs Floyd in the consulting-room. 'By jove!' Bertie exclaimed to him. 'You *do* look peaky.'

'I've been walking the streets, sir.' He stared timidly at Mrs Floyd. 'I'd no coat, and it's raw to the bone.'

'Have a sniff of this, Freshings.' Bertie poured from a brown bottle on to a handkerchief. 'It'll buck you up better than gin. I've often taken it myself. I expect you've tried it behind my back?'

'I'd never do a thing like that, sir.'

'Of course not, an honest servant like you, whom I'd trust with the cellar key any day.' Bertie sat him in a chair.

'Isn't it what you had ... that night, sir?' he asked dubiously.

'Why, so it is! I'd taken a drop too much. It can make a fool of you as easily as brandy. You'll stay right enough, having it from my hands. Go on. Big sniff, now.'

After several deep inhalations, Freshing said stumblingly, 'It makes me sort of woozy, sir.'

'Spiffing feeling, isn't it?'

Bertie poured on more chloroform. Freshings' breathing became regular, then stertorous. He started sliding from the chair like a half-filled sack. 'Help me lay him on the couch,' Bertie murmured.

'What are you going to do with him?' Mrs Floyd took the feet.

'Kill him.'

'To what object?'

'Freshings has come to us from Heaven, to which he will shortly be returning.' Bertie poured chloroform in a steady drip as the valet lay motionless. 'He is my build. He is my age. He wears my clothes. He even has some resemblance to me. Or sufficient, after he's been in the Thames a week. See how simple it is? Candy tells Scotland Yard, "Dr Randolph is the Ripper." A little later, Dr Randolph is dragged up by some lighterman's boathook. Hunt called off. Case closed. Scotland Yard delighted.'

'But how brilliant!' she clapped her hands.

Bertie diverted some drops to his own palm and inhaled. 'Wonderful fluid. I always had a good sniff or two before cutting up my whores. Here, you give the chloroform, while I do a little job. You should know how.'

She smiled, taking the bottle from his hands. 'Perhaps I've lost the knack?'

'It's a good thing to be rid of him, anyway.' Bertie stared down at the couch. 'He knew more about me than he let on. He was a sly boots.'

'How shall we take him to the Thames?'

'It's a problem I've been pondering. If we put him on a shutter, even at this time of night we should attract a crowd

268

like a brass band. We could find a hansom, and say he was drunk. But some of these driver chappies are getting dashed suspicious. Where's the obvious place to take a dead body?'

'A mortuary.'

'Exactly.'

Bertie went to the telephone in his dining-room. He wound the handle. The operator was sleepy. 'Please connect me with Islington 6.' Bertie waited. 'Hello? The Islington Ambulance Service? As advertised in the *Lancet*?' He explained that he had a dangerously sick case of smallpox, for removal at once to the isolation ward of the Whitechapel Hospital. 'No attendants will be necessary,' he added. 'I shall travel myself with the patient, accompanied by a nurse.'

Bertie returned to the consulting-room. 'Is he still breathing?' She nodded. He drew a copy of *Whitaker's Almanack* from the bookcase. 'High tide at London Bridge on the morning of Saturday, November 10, is at six-one a.m. Remarkably convenient.'

He pressed the spring of his watch. 'It is now quarter past midnight. The Ostend packet leaves on the tide from Wapping Pier, within easy walk of the Whitechapel Hospital, where we shall be taking our invaluable friend. Plenty of time to settle ourselves aboard, and to enjoy our breakfast. I much prefer reaching Paris via Ostend. The French harbour officials are becoming so unfriendly to foreigners. He *is* taking his time, isn't he?'

Bertie suffocated Freshings with one of the organdie cushions.

'No, he is not quite *me*.' Bertie looked at the corpse thoughtfully. 'Not even when half-eaten by fishes. Help me shift him to the table.'

He laid a Turkish towel over the marble top. Flicking down the knife he sliced off Freshings' nose. 'And the eyes, I think. The police photograph them, you know. The murderer's image is supposed to be indelibly imprinted. There may be something in the idea. I doubt they'll indulge in tiresome suspicions that I'm not a simple suicide, but why take risks?'

With the knife, he scooped each eye from its socket, as though finishing his breakfast eggs. He heard her retch. He said over his shoulder, smiling, 'Mrs Adelaide Bartlett, you're losing your nerve.'

'No, I'm not,' she said sharply. 'What shall you do with the bits?'

'Flush them down the Thunderer. It's terribly efficient. A little blood, this knife, don't signify in a doctor's consulting-room. What about those?' He picked up his pickle-jar of wombs with blood-smeared fingers. 'I don't much care leaving them to be picked over by a heartless pathologist, when I went to such trouble. They won't flush down as they are. You'd better slice them – there's a chopping-board in the kitchen, behind the knife grinder. Take the oil lamp.'

She returned with the organs on the scrubbed board, like catsmeat.

'I used the mincer,' she explained. 'To be sure.'

'Excellent.' Bertie was dressing Freshings in a spare frock-coat.

'Shall I fetch the weights from the kitchen scales?' she suggested. 'You'd put them in your pockets if you went to drown yourself.'

'Capital idea, Adelaide.'

'Angela.'

'Come! We're in battle now sailing under our true colours. The rest of Freshings' clothes are my discards, and the wear and tear won't show under Thames mud.' Bertie sighed, holding his cigar-case and watch. 'The cigar-case I can endure going with him. Useful identification. But my lovely watch – '

'Put it in his pocket,' Adelaide Bartlett commanded. 'So valuable an object, which you are so well known to cherish, will be conclusive proof that the man is you.'

'Quite right, as always,' he said grudgingly. 'I shall add the final touch.' George Bracegirdle's two theatre tickets were tucked into the cigar case.

'We need no luggage, when we have money,' she said practically.

'My own encumbrances will be four letters from an amazingly interesting professional colleague in Vienna, whose refreshing ideas I treasure. And a device called a safety-razor, which I bought from an American detective and find invaluable.'

The ambulance arrived within the hour, a four-wheeler, black as a hearse, one small window through the rear door. The driver stayed on his box, top-hatted, greatcoat collar up, head averted from a passenger with so deadly a catching disease. Bertie told him to take Ropewalk Lane to the back entrance of the hospital. They clopped through empty, misty streets towards the City. Bertie grinned to see policemen gaze solemnly after them from lampposts.

'Alas! poor Freshings.' Bertie and Adelaide Bartlett sat on narrow seats running down each side, knees touching over the body in a blanket. 'A fellow of infinite folly, of most excellent docility. Doubtless his soul has gone wherever the well-ironed souls of valets do.'

'Didn't you tell me once, Bertie, that what a man calls his soul is only a possessive devil? And he is saved from a life of perpetual wickedness only through its habitual laziness?'

'A man is much holier possessed of a devil than a soul. With the devil, he spends all his life struggling to be good. With a soul, only to be wicked. But where does either lodge?'

They creaked and swayed round a corner. 'In the gall-bladder, pouch of the yellow and the back bile, the melancholy and choler of Aristotle and Galen? In the slippery, unaccountable little finger of the *appendix vermiformis*? In the spongy corm of the prostate gland, root of the fruitful penile stalk? In women, undoubtedly in the womb, crucible of femininity. Descartes installed the soul in the pineal gland, a cherry on a stalk in the brain. No one else knew what to do with it.'

He quoted, ' "I think, therefore I am." I dream, therefore I sleep. I itch, therefore I share the world with fleas. But how do we know that we *really* do all three? A lame girl I saw at the Salpêtrière thought she could walk again, and she walked. But the thought was Professor Charcot's, put in her mind by hypnosis.'

Bertie glanced through the window. They were in Whitechapel. 'I agree with Descartes, the body is a superb machine made by the hand of God – or some other celestial Edison. Descartes had it powered by the mind. I prefer to think it electrified by animal magnetism, which connects us to the moon, to stars so remote they are undiscovered and already extinguished. No other doctor at the Whitechapel has read *Discours de la Méthode*,' he said proudly. 'Nor probably heard of Descartes. Doctors are dull dogs, and hospitals bookless kennels.'

A wheel scraped the familiar steep kerbstone at the turning into Ropewalk Lane.

'Mankind nearly escaped being spitted like larks on the sword of Cartesian philosophy, because our mild-mannered savant was within a whisker of murder himself. To be thrown into the Zuyder Zee by thievish sailors, but they funked. It's in the essay, *On Murder, Considered as One of the Fine Arts*. By De Quincey, the English opium-eater. Have you read it?'

'I've hardly opened a book since my husband died.'

'An affected but ingenious work,' Bertie professed. 'A connoisseur may surely assess a murder as an ideal *of its kind*, as justly as would I some sloughing phagadaenic ulcer a prime example of *its* kind. Your murder of your husband, Mrs Adelaide Bartlett, was as the most faultless moss-rose among flowers. Or amongst human flowers, as the most magnificent young female, apparelled in the pomp of womanhood. The comparisons of such happy fulfilment are De Quincey's own.'

'Must we speak of it now?' she asked shortly.

'What more fitting time?' Bertie contradicted blandly. 'A pair of cabinetmakers delivering their handiwork would talk of the furniture trade, a shopman with a sow from the abattoir would discuss butchery in general. Yours was the consummation of murder, because the ingredients were not skimped, and of such excellent quality. Murder appeals most when performed in respectable homes. In Whitechapel, it is as dull as the weather. And committed by one spouse upon the other, particularly when the wife takes the active role. The more so an *errant* wife.' He saw Adelaide Bartlett shudder. 'What became of your Methodist minister, the Reverend George Dyson?'

'I neither know nor care. He was a simpleton who nearly did for me. The stupid manner in which he bought the chloroform, the more stupid one in which he threw the bottles away, all over Wandsworth Common. He'll be the pet of some other woman. She'll benefit from all I taught him.'

'Chloroform was a piquant constituent of your recipe. Women have a weakness for poisoning, but arsenic or belladonna are a shade trite. Why did your fingers reach for it?'

'Because the unusual is unlooked for.'

'The icing on your cake, my dear Mrs Adelaide Bartlett, was your being so pretty, so young, so delicately but indubitably French. That transformed a squalid death into "The Pimlico Mystery." Tell me – how *did* you do it?'

'Chloroform on a cambric handkerchief, burned in the grate. Once he was stuporous, I emptied the bottle down his throat. He went very quickly. He was not a healthy man.'

'Had you patience, Nature might have spared you the trouble.'

'My husband had as acquisitive a grasp on life as on his grocer's shops. He would not have given up either easily.'

'You took a severe risk,' Bertie admonished her. 'Chloroform in such quantities is as obvious at post-mortem as a draught of reeking carbolic.'

'I did not imagine I should be suspected,' she replied simply. 'I was such a devoted wife.'

'All's well that ends well,' Bertie told her cheerfully. 'You were aquitted, you found a new life amid the best society, in a year or two you achieved success and respect as Mrs Angela Floyd.'

'That is what you must call me, Bertie. Adelaide Bartlett is the name of my ghost.'

'As you wish.' He made an easygoing gesture across Freshings' corpse. '*Why* did you kill your husband?'

She hesitated. 'I could not endure another minute living in Pimlico.'

They had arrived at the fever gate.

The driver whipped away his horse, glad to escape from the regions of contagion, delighted at the gold passed in compensation of his deadly risk. Bertie and Adelaide carried the body across the deserted courtyard. Bertie prized up the manhole-cover. They pushed Freshings in head first. A heavy splash welcomed him to the swift-running sewage.

'No grid, no sluice, bars his passage into the Thames,' Bertie told her. 'I have it on the authority of our hospital pathologist. He is the Charon of the London nether regions.'

Bertie quietly shut the fever gate behind them. The clocks of Whitechapel struck two in the morning. Adelaide Bartlett slipped her arms round his neck, pressing herself fiercely against him.

'Murder is *so* sensuous,' she murmured.

26

'I CAN'T believe it! I can't believe it's really him.' Janet Veale cut the cartilages of the bared ribs with her champagne-cork shaped Hey's saw.

'Obviously it is,' said Tom Dalhouse. It was four days later, the morning of Wednesday, November 14, 1888. They were alone in the post-mortem room. Janet wore a leather apron, her sleeves rolled up. He was in his suit, hands in pockets. 'Even though his face has been eaten rather ravenously by rats. That cigar case and watch were as much part of the late Randolph as his ears and nose.'

Janet sniffed. Tom wondered spitefully whether the woman would rub through the doctor. Would tears splash the purplish, green-streaked skin of the ragged-faced, cleft body on the grooved zinc-topped table?

'I do declare, I just can't conceive that a nice man like Bertie was Jack the Ripper.'

'That girl said so, plain enough,' Tom told her shortly. 'Her story stood up well in all the newspapers. I happen to have known for weeks, Randolph was concerned with the vicious place the police have just suppressed in Kensington.'

'How can anyone take the word of an unfortunate?' Janet objected. 'Particularly Scotland Yard. I'm surprised at them.'

'She was not born to a life of shame. She was an honest country girl, an orphan. She was forced into prostitution by Randolph,' Tom explained with satisfaction. 'I also happen to know that he abducted her from the hospital surgery. She was a patient of Dr Porter-Hartley's – though strangely enough, he strongly denied it when I mentioned the matter. But I looked her up in the porter's register. She lived in Star

Place, same address as that woman who was stuck like a pig with a bayonet. It's all as plain as a pikestaff.'

'The girl Farnaby might have borne a grudge against Dr Randolph, if that story's even half true,' Janet said quickly. 'It's likely she knew the real Ripper, and was trying to protect him with a *fearful* lie.'

'Then why should Randolph throw himself into the Thames? It was no accident. He'd ballasted himself with weights from his own kitchen.'

Janet lifted out the breastbone. 'That strumpet *knew* poor Bertie was going to kill himself,' she asserted. 'For some reason we'll never fathom – he was far too full of life ever to die. She plotted to make use of the dreadful event.'

'Too crafty by half,' Tom dismissed it.

'Well, I ask you, Dr Dalhouse – why, he's a small hole in his *septum membranaceum ventriculorum*,' she broke off, slitting open the heart. 'Who'd have thought it? Why on God's earth, Dr Dalhouse, should Bertie go round White-chapel ripping up filthy women?'

'There's no knowing what Bertie might have got up to. He was the queerest card I ever knew.'

'Mind you, the police still haven't said the Ripper was definitely him. They found nothing in the slightest incriminating in his house.'

'They're frightened someone might do another White-chapel murder, and make them look bigger fools than ever. Inspector Abberline says they're just going to quietly let the case drop. So far as the world's concerned, *no one* will ever know the identity of Jack the Ripper.' He nodded at the corpse. 'But I bet the murders stop.'

Janet sliced open a lung. 'Froth like soap in water. Typical of drowning.'

'Or of suffocation.'

'You're not suggesting that somebody strangled Bertie first? But he's all the other signs of drowning –' She ran the back of her knife along the body. 'The *cutis anserina*, the goose skin. The retraction of the penis.' She indicated with

276

knife-point. 'According to leading pathologists, nothing similar is observed so constantly after any other kind of death.'

'Dr Alexander Ogston has reported from America two cases of erection of the penis on drowned bodies.'

'Indeed? How singular.' Her nose wrinkled. 'Do you know, I could have sworn there was the faintest whiff of chloroform.'

'I've no doubt. Bertie was pickled in it. He sniffed it as often as his victims sank a glass of gin.' Tom smeared down his quiff. 'I only looked in to say good-bye.'

She was puzzled. 'Where are you going?'

'To America. To Boston.'

She gasped. '*Boston*?'

'The Massachusetts General Hospital. A perfectly respectable institution. It's as well esteemed as any hospital in London.'

'But Boston's *frightfully* cold.'

'I can't stand this place any longer, with so many queer things going on. And the dunderheads taking no more notice of my theories about germs than the Great Mogul's. They won't even heed my advice about such fundamental items as sewers. I expect to find our American cousins more pioneering persons. I suppose they'll give *you* my job,' he said offhandedly. 'Women seem to be all the rage in medicine these days.'

'Good-bye, Dr Dalhouse.' She extended a bloody hand. He shook it. 'And thank you for all the interesting bacteriology you've taught me.'

'My absence won't break your heart. You'd eyes only for him.' He nodded at the corpse again. 'I must confess, I often wondered why.'

Her gaze followed Tom's. 'He took me to Romano's,' she said simply.

'Well, toodle-oo. I say, the stiff does rather niff, doesn't it? I'm sure Bertie would have thought that terribly infra dig, dontcher know.'

Pushing up the end of his nose with his fingertip, he left.

Oliver Wilberforce and Ambrose Porter-Hartley were conferring in the courtyard.

'He's in there.' Oliver indicated the mortuary.

Ambrose's cheeks wobbled. 'I know.'

'Going to the funeral?'

'Does one have to?'

'Definitely not, I'd have thought.'

'Particularly after everything in the newspapers,' Ambrose agreed.

'I quite liked the knave in a way.'

'So did I, occasionally.'

'Well, it's turned out best for both of us, hasn't it?' said Oliver.

The winter of 1891 brought a terrible flu epidemic. At the beginning of January 1892, Prince George called to Dr Laking, just leaving Sandringham for London, 'By the way, I wish you'd take a look at my brother before you go. He's been out shooting, and doesn't seem well to me.' A week later, Prince Eddy died of pneumonia, aged twenty-eight. The vexations of the doctors' plot were neatly smoothed by Prince George taking over Eddy's fiancée, Princess May, who became beloved Queen Mary.

The same epidemic did for Mackenzie. 'It was rarely the lot of any member of the medical profession to influence the fate of a nation so directly as it has been that of Sir Morell Mackenzie,' said Lord Randolph Churchill. So directly, but not enough. Had his patient lived, there would perhaps have been no Great War and no Hitler.

Sir William Gull died in 1890, leaving a fortune of £344,000. Sir William Jenner died in 1898, leaving a fortune of £375,000. Dr Reid outraged Queen Victoria by presuming to marry her lady-in-waiting. Edward VIII put the clocks back permanently at Sandringham on his accession in 1936. Romano died of pneumonia in 1901, and lay in state in his restaurant. *Jekyll and Hyde* at the Lyceum ran for months.

Janet Veale spent her life as a pathologist to the

Whitechapel Hospital. She discovered Veale's bacillus, which causes a low-grade fever. She died during Dunkirk Week in 1940. Every November 14 for five years after Bertie's official post-mortem, she went alone to Wapping Pier and cast a simple wreath upon the Thames. She never married. She never knew she was to have been his ninth victim.

A British-born doctor, RICHARD GORDON claims that he became a novelist by mistake. The *British Medical Journal* started him as a writer—of other doctors' obituaries. He went on to produce 13 highly successful "Doctor" novels, which have been adapted for eight films (in one of which Brigitte Bardot made her screen debut) and sold millions of copies worldwide. He has also written a series of novels about medical breakthroughs. *Jack the Ripper* took two years of research, in the splendid libraries of old-established London hospitals, in the Black Museum at Scotland Yard, among the skeletons and specimens at the Royal College of Surgeons, and in the bleak streets of Whitechapel. Says Richard Gordon, "I was determined to discover the *real* Ripper, and I think I have got closer to him than anyone." Married to a doctor, Richard Gordon lives in London.